ANSWERING

ANNAVETA

ANSWERING ANNAVETA

by

Lorna Faith

To my husband

For believing in me, for walking beside me each step of the way, and for cheering me on in every way possible.

Chapter 1

Shremetev Estate, near the village of Noltava, Russia, April 1913

ANNAVETA TOOK A DEEP BREATH of the brisk early morning air as her eyes searched heavenward. "Is someone up there?"

Her dirt-covered hand quivered as she gripped the wooden hoe tighter, looking at the gray sky for some sign from above. None was given. She let out the breath she had been holding and winced as the motion sent a rush of pain to her bruised ribs. Her eyes squeezed shut, forcing a single tear to trail down her cheek. The flash of lightning with its echoing thunder caused her emotions to erupt. She slammed the hoe as hard as she could against the weeds, attacking them with a vengeance. *Maybe I have been doomed to a life of cruelty and misery. I must not be good enough. Papa has told me often enough that I'm stupid, worthless, and ugly, so why would I think that help could come from anywhere else? Maybe Mama's God isn't really up there listening like she believes he is.*

She bent down and pulled on the deep-rooted weed that seemed stuck. She tugged with all her strength, but nothing worked. Tears pricked her eyes at the pain of the blisters that had formed on her hands, from the stubborn weeds she'd been tackling this morning.

"Here, let me help." Pavla, her tall and much stronger friend, moved to the row Annaveta tended in the large

7

garden. "This kind only comes out when two or more people pull on it at the same time."

They gripped the tall, thick plant and pulled with all their might. The weed shifted. Digging their feet in the soft earth, they tugged again using their combined body weight as an anchor. Annaveta's knees buckled, and she stumbled against Pavla, causing them to fall to the freshly dug earth, removing the cruel enemy from the soil so that their newly planted seeds could grow without hindrance. They looked at each other and laughed at being tangled up together, the sound breaking the stillness of the gloomy morning air.

Without warning, something hard struck Annaveta's leg. She scrambled to move out of harm's way. Tripping over her long skirt, she managed to stand to her feet. Her eyes followed the length of a sculpted wooden cane that tapped a steady rhythm on the rich garden soil. Her gaze stopped, and she stared at the pale pudgy hand that bunched white as it gripped the handle tighter. The tapping stopped.

"Look at me, you clumsy wench." The threatening words behind her caused her to look up. She stared into the cold gray eyes of the estate overseer.

"Monsieur Arnaud." Annaveta swallowed her fear as she looked at him. She stood on shaky legs, her muddy hands quivering as she held them against her only work skirt, which was now covered with dirt. She heard Pavla stand up behind her, and winced as fear filled her thoughts.

She knew Monsieur Arnaud was quick to give punishment. Other girls had been pulled from their work and beaten or dismissed for a lot less.

"You both know I could have you fired for rolling on the ground laughing when you are supposed to be working." The fat of the overseer's double chin quivered as he pointed a fleshy finger at them, first at one girl, then the other. "You are lucky that right now we need workers to get the estate ready for the arrival of Count and Countess Shremetev. So, instead of getting rid of you, I will teach you both a lesson. Pavla, you will use the handcart to go shovel manure onto the unused gardens that need the fertilizer. Go at once and report to Mr. Ivanski at the barns."

Annaveta didn't dare turn her head to give her friend a glance as the sound of Pavla's footsteps faded in the sunless morning breeze.

"Now, as for you, come with me."

Panic squeezed her chest as she watched the overseer's eyes move slowly up and down her form, a lustful gleam brightening his eyes.

He grabbed her arm, nearly pulling it out of its socket as he pressed her close to his side, dragging her out of the garden. Annaveta tried to pull back, but he jerked her arm harder and tightened his grip. She bit her lip and groaned in pain, her feet stumbling over uneven clumps of dirt in the garden. Passing other garden workers, she ducked her head in shame, her neck and face burning red. She glanced up once to see Mama's tears rolling down her weathered cheeks, her one good hand covering her mouth. Annaveta's eyes misted at the heartache she saw written on her face. She had seen Mama go through enough hurt when Papa, drunk, would beat her unmercifully until he finally passed out. Her new injury, a broken arm, was held in a sling, still healing from the last time he poured out his anger on her.

Annaveta tried to give a little smile to reassure her, but she was jerked forward again, and a small sob came out instead. Panic squeezed a tight knot around her chest. She didn't know exactly where she was going, but she could guess. The garden toolshed was far enough away that her screams wouldn't be heard. She had overheard Katya, another girl who had worked here a few months ago, tell her friend that the overseer was a lustful, hateful beast. That was before she had run off the estate with tears running down her cheeks.

Monsieur Arnaud pulled her through a thick row of bushes that circled the small wooden shed. He took a ring of keys from his pocket and unlocked the door with one hand as the beefy fingers of his other hand dug sharply into her arm. Annaveta winced in pain. She couldn't let Monsieur Arnaud paw at her like he had done to the other young girls who worked here. Was this the reason they had all disappeared so quickly?

Suddenly aware of the danger that awaited her, she jerked her arm, trying to free herself from this madman. Reflexively, he loosened his grip, unprepared for her sudden movement. She hurried to distance herself from him, but he lunged, his bulky arm coiling around her middle like a hungry snake. She tried to twist away, but he only held her tighter as he dragged her kicking and screaming into the dark shed.

"Now I'm going to teach you a lesson you'll never forget." His arm loosened its bruising grip and she fell, landing on her side on the knotted planks. She moaned in pain but forced herself up on her hands and knees and crawled as fast as she could to the back wall of the small windowless building. She sat there, her white-knuckled hands clutching her knees close to her chest. Every part of her body quivered in fear as she peered at her attacker through a thick cover of tangled auburn hair. His red-rimmed eyes bore holes into hers as a slow smile crept up his portly face, baring ugly gray rotted teeth. Annaveta shrank back, pressing herself against the wall, sickened by this cruel man.

"You will get what's due you, whether you like it or not." Monsieur Arnaud's threatening tone was quickly replaced with a loud lusty laugh.

"No, Mons—" Annaveta's scream was cut off midsentence by his quick move across the room, his rough hand covering her mouth to muffle any sound.

"You'll be quiet, if you know what's good for you!" Her captor pushed her head back with one arm while his other hand slithered roughly down her curves. "Ah, this is why I like young girls." His foul breath was hot against her face as his hands continued their assault.

Annaveta swung her head to the side as he tried to kiss

her lips. She shoved against his chest with all her might, but his iron grip held her firmly. *Mama's saints or someone up there, if you are listening, help me!*

He pulled her away from the wall so fast, her head hit hard against the floor. She struggled to get up. Monsieur Arnaud pushed her to the floor with one hand and held her down forcibly with the other. He snapped off his suspenders. She didn't really know what he was about to do, but instinctively she knew it was something reserved for the marriage bed. She needed to get out of there now.

Jerking out of his grasp, she scrambled forward, trying to reach the door. But he grabbed her by the foot and pulled her down again.

"So you like this game of cat and mouse, *oui?*" Her attacker held her legs together by lodging his knees on either side. Annaveta's eyes grew wide in horror as his red sweaty face bent down to kiss her. She tasted bile on her tongue as she turned her head to the side just in time, causing him to plant a soggy kiss on her cheek. He used one hand to hold her down while his other fumbling hand ripped open the top of her blouse.

"No, Monsieur!" Annaveta cried out, struggling to break free from his grasp by pushing as hard as she could on his heavy body. His fat hand suddenly struck her cheek, and her head flew to the side, her hair still wrapped in her black head scarf. Her long auburn hair fell out of its tight bun, forming a pool of red-brown waves that circled her head. He stopped and stared at her. She flinched as the gleam in his eyes deepened.

Annaveta squeezed her eyes shut at his stare and tried to move. Her heart beat wildly as she realized she was trapped. The stench of his breath reminded her of the many times her drunken papa had beaten her. Mama had protected her when she was little, and Mama had been the one who'd gotten in trouble. These last few years, though, when her papa came home drunk in a rage, Annaveta had tried to protect Mama.

11

Usually she came away with some part of her body bruised or broken. This monster who held her captive was just like Papa, and she hated them both.

She opened her eyes and swallowed the nausea that wanted to erupt from her stomach as she heard his rapid breathing.

"Such innocent beauty. And all mine." Monsieur Arnaud's raspy voice pricked her ears as he reached out and trailed his hand over her silky hair. She tried to push his hands away, but he grabbed them and held them together in a firm grip.

"Now, be still." His quiet tone threatened her as much as his wandering fingers. His hand found the bottom of her long skirt and dragged it up. As he uncovered her legs and worked his way up with his dirty hand, he bunched her skirt. She screamed loudly for him to stop and tried to kick her legs, but she couldn't move. Terror consumed her. She froze like a trapped animal waiting for the final kill. Tears filled her eyes at her helplessness, and she tried to think of something else. *Please, help me. Whoever is listening, I need you now.*

Panting for breath, the pudgy man on top of her grabbed her pantaloons, and the sound of tearing fabric echoed in the small room.

"Stop! Have mercy, please!" Annaveta screamed as more tears streamed down her cheeks.

His loud laugh muted her screams as his hands fumbled with the buttons on his trousers.

Suddenly, through the thin walls, she heard the sounds of dogs barking and hurried footsteps. She screamed again.

Without warning, the door flew open. Splinters of wood scattered everywhere. A large man holding a shovel charged through the broken door, his face red with anger.

Annaveta watched in fear as his towering form loomed large in the cramped shed. His vivid blue eyes turned dark with anger as he took in her half-dressed body and the tears streaming down her cheeks. Her eyes widened as the stranger's cold unrelenting gaze focused on Monsieur Arnaud.

"Get off of her!" Alex stood there, his right hand gripping the shovel as he glared at the animal who held the screaming girl tightly pinned beneath him. Disgust filled him as he watched the overseer move his fleshy form off the thin girl. Alex's eyes shifted to take in the half-dressed girl-woman whose terror-filled expression changed to a sob of relief when she could move again. She shifted into a crouched fetal position against the back wall, her body trembling from head to toe. Alex felt his cheeks burning with anger.

Alex turned back to glare at Monsieur Arnaud; he couldn't believe what he was seeing. Monsieur Arnaud's pudgy hands fumbled with the buttons on his pants as his eyes darted back and forth between Alex and the door of the shed. Alex had heard her loud screams while one of the garden boys took him to find Monsieur Arnaud. He had planned on selling his family's extra seeds to the overseer today.

Alex remembered this steward from his previous trip to the Shremetev estate to sell seeds and other produce. He heard from one of the town elders in his small colony of Pleve that Count and Countess Shremetev had hired their French overseer a few years ago as a status symbol to impress other members of the Russian nobility. He had found Monsieur Arnaud sitting on the upper balcony of the main house drowning himself in Count Shremetev's vodka when he came here the last time. He didn't think the Shremetevs knew everything that went on at their estate when they were gone. Especially not the fact that their overseer was abusing their hired hands.

"You overgrown bully!" Alex shouted. His hands shook with anger. He pointed his dirt-covered finger at the shivering girl. "Look what you did. You would dare to terrorize a young girl? Maybe you just need someone your own size to fight." Alex threw down the shovel and with three strides stood in front of the man, his hands grabbing a fistful of shirt.

"*Mon Dieu*, Monsieur Wagner. Calm down." Monsieur Arnaud's shaky voice and pale face seem to be at odds with his words. Alex looked down at the man's eyes that reflected embarrassment and fear. The overseer seemed determined to explain away his actions. "Remember, if you attack me, you will no longer sell your produce here. I'll make sure all the other estates around here don't buy from you either. You will suffer, and your good name will be ruined. However, if you let me go, I will see to it that you are rewarded."

Alex couldn't believe his ears. *I caught him in the act of molesting a young girl, and he wants to reward me for my silence?* He thought of the loss of money to his family, but then just as quickly he remembered Papa's words: "Don't shrink back from doing what's right, Son. You'll live to regret it, if you do."

"This is for her innocence!" His clenched fist slammed into the man's double chin. Monsieur Arnaud made a feeble effort to fight back, but he was no match against Alex's strength. Alex punched him three times, and the overseer fell back, dazed, to the cold, hard floor.

"I trust you have learned your lesson today, Monsieur Arnaud," Alex said as his eyes took in the beaten man lying still on the floor.

Soft weeping from the corner made Alex aware of the young girl who was at the center of this mess. How could the overseer violate such a sacred trust? His heart ached with compassion as he watched her flinch with each step he took toward her. The innocence in her watery green eyes that searched his own was nearly his undoing. His gaze took in the long auburn hair that fell in soft waves over her shaking shoulders and down to her waist like a thick veil. Her shaking hands held together her ripped blouse. She pulled her knees even closer to her chest to hide her near-nakedness. He closed his eyes to rein in his unsettled emotions.

Then he reached out a gentle hand to touch her shoulder.

ANNAVETA WATCHED AS THE LARGE man moved toward her. She wiped the tears from her eyes and cheeks, worried he might be mad at her for displaying such raw emotions. With slow movements she lifted her head, her trembling arms pulling her knees tighter to her chest. She peered through stray wisps of hair to look up at this man who had saved her from the depraved hands of Monsieur Arnaud. His bright-blue eyes looked down at her with such compassion that she closed her eyes for a moment to soak it in.

Memories of her papa and of Monsieur Arnaud's attack filled her mind, and she opened her eyes in fear once again. She watched the unhurried steps he took toward her. Even in her fear, she sensed his kindness. He towered above her, his wide cheekbones and square jaw adding to his strength, and his blond hair shining like a halo in the darkened room. The touch of his hand on her shoulder caused her muscles to stiffen. She balled her hands into tight fists, her weapons at the ready.

"No. Stop!" Annaveta cried softly.

He wrapped his large arms around her shoulders and pulled her close, cradling her like a baby. The fight drained out of her as she heard his soft whispers against her hair. His low voice soothed her fears, and his gentleness calmed her. She cried until she had no tears left. Holding her close, he rocked her back and forth. She found comfort in his arms until she remembered Monsieur Arnaud. She pulled away from the stranger to look behind him. Seeing her attacker lying so still on the floor, she relaxed a little.

"Shhh. You'll be okay now." The stranger quietly placed her hand in his and with his other hand smoothed her hair. Her whimpering cries turned to quiet sighs.

Unexpectedly, all was still. No one hit her. No one yelled. The quiet moment didn't seem real. She lifted her head and peered through the tangled hair that fell in front of her face. Two of the brightest blue eyes she had ever seen looked back at her. There was no anger there — only compassion. She saw his eyes search hers, a frown marring his sun-kissed skin. He was so close, and she basked in the safety of his arms.

Then she stepped back, realizing that she was being held in a stranger's arms. She didn't know him, and yet for some reason she didn't fear him. A wonderful tingling warmth traveled up her spine as his muscled hands moved in soft circles up and down her back. She shouldn't be thinking that way. He was sure to think she was wanton. She took another step back to create more distance between them.

"He's still here." Annaveta looked over at her attacker, his large body lying unmoving on the wood floor. She stared in disbelief at him, then looked down at herself. Scratches and bruises on her arms and legs were laid bare by the shredded clothes that hung from her thin body. With shaky hands she pushed her tangled hair back from her face and held her torn blouse together. Her eyes widened as she heard a moan from across the room. She looked over to see the overseer move his head slightly as another moan came from him. Her legs weakened as fear filled her.

"Let's get away from here," the stranger said, catching her as she pitched forward. His arm went around her waist to keep her steady. He held her close to his side as they walked together toward the door.

Annaveta closed her eyes as they passed her assaulter, whose moans were getting louder. She stumbled as she hurried to get outside.

Once outside they kept walking until they were well beyond the shed and into the trees that separated the main house from the servants' quarters. She tripped over the roots and sticks that stuck up from the earth. The man stopped.

"Thank you for saving me. If you hadn't come when you

did — "

Annaveta put her hand over her mouth, suppressing sobs of relief, grateful that this unknown man had put an abrupt stop to such a horrible act. Her heart softened toward him because of his courage and kindness toward her. But still, he was a stranger. Someone she didn't know at all. He couldn't be trusted. She knew better.

She stiffened and turned away from his helping hand. She wouldn't allow herself to be drawn into the web of another man's lies and suffer at someone else's hands again. Her walls went up on the inside. Life had taught her in her short fifteen years that she couldn't trust anyone but herself.

"I did what needed to be done. What any decent man would do." The stranger's soft words weakened her resolve to push him away. "I'm just glad you are okay." He reached out his hand to help guide her through the thick green foliage. "Since it's clear I won't be selling the rest of my seeds here today, may I help you back to your home? I would feel better knowing you are safe."

"I . . . yes." Annaveta bit her lips, the shock of what she had just been through racing through her veins. She pointed the way. "Our small hut is behind the cattle barns, just past these trees. I'll change my clothes; then I need to find Mama. She needs to know what happened." She wiped away more tears. She wished the safe feeling she had when she was with this stranger would last forever. Grateful for his help to get back home, she allowed herself to enjoy a few last moments of the touch of his strong hand against her skin. His clothes smelled of horses and seeds. She took a deep breath wanting to remember this moment. To remember him.

Passing through the last strand of trees, she saw the outline of their small hut. She stopped him with a hand on his arm.

"What will happen to me? To my family?" She swallowed the fear that threatened to consume her. Her gaze darted to where they'd come from, but instinctively she was drawn back to his caring eyes.

"I hope the overseer has learned his lesson. If not, then it might mean I need to speak with the count, the next time he's here." He smiled at her, enclosing her small hand inside his large calloused one. "I'll be back in a week to see how you and your family are doing."

She just nodded and looked up at him, not knowing what to say. He held up her hand to his lips and kissed the back of it. The soft caress of his lips on her skin sent butterflies to her stomach. She stood there unmoving, watching him. His lips lingered on the back of her hand like a branding iron bonding her to him. She shivered as warm tingles ran up her arm. Finally, he let go of her and tipped his hat to her.

"I'll see you soon then." His smiling lips revealed nicely formed white teeth, and she couldn't resist smiling back. He walked a distance with his gaze fixed on her, then headed to the barn, where his wagon and horses were waiting.

Annaveta hugged her body and stared after him as he left. She wanted to remember the warm, safe feelings this stranger had stirred up in her. Her stomach fluttered with warmth as she thought of him, which quickly changed to shame and embarrassment as she remembered the overseer's attack.

She fought against the nausea that threatened to erupt. Her body trembled with fear as she hurried back to their hut. What would happen to her and her family now? What had she done?

Chapter 2

HER MUDDY FEET SLIPPED IN the lapti shoes that Mama had made from tree bark for the warm months ahead. The deep grooves in the narrow dirt road formed from yesterday's rain had made a few holes in the thin shoes, and it looked as if she would need to scrape off more bark from the trees along the river. Mama wouldn't be happy with her, not with all the extra work she'd had these past three weeks. The plowing, seeding, and planting of their small field had their small family up early and working late since they had been forced out of their old home and had moved to this new place.

Tears pricked her eyes as she remembered her mama's pleading cries as everything her family owned had been shoved into a big pile in front of their hut on the Shremetev estate. The overseer's men laughed and mocked their family as they set fire to everything they owned. Monsieur Arnaud's revenge was complete when he tossed them out of their small hut with no place to go. Later that night, they slept together huddled under the stars, but not before her papa had grabbed a willow branch and beaten her black-and-blue for what he said was her fault in tempting Monsieur Arnaud in the first place. Now, three weeks later, her back was just starting to heal.

Annaveta took in shallow breaths of the foul air that surrounded her. The rains that had poured down on the dry, cracked earth yesterday had been hoped and prayed for by the villagers, but the resulting damp air only heightened the horrible stench of animal and human waste that littered the ground around her. She kept her eyes on the rutted wagon path in an effort to dodge the recent animal droppings.

She frowned and then stopped herself. She wasn't in any position to complain about a little thing like foul odors. After what she had just been through with Monsieur Arnaud, she was glad the elders of the village of Noltava had let her papa work a small unused strip of land and live in the hut that had been abandoned by a widow and her small children.

Pushing back her black head scarf, she used her dirty sleeve to wipe the sweat off her forehead. Her only clothes, a colorless gray shirtwaist and a black skirt, had been given to her by her friend Pavla. She was grateful to have such a good friend. Looking down, she saw the bottom of her skirt soaked from wading in the river. She couldn't feel her toes. With the fieldwork finally done, she had walked the long way home, along the river. The wriggling in the basket was proof that the extra stop had been worth getting her feet cold in the icy river. These were healthy fish, and even after she had chopped off their heads, they had moved around a little bit. It looked like their family would finally be able to enjoy some meat instead of just the usual cabbage, beet, and barley soups.

She gave a sigh of relief that the planting was finished. Her sore back and limbs couldn't ruin her pleasure at being able to make a good meal this night. She could see their small hut in the distance, so she hurried, her feet slipping on the wet uneven ground. She knew the others wouldn't be far behind. Maybe this would be one day Papa would be happy, especially with a good meal in his belly and the planting done.

She shuddered as she remembered their first week in this small hut they now called home. Papa had come home, searching for kopeks in the small tin where Mama put their earnings. The money was gone. Mama explained that they needed the blessing of the priest, so he had said prayers for their family, and Mama had given their last kopek to the church. Papa had been so angry, his whole body shook. He called Mama names, and then slapped her across the cheek so hard that she fell and hit her head against the stove.

Annaveta had cried out as she heard the loud crack and then saw the still form of her mama lying on the dirt floor. The blood was already pooling around her head by the time Annaveta got to her. Papa had grabbed her arm and told her she deserved what she'd gotten. Then he told her he was hungry and ordered her to get him some food. She had just gotten the soup heated up, when he passed out on the floor. She left him lying there and rushed over to help Mama. She grabbed an old dry cloth and pressed it tightly against the side of her mama's head until the bleeding stopped, but she didn't wake up. Annaveta tapped her cheeks, but her mama lay still.

Annaveta had sat there all night with her mama's head on her lap praying her papa would die and that mama would live. She couldn't trust him. She hated him. When he was drunk, no one was safe. She hated feeling helpless, like a trapped animal. It seemed hopeless to wish he would change. It wasn't until close to morning that Mama's eyes opened. And it wasn't until the third day that Mama's dizzy spells went away. Every day since then she worked with a headache, and didn't talk about that night. It was almost as if nothing had happened. But something had triggered inside Annaveta. She couldn't make excuses anymore for her papa's actions.

Her steps quickened. Even though she had lost hope that her papa would ever change, she could still help make mama's life a little easier.

She passed a few peasant huts that lined the only rutted road through the village. Most *izbas* looked the same. They were built from logs that were poorly fit together, the large gaps filled with a mixture of mud and straw. Pigs, dogs, and chickens were outside many huts scrounging for whatever they could find to eat. It was spring again, and the small piglets, calves, and lambs were no longer squeezed together with large families inside their cramped peasant huts.

Annaveta's eyes were drawn to her friend busy hoeing the small garden plot that circled their home. She walked faster.

"Hi, Pavla. You almost done for today?" Annaveta grinned as she spied the little ones chasing a chicken. She grabbed the little girl who ran through the garden and twirled her around. Her soft giggles and flying legs urged Annaveta to go faster until she was so dizzy she fell to the ground. Annaveta laughed as she tried to get up, then stumbled and fell to the ground herself. She touched Pavla's hand and stood up this time without falling, letting out a small giggle as another wave of dizziness came over her. She hung on tighter to Pavla until her lightheadedness went away. The little girl spied the chicken and chased it to the road trying to catch it. Annaveta looked up and saw the twinkle of laughter in her friend's eyes.

"Feel better now?" Pavla put both hands on her hoe and leaned her chin on the top with a grin stuck to her face.

"I do. You don't look so good though. You have dark circles under your eyes." Annaveta raised a questioning eyebrow, while the popping sounds of little feet whisked by them once again.

"I am tired, and yes, I just finished my last row for today." Pavla took off her head scarf and wiped the sweat off her forehead. "I've been coming straight home from working at the estate garden because Mama's been feeling poorly again with this new babe coming."

Annaveta followed her friend as she put her hoe in the shed, digesting the news that Pavla's mama was pregnant again. This would make baby number thirteen.

Pavla leaned over to whisper in her ear. "You know Monsieur Arnaud is still livid. He told Mikhail, the head gardener, that you embarrassed him in front of his workers and that it can't go unpunished. He says he's going to find you and the man that helped you escape and make you both pay. So, be careful, okay?"

Pavla's worried frown caused Annaveta to stop in her tracks. She swallowed convulsively as fear filled her. Then she remembered what that evil overseer had done, and the fear changed to deep anger.

"Well, I have even more reason to be mad at him. I hate him for what he's done to me and to my family." Annaveta winced as she yanked up her sleeve. "Look. From him."

"Oh, Annaveta. That looks horrible," Pavla said, her mouth hanging open as she stared at the black-and-blue marks. "Well, you will just have to avoid him and make the best of your lot in life. That's what Mama says." Pavla's long sigh rang like the last clang of a funeral bell.

"I won't let it be my lot in life. Not anymore!" Annaveta frowned, disappointed that Pavla didn't seem to understand and feel the anger and fear that created the turmoil in her heart. Well, she supposed she couldn't be too upset with Pavla. Her friend had enough to worry about with all her work and then helping out with her many brothers and sisters.

Guilt pricked at her conscience for judging her friend. Life wasn't easy for her either. But it seemed like Pavla had already accepted that her life would be like her mama's. And Annaveta was determined that this life of struggling wouldn't be her fate forever. There had to be more to life than scraping to find the next meal and living in fear of some man intent on attacking her. She needed to be able to escape this murky life of merely surviving.

She rolled down her sleeve and picked up the basket full of fish.

"I need to go. These fish won't cook themselves. Will I see you tomorrow?" Annaveta asked, eyeing the small run-down Russian Orthodox church in the center of their village.

"You know I'll be there. Mama says we need to be careful not to offend God. You know what I mean. 'Pray to God, but take care not to offend the Devil.'" Pavla repeated the common Russian proverb as if it were ageless wisdom.

"I don't know if I believe all that, Pavla. If God is as hard to please as he seems, then I think I would rather not get too close to him." Annaveta frowned, looking again at the church as she thought of all the fasting and prayers they did. More than half the year was spent fasting. They had just finished fasting for Lent, so now they could celebrate by eating meat. She didn't understand why the church had all these rules they needed to follow. If God was such a strict judge, then she would rather have nothing to do with him.

She shook her head as if to clear out the maddening thoughts. "I need to go."

She waved a quick good-bye to her friend and hugged her coat tighter as she walked up to the shabby peasant hut that they now called home. The ground was spongy from the pouring rain the day before. She lifted her long black skirt as she made her way along the mud-caked stone path to their door. She lifted the latch, then stepped inside the dark one-room hut feeling the warmth coming from the big Russian stove that filled a quarter of the space. The white stove's color with its edges marked by simple drawings reminded her of their humble position as peasants.

She had been to her friend Natasha Dubachev's large *izba* at the other end of the village to pick up seeds and beans and had been a little jealous of their much-larger red-brick stove with its colorful tiles that displayed painted scenes of village life. The Dubachev family was better off than a lot of other peasants. She was pretty sure that Natasha's papa didn't drink away most of their money the way her own papa did.

She let the door open a crack so the fresh rain smell would overtake the musty odors that filled the small room. Since the big brick stove didn't need refueling until bedtime, she started working on making bread. With hurried hands she worked the rye flour and water with the little yeast they had to make their usual coarse sour black bread. She could hear mama's voice in her head telling her, "We need good solid food for heavy labor. Food that will hold workers to the earth. Poor is a dinner lacking bread." From the dark look of the dough, this would be solid, filling food. She hoped it was good as well. She put the loaves on the bread board and slid them into the oven just as mama moved clumsily into the hut, her arms on the shoulders of Annaveta's two brothers.

Mama's shaky hand fumbled with the head scarf that cradled her white face. Annaveta could tell she was feeling really sick. With hurried steps, she put her arm around her and helped her lie down on the sleeping bench near the stove.

"You're a good daughter." Mama's cold, wet hand touched her face. Annaveta saw that her threadbare skirt and her shirtwaist was soaked to the skin.

"Mama, I will find dry clothes for you." Seeing her eyes already closed, Annaveta looked under the bench and found a skirt that someone had given to her. There was no other shirt, so she used an old one of Papa's.

"Yuri and Nicolai, hold up the blanket please." Her brothers put down the wood sticks they used as toys and stood up to help. Annaveta smiled as they turned their backs and held the dark-gray wool blanket between them so she could change Mama's clothes. Counting on her two younger brothers, Nicolai and Yuri, to help her had become second nature to her, and many times she returned the favor. Nicolai at twelve years of age was beginning to stand as a barrier between papa's harsh anger and the women he loved. Annaveta worried that his fierce protective nature would one day get him in big trouble. Her younger brother Yuri, at seven, made her laugh and needed his daily hugs. She was grateful for them both.

Tugging off Mama's wet clothes, she rolled her mama over onto her side, managing to get the dry skirt and Papa's oversized shirt on her. Mama moaned a few times with all the movement, but fell back asleep as soon as the dry clothes were on.

Tucking the blanket around her, Annaveta was glad that

Mama was close to the warmth of the stove. The scent of baking bread was strong as she finished. She then cut up the fish and fried it in a little pig lard. Just as she was taking the bread out and putting it on the table, she heard the door creak open and shut with a thud. The heavy footsteps across the room let her know that her papa was here and ready for his supper. He sat at the table and frowned.

"Where's the rest of the food?" His eyes had a hard gleam in them that she knew all too well. "And what happened to your mama?"

"Her head hurts, so she is lying down. I caught some fish, so we're having that, and cooked potatoes." She walked to the stove to see if the food might be done cooking.

"You lazy girl. You should have started supper sooner." Papa's loud voice boomed off the walls. Annaveta put the fried fish on a plate. Then, seeing that the potatoes were done, she drained most of the water, leaving a little bit on the bottom of the pot to cream them. She hurried and managed to get everything on the table before Papa's temper got worse.

"Yuri. Nicolai. Come and eat," Annaveta called to her brothers. They dropped everything to come to sit on the rickety benches. Nicolai pushed Yuri away from him. Annaveta's body recoiled as Papa cuffed Nicolai on the side of the head. She saw her brother stiffen in anger. No words were spoken after that.

Papa bowed his head and crossed himself, sparing little time before his hands reached for the fish. Annaveta made sure she kept the platters coming until his plate was full, then she helped her brothers. She waited until everyone was eating before ladling the last small piece of fish and meager potatoes onto her plate. With her stomach in knots from trying to keep Papa happy, she wouldn't eat much of this meal. His loud belch and the thumping of his cup signaled his thirst.

Annaveta got up and hurried to the small shelf by the stove. She saw the tall bottle of vodka and with a shaky hand pulled it down. Her teeth clenched with the thought of what would happen next. She hesitated a second before taking off the lid and pouring it into Papa's waiting cup. His long drink ended with a satisfied smile that seemed charming but was only a cover for the long, hard night ahead. She hurried the boys to finish eating so they could do their chores, while she washed the dishes.

With a secret glance now and again at Papa, she knew he was draining his second full cup by the time they were all done. She motioned for the boys to get in their beds. Annaveta scrambled with quiet steps and unrolled her blanket, then lay down beside the boys, taking deep breaths to calm her nerves. She knew that by the end of his third cup her papa would be drunk, and if anyone was around, he would turn mad and start hitting.

Hearing a loud thump on the floor, she breathed a sigh of relief. Good, he's finished drinking early this night. They were safe. For now.

It took a long time for her to fall asleep.

The next morning Annaveta stood and stretched, rubbing circles on the small of her back. Yesterday's rain had moistened the dry earth just enough to make planting the seeds in the garden easier. She and Mama had gone with Yuri right after breakfast to the small plot of land behind their *izba*, to dig holes for the seeds. They had just finished planting the few seeds that had been given them by the village elders. Annaveta breathed a loud sigh of relief. Looking up, she saw the sun beginning to lower from its high perch above their village.

"Mama, you rest now. I'll make tea." Annaveta looked at her white face that stood out in stark contrast to the dark-gray head scarf she wore.

"I was hoping you would go pick some herbs today." Mama leaned on her arm as they walked to the house. She knew what Mama meant by her words. Since Papa had left today to go to his new job, this would be a good day to go looking for herbs and mushrooms and berries. He didn't like it when they left the hut. He liked them to stay at home unless they were working the fields.

"Yes. Today would be a good day." Annaveta helped her mama sit down on the bench by the table, then added more kindling to the fire in the stove. After pouring the water from the pail into the small pot, she set it on the large stove.

"Are you feeling poorly? The pots haven't banged this loudly in a long time." Mama looked over at her with an understanding smile that had Annaveta in tears.

"Oh, Mama. I'm just so angry with what has happened to us, I could scream. I am mad at Monsieur Arnaud for the evil man he is, angry at myself for somehow being in his way, and furious with God for allowing it all to happen in the first place." Annaveta covered her face with her hands and wept.

"As far as that madman's actions go, it's not your fault. It's his. You need to forgive yourself and just be grateful that the stranger came along to help you when he did. Or else we would be dealing with a bigger problem." Mama motioned for her to come sit beside her. "As for God, it sounds to me like someone was protecting you from much worse."

Annaveta sat beside her mama on the cracked wooden bench. Her eyes glistened with unshed tears as Mama's work-worn hands lifted a corner of her patched hand-sewn apron to wipe the tears that spilled down her cheeks.

"You are my special girl, little one. I'm just so happy that you're safe." Mama squeezed her eyes shut, and her lips quivered as if she wanted to say more. The warmth of her mama's love covered Annaveta like a warm blanket.

"I think I will go on that walk," she said.

Chapter 3

ANNAVETA WAVED BACK AT WIDOW Zolkin. She hurried by the old lady talking with Mrs. Grekov just outside the matchmaker's low thatched roof. She was sorry for Chenka, another village girl her age and Mrs. Grekov's only daughter. It looked as if the widow was busy making plans for a suitable husband for her friend. Annaveta pulled her head scarf further down her forehead, hoping they wouldn't stop to talk with her. She hastened her steps as she passed them.

Reaching the edge of the village, she followed along the damp path that led through the low-lying poplar trees to the meadow where she had gone once before. She knew this trail headed east toward some of the German colonies that Papa had said she was forbidden to visit. She didn't plan on walking that far — just the few miles it took to get to where there would be more plants and herbs to add to her basket.

She walked for quite a long time before the trail turned eastward. Catching her breath, she took in the quiet beauty of the open meadow and laughed as she ran and hugged the old crooked tree that sat in the middle of the open field. She dropped her basket to the ground and, pulling her head scarf off, freed her hair from its tight braid. Her thick hair swirled around her shoulders and waist as she danced in the freedom of an afternoon to spend by herself. She lifted her head and closed her eyes, savoring the sun's warm kiss and feeling the wind's warm fingers weaving gently through her hair. The chirping of birds and the crackling sounds of twigs and leaves beneath her feet added to the pleasure of the spring day.

After twirling again and again, she fell down in a dizzy heap, laughing out loud from the pleasure of the moment. A twig snapped. Her eyes widened with surprise to see the stranger who had rescued her at the Shremetev estate standing and staring at her. His arms were crossed, and a glint of laughter shone in his bright blue eyes. His intense gaze swallowed her up. She stood still and stared at him, shocked to see the man who had saved her life standing here in the meadow. His wavy blond hair was mussed, and the strong wind snapped his suspenders. He looked more like a mischievous boy than the hero she remembered.

He wasn't alone. Annaveta observed the short blond-haired girl who was looking back and forth between Annaveta and the young man, with a big smile creasing her plump pink cheeks.

"You look like the good fairy straight from Tchaikovsky's Ballet *Sleeping Beauty.*" He teased her as if seeking a response. His Russian words were laced with the recognizable German accent she had heard the last time she spoke with him. When she didn't speak, he went on. "It is good to see you again. This time our meeting is much better than last time, *ja?*" He reached out, pulled her up to stand before him, then, bowing low, he raised her hand to his lips.

Her cheeks heated as his warm lips touched her skin and lingered. He looked into her eyes with an intensity that made her step back. His eyes seemed to devour her. She watched as he took in her homemade *lapti* shoes, his gaze wandering upward, not missing her patched skirt and blouse and wind-tossed hair. These were the only clothes she had, but from the appreciative look in his eyes he didn't seem to mind. Her hand tingled from the warmth of his kiss on her skin as he let go of it.

"Yes, meeting you here is much better and safer than last time." She ran her hand up her arms to stop the goose bumps that his long kiss had unleashed. She looked at the girl beside him in an effort to change the subject. "You have a friend with you this time." She tensed as she waited for him to explain who the pretty girl beside him was.

"This is my younger sister, Clara. And I'm Alex," he said, looking down at his sister with a grin as he pulled on her braid. Annaveta covered her mouth with her hand to stop the laughter that bubbled up as she watched his sister cuff him on the shoulder. Annaveta was slightly surprised at the feeling of relief she had upon learning the pretty blonde was his sister.

"She isn't always as nice to me as she should be, but she's a good little sis." That earned him another swat.

"Don't mind my brother — he's always teasing." Clara smiled at her and nodded. "So, what's your name, and how do you know my brother?"

"I'm Annaveta. Your brother stopped the overseer at the Shremetev estate from attacking me and possibly saved my life a few weeks ago. I'm in his debt." Annaveta looked at Clara, who watched the two of them with interest. "Thank you again for saving me from Monsieur Arnaud." Her gaze flitted to his, and then she looked down at her hands as her eyes filled with tears as she remembered the horror of that day.

"Anyone else would have done the same." Alex shrugged and then frowned. "Is he still a problem?"

Annaveta thought back to that day at the estate when her family's life had been swiftly ruined by the actions of the angry overseer. She realized he didn't know that her family had been forced off the property.

"I don't know." Annaveta swallowed, trying to stop tears from rolling down her cheeks as the memories of that day washed over her. "We had to leave. So now we live in the village of Noltava. My family was removed from the estate by Monsieur Arnaud."

She dried her eyes with her sleeve and peered up at Alex. His eyebrows lifted in surprise at her words, then, as quick as the shifting wind, he frowned his lips tightly in restrained anger.

"How dare he? That low-down snake. I ought to go over there and give him another piece of my mind." Alex spat on the ground in disgust. Annaveta was shaken by his response, but soon her heart warmed toward him as she thought of his fierce protective nature and his anger at injustice. She wondered what it would feel like to be the woman who was loved and protected with such a fierce passion. Heat rose up from her belly, making its way to her cheeks. She lowered her gaze so he wouldn't guess her thoughts.

"Who is this man that has you all in a scowl?" Clara's eyebrows knit together, a look of concern written on her face.

"Monsieur Arnaud, of course." Alex spoke through a clenched jaw. "The overseer and assaulter of young girls at the Shremetev estate. He's the cursed man that threw Annaveta's family out without a place to live or work. He needs to be taught another lesson." Alex looked across the meadow, his features darkening, as if he was planning something. The look in his eyes made her worried. She had to try to stop whatever he was planning.

"No. Please don't do anything rash." Annaveta pleaded with Alex, cautiously putting her hand on his clenched fists. "If you confront him, it will just make things worse for my family. Already, my papa comes home angry, when he does come home. I don't want it to get worse." She shuddered, imagining how things could get even worse at home.

He looked down at her hand on top of his, and Annaveta removed it with haste. She tried to cover up her embarrassment by rearranging the cloth in her basket.

"All right, I won't go. This time," Alex said, the serious look on his face a promise of justice if there were any more problems with Monsieur Arnaud. "I just need to know — are you and your family doing okay?"

"We are carrying on. Mama said Papa's just found a seasonal job as a barge hauler along the Volga River. So we should be okay." Annaveta smiled even though deep inside she worried that Papa would spend all his pay on vodka, not only leaving them without food but coming home to beat Mama again. Well, there was no sense in worrying about things she couldn't change.

"Looks like it's getting late." Annaveta noticed the sun's position in the sky creeping its way lower. "I need to pick some herbs and mushrooms for Mama and then head home before it gets too late." She looked at sister and brother, nodded, then turned to leave.

"Wait." She heard Clara's quick footsteps behind her. The gentle squeeze of her hand on her arm seemed oddly soothing. "Let's see what we can find together, *ja*?" Her chatter continued. "My mama is a midwife and healer for most of the people in our colony, so I'm used to looking for herbs. What do you need to find?"

Annaveta digested this news about Clara's mama. She had always wanted to learn how to be a midwife. Maybe she would learn some things from Clara.

"I am looking for peppermint, cornflower, blackwort roots, and wild thyme," Annaveta said as she looked among the thick scattering of wild plants in the spacious meadow.

"I've spotted three of the four plants," Clara said as she rushed around like a busy bee. Annaveta looked back to see Alex sitting on the grass, his back against the big tree in the middle of the meadow. His eyes seemed hooded, his expression intense as he watched them. Annaveta quickly turned her head and followed Clara's hurried strides.

"Here they are. Here's peppermint, which is good for flavoring and to help the stomach. Cornflower will help with chest pains, colds, and fevers. At least that's what Mama tells me." Clara smiled at her as she plucked more herbs and placed them in Annaveta's basket. "Wild thyme helps in treating a cough or breathing problems. So do the blackwort roots, and I think I spotted some over by the rocks."

Annaveta listened as she went on and on about more

herbs. They even found licorice and sassafras roots to use for teas. Annaveta found many mushrooms growing in the tall grasses by rocks and poking their heads up through fallen trees. She was careful to avoid toadstool mushrooms, as those were poisonous. They searched for a long time, with Annaveta listening to Clara's chatter until the sun had lowered in the cloudy sky above.

She couldn't believe that she was speaking so freely with people who were from a German colony. She had asked her papa about the people with the strange accent when they had gone to market one day. He had warned her: *"Stay clear of those Krauts. They seemed to have missed the boat to take them back to where they came from. They are making money off of our land. Land that belongs to us. We don't need their kind around here, so stay clear of them. Do you hear me?"* She never brought up the subject again. Since then, Annaveta had gone out of her way to stay clear of any Germans. Yet, since the day that Alex had saved her from the estate's overseer, she couldn't help but see Alex as a good man instead of the enemy she had expected. She knew Papa would be angry with her if he knew she talked with Alex and Clara, so this would have to be another secret she kept buried inside. She really liked Clara and Alex and hoped that somehow she could see them again.

"I'm so glad we are becoming friends, aren't you, Annaveta?" Clara's accented Russian words fell like soothing water over her ears, making her feel warm all over.

Annaveta grinned at her. "Yes, I am, Clara." Although, she wondered just how that would work with her papa feeling the way he did about these colonists. She really wanted to get to know Clara, and maybe Alex better, so she decided to let her feelings guide her instead of her head.

"If you would like to learn more about the different medicines and herbs that my mama uses, you should come and visit us. Pleve Colony isn't so far away. We could go together with Mama on her visits and learn." Clara's pleading blue eyes, so like her brother's, pulled at something deep inside. What would it be like to get to know this family and join in the fun and warmth they seemed to share? Most of the time her family was either angry, unhappy, or too sick, and everyday living was often what Mama called "the heartache of trying to survive."

"You know I would love to learn more from your mama, Clara, but my papa will not let me come to your village or your house. You know the bad feelings that some Russians have toward the Germans. They feel they are outsiders and shouldn't have the land that they believe rightfully belongs to the Russian people. There would have to be some crisis before I would ever be allowed near your village." Annaveta shook her head, filled with sorrow at the truth of her words.

"Well, somehow I need to see more of you." Clara tilted her head to the side, thinking. "I have it! We'll meet right here in this meadow on Sunday afternoons. That would work, right? If either of us can't make it, we'll use that hollow log to put notes in." Clara pointed to an old hollowed-out log that had moss growing out of it. She clapped her hands excited at the thought. "Well, what do you think?"

"Yeah, that would work some Sundays. My parents said I need to help the other young women organize our first *Khorvody* — the round dance for young people — this coming Sunday. In my village this first spring dance for Easter will bring quite a few youths from other Russian villages together. Most of the parents, including mine, have much hope that this will be the start of serious courting for their daughters." Annaveta shook her head. "That's the last thing I want, but I must do this for my mama."

"Okay. Then maybe we can meet Sunday next?" Clara's eyes were begging her.

"Let's plan on it, and if it doesn't work for either one of us, we'll put a note in the log."

"Sounds good. See you Sunday next."

Annaveta's laughter filled the air as she watched her new

friend twirl a happy dance.

"Did you girls find the herbs you need?" Alex's voice from behind startled Annaveta, and she tripped on a loose stick and fell back into his arms. He held her with one hand on her shoulder and the other around her waist. He pulled her closer and looked down, his eyes whirling with a sea of emotions. Her body betrayed her. She seemed powerless to move away. Some part of her wanted to stay close to him, while another part sensed fear in this moment.

"Are you okay?" His whispered breath blew across her face like a caress. She lay back in his strong arms, mesmerized by him. Tingles ran up her arms and moved across her belly. Her green eyes met his stormy ones that had darkened to a deep blue.

He pulled her even closer as his head bent down to hers. *He's going to kiss me. I can't do this.* She turned her head to the side, and he stilled his sudden movement. Her body trembled in fear at his closeness.

She struggled to stand up on unsteady legs. He seemed reluctant to let her go. She pushed up and stepped back from him. She couldn't look at him. Her emotions were too close to the surface. She closed her eyes and let out the breath she'd been holding.

"I need to be heading home. I told Mama I'd be back by supper." Annaveta caught Clara's grin and smiled back. She looked at Alex's throat, as she was too embarrassed to look into his eyes. *What must he think of me? Lying in his arms like a loose woman. For shame, Annaveta.*

"I look forward to the next time we meet." Alex grabbed her hand and kissed the back of it. She made the mistake of looking into his upturned face. His rogue smile was firmly in place as his lips touched her skin. She pulled on her hand, wanting to take back the little she had surrendered to him.

"Till next time." Annaveta hurried to pick up her fallen basket and nodded at them both one last time before she hurried away.

"See you soon," Clara called out.

Annaveta slowed her steps and turned to wave back. A mistake. She saw Clara grinning, and Alex's eyes followed her every movement. He put his hat on and touched the tip as he nodded at her. She nodded and waved, a smile absent from her features. Mixed emotions swirled around in her head. She couldn't believe he had almost kissed her. Her hand still tingled from his romantic gesture. Annaveta had the curious sense of being drawn to him, and yet everything in her told her a man was not to be trusted.

Alex was the first man she had met who was handsome, gentle, and protective. What a cruel twist of fate that he was from the same people her papa saw as enemies. She would have to be careful to make sure she didn't reveal this secret to anyone in her family. She shuddered, too scared to think what might happen. She had just added another secret to her growing list. She would need to guard this one well, just like the others.

Chapter 4

SMOOTHING OUT HER THICK WAIST-LENGTH braid, Annaveta took one final look in their small mirror. Through the cracks in the glass, she studied the freckles sprinkled liberally across her nose and cheeks. Her brow crinkled as she stared at her reflection. Sea-green eyes that looked too large for her small oval-shaped face stared back. With her nose scrunched up, she tried to hide the freckles, but it didn't work. She loosened her braid a little so that the strands would cover the crescent-shaped pink scar on the left side of her neck. It was a daily reminder to be careful whom she trusted.

Straightening the new white blouse Mama had remade from someone's giveaway, she wished once more that her curves weren't so noticeable. She did not want any extra attention today. Today was Sunday and the day of her first real *Khorvody.* The *Khorvody* was meant to make couples from single young people, but she was hoping to put off having a suitor for as long as she could. She thought of all the girls her age who were excited to be at today's round dance. It seemed she would be the odd one out, because she was not happy to have to take part in the fun.

Annaveta was used to being different. All the other girls in the village were eager to be married, raise babies, and live in this village the rest of their lives. Being stuck here in this little village wasn't what she wanted, but if something didn't change, she knew this is where she would stay.

Annaveta didn't know why she longed to see more of

the world or why she was so restless. Standing back from the mirror, she looked at her form and knew that even her body was dissimilar to the girls her age in the village. Her average height and small bone size seemed to draw attention to her growing bosom, which was accented all the more by her slender waist. All the other girls seemed so well proportioned, with bigger and stronger bodies. She knew that's what most Russian men looked for in a wife, and with her small build, she clearly didn't measure up. She was sure she would have to endure the usual teasing from the boys and the mocking voices of the girls tonight. However, if it meant pleasing Mama, she would go to the dance and try to put a smile on her face. She looked in the mirror again and forced the corners of her mouth to lift.

She fingered the green-and-red festive skirt that Widow Polaski had given her, and tucked the ends of her white blouse inside the wide waistband. Annaveta had stitched the much-larger skirt so it hugged her slender waist. It hung in soft lines to her feet. It was good to wear newer clothes that fit her. Seeing her feet poking out from under her skirt, Annaveta wished for soft shoes instead of her usual tree bark shoes. Oh well, what did it matter anyway? She wasn't interested in meeting any of the men or trying to impress them. The only reason she was dressing up was her parents said it was time for her to marry. It was time. *I'll just have to find some way to escape being caught.* She would be sixteen soon. Time for her to be the added laborer in her future husband's household.

Pushing aside the hanging blanket that hung in the corner, Annaveta caught the shimmer of tears in her mama's eyes as she walked to where she stood by the stove.

"Oh, little one. You look so beautiful. So grown-up." Her voice shook with emotion, and a single tear made its way down her work-roughened cheek. The soup spoon clattered against the pot as she dropped it. "I'm so proud."

Annaveta gave her mama a tight smile as she bent down to pick up the spoon. "Mama, do I have to go? Couldn't we put this off until the fall festival?" Annaveta begged her mama, hoping that maybe this time she would relent.

"My dear. You are of age now. You know your papa and I are hoping for a good match. Remember the Russian proverb: 'Do not forsake your papa and mama in their old age, and God will not forsake you.' Don't worry — we'll make sure we ask old Widow Zolkin, the matchmaker, what she thinks of any man who shows interest in you." Mama stirred the soup quickly. Annaveta stared intently at the soup, her thoughts whirling with questions.

"Mama, look at me." The wrinkled corners of her mama's eyes only intensified the look of love Annaveta saw in her eyes. "You know the men in our village like strong women who are bigger than I am. I'm too small and look too soft for any man to want me as his wife." Annaveta repeated what she had heard — what the old village mamas said in the past about her small bones and skinny body. "Besides that, what man will want a wife who comes to him with no dowry? All men want the girl they marry to bring something to their household. Most girls have money from all the things they've made and sold. Everything I had was burned at the estate. Now, the only thing I have to offer is myself. My purity. Or at least I did until those spiteful, unmarried girls spread lies about me in the village about what happened to me at the estate. So now even my reputation has been ruined. I have nothing left." Annaveta burst into tears at the thought of facing all those mean-spirited people again.

"Daughter, I'm so sorry. I will stand by your side tonight. If you can bear all the talk, then I will also. Papa will be there too. Maybe that will help." Mama used the corner of her apron to wipe away the flood of tears blotching her daughter's cheeks.

"You and Papa don't need to come. I'll be fine." Annaveta forced a too-bright smile in hopes that Mama would believe she was okay. She didn't need the added embarrassment of her papa getting drunk at her first *Khorvody*. "I told Pavla

I would meet her, and we would walk together to help the other girls prepare for the dance," Annaveta said, wiping away the remaining traces of tears. "I'll see you later."

With her basket full of vines she had found to add to the decorations, she walked toward Pavla's house. She knew Mama's being at the *Khorvody* dance would help, but questioned what would happen with her papa there. Looking at the blue sky, she saw clouds that hinted at coming rain. She hoped it would come. Maybe the village festivities would be brought to an end early.

Annaveta lifted her skirts to avoid the dust as she walked to Pavla's house. She waved at her friend's mama. Mrs. Baranova nodded as she moved her youngest child to her hip to make room for her protruding belly. Compassion filled her as she looked at Mrs. Baranova, who seemed so worn out from having so many children. Pavla grinned at Annaveta as she scooted quickly past her many brothers and sisters who tried to grab her hand or skirt. She pulled the ribbons from Pavla's younger sister's grasping hand.

"Let's go quickly, or we'll never get away." Pavla's clipped tone matched the pace she set as they walked toward the meadow at the edge of the village.

"You found ribbons, after all?" Annaveta touched the colorful array of silk that flowed down her friend's arm like reflections of the sun from a church window.

"Mama had some hidden in her treasure box from when she was young. She saved them for me and my sisters to use." Pavla ran her fingers down the silken threads, and Annaveta moved to take the basket of food from her other hand.

"The meadow will be beautiful for the round dance when we are done decorating, for sure. I didn't really want to go. Having the other girls treat me like a loose woman is not something I'm looking forward to." Annaveta looked at Pavla, hoping for encouragement.

"It wasn't your fault that Monsieur Arnaud chose to make a spectacle of you. If their tongues wag around me, I'll

let them know the truth and put a stop to their foolishness."
Pavla bumped her shoulder in a gesture of camaraderie. "By
the way, I really like the bright colors of your skirt."

"Thanks. Widow Polaski gave it to Mama for my use."
Annaveta ran her hand along the slim waistline. "She's a nice
lady. Wagging tongues in the village tell lies about her too."

Annaveta sighed, feeling sorry for her, for Widow
Polaski's husband had died last year in a freak horse
accident.. She was especially grateful for this gift. Since then,
the wealthy Anton Dubachev had his eye on the allotment
of arable and farmstead land that the widow had cultivated
with the help of her twelve-year-old son. Pavla told her
that Mr. Dubachev had bribed the village and cantonal
authorities to take the widow's land on the false pretext that
it was not being farmed. Pavla's papa said there wasn't much
he could do, since all the male leaders of the village assembly
were under pressure from the rich village elder. So they gave
Mr. Dubachev Widow Polaski's arable allotment and a large
portion of her farmstead land. Mama had told her that now
Mr. Dubachev wasn't satisfied and wanted to get the rest of
the widow's land. She couldn't understand how something
like that could happen to a poor widow and her son. She
knew Mrs. Polaski had been working extra hard this winter
on weaving cloths and making lace to sell to make money
for her and her son. She didn't deserve the unfair treatment.

Arriving at the meadow, Annaveta saw girls from their
village, as well as some she didn't know from the two other
small villages closest to their own. Natasha and Fayina, the
two meanest girls in Noltava, stood together arranging the
many rye and dark breads on the table. Natasha's mama, the
well-off Mrs. Dubachev, was tying together some streamers
made of colorful cloths and stringing them through the
low-hanging branches that surrounded the meadow. The
youngest girls were busy fetching items and helping with the
decorating.

"Pavla, you are just in time. I'm glad you are here. It's

good to have another decent maiden in the village join us. It's much better than being forced to endure the company of the riffraff that slithers in." Natasha stared coldly at Annaveta before turning her head and giving Pavla a big smile.

"I'm glad to be here. Annaveta and I brought extra breads, as well as a few pieces to help with decorating." Pavla gave a big smile to Natasha and Fayina.

"Yes. It's good to see you, Pavla. Too bad that the trash followed you here." Faytina smirked at Annaveta.

"I think you girls must have heard a rumor that isn't true about my friend. She wasn't — "

Natasha cut in. "I admire you for being loyal, Pavla, but you should really rethink what you are doing and saying. Sticking up for her will only make your own reputation in the village worse. Then you'll never be able to find a decent husband. You don't want that." Natasha acted as if she were doing Pavla a favor. "Come and help us. The three of us can work together at this table." Natasha moved to make room for Pavla.

"Sorry, I can't. I promised Annaveta we would decorate the meadow together. Here's another basket to add to the pile." Pavla smiled as she set down her basket of rye bread. Annaveta watched their faces switch from surprise to frowns as she put down her own basket filled with *kasha* and berries she'd picked to add to the food pile. She followed Pavla to the trees and shrubs that surrounded the meadow.

"Thanks for sticking up for me. You didn't have to do that, Pavla," Annaveta said, pushing wisps of hair from her face. She knew those girls were doing their best to exclude her. She pushed down feelings of hurt, hoping they would go away, and gave a grateful smile to her friend.

"You're my friend, and you and I both know they are just trying to make your reputation worse by spreading lies. Their words are coming from hearts of envy and jealousy. They don't like it that you are prettier and full of more goodness than the two of them put together," Pavla said, handing her a few ribbons. "Let's not think about them. Let's try to have fun today. So, how should we decorate?"

The two girls worked together putting the ribbons on the many trees that surrounded the large meadow. The green grass mixed with wild yellow, purple, and white crocus flowers signaled the first signs of spring. Annaveta took deep breaths of the sweet scent of the blue honeysuckle bushes that had sprouted between the trees. She couldn't resist picking a handful of the juicy teardrop-shaped blue berries with their sweet taste.

Pavla giggled at her bulging cheeks. "If you eat too many, your mouth will turn blue."

Annaveta scrunched her nose at her friend's teasing. Soon they were joined by young teenage girls and young married women. Some older mamas and widows came to help make the borscht in the extra-large pot that perched on the iron stand the village blacksmith forged for just such events. It didn't take long for all the rye bread, sour black bread, cheese, and some salted beef and pork to fill up the table. This was the first big celebration after Easter, and all peasants, especially those without a lot of means and who were faithful to the Orthodox church, were glad to be off the fast they had religiously endured since Lent. With disciplined endurance, they waited for the few times a year they could eat meat. Rare were the days they ate with such abandon, as the church prescribed fasting for one reason or another on one hundred and eighty days of the year.

Annaveta watched as Widow Zolkin positioned herself by the big urn, stirring the soup slowly so she could observe the young people. The village matchmaker was on duty.

Annaveta decided that she would not dance with any one man too long, so the very watchful widow wouldn't get any ideas.

The single men from ages fifteen to their early thirties started arriving, bringing along the two brothers who played the accordion. They had learned to play the new instrument on their own and were often asked to play for festivals and weddings.

Pavla came behind her and whispered in her ear, "I see some couples are pairing up early."

"Look at Natasha and Vassily. They are two of a kind. Natasha's papa, Mr. Dubachev, has money and pushes his influence to get his way, and so does Vassily's papa. Seems to me the apple doesn't fall far from the tree."

"I don't understand either of them. Let's not think about them. Look over there. Standing by the accordion brothers is Sergei Smirnov." Annaveta coaxed her friend, knowing she liked the poor farmer's son.

"Annaveta, I will say the same about Misha Ivanov. He's over there with the other men, but he's staring at you. If you dance with Misha, I'll dance with Sergei. Okay?" Pavla looked down at her smaller friend. "I know you aren't ready for a man, but it's only a dance. You can do it."

"I don't know, Pavla. I'm just not ready. I think I'll just stay here and watch," Annaveta protested.

"Looks like you're too late. Your papa and mama have arrived, and here comes Misha," Pavla whispered.

The accordion players started up their first song. It wasn't surprising to Annaveta that the words of the first song spoke of the loss of a girl's freedom and the abuse she would endure once she married and went to live with her husband's family.

Do not wait, girls.
Dance now.
They will give you away in marriage in the fall.
They will not give you such freedom.
Your good-for-nothing husband will bring all his weight
down to bear on you.
He will scoff at you.
He will taunt
and abuse me for everything.

I lived at my papa-in-law's.
I created three misfortunes.
Here is the first misfortune:
I cooked some shchi — and spilled it.
Here is the second misfortune:
I made pirogi — and burned them.
The third misfortune:
I did not lie down to sleep with my husband.
And how my husband beat me.
He avidly beat me.
I had to take to my bed
from that beating;
I was in bed for three weeks.

"Would you dance with me?" Misha asked as he held his hand out. The picture in Annaveta's mind of living the life painted in the song was so real that she jumped back in fear when he appeared in front of her. Her heart pounded, and a cold chill ran up and down her spine as she looked at the man in front of her. His cocky smile made his swarthy good looks fade away.

"Are you going to make me beg?" He smiled widely, enjoying his own joke as he grabbed her hand and pulled her to his side. "Come dance with me. You'll like it."

Annaveta mouthed *help* to Pavla as she was pulled quite forcibly to the middle of the meadow, where most people were dancing. But Pavla was busy talking to some of the other village girls. There would be no help from her. Annaveta had only heard about Misha. Pavla had mentioned that he was from a nearby village and had heard other girls speak of him as a man who seemed to be stuck on himself and drank too freely.

"Well, what do you think? You get to dance with the best-looking dancer here," Misha purred as he grabbed her and pulled her so close she could feel his every heartbeat. "We make a good pair, don't you think?"

"I don't even know you." Annaveta ignored his last self-serving question as she moved to make more space between them. "Don't hold me so tight; I can hardly breathe."

"I intend to make you mine," her captor said as his eyes slid suggestively down her form.

"You might intend to, but I don't," she assured him. Her hackles went up at his leering looks and the possessiveness of his words.

"I like the fire in you," he challenged as the ballad came to an end. He held her close even after the song ended. She pushed against his chest until he finally released her. "I'll be seeing you again."

Annaveta quickened her pace as she turned and moved as far away from him as possible. With all the people moving about, she hoped she could quickly find Pavla. She walked over to the food table and poured herself some tea. Holding the hot cup with both hands, she stood on tiptoe to find her friend, then spotted her on the other side of the food tables. Annaveta hastened to her one safe haven in the storm. She passed men who gave her interested looks, but she just lowered her head. She was relieved when she reached Pavla.

Annaveta blurted out her frustration. "You are not going to believe how bold that Misha is. He intends to make me his, he says, and we've only just met. I don't intend to court or marry anyone as bold and cocky as he is. How did he even get invited here? He's from Molkov village. Usually our men don't allow outsiders to join our village dances. I just hope he doesn't plan to meet my parents."

"His cockiness is well known. Just last week Marta's brother heard Misha bragging to his friends in the village about his list of conquests. As to how he got in, look over at the men from our village. They are each carrying large bottles of vodka. Looks like he paid them off to come to the round dance," Pavla informed her friend, looking around at the many young people who came. "It's too late for your last wish. I see the matchmaker has introduced Misha to your papa and mama."

Annaveta looked over at the crowd that gathered where the path stopped and the meadow began. She saw her papa stagger toward the matchmaker. Was he drunk already? No surprise, seeing that the vodka was free. Her mama beckoned her over to where they stood with a wave of her hand and a big smile.

Annaveta wanted to hide. She wanted to be anywhere but here at this moment. She shook her head as if to say no to her mama, but Mama only made bigger gestures with her hands for her to come. She knew where this was headed. Her worst fear was coming true before her eyes.

Chapter 5

"I DIDN'T LIKE HOW YOU treated that nice young man when he was introduced to us, Daughter. The matchmaker went out of her way to help us, and you didn't even give Misha a smile. Shame on you." Papa's eyes were hard, narrowing to mere slits as he stared at her. "I know he will be coming to our village tomorrow for the *Posidelki* work bee and social afterward. I want you to do whatever you need to do to show that you are happy to see him. This is one way you can finally make up for the disgrace you brought on our family at the Shremetev estate. Do you understand?"

Annaveta had answered, "I don't like him, Papa. He's so arrogant and only talks about himself. Pavla says she heard that he drinks all the time and gets into fights when he does." Annaveta looked at her mama for her support, knowing she longed for her daughter to marry a good man, but she remained silent.

Her papa continued. "Well, Pavla isn't always right. I've heard from the matchmaker that his family is rich. That's all I need to know. He's living the Russian proverb: 'Get a wife from afar; buy a cow near.' So, you will do as I say, or you'll wish you had. Do you hear me?" Papa shook his finger in front of her nose.

"Yes, Papa." Annaveta knew she would have to obey or she would get a beating. She wanted to have a way out, but any hope for her future seemed very bleak.

The door slammed as he left their small hut, heightening

the tension in the room. Annaveta jumped back, her body's response instinctive. Her hands moved her wet rag with more vigor over the almost spotless stove, each movement emphasizing her anger. Papa's unreasonable demands spun around in her head. Maybe the anger she was feeling at being forced to marry would begin to wear away like the skin on the end of her fingers. She looked over at Mama, who was busy cooking the fish that Nicolai had caught for this evening's meal. She sighed, a mixture of frustration and resignation in the sound.

Her future would be very bleak indeed if she had to spend it with Misha. Nicolai had asked his friends about him, and they all said he got drunk regularly and thought he was the best at everything. His friends said there were some of the youth in his village who'd claimed he dallied with plenty of girls, and that there was one girl he got in trouble.

Nicolai's description of Misha didn't surprise her. One thing she knew was that she didn't want anything to do with an unprincipled man like that. For now she would have to go along with the plan, but she was desperate to figure out a way out of this mess.

ANNAVETA AWOKE TO THE SOUND of her tummy's growl as the aroma of Mama's rye bread baking filled their small *izba*. Sitting up, she groaned and rubbed an imprint on her back caused by the long night spent on the knotted sleeping bench. She remembered that today, the last day in April, was a special day for her. It was her sixteenth birthday. She knew she should be excited, but for some reason uneasiness filled her senses. Maybe it was the bad dream she'd had of her family all dying suddenly. Involuntarily she shuddered as images of their burning *izba* flooded her mind. *I really should tell Mama about my dream, but she would probably just say that*

it was just a silly dream, nothing to worry about. She looked over at Mama, who stopped what she was doing and came to Annaveta. She was being silly; of course, there was nothing to worry about. Everyone was fine.

"Happy birthday, little one." Mama put her hands on the sides of Annaveta's face and kissed both cheeks. "You are so grown-up. Today is a special day, your first *Posidelki*. You will remember this day when you are older as the day you faced your future with strength." Mama smiled at her and kissed her forehead. "I have something for you. It was my mama's before me, but now it's yours. Someday you can pass it on to your daughter."

Annaveta stared in surprise at the ring with a small ruby in the middle, encircled by delicately designed gold. She put it on her finger, and tears came to her eyes.

"Thank you, Mama. I will treasure it always." She hugged her mama knowing what a sacrifice it must have been to save it for her.

"Oh, daughter. You are such a good girl. I just want you to be happy." Mama kissed both her cheeks, then stepped back and wiped her own wet cheeks.

Annaveta watched as Mama hurried back to cooking breakfast. Looking at the ring, for the first time she felt a real connection with her mama and grandmere. She knew they were strong women who had made it through so much hardship. She was grateful for her mama's reassuring words and the gift, but she didn't feel any strength; instead, uncertainty and fear formed knots in her stomach. This was not the future she wanted, but this was what she had been given. There was nothing to be done to change it. She told herself she would go along with what Papa and Mama wanted so there would be enough food on the table for her family. She knew if she married into a rich family she could at least help them out. In her heart she knew she had to sacrifice the freedom and love she so desperately wanted so her mama and brothers could have a better life.

She looked up and saw little Yuri's mouth quiver as each of his loud snores pierced the stillness of the morning. He lay on his tummy, his little arms dangling down from the sleeping loft by the large white stove. Nicolai was sleeping on the bench beneath him. She was so thankful that at least these two brothers had survived out of the ten babies that had started in Mama's womb. Annaveta was sure that the many beatings from Papa had killed the others.

She seethed thinking of her mama's suffering. How she hated her papa. Yes, she determined in her heart to do everything she could to help take care of her mama and brothers.

Her hands trembled as she picked up her folded clothes. The sound of wood being chopped echoed through the small hut. She knew she had better get moving — Papa would be coming inside soon. With quick movements she changed into her patched black skirt and gray blouse, the only work clothes she owned. She folded her nightdress and set it neatly on top of the folded blankets on the bench. Hearing the clunk of the spoon against the pot, she looked over at Mama. She had her brown-and-gray-streaked hair pulled back into a tight bun and a kerchief around her head. Annaveta watched as she used her sleeve to get rid of the perspiration on her forehead, while stirring with her other hand. Annaveta wiped a stray tear from the corner of one eye.

This is what my life will be like soon. I'll be stirring kasha, bearing children, and being bound to a man who will control my every move. Just like Mama. But there can be no more tears. I will just have to accept it. With an angry flick, she removed the last tear from her cheek, determined to somehow survive this.

Annaveta's hurried steps made swooshing noises in the wet grass as she made her way to the makeshift outhouse behind the house. The brisk wind poured through wide-open wooden slats like a cold waterfall. She peered outside at the sky and saw the sun trying to pierce its way through dark fuming clouds that seemed ready to lash out at the unsuspecting earth beneath it. She understood their show of displeasure.

Mama had the boys up and dressed by the time she got back and was putting the *kasha* on the table. Nicolai and Yuri sat still, rubbing their eyes as Mama filled their bowls with the steaming porridge.

Annaveta wished for honey to put in their plain fare, but had learned early in life to keep her thoughts to herself or be prepared for a quick strike across her cheek from the back of Papa's hand.

"Annaveta is to help at the Posidelki today."

Annaveta watched her mama's lips form an uncertain smile as she sat down and looked up at her husband.

"Good." He glared at Annaveta. "You think on what I told you. I expect a contract of marriage for you soon. This family needs some good luck for once," her papa said, firmly shaking his finger at her.

"Yes, Papa," She forced the words from her mouth. The thought of courting and marrying any of the men she knew sent a ripple of fear through her body. She had seen firsthand the bruises of most of the women in the village and late at night had heard their screams. She wanted to escape that life to something better.

The image of Alex's gentle eyes flashed in her mind. Her heart tapped the staccato beat of the round dance as she remembered being held in his arms. She longed to feel his touch and hear his voice once again. Anticipation caused her stomach to flutter as she remembered she would see Alex and his sister on Sunday. Catching her breath, she stopped herself to take in all the sensations that flooded her whenever she thought of him. She covered her mouth to hide the sound that slipped out, and her eyes widened as she realized her attraction to Alex.

But upon looking over at her papa, she realized nothing had changed. An aching pain began in her chest, and she closed her eyes. Because of her papa's demands she would have to show interest in someone else. Alex came from the wrong kind of people, and her papa would never approve.

As Pavla hoed the last row of newly planted potatoes in the vegetable garden, Annaveta grabbed her heavy pail of water and poured it into the trenches. Widow Polaski would have a good-sized garden this year, with lots of vegetables. Covering the small holes with the soft black soil, the girls finished in short order. They stretched, rubbing their aching backs as they took stock of their hard work. A tired sigh escaped as Annaveta thought of the wood that still need to be hauled before they started supper.

"Pavla, I'll help with the outside work for Widow Polaski. Since all us girls are renting her house to use this coming year, I'll haul the wood. You could join the other girls in the house and help get the food ready for tonight." Annaveta wanted to avoid being in the same room with the other village girls for as long as possible.

"All right, I can manage that. I can't wait for the social tonight. I think the kissing games will be the most fun, don't ya think?" Pavla said as her lips puckered with the sound.

"That's the part I dread. I like it that our work benefits others, but it bothers me that we girls are expected to encourage boys we hardly know to show affection. I don't understand or want any part of it." Annaveta frowned with disgust.

"You're beautiful. You'll be chosen quickly," Pavla said, trying to encourage her.

"You know as well as I that parents and matchmakers in our village persuade men to choose girls with physical strength to bear many children and to do heavy labor. We aren't encouraged to seek love but to help our families. You're stronger than I am, Pavla; you'll be chosen first." Annaveta's frowned turned into a smile as she thought about it. "You know, this is probably a good thing. Maybe I'll be rejected for lack of strength."

"Well, don't be too happy just yet," Pavla whispered, covering her mouth with her hand as she looked behind Annaveta. "Here comes Misha wearing a big grin on his face. It looks like he likes you in spite of your beauty and lack of strength."

Annaveta stamped her foot letting her friend know that she wasn't impressed. Pavla laughed and went inside the hut. Annaveta thought about walking away, but he'd already spotted her. *He must have come from his village to join the group of young men here in Noltava for the Posidelki social.* Like most of the young men, he arrived just in time to eat the food and join in the dance. She shouldn't be surprised that he came, though. Since he had already won over most of the young men in this village by giving out his vodka at the round dance, his friends were probably eager to have him come and bribe them with drink once again.

The girls were expected to do all the work and provide the food, while the young men showed up later on with the entertainment. There wasn't much she could do to change it, but she longed to go somewhere where she would be free from all the limits that it seemed fate had placed on her. Annaveta didn't want to go back to the widow's hut, knowing that he would be there with his friends. She didn't have a choice, however, knowing her papa expected her to be there and would be disgraced by the other villagers if she didn't show up with a young man by her side.

"Hello there, my lovely flower. I see you know how to work. That's good. Once we're married, there will be a lot of it to keep you busy." Misha strolled over to her, his steps swaying and words slurring as he took another drink of the bottle he held in his tight grip.

"Misha, I'm busy." Annaveta carried her armload of heavy

wood to the back of the hut to put it in the wooden box. After dumping it in, she closed the lid, crinkling her nose at the strong stench of alcohol that surrounded him like a fog. Just like Papa.

"Misha, go back to your friends." Annaveta moved to go past him.

"No. You won't get away this time. Stay here. With me." Misha grabbed her arms, pulling her closer to him. She stiffened at his harsh touch.

"Go away, Misha. Stop it." Annaveta's angry tone grew louder as she tried to jerk away from him.

"From what I hear you don't usually tell men to go away. You would rather encourage their advances. So, I just want to test the goods for myself." He pulled her closer, harshly pressing his lips to hers. She twisted out of his arms.

"You'd better not be spreading those lies about me. I'll have you brought before the village elders," Annaveta threatened as she wiped off the imprint of his lips. She scrunched her nose in distaste at the foul smell of vodka that lingered on his breath.

"Well, soon it won't matter because you'll be mine." Misha's smile vanished, and his words turned cold. "Don't even think about changing your mind either. Because if you don't marry me, I will come after you. And if you ever marry someone else, I will kill him."

Misha's words sent an icy chill down her spine, and even in his semidrunk state, she knew he meant it. Fear wrapped strangling tentacles around her, and for a moment she couldn't breathe. She forced herself to remain calm and inhale slowly, unwilling to let the fear of what he might do intimidate her. She was determined to stand her ground against Misha. He had ruined other girls' reputations, and she didn't want to be stained in the same way. She had heard of a girl a few years ago in her village who had been branded falsely as a loose woman. Her family's gate around their *izba* had been tarred black so everyone would think she was unchaste. It wasn't until the girl confronted her accuser at the village assembly that those in authority asked the village midwife to examine her. When she had the humiliating physical examination to prove her virginity, the single young men asked the young woman for her forgiveness. They had to pay a fine, and the village officials hung a sign and made a white mark beside the tar on the parents' gate announcing to the village that the girl had been proven innocent. Annaveta didn't want to go through such embarrassment.

"No more, Misha. I need to go help the other girls prepare the food for tonight." Annaveta turned her head to the side as he tried to kiss her again. She pushed at his chest to distance herself from his embrace.

"I'll let you go for now, but only because I know I'll see you inside for the kissing games later on." Misha laughed and sauntered off, making a crooked path as he guzzled the half-empty bottle of vodka.

Annaveta silently crossed her arms and shook her head. She thought about what the evening might bring. Pavla had told her she was excited about tonight because at the *Posidelki* they would be allowed to be more intimate than at the *Khorvody* or any other social. She knew Pavla was interested in Sergei and wanted more time with him. But there wasn't any man here that Annaveta even liked.

She sighed. If only Alex were here. He would save her from Misha and the wagging tongues. But the hard feelings between the Russian peasants and German colonists made that impossible. Oh, if only there was some way to disappear tonight.

LOOKING AROUND THE CROWDED ROOM, what little courage Annaveta had sank down to her toes. She glanced at the matchmaker, who sat in the middle of a long line of older village women. They all watched closely what the young people were up to and frowned upon anyone who wasn't paired off. Annaveta knew this was only one of many such socials to come specially devised to bring couples together for marriage.

"Gather around, young ones." Widow Polaski waved her hands for them to come closer. There were ten men and nine young ladies, but one young man was the accordion player, so it looked as if everyone had a partner.

"We will start with the first song. Remember to choose your partner wisely. As the saying goes: 'Choose a cow by its horn, a maiden by her kin.'" The old ladies laughed and nodded as they heard the familiar Russian proverb. "So, men, choose your young ladies. We will have three songs and then some games." Widow Polaski nodded for the young man to start the music.

Annaveta stood back, hoping to disappear. Pavla was soon escorted to the dance floor by Sergei. They moved together in a slow-moving waltz. Soon most of the other girls were dancing with their partners, enjoying each other. Annaveta stood against the corner wall watching.

The words of the song reinforced what she already knew. Men were to choose a bride for her strength and diligence, not for her beauty. To choose a bride of spotless reputation. Well, the last requirement, according to village gossip, put her at a disadvantage. Mama had said to choose a man for a husband who was sober and hardworking. Well then, she should run far away from Misha.

Annaveta watched her friend dance and started to sway to the soothing sounds of the music. She was enjoying herself, when abruptly her hand was pulled and she fell against a hard body.

"Come, my beauty, let's dance." Misha wrapped his arms around her waist.

"Not so close, Misha. I can hardly breathe." Annaveta tried to pull his hands away, but she was no match for his strength. She looked over his shoulder at the sly stares of the older women watching. They smiled at her and nodded, talking between themselves, their tongues wagging as fast as the stitches they knitted. Her anger increased as she thought of their smiles while Misha was pawing her. It didn't look like there would be any protection from that corner.

"This social is for young people to get closer. A lot closer," Misha whispered in her ear as his hand moved from her waist to her bottom.

She turned her head so he wouldn't talk in her ear and moved his hand back to her waist. That was a mistake, for as he looked down at her he covered her lips with his own. She moved her head to the side, only to have him trail kisses down her neck. She looked at the other couples, and saw most of them were doing the same thing. She didn't want to join the crowd.

Sighing with relief, she pulled herself away when the long song finally ended.

"I need to go to the kitchen." Annaveta firmly loosened his octopus-like arms from her waist.

"Don't take too long. I'll be waiting for you," Misha said as he walked toward the drink table.

Annaveta tried her best to keep herself busy in the kitchen, making more sandwiches and putting more goodies on plates. She was enjoying having time to herself, when she heard someone behind her.

"Let me help you carry those." Misha took the two plates. "Widow Polaski has decided it's time for the games. The first one is spin the bottle."

Annaveta's cheeks turned red as she noticed that most of the girls were sitting on their man's lap. She knew how this game was played. The bottle was quickly turned, and when it stopped, the girl whom the bottle was facing was the one the fellow got to kiss.

Misha pulled her onto his lap, and Annaveta's face and neck flushed red with embarrassment. She quickly scrambled up before he could grab her and sat down on the floor. She watched as the bottle whirled around and stopped before Pavla. A shy man from their village tripped over his feet in his eagerness to give her a quick kiss on the cheek.

Annaveta smiled at her friend's red face. The bottle was spun next by Misha. It stopped and pointed to her. She cringed inside.

"Let me kish thoshe lovely lipsh," Misha said, his words slurred. He tried to get to her lips but teetered with drunkenness and slobbered over her cheek instead. Annaveta was grateful when Sergei pulled him back into his chair.

Annaveta sighed with relief when that game finished. They played a few more games and the music had begun for the next round of dancing, when there was a loud knock on the door.

Widow Polaski opened the door to let a harried Mr. Baranova inside her small *izba*. A blast of cold wind pushed him from behind, sending chills up Annaveta's arms.

Pavla's papa, with shoulders bowed and face ashen, stood facing Annaveta.

"Widow Polaski, I've come to get Miss Travotsky." He ran shaky fingers through his hair as he looked first at the widow and then at Annaveta.

"There's been a fire. I'm so sorry to tell you that your family's *izba* has burned to the ground. I've already searched along with some of the village men. There was nothing left. No survivors. We were too late." His trembling fingers wiped the corner of one eye. He lowered his head and stared at the hat in his hand.

Annaveta gasped and shook her head, unable to take it in.

She stepped closer to the solemn-faced man. Silence filled the room, and then she heard the shuffling of many feet as all the others in the room encircled her. Heavy dread filled her, and her legs went weak. She was sure she must have heard wrong. "I'm sorry, I don't think I heard you right.

What did you say about my mama, papa, and brothers?"

Mr. Baranova repeated his words. The blood drained from her face. Her arms and legs grew weak and started shaking violently. Widow Polaski moved beside her and held her hand.

Annaveta looked around and saw all the men and ladies from the *Posidelki* social staring at her. Two of the older widows each passed a handkerchief to her, as they wiped away their own tears. She sought out Pavla and grabbed her arm and held on tightly when her friend came and stood by her.

Annaveta tried to digest the news. She looked up at Mr. Baranova, hoping that it had all been a horrible mistake. But the grave expression on his face revealed the truth of his words.

"My two brothers, Mama and Papa—all dead? How could this have happened? It can't be true, it just can't." Her eyes bulged as she stared at Mr.Baranova, hoping he would take back his words of doom.

"Sadly, it is all true. I'm so sorry." Mr. Baranova looked down, twisting his cloth hat in his hands, and shook his head.

A gasp escaped her and she stumbled against Pavla, who had her arm around her. "I can't believe it. They're all gone. What will I do now?" Annaveta's dazed look went around the room silently questioning all the solemn faces that stared back at her. She looked down and rubbed the ring on her finger. "Everyone who loved me is gone. I'll never see or hug my mama or my brothers ever again." Putting her hands over her face, she sobbed as the reality of what just happened flooded her mind.

The weight of her loss crushed her will to go on. Her legs buckled from under her before everything went black.

Chapter 6

THE FIRE PLAGUED HER THOUGHTS. Had it been an accident
or had someone deliberately set it? She thought of Monsieur
Arnaud and wondered if he might have been angry enough
to set fire to her family's *izba*. She had to talk to Mr. Baranova
about that. If someone was responsible, she wanted them to
pay for taking the life of her beloved Mama and brothers.

Staring at the charred remains of her parents' *izba*, the
horror of the loss of her family splashed over her like bitter
water. It had been five days since the fire. She was going
through the motions of living with as much energy as the
aged priest who had slowly ministered at the funeral service
yesterday. Her shoulders shook with sobs, and her body sank
to the ground in hopelessness. *Why did Mama and my brothers
have to die? If there was a God up there, did he even care that she
was all alone?*

In spite of all her grief, Annaveta was relieved that her
papa was dead. Maybe it wasn't right to feel that way, but
she couldn't help it. She was so thankful that Pavla's papa
had asked her to come live with their family. He had said it
was just until they could sort through other arrangements.
They didn't have enough room for her — not with all their
children, and now with Mrs. Baranova expecting another
one.

Annaveta was worried. What would she do once she
had to leave Pavla's parents home? How would she support
herself? She could keep making the French lace that her

mama had taught her, but so far she had only been able to make one small piece every two months. The Alencon lace patterns were from Louis XVI's reign. The last one she did was a pattern of roses, sprinkled with leaves, which sadly was now burned. She had also helped Mama with midwifery, but no one in her village would ask for her, and she was sure it was because of what the local gossipers had spread about her.

The priest had said for the sake of her sainted mama he wanted to give her family a Christian service. He asked Annaveta if she had any rubles to give for the eternal memory of her family's souls. She shook her head and held out empty hands. The deep grooves in the devout priest's forehead had revealed his displeasure, but he performed the service anyway in his usual solemn manner. It seemed as if that was another thing she had failed at.

Her shoulders shook with fresh sobs. She didn't know how long she knelt there on the hard ground, mourning her loss.

As her cries lessened, she looked up at the early morning sky. Slivers of sunlight pushed their way through a canopy of heavy clouds. They mirrored the weight that had cloaked itself around her heart.

With misty eyes, she walked through the ashes, searching for the six-sided star, the symbol that her mama called her secret identity. The name sounded more real somehow when spoken in Yiddish. *Mogein Dovid*, the Star of David. She remembered Mama telling her of her childhood years in the port city of Odessa. As a little girl, Mama would often be the one to get food at the market because she got good treatment there. Mama said it was because she had red hair and green eyes. It was her light skin tone that saved her from the usual insults that the rest of her family endured. Only one other sister had the light skin and hair that she did. Aunt Esther, with her blond hair and blue eyes, was also treated like one of them.

Annaveta remembered how Mama had cried when

she learned about the 1905 pogrom in Odessa. The Jewish newspaper *Voskhod* said that more than eight hundred people had been killed. Among them were her parents and all her brothers and sisters and their families except Aunt Esther and her Gentile husband. It was a few months after the massacre that Mama finally told her secret to Annaveta and gave her the star.

Mama then sat her down and taught her to make lace. She said it was part of her heritage as her great-grandmere had been a lace maker in France in the 1820's. So Annaveta learned to weave the delicate threads together and sold some lace to wealthy women who came on market day. She would keep doing that, but she needed another way to earn money. She stood up wiping away her tears. *Why can't I find it? Mama said I should keep this forever, that it wouldn't burn or wear out. She told me the star was a reminder to trust in Yahweh, the God that brought them through the wilderness and who helped them win their battles. Well, he must be busy somewhere else.*

Footsteps scuffed the stones behind her. Her shoulders stiffened when thin arms wrapped around them. Her ash-blackened hands dabbed away a continuous trickle of tears.

"I knew where to find you this early in the morning," Pavla said as she gave her friend a fresh handkerchief. "I can't imagine losing my family, but I want to help you, Annaveta. You are my best friend."

"Just keep being my friend. That's what helps the most right now." Annaveta's voice shook with emotion. "I don't understand. Why did they have to die?"

"Oh, Annaveta, I don't know." Her friend stood beside her a solemn look in her eyes. Annaveta wiped her tears, only to have fresh ones appear.

"I suppose we need to get back to your family. Your mama's waiting." Annaveta knew Mrs. Baranova had sent Pavla to bring her home. Pavla's mama believed that idle hands were the devil's workshop and that keeping Annaveta busy would ease the sorrow. The first might be true, but not the last.

Annaveta didn't think she'd ever be finished mourning her mama and brothers. Her papa was a different matter. She was glad to finally be free of his drunken rages.

"She wants us to start the dough as soon as we get back." Pavla slipped her arm through Annaveta's. "Looks like you'll need a good washing first."

Annaveta rubbed her sooty hands on her dark-gray skirt. "I thought I might find something in the ash that could be saved as a keepsake, but everything was burned. I have nothing left." Fresh tears forged a trail down her dirty cheeks as she and Pavla made their way back to the Baranova's *izba*.

Pavla's mama sat mending some of the children's shirts and pants as they entered through the creaky wooden door.

"Go wash up, you two. Time is wasting. We need to get that bread in the oven. Papa will be back soon for breakfast." She sat in one of their two rickety wooden chairs feeding the youngest baby. "The other children will be awake soon."

Mrs. Baranova barked orders like a military sergeant. Annaveta and Pavla scurried to wash up and get started on the dough. It wasn't long before they had eight loaves ready to be baked. They stuck the first two loaves in the oven, then hurried to help the smallest four children get dressed. Annaveta heard the voices in the back room, which grew louder as she opened the door. All the little ones grabbed her hands and legs, each wanting her help. Soon they were all dressed in their threadbare but clean clothes.

The children clung to Annaveta, each begging for attention as she made her way back to the kitchen. She asked the older ones to set the table as she checked on the baking. The sweet bread and yeast smell wafted through the air.

She had just pulled out the last batch, when the slatted wooden door creaked open. Mr. Baranova walked in and stood still. The big smile on his face as he looked at Annaveta made the breadboard she held in her hands shake.

"Well, what is it?" Pavla's mama asked, frowning. Annaveta looked up from the stove wondering why Pavla's papa stood staring at her. Something in his narrowed eyes and his satisfied smile made her nervous.

"Let's all go wash up and eat. Then you can tell us what's on your mind," Mrs. Baranova said.

When the children were all seated around the table, Pavla's papa thanked God and the saints for their food and all the extra blessings they had been given that day.

Annaveta stirred her steaming bowl of *kasha* and forced herself to put small spoonfuls into her mouth. Her stomach was a jumble of nerves as she looked up seeing the finished bowls of the children around her. Mrs. Baranova told the children to start cleaning up while their papa talked with the girls. Annaveta was concerned and filled with foreboding about what Mr. Baranova was about to tell her. She knew the village elders had met this morning and so was worried that they would be sending her to live with someone else. Or maybe they didn't want her in the village at all. She knew her papa hadn't had much respect in the village because of his constant drunken stupors.

Annaveta squared her shoulders and looked up at Mr. Baranova, prepared to face her future with courage.

"Annaveta, we know you have had a very hard week with all kinds of changes. However, it seems like there will be another one shortly." He looked at his wife and seemed to gain courage from her nod. "When I met with the village elders this morning, I told them that you were adjusting well to living in our home. However, I also said it would be time soon to find a long-term solution. We just don't have enough room or money to keep you here." Mr. Baranova ran his hand through his hair as he took a deep breath.

"I understand. You want me to find a place of my own." Annaveta's words sounded calm as she spoke them, even though her stomach was in knots. She knew he was agitated because she remembered seeing him run his hand through his hair when he came to tell her about the fire.

"Actually, the elders have found a place for you. You are

one lucky girl, because there is a man who has offered to marry you, and he's willing to have it done with all speed. Next Sunday, in fact." Mr. Baranova looked up at Annaveta as his words tumbled out in a hurry. Annaveta heard Pavla gasp, and her friend moved to sit on the bench beside her.

"Who is this man, Papa?" Pavla asked as she put her hand on Annaveta's arm. Her friend's strong fingers seemed to squeeze the blood out of her arm. Annaveta tensed as she waited in dread for his answer.

"It is Misha Ivanov. He's from our closest neighboring village. He says he's been courting you with your papa's permission for a while now. Is that true?"

Clutching her throat in horror, she felt the blood drain from her face as she thought of that vile man. *Oh no, I can't marry him. There's just no way I can marry someone like him— like my papa. Somehow I need to get away from here. I need to go far away. Somewhere free from this prison sentence.* And it would need to be soon. Mr. Baranova seemed determined to be rid of her.

"Yes, he did ask my papa. He agreed that he could court me, but there was no formal contract signed," Annaveta said, hoping that would sway Pavla's papa to her side. She knew that when the contract was signed between the bride and groom's families, the couple were as good as married.

"I understand that the contract was only days away from being finalized." Pavla's papa glanced at his wife, then looked back at her. "You seem to have doubts. Do you have a good reason that this marriage should not take place?"

Annaveta hesitated, trying to choose her words carefully. She hoped that somehow she would convince them that marriage to Misha would not be a good idea. "I don't like that he drinks so much, and we don't know much about him, other than he lives in the neighboring village. Of course, the fact that he comes from a wealthy family helped my papa choose him." Annaveta's tense voice continued. "I really don't like him, and I've heard bad things about him."

Mrs. Baranova's eyebrows raised with skepticism. "What have you heard?"

"My brother had overheard conversations between Misha and his friends. He has at least two girlfriends in his village and one in another nearby village." Annaveta looked at her friend's parents, hoping they would rescue her. She added one more item to the growing list of Misha's unsavory characteristics. "My brother also heard that Misha got a girl in trouble, and he hasn't taken responsibility for his actions."

Mr. Baronova shook his head and let out a loud puff of air. "Village gossip, Annavata. That's all it is. You know as well as I do, boys will be boys. Young men exaggerate when they are with their friends, Annaveta. You should know by now that most men in the village have a drink now and then. It's the normal way. The fact that he comes from a wealthy family should sway your feelings toward him, not against him," Mr. Baranova concluded. "Besides, I think this is all hearsay. It is not a good enough reason not to marry. You will learn to like him when the deed is done. I think your parents would have wanted you to marry him, since your papa agreed to this union. So unless you can give me a better reason for not marrying, we will go ahead with the wedding as planned. On Sunday."

Annaveta's face paled, and she nodded her head for her answer. Fear and shock stilled her tongue as the finality of Mr. Baranova's words forced themselves upon her. Losing her family had been a horrible shock, but this news was almost as bad. There had to be a way to get out of this.

"I have things to do. Mama, we better plan a little celebration for Sunday. Annaveta will be a bride." Mr. Baranova stood up. After gathering his coat and hat, he left.

"Well, girls, it's time to clean up. And then we can spend a few minutes planning Annaveta's big day." Mrs. Baranova frowned and looked at Annaveta, studying her. "It's time for a wedding celebration."

Annaveta looked over at Pavla, tears brimming in her

eyes as she sat there unmoving.

"I'm so sorry. I didn't know Papa was planning this with the village elders. I don't know what to say." Pavla squeezed her friend's hand.

"There's nothing to say. What will be, will be," Annaveta said, wiping her eyes as they brought the washbowl to the table. With shaking hands she put the leftover food from the plates in the slop pail. Pavla told her younger brother to take it out to the chickens.

The dishes were washed and dried in a hurry. Annaveta could hardly think. This whole marriage arrangement seemed unreal.

Mrs. Baranova sat down beside the girls and began discussing wedding plans for Sunday. Four days away. Annaveta just sat and listened, then told Mrs. Baranova to go ahead and plan it however she wanted. In her mind, there had to be some way to escape, to get away from this awful wedding. She knew that if she married Misha, it would be like being married to her papa for the rest of her life. And that was a fate she wouldn't wish on her worst enemy.

WHILE TOSSING AND TURNING IN her sleep, Annaveta suddenly awoke. She sat up on her pallet still in a daze. The dream had been so real, yet exciting. Now she knew of a way to escape, and she knew she needed to act now. Touching Pavla's arm, she shook her awake.

"Pavla. I need to tell you something." Annaveta's relentless shaking finally woke her friend.

"What? What's wrong?" Pavla whispered, looking at Annaveta, fear filling her brown eyes.

"I had a dream. I'll tell you, and then I need to go." Annaveta spoke softly with intensity.

"Dream? Go where? What?" Pavla's voice got louder.

"Shhh. I need to tell you the dream first." Annaveta held her friend's hand as she spoke. "It was so real and vivid. I dreamed I was sleeping peacefully. Suddenly a man dressed in a long white tunic appeared and reached out his hand. I looked into his eyes, and he seemed so kind and trustworthy. He told me to come with him, that it was time to go. First place to go would be the Wagner's home in Pleve Colony. That's the home of Alex and Clara's parents. The man said he would let me know each step of the journey. He told me to not be afraid, that he would be with me."

Annaveta could only see pale features of her friend's skeptical face as the moon shone brightly through the small window.

"So, you are going to walk all the way to Pleve Colony tonight, in the dark, all because of a dream?" Pavla shook her head. "Are you crazy?"

"Maybe I am crazy. However, if I marry Misha on Sunday and live the rest of my life with the mirror image of my papa, that would prove I was out of my mind."

Annaveta had made up her mind. "I'm telling you this so you won't worry about me. However, you can't tell your parents or anyone else where I am. Okay?"

"I still think this is a foolish thing for you to do." Pavla wrapped her blanket around her as she came to sit beside her on her pallet. "What do you know about this family anyway? How do you know you can trust them?" Pavla pulled Annaveta's shoulders so they were facing each other.

"I trust Alex and Clara, even though I don't know them well. Besides, remember the night of the fire?" Annaveta looked at her closest friend and shuddered again thinking of that night. "Well, what I haven't told anyone else is that the night before, I had a dream that there was a fire and my whole family died. If only I had known that my dreams come true. Then I could have warned my family." Annaveta's gut heaved with dry heaves as she cried herself sick. She felt she was a coldhearted, horrible person because she hadn't said anything to anyone about her dream. Her family had died because they hadn't been warned.

"Listen to me." Pavla put both arms around her friend. "You are not responsible for your parents' death. I've had a lot of dreams that I haven't told anyone. How were you to know that this one dream was to be the one you should've talked about? You didn't know, and so you have to stop taking the blame. It's no one's fault that they died. It just happened."

Annaveta was desperate to believe her friend's words, but deep down guilt gnawed at her like an unwanted rodent. She would have to live with the knowledge that she could have done something to stop the fire. She wiped her tears on the sleeve of her nightdress.

"Maybe this dream is something you should listen to." Pavla's whispered words seem to carry far in the night air. "I think I'm just being selfish because I want you here with me. But I know you have to go. I know my papa won't stop until he sees you married off to some man." Pavla let out a deep sigh. "So I won't stand in your way." Pavla shook her head. "Of course, you know I won't tell anyone where you've gone. Can you let me know now and then how you are?"

"Do you know that meadow a few miles east of here?" Annaveta asked her friend. " I will put a note in the biggest log there, once a month. Leave one for me too." Annaveta smiled at Pavla with tears streaming down her cheeks. "Now I need to leave. Latch the door behind me."

"Don't you want to change into your skirt and blouse?" Pavla's anxious face looked up at her and then down at her old mended nightgown. "It's cold and dangerous out there."

"Don't worry about me. I can't have someone waking up while I'm changing. So I'll just carry my clothes and the light jacket your mama gave me." Tears welled up in Annaveta's eyes. "You're are a good friend. I'll write."

Pavla held her hand up. "Wait right here." Annaveta gathered her clothes, then wrapped the thin jacket around them and held them close to her. Soon Pavla returned with a loaf of bread and some cheese wrapped in cloth and a flask of water. "You need to keep up your strength. And here's one more thing." Pavla wrapped her best green-and-red scarf around her neck, and hugged her tightly for a long moment. She stepped back and wiped her eyes. "Something to remember me by."

"Pavla, this is the one you just made. I couldn't take it." Annaveta moved to take if off, but Pavla put her hand on top of her own.

"Please. I wanted to give my best to my best friend. Remember me?"

"You know I will." Annaveta squeezed her hand one last time before she tiptoed toward the door. Pausing, she risked a glance back to smile at her friend, then lifted the squeaky latch.

Mr. Baranova's rhythmic snoring put her mind at ease that all in the house were still asleep. A few of the children coughed but didn't wake up. Her stealthy footsteps took her outside, and with shaky hands she lowered the latch in place. She sighed with relief that she had made it this far.

The wind was chilly tonight, and the ground was cool. The biting wind sent icy pricks shooting up her bare legs. Too bad she'd had to leave her shoes behind, but she couldn't take the chance of waking someone up to find them. Pavla would be able to use her shoes.

Her hurried steps took her down the east road that lead out of the village toward Clara's home. The bright moon shone on her path, making it easy to find. She decided that she couldn't overthink what she was doing or she would lose her nerve. The angel in the dream said that she shouldn't be afraid; he would be with her. She wanted to trust him.

By the time she reached the meadow where she'd first met Clara, she was tired. Her feet were hurting from the cold ground that was littered with jagged stones. The brisk wind was chilly, slipping through the holes in her nightgown like water through a sieve. Sitting on the log, she rubbed her sore feet, which dispelled some of the achiness. She put on the thin jacket that Mrs. Baranova had given her.

Although she felt slightly warmer, she knew she couldn't wait. She needed to carry on. She was halfway there now. A distant coyote's howl jolted her to her feet and kept her moving down the path. She remembered Clara telling her if she ever needed to come to her home for any reason, to follow this path and it would take her right to Pleve Colony. Alex had told her he estimated that it was around seven miles between her Russian village and Pleve Colony. Clara had described her house as big and blue and at the far south end of the main street.

She hoped Clara's mama and papa would welcome her. Alex would be there too. She was a little nervous about what it would be like to live in the same home with him and his family — if they'd have her. Maybe the Wagners wouldn't want her to live with them. They might find her another place to live.

The closer she got, the more she worried. But she knew she had no choice but to go to Pleve Colony. Her sore feet ached with every step she took, and she hoped it wouldn't be too much further. She wondered how it would be to live in a new place with a different culture. Nothing was familiar anymore. Even the clothes on her back were borrowed. Everything that she knew was gone. Her family, her way of life. But there was no turning back. She could not marry Misha and bind her life to a man like her papa. Papa might be gone, but the mark of his cruel ways still lingered.

She wiped her eyes as the tears kept coming. Listening to Clara talk about her family had made her long for something like what her friend had. A fun, warm, loving family to live with. Maybe that's what she would find there.

The dark-blue sky faded into different hues of red and orange as dawn stretched out above Pleve Colony. Hearing the familiar sounds of dogs barking and cowbells, and the loud grunting of pigs, Annaveta smiled. The earthy hay smells mixed with the damp odor of dew on the grass made her feel as if she had arrived at a place only imagined in her dreams. She could only hope that her dreams would match real life.

She remembered Clara's description of where they lived. She hurried along the main street and walked past a large church that sat beside a small white home. Thankful that the stores were closed this early in the day, she kept going. After following the main street for a while, she turned left and then went right again. There were a few women outside beginning their chores at this time of day who frowned at her as she passed them in her nightclothes. Well, they would just have to wonder.

She stared straight ahead. Sure enough, at the end of the road, right at the bend that led to the river, was a blue house with yellow trim. Annaveta saw the cows going with the cowherd down the street, and the pigs followed the swineherd not far behind.

Her feet raw and bruised, she limped passed the gate and up to the freshly painted yellow door and knocked. The time had come. She trembled with fear, unsure of what kind of welcome awaited her.

Chapter 7

"WELL, WELL, WELL. WHAT HAVE we here?" A man with light-brown hair streaked with gray opened to Annaveta's timid knock. He looked her up and down as if he was taking her measure. Annaveta stood there shivering from fear as well as from the cold. She saw a tall woman walk over to stand behind him. Her gray-blond hair was pulled back into a loose bun with wisps of hair tucked behind her ears. Her wide smile added warmth to her blue eyes.

"*Ach*, Heinrich. *Sie ist kalt.* Let her come inside. You are welcome here." The older woman put her arm around Annaveta and pulled her close, leading her from the porch into the warm kitchen. The smell of bread baking caused Annaveta's stomach to growl. Clara was giving a plate of butter and a pitcher of milk to two little girls, pointing them toward the table. Beside her a dark-haired woman directed a little boy to sit on the bench beside two men whose features were similar to Alex's. She stepped back in surprise when Alex abruptly got up from his place at the table to come to her.

"Annaveta, what has happened?" He looked down at her, seeing the threadbare coat that covered her tattered nightgown and her hair hanging loose from its braid. He frowned as he took in her disheveled state. "Why are you dressed like that?" When Annaveta didn't answer, he added, "Well, it doesn't matter. Whatever it is, we'll help you."

Annaveta brushed away stray tears that came unbidden

as his hand gently touched her shoulder. She looked up at the man who had saved her once before. She was moved by the worry in his voice and could hold back no longer.

Annaveta broke down, covering her face with her hands as a flood of tears ran down her cheeks. Arms went around her, pulling her into a tight embrace. She cried until she had no more tears left. All the while Alex whispered encouraging words into her ears.

Her story erupted. "There was a fire—"

"Shhh." Alex soothed. "Don't talk about it now. You can tell us later. For right now, just rest, and we'll get some food in you soon."

Annaveta relaxed in his arms until she became aware of the silence in the room. Pushing back from the arms that encircled her, she looked up into cornflower-blue eyes that were filled with concern for her. She pulled Alex's arms away from her waist. Heat surged up her neck to her cheeks and she looked at the floor, embarrassed to have melted down like that in front of Alex and Clara's family.

"It's my turn, big brother."

Annaveta smiled as her friend Clara gently shoved her tall brother aside. "Annaveta, my friend. I'm so glad you came. We were just about to have breakfast. Why don't I help you bring your clothes to the girls' room and then we'll eat."

Mrs. Wagner squeezed Annaveta's shoulder. "*Ja,* Annaveta. Go with Clara. She will find you something to wear. Then we will fill you up, *ja?*" Annaveta nodded and smiled at her kindness.

Clara took her hand and led her to another room beyond the warm kitchen. Even with her head lowered, Annaveta could feel the curious gazes of the other family members at the table.

"We don't have a lot of time. Why don't you change here quickly, and then we'll eat breakfast. Are you okay? What happened?" Clara's words soaked through her skin like a warm hug.

Annaveta fumbled with the few buttons on her nightgown as her hands shook with the retelling of the fire that killed her family.

Clara's hands flew to her chest, her mouth falling open as Annaveta told her story. "I'm so sorry, my friend. I can't imagine what you're going through right now, but you know I will help you anyway I can. I know my parents will welcome you to stay here with us." With her tears flowing freely, Clara gave her another big hug. "You look like you haven't slept for days. We'll first get food in you, and then you can rest." Her friend's words cheered her as she helped her button up her blouse. Clara brushed Annaveta's waist-length hair, braided it, and looped it around her head. "There. You look beautiful."

Clara pulled her by the hand, but stopped as she heard the sound of loud voices in argument. Clara put her fingers to her lips, signaling Annaveta to silence. Annaveta watched as Clara shook her head and frowned.

"What is it?" Annaveta was curious. She heard a younger woman's loud voice as well as the calmer tones of Clara's parents, speaking in German. They were sounds of disagreement.

"Inga is making a fuss that you've come to stay with us." Clara shook her head and placed her hands on her hips. "Sometimes she makes me so mad."

"Who is Inga?"

"She is my oldest brother Helmut's wife. I'm thankful she's now part of this family, but sometimes she tests my patience with her negative words." Clara shook her head, her mouth forming a thin line as she stared at the door that separated her room from the kitchen.

"Maybe I shouldn't have come here." Annaveta looked uncertainly at her friend. "Your home was the only place I knew of that I could come to. I don't know where else to go. I hope your parents let me stay, but I don't want to be a burden to your family. Your parents already have enough mouths to feed. And I really don't want to be the cause of fighting in your family."

"Nonsense. You are welcome here. Trust me — my parents will be happy for the extra help on the farm, especially now that it's planting time." Clara's smile reassured her. "Inga is just overly concerned what everyone will think, with our family having a Russian living with us. She says it's just not done, Russians living with Germans." Clara huffed. "Well, there's a first time for everything. Come, let's go eat."

Smells of licorice-scented tea, fresh bread, and porridge floated through the air, making Annaveta's stomach rumble again. When they came to the kitchen, everyone moved to take their seat on the benches around the large wooden table. She overheard Alex say in Russian to his younger sisters that they should speak in the language of their guest. Annaveta smiled at him. She knew that it was required by law for all children to learn the Russian language in schools. She remembered Clara had told her that Oma — her grandmama — was the only one couldn't really speak Russian, but her parents spoke the language. They needed to speak Russian, especially on market day, when Russian traders came to the colony.

Annaveta looked around at all those seated at the table and thought it might be good for her to learn their language. It would make it easier for everyone.

"Someone's hungry," Mrs. Wagner said, hearing the loud rumbling from Annaveta's stomach, as she placed the porridge in the center of the table. "Well, there's more than enough. Come, sit down, girls. There is a place on the bench beside Erika and Katarina."

Annaveta sat beside the smallest girl, who looked like she was the youngest. Her little hand grabbed Annaveta's larger one as she looked up at her with a gap-toothed smile. She seemed like she was full of mischief. Annaveta squeezed her hand and grinned back. She noticed the red-gold braids hanging to her waist and knew from Clara's description she must be Erika. She glanced at the other sister with blond braids, who was peeking up at her from her hiding place behind her sister. The shy one was Katarina. Across from her sat a young wife with a small son between her and her husband. The dark-haired woman with big brown eyes was so frail, her cheekbones stuck out. She was shushing her young son. His brown eyes were filled with tears as he wiped them with his fist. Annaveta's eyes went back to his mama. Her brows were knit together in disapproval as she stared back at her. This must be Inga, Clara's sister-in-law. The one who didn't want her here. Annaveta gave her a tentative smile. She didn't smile back.

Annaveta abruptly shifted her gaze and found herself looking across at a buxom gray-haired lady that could only be Clara's oma. She sat at the end of the table with her three older grandsons. She had a twinkle in her eyes as she looked at Annaveta. Clara's oma reached over and squeezed her hand. The three older brothers sat on either side of their oma, but only one had welcomed her so far. As she glanced at Alex, he gave her his rogue smile. She could feel the heat rising from beneath her fitted gray blouse and up her neck. She lowered her eyes to stare at her plate.

Mr. Wagner rose to stand with the rest of the family. Annaveta wondered what they were doing, but she stood as well. Mr. Wagner, with eyes closed, began speaking out loud in German as the rest of the family joined in. She understood that they were praying together, and she lowered her head. When Clara's papa said amen, the family sat back down, sitting very still as they listened to the words Mr. Wagner read from his well-worn Bible.

He read the morning verses in German, so Annaveta understood only a few words, ones that Clara had used before. Praying and Bible reading seemed to be a part of the family's daily routine, and they seemed to believe what they were saying. She didn't know what to make of it, so she just listened. It seemed so different than the Russian Orthodox church that she had been raised in. In her home they bowed and prayed to the saints when they came through the door of their *izba* and saw the many icons on the wall. They crossed themselves when they prayed and listened to the priest read Scriptures at church and joined in the required fasts. It all seemed only a ritual. She was surprised that the family around this table listened so closely to the Bible reading. She looked around at the bare walls, free of icons. It would take a little getting used to.

Right now she was glad she didn't understand the words Mr. Wagner was speaking because her circumstances didn't match with all the promises of a good and loving God. To her it seemed like God had turned his back on her when he let her family die. She angrily wiped away more tears.

After the prayer, most of the family devoured their food as if it had been a week instead of a few hours since their last meal. Annaveta was so worn out from lack of sleep and worry that she could only eat a few bites. When the smaller children were done eating, they were sent off to wash the dishes and clean their rooms.

"We would like to hear what brought you to our home, Annaveta." Mr. Wagner looked at her with a directness that was disconcerting. "I am also wondering if I need to watch for strangers arriving on our doorstep looking for you."

"Give her a chance to explain, Heinrich." Mrs. Wagner smiled as she patted her husband's hand. Her warm smile gave Annaveta courage. "Don't be afraid. You are with friends now."

Annaveta looked at Clara's parents and nervously began. "I was at our youth *Posidelki*, which was held at one of the village widow's homes. There were other adults there overseeing the games and dancing, when suddenly my friend Pavla's papa came to the door. He came to tell me a fire had burned down our *izba* so quickly that no one knew it was happening until the fire was out of control. My parents and two brothers died. The horrible part is that one of the village elders suspects that the fire was set on purpose."

Annaveta used her sleeve to wipe away tears that wouldn't stop flowing. "Pavla's papa found a cigarette lying beside a broken vodka bottle in the rubble on the west side of our *izba*. Large footprints in the ground were found that went to and from our hut. Neither of my parents smoked, but my papa did drink vodka. I just can't believe he would set fire to our home. I don't know who would be so mad at us that they would want to be rid of us." Annaveta caught her breath, feeling uneasy with the lie. "Well, maybe there was someone. Monsieur Arnaud would have been mad enough at me to start that fire. He's the overseer at the Shremetev estate, where our family used to live. I feel sick that I wasn't there to help my family. Maybe if I had been at home, I could have stopped the fire from killing them."

Clara put her arms around Annaveta's shaking shoulders. "We are sorry for all you have lost." Mrs. Wagner's eyes had filled with tears. "We will pray every day for God to show you his peace and comfort."

"But why did you come to us?" Clara's papa questioned.

"I first stayed with my friend Pavla and her parents, but yesterday her papa came to tell me that I would be married on Sunday to a man I don't even know. I remembered Clara saying that I would be welcomed here if ever I needed to come." Annaveta hesitated before telling the next part of her tale. "Then last night I had a dream. It was so real, I knew I needed to come. A man in white reached out his hand. I saw his eyes, and he seemed so kind and loving. So I took his hand. He said it was time to go. The first place he wanted me to travel to was the Wagner home in Pleve Colony. The man said he would be with me every step of the way and to not be afraid. So that's why I'm here. Right now I don't have any other place to go, but I'll try not to be a burden if you let me stay for a little while."

"Can't say I've ever had a dream like that," Mr. Wagner said to her in Russian. "But God did give dreams to many people in history, like Joseph and Daniel. It's in the Bible, so

I think God is speaking to you through your dreams. Joseph's dreams were of the future when his brothers and papa would bow down to him. Later when he was promoted to second in command over all of Egypt, his dream came true. So if the angel told you to come here, then we will accept this as God's will. Let me read the chapter in the Bible where it talks about Joseph's dream." Mr. Wagner's read from the Bible, translating into Russian, and looked at her, his direct eyes piercing through her own.

"I've never heard Joseph's story before. It's curious that people in the Bible were given dreams from God that directed their lives." Annaveta sighed a contented sigh, feeling hope that maybe her own dreams was somehow God leading her too. Maybe she would learn to read German so she could read more about the dreams of these people.

She looked up as Mr. Wagner continued. "Clara was right in telling you that you are welcome to stay here for as long as you need to. I don't remember any other Russian who stayed in Pleve Colony, so it will take our friends a little while to get used to seeing you here. Be patient with them. Some of the people still remember the market day a few years ago when a Russian man and one of the colonists got into a fight, and then a few more men and boys took sides. Some Germans got badly hurt, and so there are some colonists who are suspicious of any Russian they see." Mr. Wagner rubbed a hand through his hair, and wrinkles creased his forehead. "However, like my wife said, you are with friends now. We'll teach you our ways. You just need to be willing to learn and help out where you are needed."

"Thank you for letting me stay. I'll try to learn quickly." Annaveta sighed with relief, her shoulders relaxing with his words of acceptance. She looked around the table and noticed everyone quietly listening. Alex stared at her and nodded. He looked like he was listening intently to their conversation. Self-consciousness flooded her.

"Just one thing more." Mr. Wagner looked at his wife and

then back at her as if searching for the truth. "Will someone come from your village to our colony to try to find you?"

"I'm quite sure no one will come here." Annaveta looked at Clara's papa, hoping her words would prove true. "The only person who knows I'm here is my friend Pavla, and I asked her not to tell anyone."

"Well, if someone does come looking for you, we'll send them on their way," Mr. Wagner assured her. "I think you're the first Russian we've had stay in our colony, so news will spread fast here." Annaveta lowered her head, despair washing over her. "Don't worry, in our family, we don't worry about the gossipers around us."

"Enough questions for now, Husband. Annaveta looks worn out. Time for you to lie down, my dear," Clara's mama announced as she put her arm around Annaveta's shoulders. "You have one day of rest, and then tomorrow we'll teach you what we do around the Wagner house and in Pleve Colony."

"Thank you for being so kind," Annaveta said as she got off the bench. Alex gave her a big smile as he walked to the door to go work outside. She was glad that Clara and Alex were both such good friends. She put her hand to her stomach to stop the butterflies that swirled there whenever Alex smiled at her. She scolded herself for being so weak around him. Picking up her pace, she walked with Clara and her mama to another room. The straw-filled mattresses resting on homemade wooden bed frames looked so inviting to Annaveta's weary body.

"Let's tuck you into bed, and I'll come get you for lunch." Clara chatted as she helped Annaveta out of her clothes and into one of her old nightgowns.

"Thank you for everything." Annaveta squeezed Clara's hand as a few tears made crooked lines down her cheeks.

"You're my friend. What else would I do?" Clara unbound Annaveta's thick braids and brushed her hair until it looked like a shining pool of red-brown waves. "I'm happy you're here. Just think — now you'll be able to get to know my brother even better."

Annaveta gave her a friend a worn-out smile. "What makes you think either of us are interested in being more than friends?"

"I have eyes." Clara threw her a saucy grin as she left the room. Annaveta pull the blanket up to hide her own grin as she snuggled under the warm blankets.

LUNCH WAS A HURRIED MEAL with everyone eating quickly so they could get back to work. Clara woke her up and helped her dress just in time for the noon meal. It was just the women and children at home today. The men were finishing up their last day scything the wild hay in the community *wiese*, which was the meadowland.

"We need to clean up the rear courtyard so there's room to put the hay," Mrs. Wagner directed everyone. "Children, you stay here with your oma. Papa thinks they will be back with their last load of hay by midafternoon."

"I'm worried about Jacob. His temperature seems higher today." Inga frowned and looked at Annaveta. "All the changes happening around here lately sure aren't helping."

"Oma will see to it that he rests and has plenty to drink." Mama Wagner switched to German and spoke to Oma quickly in her native tongue.

"*Ja, ja. Mach schnell.* Get it done." Oma waved them off as the women went out into the cool air.

Annaveta straightened the clothes borrowed from Clara. They hung loose on her slender figure, but they would do. She was grateful for all they had done to help her already. She put on the gray kerchief Clara handed her. All the women had their hair wrapped to keep out the dust and hay. The air outside was warm for the middle of May, so none of them wore jackets. It was so good to be working outside, with the sun on their backs.

"Let's move the lighter machinery over to the far corner and clear the place on the side of the barn for the hay." Mrs. Wagner led the way to the plow and other farm machinery.

With all four women working steadily through the morning, they were able to move the farming tools to the far corner of the yard and clean up the remaining debris. Annaveta turned her head at the sound of horses' hooves and the creak of the hay wagon. Good, they'd gotten the yard cleaned up just in time.

"*Gut*. You cleaned up a spot for the hay. We could use your help unloading it." Papa Wagner smiled as he used his shirtsleeve to wipe the sweat off his forehead. "Many hands make light work."

Alex jumped off the wagon, landing softly right in front of Annaveta. He looked down into her startled eyes and winked. She just stood there watching him until Clara nudged her elbow. Inching forward, her legs moved stiffly from her long walk last night. She was so tired. Clara tugged her hand and helped her to where Mrs. Wagner and Inga were working. Annaveta listened to the easy camaraderie between Alex and his brothers, his papa, Clara, and his mama. Catching her breath, she remembered the pain of her loss of family. She remembered how she and Mama would talk about all that was going on in their lives, the good and the bad. She missed laughing and the deep heart-to-heart talks with Mama. She missed the teasing and wrestling with her brothers — Nicolai the tease and little Yuri her big helper. Swallowing the lump in her throat, she tried to dispel the deep pain that stabbed her heart at their loss. She hugged herself as she revived the memories of her family. She couldn't allow herself to forget them, no matter what.

Alex and his brothers and papa moved the wagon closer to the unloading area. The men took turns throwing down the hay, and the women gathered and stacked it in piles. With a lot of heavy lifting and sweat they had it done just as they heard Oma ring the bell for supper. They then covered the hay with a tarp and tied it down.

"There, that should keep the hay nice and dry even if we get some bad weather." Papa Wagner's words had the firm tone of experience as he tied down the last corner of the tarp.

The clouds bulged dense and heavy from a darkening sky as they made their way to the house.

Alex frowned as he looked up. "Looks like we're in for a good downpour."

"If it rains tonight, we will be fixing things tomorrow. We need to mend some harnesses and other tools." Papa Wagner spoke loudly over a clap of thunder as he tried to keep up with his sons.

Alex opened the door for Annaveta and gently put his hand under her elbow to help her up the stairs. Annaveta shivered at the warmth of his rugged skin caressing hers. His touch made her want to linger, but she knew she shouldn't encourage him. She did not need a man in her life right now. She'd had enough changes lately.

Annaveta quickly found Clara scrubbing her hands and face in the washbowl that was located next to the entrance of the house. She copied her friend's actions, getting rid of the dirt on her skin.

"*Kommen Sie, bitte.*" Oma waved her wrinkled hand at Annaveta and stood by the table waiting for her.

"Why does she stand there waiting for me?" Annaveta whispered in Clara's ear.

"My kindhearted oma has decided to take you under her wing and make you her favorite." Clara winked at her and translated her oma's words. "She wants you to come to her. It means you are accepted as a honored guest in this home."

Annaveta walked up to Clara's oma and smiled while she took her by the hand to help her sit down. Oma patted the bench beside her, to signal Annaveta to sit down next to her. The homey smell of the stew and fresh bread Oma made filled the air.

"It's good we got the last load of hay home and covered today." Mr. Wagner peered at the window as the sounds of hard rain pelted against the house. "Let's give thanks for our many blessings this day."

Everyone had worked up an appetite, and most of the food was gone in short order. Only Oma and little Jacob pecked at the food on their plates.

"What's wrong, Oma?" Mama Wagner was concerned at her mama-in-law's pale face.

"Ich fuhle mich nicht gut." Oma pushed her plate aside and continued talking. She stood unsteadily on her feet.

Clara sat on Annaveta's other side and translated the German words that Oma spoke. "Oma said she's not feeling good. There might be a flu going around. She said her head is dizzy, and her stomach is rolling around."

"I'll help you to your bed," Mrs. Wagner said. "Little Jacob had a bad case of dizziness today too. Girls, you can start the dishes while Inga puts away the food when everyone's done eating." Mrs. Wagner organized the jobs that needed doing as she put her strong arms around Oma to ease her way to her bed.

Clara took the boiled water and poured it into the dishpan while Annaveta collected the dirty dishes. Alex's hand lingered on hers as she took his dirty plate. She blushed as his eyes searched hers. She quickly looked down and hurried to the kitchen.

With the kitchen all cleaned and the pans set out to bake the morning loaves of bread, Annaveta helped Clara get her sisters ready for bed. Katarina and Erika both wanted Annaveta to help with something, so she brushed their hair and sang a few Russian lullabies to settle them.

"Could you sing one more?" Erika begged after Annaveta had sung two.

"All right, one more. Then you must go to sleep. Agreed?" Annaveta impulsively gave little Erika and Katarina each a hug, the image in her mind of two little brothers causing her embrace to linger.

"So nice." Katarina sighed and closed her eyes as she listened to Annaveta sing.

"Annaveta, you are full of surprises." Clara slipped her arm through her friend's as they tiptoed away from the sleeping girls. "You have such a clear, beautiful voice."

"Mama always encouraged me to sing. She said it calmed her. So I thought it might help the girls fall asleep." Annaveta gave her friend a shy smile.

"I think you will be doing a lot more singing around here from now on." Clara took her by the hand to check on Oma. They walked into her room, where her frail body lay on the bed. Annaveta's chest ached as she saw Oma lying so still, her face pale against the pillows. Mrs. Wagner had given Oma some herb tea and brushed her hair. Annaveta smiled as Oma closed her eyes, and she heard her whisper something in German. Clara tugged on her hand, motioning for them to leave, perhaps thinking she was ready to sleep.

"Wait," Mrs. Wagner said, pointing at Annaveta. "We thought we heard an angel singing in the other room. What a wonderful gift you have. Oma said she would like you to sing her to sleep. Would you?"

"Of course." Annaveta sat by Oma's feet and sang in her clear voice. The family matriarch was holding her hand to her stomach, and her forehead glistened with sweat. With effort, she opened her eyes a little and reached for Annaveta's hand.

Oma whispered something to her in German. "You were sent to us as a gift," Clara translated.

Annaveta grew still. "You are the first person who has ever told me that." She wiped the slow trail of tears falling down her cheeks. As Oma gently held her hand, Annaveta couldn't believe that someone would consider her a gift. She had been told by her papa while growing up that she was a bad girl who couldn't do anything right. Imagine — someone actually thought she was a gift.

She was so glad the angel had led her here to this home. Sitting here with Clara's oma reminded her of the gift she had been given. The gift of getting to know this family and feeling their love. She squeezed Oma's hand one more time. It felt good to belong.

Chapter 8

OMA'S FEVER WAS FINALLY GONE after two days and nights of ongoing shivering and nausea. Mama Wagner had given Oma milkwort tea to bring down her fever, and had stayed up for both nights Oma had been sick. Annaveta had been up early so had taken over for Mama Wagner, singing songs to calm Oma. Her fever finally broke in the last hour.

"How is she doing?" Clara walked up to her oma's bed, her forehead puckered with lines of worry. She looked at Annaveta as she knelt by the bedside.

"She's sleeping peacefully now. The fever has finally broken, so your mama said she should be okay now." Annaveta looked at her friend's bloodshot eyes and ran her hand down Clara's disheveled braids. "You can finally rest now too. No more worrying."

"Oh, I'm so glad she's on the mend." Clara let out a big breath and pressed both hands to her face. "You don't know how much I've prayed and worried. Thank you, Annaveta, for singing to her and helping Mama take care of her."

"I feel like I've become attached to your oma." Annaveta squeezed her friend's hand. "It's been good just to be by her side. She's important to you, so she is important to me too. Besides, my grandmama died before I was born, so I like getting to know your oma. She's so nice, and she seems to just love me for who I am."

"Girls, come. Let your oma rest," Mama Wagner whispered, shooing them out of the room where the sick family matriarch was fast asleep.

For the rest of the day they baked and cleaned. Annaveta and Clara took a broom and dustpan to all the bedrooms, the living room, and the kitchen while Inga and Mama Wagner baked. Erika and Katarina took turns watching over oma. By the time supper was almost ready, all the rooms had been dusted and washed, and even the summer kitchen that was attached to the house had been cleaned as well.

"It's nearly time for supper. It always feels good to have most of the baking done so we're ready for the next week. Now there's fresh bread to go with our usual Saturday meal of *schnitzopp un krepbel.* Good for a rainy day. You girls can go ahead and set the table."

Mrs. Wagner walked over to where Inga was taking out of the oven the meat that was tucked inside the cooked bread-like dough. Clara and Annaveta put the plates on the table.

"How does it taste?" Mama Wagner picked up a small misshaped piece to taste. She nodded and smiled. "I'm hungry already. The men should be coming inside soon."

"*Gut.* I'm glad we made a pot of borscht soup for Oma. It'll be good for Jacob to eat something soothing to help his sore throat." Inga looked over to where her son was playing with wooden blocks on the floor with Katarina and Erika.

"Last time I checked, it seemed like his fever was gone. He should sleep better tonight." Mama Wagner squeezed her daughter-in-law's shoulders. "We'll keep praying and doing all we can to help him. God will heal him."

Annaveta watched Inga shrug off Mama Wagner's hug. She wondered why Inga responded with so much bitterness to the people around her who loved her. She supposed the longer she lived with the Wagners, the more she would learn their ways and their secrets. That meant that this family would learn the emotions and past events that she kept hidden too. Her forehead creased at the thought.

"Cheer up. It's Saturday night, and tomorrow is a day of

rest. There's a lot to be happy about." Clara pulled her hand. "Mama said supper was ready. Let's go find the girls and call the men inside." When the rest of the family was on their way in to eat, she helped Clara set the table. Her empty stomach rumbled loudly in anticipation as pleasant aromas of pastry, meat, buns, and cheese arose from the table.

Supper was unhurried, as the cows, calves, and pigs had already come home with the herdsman, and the women had already milked and fed the cows. Everyone was hungry and talked about the work to be done in the fields and gardens. When Alex wasn't talking to his brothers or his papa, his eyes had a look of interest as they stared at her. It pleased her that he found her attractive, but she didn't really know what to do about it. So she busied herself talking to Clara and her younger sisters.

After supper Ernest said to Alex, "Why don't we play a few rounds of Crokinole? If I win, you do my extra chores for a week, and if you win, I do yours."

"All right." Alex went to the small cupboard where they kept a few games. "This is the best present Uncle Leo has sent us yet. It's also been a good way for me to get out of doing chores, thanks to your losing pattern, Brother."

Ernest gave Alex a friendly shove at his brother's teasing words. They all sat at the kitchen table, and Alex placed the circular board in the middle. The two brothers gathered their different-coloured wooden discs and took turns shooting for the small indented circle in the middle. Annaveta watched in fascination.

"Uncle Leo said this game was first built in Ontario, Canada, in 1876 by a Lutheran. So he thought we would like it." Clara smiled and looked at Annaveta to explain. "He's Papa's youngest brother who moved to Canada ten years ago. He keeps telling us to move there and sends us gifts so we'll be reminded there's lots of land and money to be made. His wife, Aunt Martha, has written that she would love to have help with their four little ones. It seems every letter has some kind of hint in one way or another. Somehow I don't think Papa's very interested in moving. I can't imagine moving away from my home."

"Really? To be able to go to another country — now, that would be a great adventure." Annaveta looked upward, dreaming of freedom and the opportunity such a move would give her.

"Maybe someday your chance will come." Alex winked at her as his wooden disc knocked Ernest's discs to the out-of-bounds corners of the board.

Annaveta gave him a wistful smile at his big dreams. Her dream was to travel and live in a place where she could decide her own future and not be forced into one. It was only a dream, however, because there was no way that would ever happen for her.

Ernest's loud roar of defeat caused Annaveta to jump from her seat. "How did you win again? You have all the luck."

"It looks like I won't be doing my extra chores for awhile." Alex laughed and lightly punched his brother's shoulder.

"You know we're going to have another round again soon, don't you?" Ernest stared down his brother.

"Of course. I know how much you enjoy the extra work," Alex retorted. Ernest's loud laughter rang through the air as he left to go have a drink with his older brother and his papa. Clara left the table to make some more tea and to go sit with Oma for a while.

Annaveta looked around. Everyone had left, and she was alone with Alex. She looked up at him and saw him smiling, pleased with his latest win.

"Do you want to learn the game, Annaveta?" Alex's eyes twinkled with mischief.

"Sorry, I don't want to do your chores," Annaveta teased.

"Well, even if I win, you won't have to do my chores." Alex stared at her thoughtfully. "However, now that I have some extra free time, how about I teach you this game and show you how to ride a horse and maybe some other things?" His rogue smile was back. She didn't know what he meant by "other things," but she did want to learn to play this game.

She nodded. "All right, that might be fun." Annaveta liked watching his large arm muscles move when he shot the button.

Alex put her half of the Crokinole buttons into her palm. His fingers brushed hers, and his eyes twinkled as a lop-sided grin appeared on his handsome face. She was determined not to let herself be drawn to him, though he was getting harder and harder to resist.

"Okay, let's play." Annaveta had to do something to squelch this attraction she was feeling.

"It'll have to be a short game. The bell for vespers will ring soon." Alex put his button on the board and showed her how to shoot. He was able to get his in the small middle circle on his first try. "Your turn."

Annaveta tried shooting, but her button didn't go very far. Her shooting finger seemed weaker than his.

"You're holding your hand at too much of an angle. Let me help you." Alex came behind her on the bench and put his hand on hers. "Hold your hand in a loose fist and shoot with your index finger. Your shot will be much straighter."

Annaveta could feel his chest against her back, and his blond curls on his head tickled her cheek. She could hardly concentrate. Her shot went crooked again.

"I don't know what I'm doing wrong." Annaveta turned her head to look at him.

Her nose touched his cheek. "Sorry, I — " She quickly moved back.

"I'm not." Alex curved his neck so he could look into her eyes. "You have the most beautiful sea-green eyes I've ever seen." He took his hand off hers and tucked in a loose wisp of curl behind her ear. From there he traced her eyes, nose, and cheekbones. His touch was so tender.

Annaveta was transfixed by this man. He then trailed his

fingers along her jawline and gently caressed the curve of her lips. Her insides quivered.

"I've wanted to taste your lips since we first met." Alex's eyes darkened as he focused on her lips. Mesmerized, she watched his head lower toward hers and his lips found her own. He put his hand behind her head and pulled her closer as if one taste wasn't enough. Her hands reached for him with a will of their own.

Suddenly she heard a bell ringing far away. Annaveta pulled back from Alex's embrace.

"How's that for bad timing? That's the bell for vespers." Alex looked at her, disappointed at the interruption. "That kiss was better than I'd hoped," he whispered as voices and footsteps from the other room came closer.

"Well, vespers has begun. It is Holy Day," Alex's papa said to everyone. "We should all get to bed so we are ready for church tomorrow."

Annaveta lowered her head so Mr. Wagner wouldn't see her face. She busied her hands with cleaning up the buttons from the game. She was sure everyone would be able to see the signs of a first kiss if they looked close enough. Annaveta risked one last look at Alex, and she found him looking at her like a cat that found the cream. Her face heated.

Clara walked up to the table and grabbed Annaveta's hand. "Your face is flushed. You're not getting sick now too, are you?" Clara asked with concern, putting her hand on her friend's forehead.

"I'm not sick. I'm probably just tired," Annaveta said, hoping to discourage anymore questions.

"Me too. I'm glad tomorrow is Sunday. You'll get to meet my friends at church. Later on we can go for a walk and just relax. I love Sundays." Clara sighed with contentment.

Annaveta frowned. She knew there often were bad feelings between the youth in the German colonies and the Russian villages. Once Clara's friends found out she was Russian, she was sure there would be no end of bad comments. She knew she need to be prepared that she might stick out as very different from them and that they might not accept her. But she hoped she was wrong and it would be a good experience when she met Clara's friends tomorrow.

THE SMALL BELL ECHOED IN the silent street as the Wagner family rounded the last corner approaching Main Street. Annaveta saw hundreds of people dressed in their Sunday best enter the towering rectangular-shaped stone structure. She looked down at the tight skirt and blouse she had borrowed from Clara. She was glad for the black wool jacket that hung over her white blouse and dark-blue skirt. With her hair pulled back in a loose braided bun, she felt much older than her sixteen years. She looked at Clara beside her, with her blond hair swept up in a similar style that accented her big blue eyes and straight nose. She thought her own freckles and green eyes made her appear younger than her age.

Annaveta saw other girls and young men waiting at the top of the landing with their families. She worried what sort of welcome was awaiting her. Instinctively she tensed.

"Relax. Don't worry about them." Alex's reassuring smile as he walked up to greet his friends didn't help much. Annaveta looked at the young ladies who came to welcome the Wagner family. She noticed many of them stood as close as they could to Alex, hoping for his attention. Ernest had already paired up with a cute tall girl also dressed in a long black dress with rows of buttons up to her neck. There were other girls dressed in similar dresses. A few of the girls gave Annaveta a withering glance as Clara introduced her to each of them. Annaveta made a mental note of each of their names.

"So you have come here to stay?" Catherine, a pretty

blonde, spoke to her in Russian. "Well, just don't try to take one of our guys. We don't respond nicely to girls who do that."

Catherine gave a knowing look to her friend, Greta, who stood rigid with her arms crossed beside her. Annaveta didn't know what to say, so she just pasted on a smile, her eyes searching Clara's.

"Annaveta is my friend. I hope that she will be treated with kindness while she lives here in our colony," Clara said pointedly to her friends. The other girls only shrugged and started talking among themselves.

Without warning, three loud bells reverberated through the air. The people who were talking beside the schoolhouse and along the street filed slowly into the church. Annaveta was amazed at the height of the large six Grecian-like tapered columns that stood like a barricade to the front doors. She saw Alex hurry to catch up with his friends.

Alex glanced behind and winked. Annaveta smiled nervously back at him and watched as he disappeared with his friends up a set of stairs. She followed Clara to the corner of the large foyer.

"The single men sit in the balcony," Clara explained as she watched her brother leave. "Papa reminds us often that this church was built in 1842 in what was called *KontorStil* or Official Style. It seats more than one thousand people and really is the mainstay of this colony. The bell rung by the sexton is used not only to mark the start of vespers but to announce the death of people or to warn of fire or blizzards," Clara explained as they hung their jackets on large hooks in the entrance.

"You have a priest?" Annaveta walked through to the sanctuary to see the pews filling up fast and thought of the much smaller parish in her former village of Noltava.

"We have Pastor Michael Sommelt. He has been here since 1901 and has done a lot to help the people in this colony. However, he only preaches here every other week because he's needed in other colonies," Clara whispered as she took her friend's hand. "Since you haven't been confirmed into our church, we need to go with my little sisters to the Sunday school classroom. Only confirmed young people and adults are allowed in the sanctuary." Annaveta peeked into the sanctuary and noticed that the women sat on one side and men on the other side. Clara's friends were seated in the last three rows.

The organ played the opening hymn as Clara tugged on her hand to take her to their Sunday school class.

"I don't read German." Annaveta grimaced when they got to the door and the teacher handed them lesson books. "I guess I need to learn." They sat down in a large room filled with many young people their age.

Clara playfully nudged her shoulder. "That's okay. I'll explain as we go."

Annaveta learned the lessons quickly, so that by the last page she had the ten commandments memorized. When they stood to sing a song together, she noticed the girls seated next to her staring. She squirmed and averted her eyes from all the attention. Finally the singing ended. They remained standing, and the teacher bowed his head and prayed. Annaveta only understood a few words, as he spoke in German. After class was done, Clara translated the words to the Lord's Prayer that the teacher was praying. Annaveta was determined to start learning her friend's language.

They heard the three bells ring to mark the end of the service, and the young people filed into the foyer along with the rest of the adults.

"Women leave first and then the men," Clara whispered to Annaveta as they watched the women file out of the sanctuary. "Our tradition is for people to leave in order from oldest to youngest."

They all filed out and went to wait in the churchyard as rows of horse-drawn wagons pulled up to the street. Annaveta and Clara waited for Mrs. Wagner, as she was busy talking to some friends. Mr. Wagner then fetched his wife, and they left together with little Jacob hanging on to his oma's hand. Alex came to help his oma onto the wagon as Inga and Helmut also went with Mr. and Mrs. Wagner.

"We're having the Hoffs over for Sunday meal. So come home quickly," Mrs. Wagner said to Clara, her voice barely discernible over the creaking wheels of the wagon.

"That means you'll get to meet the handsome Hoff brothers Jacob and Joseph," Clara whispered, her eyes bright with mischief. "Of course, they're probably coming over so that both sets of parents can get to know the other's family better since Rachel and Ernest's relationship is getting pretty serious. I wish Mama would ask the Koch family over some Sunday so I could get to know John better."

"Ah, so the handsome brothers have competition." Annaveta nudged her friend's shoulder as they hurried their pace through the last street toward the Wagner's home. Sounds of children's laughter welcomed them as they walked up the now-familiar street. Coming through the door, the smell of chicken and potatoes with pickles made her stomach rumble.

Mama directed them as they took off their coats. "Wash your hands and set the table, girls."

It didn't take long before the big table was filled with all the adults and children. Annaveta sat on the wooden bench beside Katarina and Erika to help them put food on their plates. She looked down the table and saw Rachel and Christina also serving their little sister and brother. The girls kept up a constant stream of chatter about their side projects of stitching little pillows and other pretty keepsakes.

With the lunch dishes all washed and dried, the parents asked the older children to go outside with the younger ones for fresh air. Annaveta stuck close to Clara's side, as she wasn't sure about these new people. They walked around the yard between the barn and farm tools, where the wildflowers were blooming. Suddenly she was hit softly in the arm by a ball.

As she turned, she saw Jacob's deep-brown eyes looking intently at her. He spoke to her in German. Annaveta didn't understand and saw Alex frown at his friend. Clara explained what he said, which was, "Let's see if your throw is as perfect as you are." Upon understanding, Annaveta's face heated with discomfort.

"He, sind sie nicht der einzige stier im stift, Bruder." Joseph was the fun-loving younger blond brother that had a ruddy appearance his brother lacked. Joseph continued in German, an appealing grin on his face.

Clara whispered in her ear what he was saying. "He told his brother that he's not the only bull in the pen. And now he's saying to you that you might not understand his words, but he thinks you will understand his actions better than the clumsy words of his brother." Annaveta blushed when Clara added, "I think they're fighting over you."

Joseph pulled up a wildflower he found in the yard and, bowing, handed it to Annaveta. She took it, looking at him cautiously, a small smile forming on her lips.

"Both of you stop with the flattery already." Alex spoke firmly. "She's new here, and you are making her uncomfortable. Let's go play anti-over by the barn." He picked up the ball and leaned down to Annaveta's ear. "I'm going to catch you yet."

Warmth flooded her face as she listened to his words. With a hooded gaze she watched Alex swagger back to his friends.

He may think he's going to catch me, but he doesn't realize I don't want to surrender my freedom to a man. I wonder just how relentless he'll be?

Chapter 9

WITH HANDS NUMB FROM THE cold river water, Annaveta pounded the last of the washed clothes with the wide paddle. Balancing herself on the narrow planks, she bent over once more to rinse out the final pair of men's pants. Her cold hands were barely able to squeeze out the extra water.

Fingering back wisps of hair, she watched other girls her age help their mamas. It was wash day for the Pleve colony, and the River Medweitz, which flowed into the Volga River, was where they rinsed their laundry. She was glad that Clara and she could help with the laundry for Mrs. Wagner, who was at home tending little Katarina and Erika. Last night and this morning they complained that their tummies hurt, and they each had a fever. Clara's mama had been cooling them off again before they left this morning. Inga stayed behind to help with making meals.

Rinsing the men's pants in the river reminded Annaveta of the many times she had helped her mama wash their clothes in their small barrel at home. Her mama would flick water at her in fun as she washed, then Annaveta rinsed and helped hang up the clothes on the string tied between two trees outside. They had been so poor, yet Mama always tried to make her and her brothers smile. Tears welled up in her eyes. *There are so many things I miss about you, Mama.*

"No time for dawdling, Annaveta," Clara announced behind her. "Let's get these wet clothes home and hung up to dry. By the look of the sun, it must be almost noon."

"Good," Annaveta choked out as she quickly wiped her eyes, picked up the heavy basket of wet clothes, and set it on her hip.

"Hey, are you okay?" Clara stood in front of her, her forehead wet with sweat, the water from the wet clothes in her basket dripping down her skirt. She gave Annaveta a big hug.

"There, now we're both soaked." Clara's face was filled with mischief, but her smile quickly changed to a frown as she studied Annaveta's teary eyes. "Are you thinking of your family?"

Annaveta nodded as she sponged off the tears with her sleeve.

"Seeing other girls with their mamas is kind of hard. I remember how Mama would play games with us kids so that even though we worked hard, it never seemed like it," Annaveta whispered, giving Clara a weak smile. "I miss her more than I thought possible. I needed that hug today, thanks. You're a good friend."

"What are friends for?" Clara squeezed her arm and pulled her up the hill. "You are part of our family now. I'm so glad you're here."

Annaveta thought of how much Clara, Alex, and their whole family had already helped her. They had given her a home when she had no other place to go, offered their protection, and treated her like family. She had so much to be grateful for. Yet, she harbored the fear that Misha or Monsieur Arnaud would find her. They both had threatened her, and it had her worried. However, it seemed unlikely they would come to a German colony to look for her. Yet even the smallest chance of either of them finding her knotted her stomach. If they found her, they would do all they could to make her leave this colony. She knew both those men never stopped until they got what they wanted. Hopefully Pavla hadn't said anything to anyone about where she was. She would just have to stay alert, as she had been doing.

"Come around to the back of the house." Clara tugged on Annaveta's basket. "We'll hang the last of the clothes there. Mama said to hurry because lunch is ready."

They hung the wet clothes on the already full clothesline behind the house. Then with damp skirts and numb hands, they headed inside the house.

ANNAVETA TOOK A BREAK FROM hoeing the vegetables that the Wagners had planted in the *hinnerhof* and glanced over at Clara and Inga. For three days they had been hard at work hoeing the beets, carrots, and peas. Both of them seemed to have more energy than she had. Annaveta was a little discouraged by the large plot of growing vegetable crops as she imagined all the hoeing and weeding that would need to be done. Clara's mama had reminded them that this harvest would need to last the family throughout the winter. Annaveta was amazed at what a diligent, hardworking family the Wagners were. Somehow, even though she had always worked hard, there had never been enough for their family. *That's because my papa took whatever rubles he could find and came home drunk.* She pulled her kerchief closer to her brows as if to cover up the bad memories.

Clara glanced over at her, and she gave her a tired smile. Her shoulders were aching and her fingers were starting to form blisters, but she told herself she could make it until the last two rows were done.

"I'm sure you're not used to all this hard work." Inga taunted Annaveta as she finished her row. "I guess there're a few things you'll have to get used to — or you could just go back to where you came from."

Annaveta looked at Inga and then to Clara without saying a word.

"She's a hard worker and learning quickly. Even Mama

103

says so." Clara aimed a dark look at her sister-in-law as if daring her to make another unkind remark.

"Hmm. We'll see, I guess." Inga picked up the drinking cup and dipped it in the pail of cool water, taking her time as she dipped it in twice before handing it to Clara.

Annaveta fumed at Inga's mean comments. She didn't think she had done anything to upset her, and yet Inga still treated her like an unwelcome guest.

"Looks like it's close to suppertime." Clara looked at the sun's position, which was moving closer to the horizon. "We need to water the plants quickly. Mama said to come back to the house after we're done watering the garden. We'll need to do the rest of the weeding tomorrow."

Watering the plants didn't take long with all three of them working. After gathering the hoes and buckets, the three of them walked around the large garden. Annaveta stopped and looked through a hole in the fence to see a large field with hundreds of lambs and calves busily eating the green grass. She giggled at a black-and-white spotted calf that seemed to be whispering in its friend's ear. She imagined they were planning to run away from the herdsman. The herdsman was a tall, skinny man with dark pants and a light-colored tunic that was belted around his waist. The animals moved forward together as they heard the tap of his long stick. His straw hat fell off as one of the calves bucked against him. She laughed at the young bull calf's antics. She turned her head quickly as the herdsman looked around to see where the laughter had come from.

"Annaveta. Quickly now." Inga waved her arm; she was already at the house. "If the herdsman is rounding up the animals to bring home, then it's time for supper."

"Coming." Annaveta hurried her steps. Her long skirt swished loudly as she caught up with the two women. She hoped eventually Clara's sister-in-law would accept her. The constant flood of critical remarks hurt her feelings, but maybe she would just have to get used to it. Inga reminded her of the girl who warned her off Alex on Sunday. If Alex's kiss the other night was any indication of where his passions lay, it didn't seem as if he was too attached to that girl. She would have to just wait and see, but she didn't want to get too close to Alex or any other man. At least Clara accepted her for who she was, and for that she was grateful.

When everyone was seated around the table, Papa Wagner gave the blessing. Annaveta's pulse raced at the intimate look Alex gave her from his place across from her. Was he remembering their heated kiss from the other night? The ardent look in his eyes as he stared at her convinced her that his thoughts matched her own. She lowered her eyes, breaking the connection between them. Instead, she focused on the borscht soup in front of her. Her thoughts were a whirlwind of confusion and doubt about so many things. She didn't need to add falling in love to the mixture.

"Clara, I was wondering if you and Annaveta could go get more water from the town well. We are in short supply today, what with using it for housework, watering the garden, and the laundry." Mama Wagner looked at her oldest daughter, weariness etched in every line on her face from tending to her sick family. Oma, Jacob, and her two youngest daughters were starting to mend.

"Of course, Mama. We'll each carry the wooden water yoke so we can bring home extra drinking and cooking water." Clara nodded at her mama and hurried to finish her soup. "Since we're talking about wells, Mama, you should tell Annaveta how you and Papa met." Clara gave her mama a big smile and winked at Annaveta.

"*Ach*, that was so long ago." Mama Wagner passed the bread around once more.

"Please, Mama. It's such a great story," Clara urged.

"All right then." Mrs. Wagner smiled, looking at her husband. "I had walked from our house on the other side of this colony, carrying my empty buckets with the neck yoke on my shoulders. I was at the well, and I set them down on the ground intending to fill them. I reached for the rope that held the bucket to dip in the well, when I slipped. I would've fallen in the well if your papa hadn't grabbed my legs and saved me. It seemed like he just suddenly appeared, but later he told me he had been watching me from the side of the blacksmith shop. He ran to save me when he saw that I was in trouble, and then took the time to dip the buckets in the water for me and to fill them up. He was so handsome, I just stood there watching his strong muscles at work. I felt a little like Rachel meeting her Jacob for the first time." Mama looked at Papa Wagner and winked. He shook his head, but the shine in his eyes gave away his delight. "We kept talking and getting to know each other, until one evening when we went for a walk, he gave me a braided bracelet that he had made with my name on it. It was in my favorite colours of brown, green, and yellow. He told me it was his promise to love me. A three-corded strand is not easily broken. I've worn it ever since that day." Mrs. Wagner fingered the faded braided bracelet on her left wrist and smiled.

"What a wonderful story." Annaveta had a wistful smile as she saw the gentle glances that passed between Clara's parents, even after all these years. Her parents had never had that kind of love for each other. She had never known another couple that did. Until now.

"Thanks, Mama." Clara got up to bring a stack of dirty dishes to the sink.

"*Ach*, you're welcome. Clara loves the stories. She is a romantic at heart." Mrs. Wagner kissed her daughter's cheek. "But I wouldn't have you any other way."

Annaveta sighed, missing the closeness she had with her own mama in moments like this.

Rubbing her fist against her chest, she tried to massage away the ache that came to her chest at memories of her mama's hugs and encouraging words. She looked over at mama and daughter and tried to smile through the pain.

Soon most of the men had left the table, and Annaveta

stood to help collect more dirty dishes. Alex handed her his bowl, deliberately running his fingers across her hand. She looked at him, trying to still the tingling in her belly. Moving away quickly, she picked up more dishes.

His warm breath tickled her ear as he bent over to whisper to her. "I look forward to seeing you later." She jerked almost dropping the dishes in surprise. The rumble of his chuckle faded with the sound of his footsteps as he left the house. She stood with the dishes in her hand trying to calm her tremors. *Why does he always affect me so strongly? I don't want his attention right now, even if he makes me feel special. No good can come of it. I must do what I can to avoid him.*

"Annaveta, let me help you bring those dishes to the washing bowl, and then we must get water. As it is, there's only enough left to wash the dishes," Clara said, picking up the leftover bowls.

They completed their task in a hurry and set out for the colony well. Feeling the sun shining on her skin, Annaveta was glad to be in the fresh air again. So far the weight of the wooden yoke on her shoulders was manageable. Clara had picked up two hand-carved five-foot-long yokes from their woodshed and put them on their necks. The four-gallon pails hanging on hooks at each end made her wonder just how heavy this would be with full pails.

Clara waved at Pastor Sommelt as they passed the churchyard. He gave a quick wave and went back to his conversation with Rachel's mama.

"I wonder if they are talking about a fall wedding," Annaveta said to her friend as they passed the newly finished brick blacksmith shop on their left. Clara waved at more people she knew.

"Mrs. Hoff might hint at an upcoming wedding, but when couples are courting, it's mostly hush-hush around here." Clara winked at her. "I think you know what I mean."

Annaveta rolled her eyes at her friend and didn't respond. She didn't need the reminder that she had nearly been married only a few weeks ago or that she was trying to avoid falling in love with her brother. She knew Clara longed to see her and her brother as a couple, but Annaveta just wasn't sure she wanted to go where her heart was telling her.

Hearing laughter, they rounded the corner to see most of the same girls they had talked with on Sunday standing by the well. The girls were dressed in their best work clothes with swaying ankle-length skirts made of the finest black wool. They were laughing with a few of the younger men who appeared to have found the pretty girls standing by the watering hole too hard to resist.

Looking up, she saw the three men stare at them as they made their way forward. The girls at the well looked at Clara and Annaveta and stopped laughing. Annaveta's whole body tensed as she saw the pretty blond girl from last Sunday suddenly frown at her.

"That's Catherine with Rachel, Maria, and Greta," Clara whispered, pointing out the different girls standing by the well. "Don't let their words bother you. Let's just fill our pails and go."

Clara and Annaveta tried to walk around the girls, but they moved to stand in their way.

"So you're still here?" Catherine crossed her arms over her generous bosom as she stood in front of her in her tight-fitting ivory blouse. Her shiny blond hair was pulled loosely back with stray tendrils blowing in the wind. She spoke in fluent Russian, as did all the young people in the colony. Clara had told her it had been required for all school age children to learn Russian, since the government encouraged Russian German immigration in the last fifteen years. At that moment Annaveta wished she could pretend she didn't understand Catherine's words. "I thought you would have realized already that you're not welcome here. You should go back to where you came from."

"The Wagners asked — " Annaveta started but was interrupted.

"I don't believe they asked you to stay because they wanted you. I think they thought they had to because they felt sorry for you." Greta said, a tall brown-haired plain girl with dark-brown eyes that seemed to shoot fire as she spoke. "Face it. It's time for you to head back to your little village. Go back to your shiftless life with your good-for-nothing Ruskie friends."

The slur against her pedigree was something that Annaveta had heard before between young German and Russian boys. When Germans visited Noltava or when Russians came to Pleve Colony on market day, young boys of both backgrounds insulted and made rude gestures to each other. What hurt was that these girls thought the Wagners, who had been so loving and kind, didn't really want her here with them.

She looked over at Clara, who was busy talking with Rachel.

"Well, for now that's where I'm staying." Annaveta refused to be bullied by their rude words. "If the Wagners want me to leave their home, then they can tell me. Not you."

"Oh, they'll tell you to go away. Won't they, Greta?" Catherine smirked at her, then gave an unpleasant laugh as she looked at her friend. She raised her eyebrows like a queen giving orders. "Watch and see."

Annaveta shrugged her shoulders in a dismissive gesture, but inside she thought their words sounded a bit like a threat. Before she could say anything, Clara came to her side and helped take the shoulder yoke off her sore back. Annaveta returned the favor and then they started walking.

"We need to get going. Mama said to hurry back with the water." Clara moved forward, forcing Catherine and Greta to move aside. "Come, my friend."

Annaveta followed Clara, keeping her eyes on their destination — the well. She inhaled deeply of the moist air that seemed to sink deep into her pores like a restoring oil. She kept walking until she reached the well. Clara lifted the lid on the large open hole that was encircled by two layers of brick. She pointed to the bucket that was suspended by a rope next to the well's opening.

Annaveta's hand was still shaking from the confrontation as she reached for the water bucket and a shadow suddenly fell across her hand. She looked up surprised to see Joseph Hoff looking down at her.

"Want some help?" His big brown eyes searched hers as he reached to take the bucket from her hand. He spoke Russian with a heavy accent, so she had to listen hard to understand him.

"Uh, sure. Thanks." Annaveta let him take the bucket from her trembling hand.

"Hey, don't worry about those girls none," he whispered, trying to comfort her as he lowered the bucket into the well. "My sister used to hear their insults when they teased her about stuttering. She's learned that it's people who are little on the inside who need to make other people feel little. Now she just smiles at them and doesn't respond to their insults."

"Thank you for your kindness." Annaveta spoke softly as her eyes brimmed with tears. She looked up at him, her lips shaking from the surge of emotions that flooded her.

"Oh, now I made you cry." Joseph's woebegone grimace almost made her laugh. "Even when Mama cries, I try to make her laugh or do something to make her happy. Anything to take away the tears."

"Ah, now I know you better. Underneath all that humor is a soft heart. I like it," Annaveta said, wiping her wet cheeks with her sleeve and giving him a smile. She looked over at Clara, who was handing over more empty pails for Joseph to fill.

"Think you have me figured out, do you?" Joseph teased her, flicking some water at her from the pail he just pulled up. Annaveta laughed at his fun and dipped her fingers into the water to shoot some back at him.

"No you don't." Joseph grabbed her hand and held it tight.

Then he gently turned her hand over and placed a tender kiss on the inside of her palm.

Annaveta just stood there, unsure of how to respond to the quick change in his demeanor. First teasing and laughing, then flirting. He still had the young boyishness in him that she enjoyed in her brothers. That's how Joseph appeared to her. He was like the brother she was missing in her life. She relaxed.

"Hey, you two." Clara stared at them, her hands on her hips, her two full pails of water at her side. "Time to stop playing and start working."

"Clara's right; we need to get to work. So, are you going to fill the other bucket?" She looked at him with a hopeful expression. She hoped the distraction would cause him to forget his teasing ways.

"No, he won't." A low voice, filled with resolve, seemed to come out of nowhere.

Annaveta turned and saw Alex standing behind her, his stern eyes glued on Joseph.

"I saw your papa at the blacksmith's shop. I think he's waiting for you." Alex took the pail from Joseph's hand, forcing him to move aside. He poured the water into Annaveta's two pails, then started on Clara's. "I'll help the girls finish up. Mama was wondering what was taking you two so long. Now I know why."

"There's no need to be pushy, Wagner." Joseph's face turned red. His mouth drew into a tight line as his chin went up.

"I just wanted to remind you of your place." Alex, just slightly taller than Joseph, looked down at him, piercing him with his eyes. "And it's not your place to kiss Annaveta's hand."

"I suppose that's your own private spot?" Joseph mocked him with his hands on his hips.

"As a matter of fact it is." Alex glared at his friend as if daring him to challenge him.

Annaveta gasped with shock, her face heating with mortification. She saw Alex's intimidating look as he stood with his hands on his hips as he faced Joseph. Joseph's face turned red as he tried to think of a response to Alex's bold words. The tittering laughter of the girls behind her was the final straw. She turned quickly and walked at a half run–half walk past the bullheaded men and sarcastic girls without looking back.

"Annaveta, wait!" she heard Clara call behind her. "What about the water?"

Annaveta didn't stop. She figured since Alex was so interested in controlling things, he could take charge of the heavy pails of water that she'd left behind. She walked as fast as she could hoping that would drain some of the anger she was feeling. It was all too much. Trying to settle into a new culture, being told she wasn't wanted by Clara's friends, and now Alex claiming her in front of everyone and nearly starting a fight to do it. She had to get away from this man who wanted to control her.

She didn't want to be subjected to the kind of control she'd faced with her own papa.

Chapter 10

FUMBLING WITH THE BUTTONS ON her oldest work blouse, Annaveta hurried to get ready to go. It had been a long, hot summer with the occasional rain. Now they were nearing the end of August, and all the hard work they had put into the garden and the fields had resulted in what looked to be a bumper crop.

Today was the start of three weeks of harvest, and today would begin the hardest work of all. She didn't know how she would be able to work alongside Alex day after day, around the clock. Somehow she had managed to avoid being alone with him since that day at the well. She could tell he was miserable when he looked at her, his eyes filled with entreaty. Annaveta was no longer angry, but she didn't really know what to do with her confused feelings. On one hand she really liked him, but on the other she didn't like that he thought he could stop her from talking with other men. So for now she would try to stay out of his way.

After braiding her hair, she looped it back into a low bun. Clara had already left with her mama to milk the cows, so she hurried to the barn. The milking needed to be done before the cow herdsman came by their house.

Wiping the sweat from her forehead, she found her stool and put it in place by her cow, whom she had named Liza. Liza was gentle except she swished her tail at her every chance she got. Mrs. Wagner let her milk the gentle cow — not the feisty one that Clara usually had. Clara gave the nickname Crazy to the cow she milked. Annaveta smiled at the fitting label. She leaned her head against the curve of her hind shank as her sore hands finished milking, then gave Liza's rump a gentle pat.

Clara was removing the old hay and putting fresh straw down in the stalls as Annaveta led her old black cow to the end of the road where the other two milk cows stood chewing their cud. The herdsman was just coming down the lane, followed by a wide row of Pleve Colony's cows. Annaveta watched fascinated as the Wagner's three cows stepped automatically into the line behind the herdsman. Next were the calves and pigs. She would get them ready for the herdsman that would take them to large grazing fields outside of town. Just like every day, he would come for them soon.

Annaveta pulled down her kerchief to dab at the moisture on her forehead. She could tell it was going to be another hot day. Clara's papa said the crops ripened during the heat of the summer. Which was why today was the first day of harvest.

"Annaveta, *mach schnell*. Come." Clara stood at the door waving her indoors. "Papa wants to eat in a hurry so we can get going." Katarina and Erika poked their heads out beside her.

"It's going to be fun. We get to sleep in tents." Erika ran and grabbed her hand, tugging her inside. Everyone was seated at the table, ready to eat, waiting for her.

"Sorry I'm late." Annaveta grimaced at the impatient gesture from Helmut and Inga and sensed subdued tolerance from Mr. Wagner as his hand tapped the open Bible in front of him.

After they stood to say the Lord's Prayer, Mr. Wagner gave thanks for the morning's meal and read the Bible verses for the day. The porridge and rye bread was a fitting meal for the grueling day that lay ahead.

"We'll be loading up supplies for harvest on the long wagon. Today we go to the far fields." He looked over at

Oma. "Mama, you will be okay here with Inga and Jacob?"

"*Ja, gut, mein sohn.* I'll be fine," Oma sat next to her son eating only a little food. "I will pray that you get all the harvest in soon, and for safety." Oma patted her son's hand. Heinrich had taken over the family farm when Oma's husband died, which Clara had explained to Annaveta was a custom among all Volga German people. Oma was a honored and respected elder in this house, and she loved her grandchildren. Annaveta was glad to feel the love of Clara's oma. She would miss her while they were gone.

"Pray that the weather holds out. It's nice and hot now, but we know here on the Volga steppes that the weather can change as fast as the wind." Mr. Wagner finished his meal, patted his mama's hand, and stood.

One by one the family finished their food and started gathering what they needed to take. The tents, equipment, bedding, and kitchen supplies had already been piled in the back of the wagon, so they each gathered an extra set of work clothes and old sweaters and jackets to take to the site.

Clara had explained to Annaveta that gathering the harvest was when the real workload began for their family and the rest of the families in the colony. Unlike the opening of spring's seeding operation, which was dictated by the village elders, the harvest of their crops was decided by the papa and head of each household. Their crops of wheat, oats, sugar beets, barley, millet, flax, tobacco, and sunflowers were ripening. Here on the Volga steppes, once the grain crops were mature, there could be no delay either in beginning the reaping or in finishing the threshing. The village was quite deserted during harvesttime.

The red and orange hues of the sun peeking over the horizon signaled the dawn. Sitting on the flatbed of the wagon, Annaveta took off her kerchief to enjoy the morning air. Erika and Katarina scrambled in between Annaveta and Clara, cuddling close. Waving good-bye to Oma, Inga, and little Jacob, Papa Wagner signaled the horses to move forward.

"It looks like a cloudless sky today, Papa," Alex said, shifting beside his brother Helmut so he could look up at his papa. "Since we just had a big rain, hopefully the weather will stay warm now until we can get this crop off."

"Lord willing, Son. Last week when we checked the crops, I tasted a few kernels of grain. They are ready to go. We should be there by lunchtime." Papa Wagner sounded glad. "It will be good to get the harvest in. Looks like we left earlier than many others from the colony. Is that the Hoff wagon behind us?"

"*Ja*, they are eager to start too." Mama Wagner looked back to wave at their friends.

Annaveta looked over and smiled at the Hoff family. The heat of embarrassment flooded her cheeks as she thought of the incident at the well. She hoped Joseph didn't have hard feelings about it. She caught a glimmer of his smile just before their wagon turned off into their field. She sighed with relief. At least Joseph wasn't going to be a problem, but she didn't know if she could say the same for Alex.

The sun was shining brightly overhead by the time they reached the fields. The wheat fields that rippled in waves that seemed to touch the sky like a golden-white ocean. They stopped the wagon near other field equipment that the men had brought over the last week in preparation for the harvest. Unloading the supplies from the wagon was a heavy job. It took all four men to lift the three heavy barrels of water that were needed to last the week.

"Girls, I'll need you to help haul the food to the table by the fire pit. We'll set up an outdoor campfire there." Mama Wagner pointed to a small hole filled with leftover ash and stones. "We've packed extra food, since Uncle Johann and Aunt Bertha and their four boys and five girls will be helping with our harvest, just like we'll help with theirs."

"Oh good. I love my cousins. I've got to tell Katarina." Erika's red braids bounced as she skipped over to the wagon to find her sister.

"Let me tell you, my friend, there is no bunch as loud and wild as my cousins." Clara's eyes danced as she looked at Annaveta.

Annaveta smiled. "Well, I guess they'll add excitement to harvesttime."

"True enough." Clara shook her head laughing.

Annaveta massaged her arms and shoulders, trying to ease the pain from hauling all the food and supplies. And this week was just beginning. She groaned as she went to help Clara lay out the straw and blankets for the beds in the two tents. The men had just finished setting up the tall, round tents. Each one had a hole in the center and a vent at the top to let out the smoke from the fire.

"These are copies of the *Kirghiz*-style tents. It's good we have them. They work well for harvesttime," Clara explained, seeing Annaveta's curious expression. "The Kirghiz were the same Turko-Tatar tribesmen that lived two hundred miles eastward from the Volga Germans across the Ural Mountains. They attacked the first colonists who had moved here from Germany with Catherine the Great's invitation to settle the land along the Volga River. The Kirghiz tribes captured or killed over one thousand Volga Germans. I'm glad I didn't live back then." Clara shuddered at the thought. "Every Volga German has been told the story of the Kirghiz raids, even though we are friends with them now. I remember a few times when we were naughty, Oma would threaten that the Kirghiz would come get me. I would go to bed worried until Mama calmed me down."

Annaveta stared at Clara's expression of mock terror, which inspired giggles in both of them.

"What's so funny?" Alex tugged on his sister's kerchief and pulled gently on Katrina's and Erika's braids as they danced around him.

"Oh, you wouldn't understand," Clara told her big brother, playfully swatting his hand.

"Mama says to come for lunch." Erika tugged on Annaveta's hand. It seemed she had a new little friend. They left Alex with an unsatisfied frown as they walked to the makeshift fire pit. Papa Wagner had just finished setting up the iron tripod over the pit, placing the large cast-iron pot filled with water on it. The tripod was shaped like an open-faced pyramid with a hook from which the pot hung over the smoldering fire. Surrounding the fire pit were large logs to sit on and a folding table that Alex and his papa had made. Mrs. Wagner had just finished covering the table with sliced rye bread, pickles, fresh peas, and sliced chicken.

"It's all ready to eat." Mama Wagner looked around at everyone. "It's just cold sandwiches today. Something cool for an extra-hot day."

After Clara's papa gave thanks, everyone lined up and made their sandwiches.

"We will start on this field closest to us today." Mr. Wagner was the last to sit down. He began chewing his chicken sandwich while looking around at his family. "That way we'll be able to cross this field with our wagon to get to the next one, and so on. We'll work until sundown so we get it done while the weather holds out. Mama, you and the girls bring lots of water; we'll be needing it today."

With the men leading the way to the corner of the field, the girls followed, each carrying a pail of water and a few cups. Alex and Ernest each had a *reff* — a frame for carrying loads on one's back — and attached to the reff was a cradle scythe. Alex started swinging his scythe, swathing the first piles of freshly cut rye. His brother Ernest then made a new row beside that one. Clara and Annaveta followed Alex, gathering armfuls of the reapings with their bare hands and tying them into bundles. They didn't use fiber twine, as it was too costly. Instead, twists of rye straw were used with the beaten-out ends skillfully knotted. Annaveta watched how Clara bundled and tied, then did the same. Annaveta looked back to see Helmut and Clara's mama and papa walking behind Ernest's swaths, bundling and tying. Katarina and Erika kept up with Annaveta and Clara as they helped each other. Alex was sweating profusely, beaded moisture dripping from his forehead and hair as he continued to swing the scythe.

The last of the bundles of rye were carried to the family threshing site just before the sun went down. Exhausted and thirsty, they each took turns drinking the now-lukewarm water until it was completely gone. Tired but glad to be half-done with the field, they walked over to eat the warmed-up stew that Clara's mama had made.

Katarina didn't even finish her plate before she fell asleep on Clara's shoulder. Erika finished her food and asked Annaveta to come with her to hear her prayers and tuck her in. Mama Wagner told her to go ahead and get to bed herself. Annaveta was so weary that after helping Erika and Katarina to bed, she promptly fell asleep on the thin blankets that lay on the straw beside them.

Clanging pans woke everyone in their tent in the morning.

"*Wachen sie, auf!* It's time to get up. We have plenty of work to do today," Papa Wagner called out as he struck the pots three more times.

Annaveta sat up in bed, scared, as the loud sounds of pans reminded her of the Russian village's clanging bells when there was a fire. She fought off the memories of her recent loss that now filled her mind. Wiping away tears, she found her long dark-gray skirt with her brown work blouse that she somehow had folded last night. Then she went to wake the girls, who had slept through the loud noise. Clara quickly got dressed as Annaveta helped the younger girls with their hair, making tight braids that hung down their backs. Then Clara and Annaveta helped fix each other's hair. After putting on their head shawls, they made their way in the early morning light to the campfire.

"We will have *kasha* today and our usual *steppe* tea." Mrs.

Wagner put a small handful of leaves in the pot of boiled water. "We'll feel like we have energy again after some solid food." Annaveta sat beside Alex on the log, as all the other places were taken. Her cheeks turned red as she glanced up at him and caught his crooked smile. She quickly ate her food and drank her hot tea, almost burning her tongue.

Mr. Wagner got up, and with help from Helmut, Ernest, and Alex, they hitched the horses to the wagon. They made their way to the half-finished rye field, and Annaveta hurried to join Clara and her mama as they put the leftover food in a cool wooden box they kept in the tent. Carrying more pails of water, the girls walked to the field where Helmut and Mr. Wagner were scything.

"Make sure your head scarf is down low over your forehead, Annaveta. Feels like today is going to be extra hot, and you don't want sunstroke." Clara pulled hers lower as she walked toward the wagon and the sun peeked its yellow head over the horizon.

Annaveta pulled her head scarf down so she was just able to peer out from under the fringe. She caught up with Clara and hopped on the back of the wagon just as Mr. Wagner got the horses moving. They reached their destination in good time.

Alex spoke. "This new scythe we're using was invented by one of our own Volga colonists and works much better than the Russian sickle that you're used to." Alex explained. "There're a lot of things we do better." Annaveta raised one eyebrow, casting doubt on his comment but leaving it alone.

Annaveta was glad when they got back to work. She stopped as everyone else ran ahead, and Alex came to stand beside her. He tugged her head scarf lower on her forehead and ran his thumb down her nose, letting his slow-moving finger graze her lips. An unspoken promise was in his touch, echoing his last words. She pulled away from him as his head bent closer to her own. She reminded herself that being so near Alex wasn't good for her. His possessiveness was something she didn't like because she knew where it would lead.

Alex released her arms reluctantly, a frown on his brow. "I'll find you later," he promised, turning as he heard his papa call his name. Annaveta hurried to where Clara was tying her bundle. Thoughts of Alex twisted in her mind like the sheaves of rye she gathered in her arms. He seemed determined to win her over even as she resisted his advances.

She looked over to where he worked alongside his brothers with a big smile on his face. She frowned and saw the other women were far ahead of her. She shook off her thoughts and followed their pattern, picking up their natural rhythm as they worked. The morning hurried by as they finished row after row. Soon the faint tolling of bells from their village announced lunchtime as everyone moved back toward the shade of the tree and the makeshift tarp.

"Did you hear that?" Annaveta turned to ask Clara, who sat beside her on the knotted pine log.

"*Ja.* Those are the church bells tolling the midday chimes. They ring every day in our village, but with us being so far away, they are hard to hear," Clara explained after she finished her drink of water.

Annaveta thought all these homey sounds like the bells, mixed with the smells of sweet clover that surrounded the fields and the malty odor of rye, would linger in her memory after she was long gone from here. She closed her eyes to rest, glad for a few moments to unwind.

Clara touched her shoulder to wake her up. She must have drifted to sleep, because it took a minute to realize where she was. She got up and followed the path Clara's two oldest brothers were making with their scythes. She hurried to pick up what she could, then quickly tied it into bundles. The sun burned extra hot this afternoon. Annaveta was constantly brushing off sweat from her forehead with her sleeve.

She looked up, tucking her hair into her head scarf, when she noticed that Alex had taken Helmut's place on the scythe. She watched as he moved fast and followed an easy rhythm, cutting even swatches of rye. Annaveta noticed his blond hair was uncovered and that he was constantly wiping his brow.

Looking at the others, she saw they too were swabbing the moisture off their foreheads and necks. She continued working as the blistering sun pricked at her skin. She was dreaming of finishing up the harvest and being back home again, when suddenly she heard Mrs. Wagner cry out. She looked up and saw Alex's legs buckle beneath him.

"Alexander! My son, what is the matter?" His mama ran as quickly as she could to his side. Kneeling among the twists of straw, she cradled Alex's head on her lap. "*Meine kostbarer sohn.* What has happened?" She slapped his cheek to wake him up.

The sound of running feet echoed the thumping of Annaveta's racing pulse. She stared at Alex, scared as he lay there pale and unmoving. His family was crowded around him, everyone asking the same question. What happened to him? No one seemed to really know. Annaveta thought about this big man who was so strong and yet so gentle with her and with his family. He stood by her, was her protector, and did so much for her. Her stomach clenched with knots of panic as she thought the worst.

He can't die — he just can't! I don't know what I'd do if he died. In that moment Annaveta realized how much she truly did care for him and how much she would miss his teasing, his fun-loving manner, and all the ways he took care of her. She raised her eyes as she pleaded. *Please, God, if you are up there, make him live. He needs to get better, because I really need him. And not just for me — his family loves him so.*

Chapter 11

ANNAVETA FROWNED AS SHE STOOD and rubbed her aching back. They still had one more row to go to finish this field. The sun had long since gone down, so they were working by the light of the moon. She couldn't wait to be done so she could see how Alex was doing.

Mrs. Wagner had brought more water to the workers a while ago and told them that Alex's head had hurt so badly that he had been sick to his stomach. He had finally fallen asleep after she cooled him down with a sponge bath. Annaveta was worried about him. She knew she wouldn't be able to rest until she saw him for herself.

With the last rye field finished, she helped the others carry the remaining tied bundles to the threshing site. They each scooped their own dish of the stew that Mrs. Wagner had left on the table for them. Sitting beside Clara, Annaveta kept glancing nervously toward the tent she knew Alex was sleeping in.

"I can tell you won't rest until you see my brother." Clara stood up when they had eaten their full. "Come on then."

They went to the men's tent while the rest of the family finished their food. They quietly opened the flap and looked inside. Alex lay still and white with only a thin blanket over his lengthy body. Annaveta went to kneel beside where he lay. He looked like death. Her hand that touched his forehead burned to the touch. Seeing a pail beside his pallet, she rinsed out the cloth and gently cooled his forehead and neck.

"Try to get better, Alex. You must get well." Annaveta's voice trembled as she spoke softly to him. With one hand holding his and the other cooling his forehead, she whispered encouraging words to him. All of a sudden his weak hand squeezed her own. His eyes flickered for a second, and then he slept again.

"I could feel that. Thanks for letting me know you are listening." A tear escaped and ran down one cheek. "Now I know you are going to be okay."

A hand squeezed her shoulder and drew her out of a deep reverie.

"Annaveta, time for everyone to go to bed. Now, don't worry anymore. Alex will be okay." The warmth of his mama's embrace helped her believe it would be true. "The men are putting out the fire and getting things ready for morning. Time for us women to get our beauty rest."

Annaveta got up and took one last lingering look at the one man who frustrated her and yet whom she cared for more than any other. He needed to get better and soon.

Her quick pace covered the short distance between the two tents in short order. Clara was already fast asleep when she stepped inside. Annaveta hurried to get her own work dress off and settled in between Clara and her small sisters. She lay there thinking about how pale and helpless Alex looked, and tears rolled down her cheeks. She shouldn't have been so mean to him, and decided to be much kinder to him from now on.

It wasn't until much later that she finally fell asleep.

ALEX ROLLED OVER FIRST ONTO his stomach, then back to his side. He was wide awake and feeling weak, but so much better. His stomach growled as if in agreement. He was ready to help with the harvesting today.

He picked up the wet cloth and dipped it in the pail by his bed, then sponged his face. Smiling, he remembered the few times Annaveta had come to his side, talking to him, her gentle touch with the cool cloth helping him feel better. After Mama had fed him his broth last night, Annaveta, his angel, had come in. He had pretended to be asleep so he could listen to her singing. Her lullaby was the sweetest sound he had ever heard. Her clear voice calmed and drew him to her. That's why he lay so still last night when she sang her lullaby. He knew she would leave if she guessed he was awake. She was as skittish as a newborn colt and twice as feisty.

He thought about her past. It wasn't surprising that Annaveta was still unsure about him. After all, it had been the men in her past who had hurt her. First, her papa had abused her, and then Monsieur Arnaud's brutal attack had filled her with terror. That she was resisting him was not surprising. He was sure she put barriers up so her heart wouldn't get battered again. Having to deal with being thrown out of her home and then dealing with the shock of her family dying in that fire was more than any person should have to handle, and yet she made it through. He was amazed by this beautiful redheaded Russian woman who had entranced him since the first day he saw her. She had strength, dignity, courage, gentleness, and compassion all bundled up in one beautiful package. To him it didn't matter that she was from a different culture or even held a different belief because he knew God would take care of that. He knew there was some reason that God kept putting him in her path to protect her and help her. He would trust that he was where he was supposed to be. Knowing all the hurt she must carry inside from all she had been through, he couldn't help but hope that soon she would give in to her feelings for him. She still held him at arm's length, not wanting him to see too deep inside her heart. To be honest, her brush-offs stung his pride and caused him no end of hurt. Somehow he had to try to get through to her. To let her know he was falling for her. Hard.

Alex didn't know if he should let her know how much he needed her, but he didn't think he would be able to stop himself. He yearned for her like a dying man longed for water. He knew each day he found it more difficult to take things slowly. He would, though. Somehow he would show her that he was someone that she could trust. He would protect her, help her, keep his promises to her, and love her. Whatever it took he would do it to make her his own. And pray that she never had reason to not trust him again.

ANNAVETA LOOKED UP AND SAW Alex take weak steps toward the campfire. She sipped her tea as she watched his mama give him a big hug. After three days of being sick, he was finally up and ready to join them again. She smiled as he talked with his family.

"Had a nice vacation, did you, Brother?" Ernest swatted his arm as he walked passed him for more porridge.

"*Ja*, some vacation." Alex scowled at his brother. He took his bowl of porridge and sat beside his papa.

Alex's papa looked at him with concern. "Do you feel some better now?"

"Mama took such good care of me that I think I'm ready to get back at it." Alex spoke with confidence.

"Well, mama said you could help this morning. She wanted you to rest this afternoon," Papa said, drinking the last of his tea. "It's cool this morning, so we should be able to work faster today."

"All right, I'll go easy today. Tomorrow, though, I'll be ready to work full days," Alex assured his papa.

"We'll see. Let's get going, everyone." Mr. Wagner led the horses and wagon out, and they piled on as they headed farther out to the last wheat field.

Annaveta heard Alex sigh in frustration. She knew he

wanted to work as hard as his brothers, but she secretly thought his mama was being wise to make him take it slowly.

She jumped when she heard movement behind her.

"I thought I heard angels singing in my dreams last night," Alex whispered in her ear as he squeezed in between her and Clara.

"I'm glad your dreams are so real." Annaveta gave him a knowing smile. "It will help you heal faster."

"I wonder if I could hear this angel sing again?" Alex's vivid blue eyes caught hers..

"I guess that's always possible." Annaveta teased him with a vague answer, knowing he wanted more. She looked up at him and realized her thoughts about him had changed a little. He had become not only her protector but someone who cared for her and listened to her. The little flashes of hurt she had seen on his face when she resisted him hurt her too. She was ready to let him into her heart, a little—to try to trust him more. She longed for more moments like this one.

Alex rubbed her shoulder with his own. "I might have to lure her to my lair with tempting treats. Maybe then the angel will bestow her kindness on me."

"Maybe." Annaveta's musical laugh lingered in the air as the rolled to a stop. She saw him smiling at her, and she jutted her chin out in a teasing grin before she joined Clara.

She shook her head at his antics. He was definitely feeling better.

ALL THE FIELDS WERE FINALLY finished. It was the middle of their third week of harvesting, and now they were at the threshing site. Clara said if they didn't get through threshing the grain today, then it would be done tomorrow if the weather held out.

Annaveta watched in amazement as two large horses

trotted briskly around the grain. The smooth heavy stones they pulled bumped and rolled gently over the knee-deep layer of wheat that was spread over the flattened ground that had been made into a threshing floor. Clara's cousin Benjamin, the middle child of twelve children, rode the horse closest to the center of the circle. Alex had showed him what to do since he would most likely be helping both families with threshing the grain. Little Benji seemed to love the matched chestnut horses, as he patted and rubbed their necks while riding. His small body rocked with the horses' rhythm as he went round and round driving the team.

At one point the hot sun seemed to put him asleep. His head started bobbing up and down, and his eyelids drooped.

Helmut dashed a bucketful of water into his face as he rode by. Startled, Benji let one of the reins fall. He smiled sheepishly at Alex, who was nearby. Alex gave him an encouraging nod.

Annaveta gasped and put her hand to her mouth as she nervously watched the small boy.

"He'll be okay," Clara said. "Helmut needed to wake up my little cousin. We had a funeral last year for a little eight-year-old neighbor boy from the village who had fallen asleep on a horse during threshing. When he fell off, he was trampled under the heavy threshing stones." Clara whispered with a visible shudder, "So it's good Helmut moved quickly."

Benji led the team around the circle a few more times until the mass of grain went down to half its depth.

"*Wenden!*" Mr. Wagner called out, holding his hand in the air. Clara explained that this was the point in threshing when they stopped to turn over the grain. Annaveta watched as Alex helped Benjamin lead the team of horses off the threshing floor. All available hands from both families of Wagners attached the packed mass with wood-pronged forks to turn it over. Alex then led the horses for Benji back onto the threshing floor, and they started circling again. After switching back and forth three times, Mr. Wagner shook the stalks to separate the kernels from the straw.

Everyone got busy. They all helped shake the straw vigorously forkful by forkful to get the kernels out. The empty heads of straw were tossed aside to be stacked for fodder as food for their animals, which was given to each family that helped. When the grain was shaken free, the stones were moved one more time onto the threshing floor to process any kernels that had not yet been thumped and trodden from their husks.

"Time for the piling," Clara moved to gather and pile the grain together, which would then be run through the fanning mill later in the evening. Annaveta just followed her friend hoping it wouldn't take her too long to learn.

The hot sun had most people wiping their foreheads with the backs of their sleeves. Annaveta pulled her kerchief farther down her forehead, hoping to avoid a sunburn. With her auburn hair and light skin, she had to be careful in the hot sun. Just like someone else she knew.

She looked up at Alex and was glad that he had chosen to wear a straw hat ever since he started helping with the harvest again.

"I know I'm going to be covered in freckles by the time harvesting is done," Annaveta whispered to Clara as she used the back of her sleeve to wipe away the sweat dripping from her forehead to her nose.

"If that's the worst of your worries, then you should be thankful," Clara said, wincing as she rubbed her back. Seeing the workers move to the fanning mill, they knew their rest was over.

They worked together to gather and pile the grain to get it ready. The men worked on piling the grain while the women gathered the straw to put into large bundles for fodder for the animals. Both families worked quickly trying to finish before nightfall.

A loud rumble pierced the quietness. The workers looked up and saw the dark sky overhead. A storm was on the way.

"Mach schnell!" Mr. Wagner called out, giving more shovels to all the men while the women held the grain sacks open. Just as the heavy rain started coming down, they finished putting all the grain into the separate sacks. Finding the heavy canvas tarps that he had the foresight to buy in the spring, they covered the many grain sacks that they couldn't fit under the large wagon. Assaulted by the heavy rain, they all ran under the large canvas that was hung over the long thick rope covering the eating area.

"I'm so glad to be done." Annaveta heaved a heavy sigh as she came to stand close to Clara. Her hair had fallen out of its braid and was hanging down her back in wet strands. She squeezed what water she could from the ends. Mrs. Wagner walked around handing out towels here and there to the many people who huddled under the large tarp. Annaveta shared one with Clara and her two little sisters.

"I didn't realize how hard working a large field is. It's even more work than gardening," Annaveta mused out loud as she remembered the hard work she did at the Shremetev estate.

"You're shivering." Alex pulled off his jacket as he came to stand between Annaveta and one of his cousins. Putting his arm around her, he covered her with his jacket. Annaveta held it open so that Clara could share with her.

"Thank you." Annaveta gave a quick smile as she glanced up and saw some of Alex's brothers and cousins smirking at them and making jokes between themselves with knowing smiles. Annaveta lowered her head as her cheeks heated with embarrassment.

"They're just jealous. Don't worry about them." Alex playfully bumped her shoulder. "So, have you had enough of harvesting yet?" he said as he reached his hand up and pulled out a stray piece of straw from her hair. "You look tired." The back of his hand gently brushed against her cheek. She wanted to lean into him as if by getting closer she could soak up his compassion and strength. Instead, she tried to keep her emotions under control.

"I enjoyed helping with the harvest, but I feel so tired I can hardly move." Annaveta looked up at Alex, noticing for the first time the dark circles under his eyes. "You look like you could use a week of sleep."

Alex leaned closer and whispered, "I feel like I could. You, on the other hand, still look beautiful even after weeks of hard work and not enough sleep."

Annaveta didn't know what to say, so she looked down and busied herself with tucking the blanket in around Erika.

"Not hiding from me, are you?" Alex teased. "I don't mean to make you uncomfortable. I just can't resist saying what I feel when I'm with you." His rogue smile was back. She blushed.

"The sandwiches are ready for everyone. We'll give God thanks for finishing the harvest on time and for the food. Tomorrow is another early day." Mr. Wagner said grace and had barely finished the amen, when the young ones in the family moved toward the table loaded with sandwiches. It was a tight squeeze to fit everyone under the tarp, but somehow they managed the task.

"I'm starved." Annaveta was glad for a reason to change the subject. She was getting uncomfortable.

"Okay, I'll let you off the hook this time," Alex said, his warm breath tickled her ear.

She leaned down to take Erika's hand to help her get her food, unsettled by his compliments. From somewhere deep within she knew the reason. She didn't believe she was worthy of any of it.

Chapter 12

ANNAVETA SANG SOFTLY TO HERSELF as she helped with the baking. Today was Saturday, so all the baking for next week's supply needed to be done today. The last loaves of bread were in the oven, and Annaveta was helping Inga make the sheet cakes. They had toppings of cherries, diced plums, and apples, a few of which Annaveta had sampled already. Clara had gone with her mama and papa to bring their portion of grain to the community storage and to the miller, Mr. Mueller, who would grind their wheat into flour.

"Helmut tells me you were a big distraction for Alex during harvesting." Inga frowned, piercing Annaveta with her small dark-brown eyes. "You better start considering how your actions affect this family and our position in this community. Already most people in this colony wonder about you because you're not really one of us. If you are hoping to catch Alex, you might as well give up on that now. Catherine is almost finished making her wedding dress. I wouldn't be surprised if they marry this fall with all the other couples."

Annaveta tried to keep a smile on her face even though Inga's words brought jealousy, confusion, and anger. He was getting married? How come he was constantly flirting and flinging all those pretty words in her direction then? Was she just a little fun on the side for Alex until he could get back to Catherine? If that was true, she would need to tell Alex stop toying with her and to focus on his wife-to-be. Alex seemed like someone who was honorable. He seemed like someone who wouldn't hurt another person on purpose. Was she wrong about him? Was he not someone she could trust? Her hands made fists in anger at the thought of his deception.

Annaveta eyed Inga, feeling the strong dislike that Clara's sister-in-law had for her. Inga seemed wound up as tight as a ball of yarn. Her stance matched her hair — closed in and pulled back. Annaveta didn't really know what to say. She knew Inga didn't like her, but she wouldn't lie about something like that, would she?

"I'm trying my best to follow what Clara and her mama tell me to do. I can't do more than that," Annaveta said, hoping to end the discussion.

"What about Alex?" Inga probed further.

"Alex is a good man. If it's true what you say, then I hope he and Catherine will be happy," Annaveta said out loud, although inside she was a quivering mess.

"Well, I'm glad you have some sense." Inga gave her a smug look as she took the bread out of the oven and placed it on the cooling rack.

Annaveta ignored Inga and put the first sheet cake in the oven. She couldn't wait until Clara came home so she could work with her and not have to listen to Inga's ceaseless prattle.

Jacob came running in with dirt on his hands and face from playing outside. "Mama, Opa said I could help him, the next time he builds something with wood."

"Look at you, all dirty," Inga scolded. "You know better than to come running in here with dirt everywhere. Come, let's get you cleaned up."

"Sorry, Mama." Jacob's face went from excited to sad as he held up his little hands for his mama to wash. "Don't you like it that Opa is going to teach me?"

"Opa's not the only one that teaches you things, you know." Inga finished washing his face, her voice sounding irritated.

"You and Papa teach me things too. I love you, Mama." Jacob gave her a hug.

Annaveta was busy washing down the kitchen table, listening to the exchange between Inga and her son. Concern and love filled her heart for little Jacob. It was sad that the one he loved and came to when he was excited about something was so critical of him. It reminded her of her own papa. She had never measured up or done enough things right to please him. She had worked hard, helping to earn money for the family and helping out at home, and still she had never received a kind word. Her papa thought that by marrying Misha she would finally do something that was of worth to the family. He had told her in no uncertain terms that marriage to Misha was the only way that she could make up for the sins to her family and to others in the village. It was the only way she could have a chance to become something more than a worthless, lazy girl and become someone who would finally have a decent name as Misha's wife. He said he didn't care what Misha did with her after they married, he just wanted the deed done.

The memory of her papa's rejection stung like a deep wound that was cut open, making her bleed once again. She put her arms around herself as feelings of insecurity, rejection, and abandonment forced their way to the surface. She swallowed the tears that threatened to spill over.

Unexpectedly, Clara burst into the house full of energy. "Guess what? I talked with Rachel today. She says she's planning on having us girls at her house some evening next week. Most people are done with their harvest, so she thought it would be the perfect time for some of the unmarried girls to have fun together. Isn't that a great idea?"

"Sounds like fun. Who is she inviting?" Annaveta needed to ask, hoping that Catherine and Greta weren't going to be there.

"You met most of the girls on Sunday that will be coming to Rachel's house. Most of them are Rachel's friends." Clara seemed happy about it, but Annaveta's heart sank. "We'll each take the stitching we've been working on in the evenings. Maybe even play a few games."

"I don't really want to spend an evening with those rude girls again." Annaveta grimaced as she remembered them from the incident at the well.

"Oh, please say you'll come. I need you there." Clara's crestfallen face looked into hers, and Annaveta's heart softened. "Those other girls only tolerate me; they're not my friends. Rachel gets along with them, but her mama is forcing her to invite all the young unmarried ladies from church. So, you see, she has no choice. But I really need you to be there. We can help each other. Please, Annaveta?"

"Okay, I will. But I'm only doing this for you." Annaveta laughed as Clara grabbed her hand and dragged her to their bedroom.

"You know what the best part is?" Clara whispered as if she was giving away a big secret. "When the girls get together at a house for visiting, the boys knock on the window and ask to be let in. I hope John Koch can come. He only has one older brother who is married, and the rest are sisters."

"Why don't you ask Rachel to invite his sister? Then he would feel more comfortable coming," Annaveta suggested, happy that her friend was showing an interest in someone.

"*Ja*, I will do that. I don't know Maria that well; she's so quiet. I'll see if Rachel can invite her tomorrow," Clara said, seemingly happy with the whole idea.

Annaveta was glad that Clara was interested in John. He was a helpful son to his aging papa and crippled mama. Mrs. Koch's arthritis was so bad that she couldn't walk anymore without a cane or someone helping her. Annaveta admired that he was such a hard worker and so kind. Those traits reminded her of Alex.

She cringed as she thought of the possibility that Alex would show up at Rachel's home and pay attention to Catherine and not to her. Inga's words about Alex and

Catherine's close relationship rang in her ears. It made her mad and jealous just to think of the possibility. Tonight, if Alex showed up, she would know whom he preferred. Annaveta didn't think Catherine was willing to give him up so easily. She wasn't ready to admit even to herself that she was already starting to care for him. More than she should.

The day passed quickly. With the hard work of baking for the next week finished and the preparations for Sunday's meals all ready, the women worked hard cleaning the house and sweeping away the big stones and clutter outside their house. The men were busy moving the fanning mill and threshing stones under cover for the winter and fixing their tools. Next week they would start seeding rye and winter wheat since it was already the middle of August.

GLAD FOR A SUNDAY AFTERNOON to herself, Annaveta walked a well-worn path to the river. Clara had decided she wanted to rest, and most of the others were napping or playing games. Annaveta had told Clara where she was going and that she would be back in time for their usual light supper.

She walked down the bank leading to the river and found a shady spot under a pine tree. She lay on the grass listening to the birds singing and the lilting sound of the water trickling along the bends of the Medweitz River. Thoughts of the Sunday morning sermon, which Mrs. Wagner had translated for her, ran through her mind. Even though she was understanding simple German already, the more complicated words still confused her. The pastor's message was about forgiveness and taught that when people offended and hurt you, you needed to forgive as Jesus did. Seventy times seven. That was hard to do. Especially when there were so many things people did that hurt. Did you still have to forgive them even after they were dead? Nausea threatened to choke her as she thought of all the wrongs that she held against her papa. How could she forgive all the wrongs he had done? She would have to talk to Clara about that. Maybe she could help her understand.

Suddenly she heard the crisp sound of crackling leaves behind her. She sat up and turned her head to look around her, holding held her hand above her eyes to block out the sun's glare. The sun overhead was so bright, it took a while for her eyes to adjust. Behind her was a forest of trees that seemed to hold many secrets. She couldn't see anyone there, so maybe it was just an animal skittering across the ground.

Still, she couldn't shake the feeling of being watched. She was nervous at the thought that someone could just stare at her without her knowing it. Tingles went up her arms and down her legs. She got up. Walking up to the first row of trees, she tentatively looked around and up and down. Seeing nothing, not even any animals, she moved forward looking for any signs of an intruder along the hard-packed earth. Feeling bolder, she walked further into the darkness of the woods, when she saw something white move against one of the trees. She moved closer.

There, hanging from the branch by a string, was a note. With the sun barely slithering through the row of trees, she couldn't read the words. She detached the string from the tree and clutching it tightly in her hand made her way toward the sunlight. She read the words.

"Annaveta. Remember the footprints you found outside your parents *izba,* the day after the fire? That was me. Remember the gossip about you that ruined your reputation in your village? That was me. I'm watching you. It won't be long now until I have you."

Annaveta gasped in horror as she read the horrible note. Who would write her such threatening things? There were only two people she could think of. It was either Monsieur Arnaud, who had been so mad at her he'd kicked her family off the estate, or Misha, who demanded to marry her. How had either of them found her? She believed her old friend Pavla, was too loyal to have told anyone where she was living, so who would have found her here? Or could there be someone else who was crazy enough to write this note?

She knew she needed to get away from this place. Her legs took her as fast as they would fly to her one safe haven, the Wagner home. She slowed down enough to look behind her to see if whoever wrote the note was following her. Even though she didn't see anyone, she moved faster anyway. Fear crawled up her spine.

Gasping for air, she made it to the Wagner home, went through the gate, and secured it behind her. She leaned against the tall wooden gate, trying to regain her breath before she went inside. Hesitating, she nervously straightened her skirt trying to calm her shaking hands. She had to think what was she going to do. It wouldn't do for her tell them about the note — at least not yet. The Wagner family didn't need the extra worry. What was she going to do? Maybe it would all blow over. She frowned. That wasn't likely. When the time was right, she'd tell Clara. But until she could figure out a plan, a way to stop her assailant, she had to pretend that everything was normal. Now her life here would no longer be peaceful. Someone was after her, and now they probably knew she lived at the Wagner home. *My world is a mess again. I am no longer safe. I'll need to always be looking around everywhere I go, watching to see if someone is waiting to catch me in an unguarded moment.*

Alex came around the corner of the house about to go inside, when he saw her. Annaveta tried to slow down her breathing, but her hands were still shaking as she drew in ragged breaths.

"What happened? Were you running from someone?" Alex put his hand on the gate behind her.

"I ran from the river. And as far as I know, no one was chasing me." There, that should stop the questions. At least she told the truth, even though she left out a few important facts.

"If no one was chasing you, why are your hands shaking so much?" Alex bent his head close to hers and stared at her for a long time. "You are afraid of something, Annaveta. I can tell by the way your eyes keep darting back and forth and the fact that you've looked over your shoulder at least three times since I came over here. So, tell me what's going on. I'm not moving from this spot until you do."

"Oh, all right. But you have to promise not to tell anyone else." Annaveta waited for his nod before she described what happened. "I was at the river, relaxing, when suddenly I heard a noise behind me. I didn't see anyone close to where I was, so I wondered about it. By the time I got to the trees, everything was quiet again. I walked a bit further, and then I saw this note hanging from one of the trees." She handed it to him to read, wondering what he would think.

"Whoever this is from, he's threatening you." Alex ran a large calloused hand through his hair, and a frown appeared on his forehead. "It sounds like whoever this person is not only killed your family but tried to ruin your reputation and has followed you here. Is there someone besides Monsieur Arnaud who is angry with you?" Alex's hands balled into fists, and he marched across the yard. Annaveta watched as he looked through the trees and behind the machinery, staring hard at the area by the river from which she had escaped.

"Misha might be mad at me too because I refused to marry him and ran away from Noltava so he couldn't find me." Annaveta closed her eyes as she realized she wouldn't be safe here. Not really, now that this madman had found her. "What do I do?"

"We need to make sure you're safe. No more walks by yourself. You need to always be with someone else, okay?" Alex put his hands on her shoulders and sighed when she nodded. He pulled her close and ran his hand up and down her back, like she had seen him do with a frightened horse.

She soon calmed down.

"I know what we need to do." She pulled back from his embrace and looked up at him hoping he'd agree. "I need to get to the meadow to put a note in the log for Pavla, asking her if anyone came to Noltava asking about me. That would give us a clue as to who wrote this note."

"Sure, that could help us." Alex tugged on her head scarf and smiled. "We could go next Sunday afternoon. It would be good to get some answers."

Annaveta couldn't keep fear from filling her thoughts as they walked up to the house. Who wrote the note? Was she no longer safe here at the Wagner home? Would she and Alex find answers before whoever it was did something worse?

AFTER PLACING THE LAST CLEAN dish away after supper on Wednesday night, Annaveta hung up the drying cloth. Her stomach was in knots. Not only had she hardly slept since finding the note on Sunday, she was now worried about this evening. She didn't know how this night was going to go at Rachel's house. Especially with Catherine and Greta both there. She was glad Clara was excited, but she would much rather stay home.

Clara had told her that Rachel's papa and mama were coming to the Wagners for a visit. During most of the year, except for harvesting, Papa Wagner had the men come over so he could read the newspaper to those who couldn't read for themselves. He picked up the German newspaper as well as the paper from St. Petersburg whenever it was available. He would often comment and give his opinion on whatever he was reading at the time. Mama Wagner and her friends sat in the sitting room with the other ladies making sure their hands were busy. They either brought their spinning wheels, yarn, knitting needles, or embroidery work to keep them busy while they were talking with one another.

Annaveta found Clara in the girls' room, already busy brushing out her long blond hair. It hung in waves down to her waist.

"Your hair is so beautiful, Clara," Annaveta said as she went over to find the dark-green skirt and ivory-colored blouse that Clara was letting her borrow. "Too bad you can't just leave it hang loose like that. John would propose to you tonight."

Annaveta smiled as the look on Clara's calm face switched to one of panic.

"Don't tease me. I'm already nervous enough as it is." Clara stuck out her tongue at her friend's teasing. She put her hair up in a neat braid that looked like a coronet. "So, how do I look?"

"Your hair is like spun gold, your eyes like the blue sky, and your lips red like roses, my fair maiden." Annaveta giggled, then got serious as Clara put her hands on her hips. "Seriously, you look great. I like that dark-blue skirt and matching jacket on you. You really are good at sewing."

"Thank you for that. I feel better already." Clara moved toward Annaveta. "Here, let me help put your hair up. We need to hurry."

It didn't take long for them to get to the Hoffs' home. Rachel was busy admiring a sampler John's sister Maria held in her hand when Clara and Annaveta arrived. Annaveta looked around the sitting room and saw Catherine, Greta, and a few other girls that she had met at the Lutheran church. They were busy talking with each other but stopped visiting long enough to greet the new arrivals as Clara and Annaveta came in.

Annaveta and Clara both gave their greetings, but didn't get a response from Catherine or Greta.

"Does anyone want some tea?" Rachel asked, wanting to get everyone settled comfortably. "I think that's everyone now."

All the girls said they wanted tea, so Annaveta offered to help. When all the girls were served, they sat down on the handmade cushioned wooden chairs that littered the Hoffs' sitting room. Annaveta sat next to Clara and pulled out her embroidery. She was working on a design that she had sketched onto white cotton pillowcases. They were pictures of a little girl and a little boy walking in a field of flowers. She was just finishing the flowers on one of them. Annaveta wished life were as peaceful as her picture portrayed. Fear gripped her mind again as she thought of the note, and she looked around hoping to distract herself from her thoughts. Clara liked knitting, and she was halfway through a sweater that she was making for her mama. Some of the other girls were mending, working embroidery, or making use of the spinning wheel.

"I love the pattern on your pillowcase. Where did you find that?" Maria asked quietly, sitting on her other side. Her light-brown hair was pulled tightly off her face. Big round eyes looked at Annaveta's work with admiration.

"I drew it when I was watching Clara's sister and nephew one day. I couldn't resist." Annaveta smiled and looked at Maria's sampler. "I like yours too. Is that a poem?"

"It's my mama's favorite verse from First John chapter four. It says 'God is love.'" Maria whispered, "I'm hoping to have it done by Christmas to give to her. She can't really do needlework anymore because of her stiff hands, so I try to do what I can."

Annaveta liked talking to Maria. It seemed like she had made a new friend. Maria understood what it was like to have the concern and responsibility to take care of family. Although right now she didn't really agree with the words she was stitching. God certainly didn't seem very loving or real in her life. Everyone here seemed to have such normal lives, and here she sat full of fear that her family's killer might be after her. Oh, the irony of life. But, she didn't want to dwell on her worries tonight.

She looked over and admired Maria's steady hands as she worked. "Your stitching is so fine and even. I'm sure your mama will love it," Annaveta said, hoping to encourage her.

She looked up to see what the other girls were working on as she looked around the homey room. Most of the girls were chatting while they knitted or stitched. It looked like Rachel was embroidering some white pillowcases too, getting ready for her big day.

"I wonder when our men will show up. I can hardly wait for them to get here." Catherine spoke to Greta but announced her words loud enough for Annaveta and the rest of the girls to hear. "Too bad there will be one or two girls without men at their side tonight." This last comment was said as she looked directly at Annaveta.

Annaveta didn't respond but started her stitching, determined not to let the snobby Miss Catherine know her unkind words bothered her.

Suddenly there was a rap at the window. Rachel, as the hostess, stood up to open the curtain to see who was there. From her place in the corner of the room Annaveta had a clear view of the window and saw the group of men who stood outside, wearing wide smiles as they peered into the room. She saw Alex joking with one of the other men f rom their village. Rachel waved them around to the door.

"Thought we might join you for some of your tea and goodies," Ernest said as Rachel let her boyfriend and his other friends inside. It didn't take long for the men to find their places beside their favorite girls. More chairs were pulled out, and soon Clara had John sitting beside her. She saw a young man, Dietrich, sit beside Catherine, but Catherine lifted up her chin and looked the other way. Annaveta frowned at Catherine's uptight ways.

When a large calloused hand touched hers, her heart did a little dance.

"Would you like some more cake?" Alex's deep voice

spoke beside her. Annaveta looked up at him, confused and relieved all at the same time.

"Uh . . ." Annaveta's words were interrupted. She glanced over at Catherine just in time to see her stand up suddenly.

"So that's the way it is." Catherine huffed, stuffing her needlework into her large handmade bag. "You hussy. I bet I know what you offered him to get him to come to your side so easily. It doesn't matter what village you live in, does it? You just ruin people's lives wherever you go. Wait and see — you'll both regret your choice tonight."

With those spiteful words lingering in the air, Catherine grabbed her stitching and tugged Greta's hand, and they walked out the door.

Annaveta gasped, feeling humiliated at Catherine's insulting words. Her eyes stung with unshed tears, and the sampler shook as she held it in her hand. Would everyone now see her as a loose woman, even though she had done nothing to deserve it? With unhurried movements, she glanced around the room, hestitant to face the censure of all the others. Most of the other girls were long-time friends of Catherine, and the glowers she saw on their faces only reaffirmed that. Annaveta looked over at Clara, and she sighed with relief to see that someone was on her side.

Feeling Alex's warm hand cover hers, she looked up at him, feeling the shame of the moment, her heart asking the words her lips couldn't. Alex's frown of disapproval as he looked from the door and back to her seemed to be her answer.

Chapter 13

PLOWING THE FIELD THAT HAD been left unfinished due to
the recent heavy rain, Alex hurried the horses along. He had
spent the last two days in this field and was just now able to
plow the last row so they would be ready for winter. Now
if only the weather would hold out until they could finish
planting the winter wheat and maybe some rye.

Since today was the first day of September, they were
right on schedule with the farm work. Papa would be
expecting a good report when he got home tonight. Papa,
Helmut, and Ernest were working in the other fields closer
to home, getting a head start on seeding for the winter. He
would be late for supper again, but today would be his last
day being away from the family. Who was he kidding? It was
a certain redheaded miss that he couldn't wait to see again.

Alex frowned. She had been avoiding him again. Since
the evening at Rachel's house, something had changed. No, it
had changed before that, and he'd been too busy to find out
what was wrong.

He'd noticed the dark circles under Annaveta's eyes in
the last week or so and assumed she must be really worried
about the note. He didn't blame her. Somehow he needed to
stop whoever was terrorizing her. When he had asked her to
stay near the house and not go anywhere without someone
else by her side, she didn't seem happy with that idea. And
now that he was working so much in the fields, he couldn't
be there to protect her He hated the fact that he couldn't

ensure her safety. Asking his papa or brothers to watch out for her was out of the question, as he had promised Annaveta he wouldn't tell anyone else about the note. It seemed his hands were tied. God protect her. He breathed his prayer heavenward.

But Alex suspected there was more than the note that was troubling her. She had been keeping him at arm's length this past week. Ever since that evening at Rachel's house, she had hardly spoken to him. He wasn't sure what he did, but he thought he should explain to her about Catherine. Yes, he used to spend more time with Catherine and at one point had considered courting her. But since he'd met Annaveta, he was drawn to the tenderhearted, feisty redhead in a way that he had never been drawn to the cool, attention-seeking blonde. He needed her to know that she meant more to him than Catherine ever would. If he could have the chance to talk to her, maybe she would open up to him. Somehow he would find out the truth to her mood.

ANNAVETA FOUND IT NEARLY IMPOSSIBLE to focus this morning on gardening. The dream last night had scared her. She had woken up in the middle of the night holding back a scream. In her dream, a dark-haired man hid behind some machinery on the Wagner's farmyard. As she walked out into the yard, she saw the glint of metal in his right hand. A gun was pointed straight at her.

She was afraid of what might happen. She flexed her hands, rewrapping the rags around her fingers as she tried to shake off the fear that plagued her this morning. The blisters that had formed in the last few days were really stinging today. It helped to focus on that pain instead of the other. Too bad her other problems couldn't be fixed as easily.

"Do you want me to finish the row?" Clara came up

behind her, pulling her kerchief down lower to soak up her wet forehead. "Here, you take the sack and gather the potatoes, and I'll shovel."

"Thanks. That would really help." Annaveta sighed in relief as she traded the shovel for the sack. With Clara working fast, it didn't take long for them to finish the row. It was good to be finished with the potato harvest.

"Girls, good job. We'll get home and see what Oma has made for supper." Mrs. Wagner loaded their potatoes in their handmade carts. Erika and Katarina carried smaller bags, and Jacob dragged the shovels behind him. Inga was frowning and swatting at the mosquitoes as she made her way to the water bucket. Everyone took turns drinking before leaving.

"The sun is starting to set, so we'll need to hurry so we can milk the cows and get supper for the men." Mrs. Wagner quickened her pace as she pushed one of the handcarts.

The men were just getting home at the same time they arrived at the door. They all quickly washed up and sat at the table laden with chicken vegetable soup and sliced bread. Oma was smiling at them all. She reached over and patted Annaveta's head as she sat down at the table.

The warmth of Oma's touch surged all the way down to her toes.

"That means she likes you," Clara whispered in her ear, grinning at her oma. Annaveta sat there feeling her heart open up a little more to this family. Clara's oma, the matriarch to whom the family looked up to, had given her the gift of acceptance into this family.

"Where's Alex?" Clara asked her papa after they gave thanks.

"He should be coming home soon. He was plowing the far field today," Papa said, looking out the window at the sun setting. "Glad the weather has been good this week. Tomorrow is Sunday. It'll be good to rest from this week's hard work."

Annaveta was glad tomorrow was a rest day. She didn't

mind keeping busy at the Wagners, but it was good to have time to herself, something she didn't get very often. Thoughts of the unknown man, with his threatening note, crowded her mind. Now this dream tormented her thoughts too. She hoped that whoever gave her the note would just disappear — not only for herself but for this family. When she reread the note this morning, it seemed like he wasn't going away anytime soon. The responsibility for any trouble that followed her from her past to her present weighed heavily on her shoulders. Just thinking about the possibility that any of the Wagner family could get hurt because of her made her sick to her stomach. Since she'd had the dream, thoughts of telling the family—to warn them of what might happen — dominated her thoughts. One thing was sure — she would stay alert for signs of an intruder.

With the supper dishes washed and dried, it was Annaveta's turn next in their portable cast-iron claw foot bathtub. Clara's younger sisters, little Jacob, and the other women had already had their turn. She knew she couldn't soak for a long time, as the men were still waiting, but as she sank into the tub that was surrounded by curtains in the kitchen, she sighed out loud at the hot water massaging her muscles.

She was amazed by such luxury. No one she knew in her village had one of these tubs. Her family had always used a pail of warm water and sponged their bodies when they got too dirty. She closed her eyes, letting the hot water soothe her. After a few moments she washed her long hair with Clara's lavender-scented soap. Clara said her Uncle Leo from Canada had sent it to her and her sisters when he had shipped Mama's Mason jars. Letting the scent soak in her hair awhile, she relaxed, enjoying the few moments of quietness.

With the sound of the door opening and closing, she heard footsteps and the soothing tone of Alex's voice as he spoke with his brothers and papa.

She hurried to rinse her long hair, and got out of the tub. Drying herself off, she realized she had only brought her long nightgown to dress in. Maybe if she walked fast she would be back in the girls' room before anyone knew it, and hopefully no one would see her. After towel-drying her hair, she quickly finger-combed it before picking up her clothes and leaving the room. There was no way around it — she had to walk by the big kitchen table to get to her room. Good thing she heard the men's voices outside on the front porch. She opened the curtain that hid the bath and hurried forward.

ALEX SAW ANNAVETA TRY TO sneak across the kitchen and slipped in behind her. His strong hand lightly touched her shoulder. She stood still and twisted her head, her mouth hanging open, her body turning to face him.

Alex stared into a pool of sea-green softness that he thought he could drown in. He held a sandwich in one hand while his other hand remained on her shoulder. His mesmerized gaze traveled the length of her. Her wet hair reached her waist, adding dampness to her already thin nightdress. She moved her arms to cover herself as she saw his eyes roam her outline through her nightdress.

"Alex, I should go." The unsettled tone in her voice broke through the enchantment of the moment. She wrapped her arms around her waist and lowered her head, causing her wet hair to fall over her face.

"Don't be afraid. I won't hurt you. You can trust me." He put his fingers under her chin so she could see the sincerity in his eyes.

She looked up at him with a sweetness he couldn't resist. He took in her freshly washed clear skin and lavender-scented hair and leaned his forehead against hers. His hand moved from her shoulder to her hair, lightly touching the length of it. Annaveta's look of innocence mixed with longing tugged at his heart. He was entranced by the intense look in her eyes.

"You're so beautiful," he whispered as he put his sandwich on the table. He moved closer to her while his other hand gently traced her eyebrows, her upturned nose, rosy cheeks, and finally her full pink lips. She closed her eyes, and he heard a long sigh escape her lips. She didn't resist when he moved closer and bent his head so he was looking down into her eyes. He put his forehead against hers, willing himself to not scare her with the intensity of his ardor. When she didn't pull away, he moved his lips in a featherlight motion across her forehead as one of his hands framed her delicate cheek and his other hand moved to her waist. He tugged her closer, savoring the moment, when she finally relaxed against him.

Suddenly the porch door opened.

Annaveta quickly moved back. He saw her face and neck flush red as she looked toward the door. Alex turned toward at the sound and saw Ernest with his hand on the door looking back, talking to his papa.

"I've got to go," Annaveta whispered, looking up at him and backing away, confusion filling her eyes.

"I know," Reluctance filled his voice. He kissed his finger and placed it on her moist lips, a promise in his touch. He was rewarded with a shaky smile before she turned quickly, hurrying toward her room.

Alex went to pour a glass of water. He was feeling hot all over and needed the liquid to cool off. He took his glass to the table and was sitting there reading the newspaper by the time his papa and his brothers came inside.

ANNAVETA HURRIED OUT OF THE kitchen to the bedroom she shared with Clara and her two sisters. Her hair was almost dry by the time she crawled in beside Clara. She flushed as she thought about her run-in with Alex and their few stolen moments. She couldn't seem to stop thinking about him. She had let him kiss her. Again. What was she thinking? She certainly didn't want to give the impression that she was a loose woman — or worse yet, that she deserved the reputation that people had given her in her old village of Noltava. She certainly couldn't fault him for kissing her though; she had just stood there like a dolt, mesmerized by him. It made her heart beat faster just thinking about it. Somehow her mind had to win the battle over what her heart was telling her. She just didn't know how to do that yet.

WALKING UP THE STEPS WITH Clara to the Lutheran church, Annaveta saw many of the same girls that had gathered at Rachel's house standing around and talking. Catherine and Greta were there also, whispering something between themselves as they looked over at Annaveta and then back again to their friends. Annaveta couldn't shake the feeling that they were talking about her. However, she did her best to smile as she walked past them. She hung on to Clara's arm as she led her to the foyer toward the back of the church on the women's side. Soon the other girls followed them inside. A few girls their age gave Annaveta a look of dislike and moved as far away from her as possible.

"Those girls are acting strange. Have you seen all the frowns I'm getting today?" Annaveta asked Clara.

"I know. I saw Catherine and Greta had all those same girls gathered in a circle whispering to them. I wish I knew what the big secret was," Clara whispered. "I have a feeling, since we weren't included in their little group, that it has something to do with us. I'm sure we'll find out soon enough."

When their class was over, Annaveta pulled Clara

quickly to the foyer. As they were putting on their jackets they overheard some ladies talking. Clara leaned close and put her finger over her lips to signal silence. Clara whispered in Annaveta's ear, translating what words she could hear.

"My daughter heard . . . news from Catherine about Heinrich and Maria Wagner's Russian girl they have staying with them. Did you hear?" An older lady with a large nose and double chin, wearing her Sunday best, questioned her friend.

Clara frowned at Annaveta as she repeated the lady's words.

"*Nein.* What is it?" The other younger lady was so thin her cheekbones stuck out. She leaned her head with its tightly styled bun closer to hear the news.

Annaveta looked at Clara, her heart in her throat, waiting for the worst.

"She said . . . Wagner's boarder — you know, the Russian peasant girl they took into their home? Her name is Annaveta or some strange-sounding name like that . . ." The older woman scrunched her nose as if preparing for the worst.

Clara put her finger to her mouth, to hush Annaveta.

"Catherine heard from people in that girl's Russian village that Annaveta is an impure girl . . . reputation of being a loose woman . . . many different men. Heard it from someone . . . Count Shremetev's estate."

As Clara translated the German words, Annaveta stifled a gasp. How would Catherine have heard anything—unless she went to Noltava and asked the villagers there. Annaveta shook her head in disbelief that Catherine would stoop so low and be so mean and spiteful.

"Well, I'm not surprised." The thin woman gave an exasperated look. "Think about the loose morals they have. At least our youth have to go through confirmation and are raised reading the Good Book."

Anger rose to the surface when Clara translated the words.

"We don't all have loose morals; only some do . . . which I'm sure is not that different from this colony," Annaveta whispered to her friend, irritation flooding her tone. Clara hushed her again so they could hear the rest of the ladies' conversation.

"I know. I'm worried to have her living here in our colony. We can't have our girls — or worse, our sons — keep company with a girl like that." The older lady's double chin wriggled as she shook her head. "We . . . talk to the other parents, to make sure . . . agreement. I knew trouble would come of Heinrich and Maria's inviting that Russian peasant girl into their home."

With that the two women walked toward the front doors, where more women were speaking in hushed tones.

"Well?" Annaveta couldn't wait to hear the last words these old ladies had to say about her.

Clara put a hand on her arm as if to hold her in place. "Seems like they aren't wanting you here, keeping company with their sons and daughters. They said something about talking with other parents and coming to some sort of agreement. I didn't catch every word. Sounds like they are bent on having you stay away from their children. Don't worry about them. My parents and I want you here with us, so we're not going to worry about what some gossiping ladies say. Okay?"

Clara put a hand on her shoulder when she saw Annaveta's face.

"What is it? You're as white as your blouse." Clara looked into her face demanding answers.

"So, this was Catherine's plan." Annaveta stood motionless. "She meant to spread rumors about me and in that way ruin my reputation here."

"Come on." Clara grabbed Annaveta's hand and tugged. "Don't think about it. I know it's not true."

"I think I should come up with a plan to expose the lie that Catherine is spreading to everyone," Annaveta said firmly, her lips a thin line of anger.

"Let's take some time to think and pray about it." Clara squeezed her arm and pulled her along. "The walk home will do us good."

Annaveta was too stunned to move her feet, so she let Clara tug her down the steps. They passed both the older and younger ladies who were scattered on the steps and all over the churchyard. Most of the ladies they passed looked at her with scorn in their eyes. Annaveta kept her head held high as she walked. She didn't want them to think that she was intimidated by their glares. She looked away from them and saw Catherine and Greta talking together. Catherine folded her arms and gave Annaveta a smug smile as she walked by.

As they started down the street, Annaveta noticed Catherine corner Alex. He looked altogether too relaxed in her presence. She knew Catherine was probably poisoning his ears with her version of the truth. Annaveta knew she would need to explain all the gossip regarding her reputation to Mr. and Mrs. Wagner when they got home.

Rounding the corner to their street, Annaveta looked past their house to the darkness of the trees at the end. She shivered as she remembered the threatening note and the scary dream. Hearing their family dog Zucker howling, Clara looked at Annaveta.

"The old people of our colony believe that when a dog howls a mournful sound, it means that death will visit the house." Clara shivered as they reached the steps to the house. Zucker howled again.

"Let's not think about that." Annaveta shook her head thinking of her mama's own beliefs in the power of spirits and her fear of the unknown. She didn't believe all that and hoped Clara would stop talking about death. There had been too much of that lately. Her eyes welled with tears as she looked at the dog. "Here, I'll go get the old cow bone lying over there that Zucker was chewing on. That'll make him happy. You go on in." Annaveta walked to the middle of the muddy yard, stepping on stones to avoid the puddles. "Zucker." She called for the friendly black dog to come fetch his bone.

As she bent down to pick up the bone, something whizzed by her head.

The loud cracking sound split the air. Annaveta's purse flew out of her hands and landed far behind her. Without thinking, she ran back to pick up her purse. Her mouth gaped open in shock when she saw that a hole, the size of a ruble, marred the right side. Seeing a flash of movement behind a couple of trees made her turn and run.

"Run, Zucker!" Annaveta called behind her, Zucker on her heels as she heard another ear-splitting boom. "Clara, open the door!" she yelled at her friend who stood unmoving at the threshold. Pushing the door with all her might, she pulled her friend into the porch and slammed the door behind them.

Both girls stood there shaking, staring at the purse in horror. They listened for more sounds but suddenly all was quiet. They were motionless afraid to move.

Zucker was still howling when Mama and Papa and the rest of the family came through the door. They came home from church quite a bit later than she and Clara.

"Did you hear the gunshots?" Clara rasped, her wide-eyed gaze looking at her papa.

"I heard something loud, but it was hard to know what it was over Zucker's loud howls." Papa patted her shoulder. "What has you so worried?"

"Here. Look at this." Clara grabbed Annaveta's purse and showed it to her papa. "Someone shot at us and put a big hole in Annaveta's purse."

"First the horrible rumors at church and now this?" Mrs. Wagner gasped and put her hand on her bosom.

"This has gotten out of hand. And on my own land too." Mr. Wagner shook his head, the look in his eyes turning as hard as steel. "Come, boys, lets go take a look." Annaveta watched Mr. Wagner grab his gun and leave the house with his sons following close behind. Alex stopped to look at her, his eyes wide with concern.

"I'll be back soon." He whispered to Annaveta before he followed his papa.

"Sit down, girls." Mrs. Wagner pulled out a chair for Annaveta and Clara. "Your hands are shaking. I'll make some tea to help you relax. We'll know more when the men come back inside." She pulled the purse from Clara's tight grip and traced her finger around the hole, shaking her head in what seemed like disbelief. It wasn't long before all the men returned.

"Found some footprints, but whoever he is, he's long gone," Mr. Wagner told his wife as he set the gun by the door.

Alex sat at the table beside Annaveta, concern in his eyes. He squeezed her hand in reassurance. "I can't believe someone shot at you. Are you okay?" His words and the warmth of his hand brought comfort. "I'll explain to my family why someone is trying to harm you, okay?"

"No, I should do it. I think they need to hear it from me." Her lips formed a tight line, and she nervously twisted her hands as she took a big breath and spoke up. "I need to tell you all something before the gossip or the attacks get any worse." She looked up to see the whole family watching her closely. She swallowed the fear that tried to stop her next words. "Last Sunday, when I was walking down by the river and just relaxing, I heard a noise behind me in the trees. I turned around and couldn't see anyone, so I walked closer hoping to find out if someone was there. When I walked further, I stopped when I saw a white note hanging from a branch. The note said 'Annaveta. Remember the footprints you found outside your parents *izba,* the day after the fire? That was me. Remember the gossip about you that ruined your reputation in your village? That was me. I'm watching you. It won't be long now until I have you.'"

Mr. and Mrs. Wagner's eyes widened with shock at

her story. Remorse clung to her like the mud stains on her skirt. She wasn't sure if they would ever come clean. "So, the reason there's danger here is because of me. This madman is after me, and I brought all this trouble to your home. I'm so sorry. I never meant to cause such trouble and worry for your family." She bit her lip and forced back the tears that wanted to come.

"*Ach*, Anna." When Mrs. Wagner shortened her name it sounded like an endearment to her. "We are glad you came to our home. How could you have known someone would come chasing after you?" She put her arms around Annaveta in a warm hug that melted away some of the fear and worry from her mind and body.

"*Ja*." Mr. Wagner, a man of few words, nodded his agreement. "Even though the truth has come a little late, I'm glad you told us now before something worse happened." He nodded at her and looked at his sons, running a hand through his gray-streaked hair. "*Ach*, what next?"

"How do we know she's telling the truth?" Scorn laced Inga's words as she folded her arms across her chest. "She could have lied to us and written the note herself."

Alex frowned at his sister-in-law. "Maybe she could have forged the note, which I don't believe she did. But the gunshots you just heard outside were very real. Besides, I know that there's at least one person who would be angry enough to try to find Annaveta, seeking revenge."

"Who would that be?" Mr. Wagner looked at his son, a question in his eyes.

"Monsieur Arnaud, the overseer at the Shremetev estate," Alex blurted out. An apology lingered in his eyes as he looked at Annaveta. "This is what the gossip you heard at church is about. Someone has gone to great lengths to talk to the village people of Noltava and has been spreading a story that isn't true. They are trying to ruin Annaveta's reputation."

Humiliation's hot jabs prickled Annaveta's skin. She averted her gaze from the family to look down at her shoes.

Alex took a deep breath and continued. "Remember in the spring when I brought the seeds to sell to the estate?" A few nods encouraged him to tell the whole story. "Well, when I got there I found Monsieur Arnaud attacking Annaveta, bent on ruining her. And all because she had disobeyed the rule of silence between workers by talking to her friend Pavla."

Loud gasps filled the room. Annaveta kept her head down in shame. "The overseer had dragged her into an old shed and was attacking her. I'd heard Annaveta's loud cries from outside and ran into the shed to see what was the matter. I came just in time. He was speaking obscene things and was about to ruin her. I pulled him off her and used my fists to teach him a lesson he wouldn't soon forget. So Annaveta is a victim in this whole mess. I was there; I know what happened. It's not her fault that Monsieur Arnaud is a lecherous man." Alex stopped for a moment before continuing. "However, there is another man who might be angry enough to make trouble. Annaveta's papa planned for her to marry Misha. He's a man from Molkov, a village close to Noltava. He had started the process for the marriage contract between him and Annaveta, but it was never completed, as Annaveta's papa died before it was done. Then she came here. So we need to protect her from whoever is out there trying to scare her and us." Alex's jaw tightened in anger, and a resolve came over his face.

Annaveta slid down in her chair, her neck, face, and ears feeling impossibly hot from the embarrassment of the moment. Her stomach dropped with dread, and she closed her eyes as Alex's description ended. She hadn't wanted anyone to know, but knew it was best that Mr. and Mrs. Wagner were told the whole truth. Tension knotted her shoulders as Inga's words filled her ears again. Maybe they would all want her to leave now.

The air seemed thick with tension. Slowly, she looked up to find everyone thinking in silence. She watched Alex's fists clench at his side as he looked at his papa and brothers. "Well, it seems to me like someone wants to do more than just give Annaveta a bad name. I'm going to go look one more time and see if I can find this sick man." He looked at his brothers. "Who wants to come with me?"

Chapter 14

THROUGH THE SMALL WINDOW IN the summerhouse, Annaveta could see the men in the yard making the *mistholz* for their fuel supply for another long, cold winter. The weather had been very good today. It seemed almost too calm, with only one dark cloud in the sky waiting for the right moment to pelt them all with heavy rain. The men were hard at work, hoping to get done soon. It had been a little more than a week since that madman had shot at her, and even though Alex and his brothers had looked, they couldn't trace his steps farther than their farm. Alex had been so concerned for her since that day. Every day he asked how she was doing, and she found his eyes staring hard at her at the oddest moments. Tingles ran up her arms as she thought of his care for her. Truthfully, she hoped it didn't end. Seeing him outside, helping his brothers and papa, she was reminded what a loyal and kind man he really was.

Making the *mistholz* was a dirty job, but one that was needed for the cold winter months. Papa Wagner had explained at breakfast that a colonist named Risch from Messer on the Bergseite had come up with this slow-burning, odorless type of fuel that was used in cookstoves to heat homes in the cold winter months. This mixture of manure and other litter from the barn stalls replaced wood, which was in very short supply. Colonist Risch got a medallion from the Russian government for his discovery that helped German colonists and also the country. Annaveta thought it would smell horrible and was surprised that it only had a faint odor. In the spring they had already compacted the mixture by driving the horses around it, pulling a stone to roll it flat. Now that the sun had dried it, they were cutting it into small blocks with a flat spade to let it cure in the sun. She watched them put the small bricks against the front of the barn, where they would cure until the weather turned.

The women were all in the summerhouse making syrup from the many watermelons they had taken in from the field in the last few days. Annaveta had helped haul in the big load with the rest of the family. There had been many wagons loaded with watermelons all over the colony in the last few days. The entire village smelled like sweet watermelon syrup.

Clara's mama put two big pots on the large stove and added extra fuel so the water would boil quickly. Annaveta looked away from the window and washed the dozen or so watermelons she had in front of her. Then she sliced the green globes into halves, then quarters, and then into inch-wide strips. Next, was the messy job of picking out the seeds and putting the seedless chunks of pulp into bowls. She had watched Clara and had been a fast learner. When they had about one third of the watermelon pulp in a large bowl, Mrs. Wagner cleaned Katarina's and Erika's feet and had them stomp the pulp until all of it was mashed. When most of it was in liquid form, Annaveta, Clara, and Inga worked together to press the watermelon liquid through a strainer into the big pots they had all carried here from the house. They filled up two big pots with the liquid they had from one third of the watermelons.

Mrs. Wagner peered into the large iron kettle. "*Gut.* Now we let it boil down a little ways. Our taste buds will tell us when the syrup is sweet enough." She piled another row of large watermelons on the long counter, close to where Inga, Clara, and Annaveta worked side by side. Mrs. Wagner walked over to Katarina and Erika, sitting with their feet in clean water, and set them to work washing watermelons until it was time for them to stomp the pulp again.

"I see it's almost noon, by the sun's position, and we have only just finished a third of our watermelons." Annaveta sighed as she looked out the window caught in her thoughts of what had happened three days ago. When Alex and his brothers went searching to find the dangerous man who had shot at her, they couldn't find him anywhere. They saw footprints, but even those were hard to see because of the thick covering of fall leaves.

Once the boys had returned, Mr. and Mrs. Wagner had talked to the family about how to protect Annaveta. They all agreed that Annaveta would stay close to home unless one of the men was with her as protection. As for the gossip, Mrs. Wagner was sure it would stop once the people in the colony saw that Annaveta lived a chaste, productive life in their home.

Annaveta hoped the gossip would disappear along with whoever was coming after her. A tremor of fear caused her hand to shake, and she nicked herself with the knife. She grabbed the end of her apron to stop the blood from getting on the watermelon.

Mrs. Wagner walked over and frowned. "It's almost time for our lunch break, which is good, as it seems like you could use a rest." She put Annaveta's finger in a bowl of clean water, and then wrapped it with a clean strip of cloth. "Are you worried today?" Mama Wagner asked in heavily accented Russian, tying a strip of cloth into a makeshift bandage. Throughout the summer, Annaveta had learned different German phrases from Clara and from listening to the other family members when they slipped back into their native language. She could now understand most of the simple German phrases.

"I was just thinking that I am thankful to be so protected here in your family. I'm scared that whoever is after me will hurt you all. I don't think I could live with that." Tears slid down her cheeks. She wiped them away with shaky hands.

"Come here." Mama Wagner wrapped her long arms around her in a big hug. "Don't you worry about us, the *gut* Lord will protect us. All of us. Do you hear me? Now, no more borrowing trouble. Work is what you need to get your mind off your fear."

"Thank you. For everything." Annaveta looked at Clara's mama, feeling the warmth between them. She was so happy to be here.

Clara giggled as she nudged her way into the hug. "Hey, I don't want to miss out." Clara hugged her mama and friend, pulling back to kiss Annaveta's cheek. "You will be okay. We'll help you get through this. We are here for you and love you. Don't forget that."

"*Ach.* We all need each other." Mrs. Wagner gave them each one more hug before she moved to help her younger daughters with their tasks.

"You are the best of friends, Clara." Annaveta impulsively hugged her friend again, so thankful for her. She was overwhelmed that this family would just love her for who she was instead of chiding her for all the things she did wrong. They stuck by her and didn't abandon her even when things got hard. It was a blessed relief from the strict censure that she was used to.

Annaveta reached for her knife and got back to work slicing her watermelon into sections. This time the work seemed easier. Clara and Inga were already busy cutting into their second watermelon. Katarina and Erika were learning from their mama, but it looked as if they were doing more eating than cutting. She sighed as she saw the two barrels that needed to be done today. This would be a long day.

"It looks like a lot, and the truth is we'll probably be here until midnight, but when you taste the sweet syrup from the watermelons, you'll say the work was worth it." Clara looked at her and slipped another wedge of watermelon into her mouth. "Oh, these are so sweet. Try some."

Annaveta sliced hers into sections and took a wedge in

her mouth. She nodded to her friend, enjoying the watery sweet sensation.

"Just don't eat so much that we have nothing left for syrup," Inga reminded them in a strident voice. "We would all like to enjoy some."

Annaveta noted her frown. She then looked at Clara, who gave her a small grin. She shrugged and went back to work.

Oma came to the summerhouse a few hours later holding hands with Jacob. She spoke quickly in German to Clara's mama.

"The sandwiches are on the table. Would one of you girls tell the men the food is ready? Oh, and take this pail with peelings to give to the pigs to eat." Mama Wagner gave the pail to Clara and shooed them out the door. Clara quickly untied Annaveta's stained apron and then her own, and went back to hang them up in the summerhouse.

"I need to go to the outhouse. Can you take these peelings to the pigs?" Clara handed her the heavy pail and hurried away to the outhouse. Annaveta slipped to the back of the barn and poured the slop into the pigs' trough, smiling as they came squealing to the food. She walked further to where the men were working.

"Lunch is ready." She smiled at Alex's wink. Carrying the empty pail, she sauntered through the yard, deciding to go through what few trees there were as she made her way back to the summerhouse.

She was almost through the jagged row of trees when she spotted it. Another white note hung from one of the spindly branches. Fear rushed through her and lodged in her throat until she couldn't seem to breathe. The pail dropped out of her hand. She swallowed and looked around. Alex started walking in her direction, but she couldn't see anyone unusual in the yard. After pulling the note off its string, she held it for a minute with a hand that shook so badly she couldn't read it.

"What are you still doing here? I thought it was time for

lunch." Alex squeezed her shoulder, and she turned toward him. "What's wrong? Why are you shaking?" His furrowed brow filled with concern gave her comfort.

She handed him the note. "Read this. I just can't." Annaveta put a hand on her throat in an unconscious act of self-preservation.

"Another one?" Alex's tight lipped facial features said it all. He opened it up. "It says, 'Annaveta, you had better go back to your own village where you belong or next time the bullet won't miss.'" He looked around, his hands on his hips as if daring the man to show himself. "Who is this guy anyway? He must be a coward who is afraid to show his face. He makes me so angry."

He crushed the note in his hand, and Annaveta imagined it was the madman's head. Her heart raced at his unfailing protection. She couldn't help herself from treasuring him a little more each time he doted on her. She watched as he looked at the ground and walked toward the barn, looking down. "These are unusual boot prints with a small star on the heel of each boot. Let's see where these lead to."

Annaveta grabbed Alex's hand, needing to feel his strength as they followed the tracks behind the barn. Bending low, he found where the prints disappeared over the fence into Pleve Colony's grazing field. "Well, now we know how he is finding his way into our yard. I'll need to talk to Papa about securing our fence against intruders." He stood looking as if he was planning a strategy. He was always looking out for her. Since that first day they met, when he had saved her from the depraved hands of Monsieur Arnaud, he had been her hero. Her breath caught in her thoat as she realized that her feelings for him were growing and she didn't want them to stop.

"It doesn't look like he's going to give up, is he? He means to haunt me forever. I'm so afraid, Alex." Her eyes stung with tears that threatened to spill as she looked up at him.

"Ah, *meine liebe*. I'm so sorry this is happening to you."

Alex pulled her into a close embrace, whispering words of comfort into her ear. The gentle circles he drew on her back soon made her forget her fears. He tilted her chin up with his fingers, and his lips melted into her own. She put her arms around his neck and pulled him closer. In some deep part of her she needed his reassurance of his care for her. That he would be her protector once again.

Hearing a bell ringing, Alex pulled away.

"That's Mama ringing the bell, reminding us that lunch is ready. We had better go." Alex put his hands on either side of her face and looked deeply into her eyes. "I don't want you to worry. Somehow we'll protect you and get this vile man out of your life." He then took her hand in his as they hurried to the house.

They came through the door and washed up quickly as everyone else was already waiting at the table. Annaveta hurried to sit beside Clara, and Alex sat by Ernest.

"Did you get lost finding your way to the house, Brother?" Ernest looked at Annaveta and then back at Alex with a meaningful look.

"I'm here, aren't I?" Alex looked at Annaveta, then at his papa, who was clearing his throat.

"Boys." Mr. Wagner's stern look stopped Alex and Ernest from talking. He blessed their meal, and then Mrs. Wagner started passing the big plate of sandwiches.

"Looks like there's a storm coming in," Clara's papa said as he looked out the window. "We'll need to cover the *mistholz* real good, clean out the stalls, and put fresh hay for when the herdsman brings home the cows today."

"We'll be cooking watermelons in the summer kitchen for the rest of the day. We're trying to get lots of syrup cooked for the year," Mrs. Wagner told her husband as everyone finished their sandwiches. "It seemed like last year we barely had enough. So this year we make extra."

"Katarina and I are learning how to make syrup too, Papa," Erika declared, her red braids bobbing with the rhythm of her words.

"*Ach*, that's good then, Daughter. You'll be well able to take care of a home when you get older." Her papa pinched her cheek and smiled. Erika giggled.

With the sandwiches done, Alex cleared his throat. "We found another note among the trees between the barn and the outhouse." He told them what the note said and saw the frightened looks around the table.

"He boldly walks on my land and threatens one of ours?" Mr. Wagner ran his hand through his hair. A habit he did, Annaveta noticed, when he seemed stressed about something. "Well, it looks like we'll have to be even more careful around here now. Annaveta, you will not go anywhere in the yard by yourself. Even to the outhouse. Right now that's the only way I can think of to protect you." Alex's papa sat there frowning as he looked at her. "We will keep praying for the man to be found and for Annaveta and our whole family's protection." Mr. Wagner kept running his hand through his graying hair.

"I will do as you say." Annaveta spoke to Mr. Wagner, feeling guilty for all the trouble she had brought to his home. She wanted to do whatever she needed to, to help this family who had been so kind to her.

Soon everyone got up from the table. Oma waved the women off, telling them she would take care of the dishes. As they walked outside, they saw the lightning streak the sky with a loud crack. The men hurried over to the barn to cover up the manure bricks. The women continued cooking the syrup.

By midafternoon they had the counter mostly covered in jars of syrup and only half a barrel left to cook through.

Hearing footsteps running through the rain-spattered yard, Annaveta hurried to the door. She saw the herdsman talking with Mr. Wagner. Alex ran over to the summer kitchen in a hurry.

"Looks like the cows have been spooked and have run who knows where. We need to go look for them. Keep supper warm for us." Alex rushed his words as if they couldn't come fast enough. "Papa's worried, but I'm sure we'll find them."

Annaveta watched as Alex, his papa, and his brothers mounted their horses in the pouring rain. Lightning streaked across the dark sky, bringing with it a sense of foreboding.

"It's no use worrying. The boys will do their best to find those lost cows while we do our best here to make syrup from these watermelons," Mrs. Wagner advised them. "We'll pray that they'll find the cows quickly, and that they'll come home safely."

All of them got back to their tasks, with Katarina and Erika working closely with their mama. In a few short hours they were filling the remaining jars with the rest of the syrup. Looking at the many rows of jars they had made Annaveta feel good. They were stocking up for winter with the vegetables and now syrup. A few days ago they had harvested the sunflowers, pounding the seeds out with a short paddle-like cudgel. It had taken all day to clean and sack them, but then they took the sacks to the colony's oil mill. They would be able to pick up their processed cooking oil from the mill next week. Mrs. Wagner knew the formula to make baking soda from the stalks of the sunflowers, and Annaveta had learned how to do that yesterday. Now all they had left was to gather the licorice roots for tea and cabbages. But that would have to wait until the rain stopped.

After washing out the large cast-iron kettle and wiping off the sticky mess they'd made, they returned to the house, where Oma had a stew kept warm for them.

The men still weren't back when they were finished, so after cleaning up and washing the watermelon syrup off their hands, Mama Wagner encouraged the women to go to bed. She said the men would wake them if they needed them.

Annaveta envied the soft snores of her friend as she slept peacefully beside her. Fear of the man who was determined to scare her and fear of the unknown kept her mind racing. It wasn't until much later that she fell into a fitful sleep.

ANNAVETA WOKE UP EARLY THE next morning, hearing loud voices coming from the kitchen. She quickly dressed herself for the day, but Clara held her back from leaving the room.

"Wait until they're done," Clara whispered. "I've learned from experience to not get in the middle of my parent's disagreements. It must be bad though, because I think Papa just said he's not hungry."

The door slammed with a loud thunk as the sound of footsteps echoed in the still morning air. Clara tugged on Annaveta's hand and nodded to her little sisters.

"Okay, we can go to the breakfast table now." The girls walked quietly to the kitchen and saw Clara's mama sitting very still, looking out the window. She turned her weary face to them.

"Come and sit down. I'll pour the porridge into your bowls." Mrs. Wagner's face held a look of surrender. "I'm sure you heard Papa and me arguing. He's determined to go talk to a medium or diviner to try to find our lost cows. In case you haven't heard who that is, it's someone who can see into the spirit realm to find answers. I don't feel that's the right thing to do, but he says that's what Catherine's papa, Mr. Eberhardt, did to find their cows last year. He said he found them the next day."

Mrs. Wagner walked over and kissed her two youngest girls on their cheek.

"Will we be okay, Mama?" Katarina asked with tears in her eyes.

"*Ja, meine liebe.* We are going to be fine." Mama Wagner wiped the tears from her sensitive little one's face. "We'll just keep praying, *ja?*"

"The rain must have stopped sometime last morning, so after we're done with breakfast, we'll go gather the licorice. With the handcart we should be able to get enough tea to last us through the winter." The little girls calmed down upon hearing their mama's voice. "Annaveta, maybe you should stay at home, with all that's been happening here lately."

Annaveta helped Clara as they worked to finish their dishes in a hurry. Oma had put on her shoes and light jacket to come with them today. Annaveta really wanted to come, but wanted to listen to them.

"Isn't Helmut working in the barn, Mama?" Clara stopped to look at her mama. "Couldn't he come with us for the little time that it takes for us to pick roots, so Annaveta could come with us?"

"*Ja*, you're right. Helmut probably could do with a break, and then we would have the added protection. I'll go talk to him." Mrs. Wagner went outside, and it wasn't long until she was back with Helmut at her side.

Annaveta smiled. She was glad she would be able to come today. She was starting to learn more of this family's ways and their language. They walked about a mile from the colony to where there was a little valley with lots of short shrubs and green plants.

"*Wir stoppen hier.*" Oma stopped and pointed at a tall green plant that had pink flowers shooting up from all sides. "We will take the plant out by the root. I'll show you." Annaveta was amazed at the energy of Clara's oma. She tugged on the plant with both hands until the root sprang free from the ground. With her hands she brushed off the dirt and put it in the handcart.

"Now it's your turn." Oma pointed at Annaveta as they walked down the hill and saw another flowering plant. Annaveta was pleased that she was finally understanding this older lady who had been so kind to her.

Annaveta tugged hard until the root popped out of the ground. "I did it." She smiled at Oma, pleased that she was able to help this family.

"*Gut.*" Oma's wrinkled hand patted her own, and they kept picking with the other women until the cart was full.

Annaveta knew this family drank lots of tea, but she was amazed at how full the cart was. She had watched them at mealtimes and between meals drinking their *steppetee* made from licorice root.

Annaveta appreciated all the green grass, wild flowers, and different herbs that were plentiful here. She noticed Helmut not far from where she was keeping an eye on all of them and searching the border of the meadow for signs of a stranger. She stayed close to Oma. The dark shadows hidden in the thicker foliage seemed to play tricks on her mind. She swallowed the fear and resolved that she would be a help today, not a hindrance.

They gathered what they could. With all the women, along with Jacob, working together, they found enough roots so that the handcart was overflowing.

Looking at the position of the sun, Annaveta knew they needed to hurry to get home for lunch.

"We'll scrape and wash these roots after lunch in the summer kitchen. Girls, you can take the handcart." Mama Wagner hurried them into the house, while Clara and Annaveta went to the summer kitchen, laying out the roots so that they could dry. Once the roots were spread over the table and counter, they hung up their aprons and went back to the house for lunch.

They got back just when the men did. Annaveta looked at Alex as he tied his horse's halter to a long rope that was tethered tightly to the fence. The horses were busy eating all the green grass they could get to. Giving his horse a final pat on the rump, Alex walked toward her. His frown said it all.

"We were told where to find the cows." Alex shook his head as they walked toward the house. "Papa asked the medium to find the cows, and I just don't feel good about his decision. Helmut and Ernest said it didn't bother them, but it bothers me. Herr Wexler went into some sort of trance and just sat there until a much lower voice that didn't sound like his spoke through him and told us where to find the cows. I tell you, it gave me the shakes all over." He ran his hand through his hair just like she'd seen his papa do that morning. He was really nervous about this. Annaveta thought about the many mediums she had known about growing up. It seemed so common, so she wondered why Alex would be worried about it. Alex opened the door to the house, and she could hear Mr. Wagner talking to his wife.

"Well, Herr Wexler, also called Wise Wexler, told us where the cows are." Papa Wagner looked at his wife with a satisfied smile. "So, we'll go get them right after lunch."

"Where did he say they were?" Clara asked.

"He said we would find them grazing about six miles east somewhere along the road to Kolb." Papa Wagner ran his hand back through his hair with a smile. "Well, time will tell if Jacob Wexler is wise or not."

Alex's mama didn't say anything as she sat down at the table with the family. Annaveta noticed that even Alex glanced with concern at his parents.

With the meal finished and the men on their way to find the cattle, the women went to the summer kitchen to get the roots sorted out. They scraped and washed all the roots, then let them sit out. Clara and Annaveta were sent to the attic once the licorice roots were dry to hang them from the rafters. The smells of herbs, sausage, and wheat filled the air, and they were glad to leave the pungent aroma when they closed the latch on the attic door.

"The attic is where most people in the colony store their dried food. It keeps it dry as well as handy. It sure makes for a strong smell up here." Clara giggled, plugging her nose.

Annaveta tried to hold her breath as she carried more roots up the ladder stairs. She, too, was ready for fresh air by the time they finished hanging the last load of licorice.

Slicing the potatoes and putting them in the chicken stew for supper, Annaveta savored the smell. It would be good when the cows were found. It would one less thing to worry about.

"There they are. I see the dust." Jacob was looking out the window that faced the street. "They are bringing the cows home. They found them!"

Mrs. Wagner just shook her head as she continued to stir the stew. It didn't take long for the men to settle the cows in their pen. Mr. Wagner walked through the door, wearing a smug smile on his face.

"See, Mama, I guess Herr Wexler is Wise Wexler after all. The cows are home." He snapped his suspenders for emphasis as if daring her to dispute it.

"Well, Heinrich, I am glad the cows are home. I really am. It's the way we found them that worries me. You know as well as I do that the Good Book says to not ask for help from mediums." Annaveta listened closely as Mrs. Wagner got out her Bible and read softly. She looked at Mr. Wagner and saw him frown. Mrs. Wagner didn't move from her spot at the stove. The churning sound of her spoon stirring the stew echoed in the silent room. "God takes it seriously when we don't listen to him. But I know he also forgives us when we tell him we're sorry. I think maybe that's what we need to do."

Annaveta let out a sigh of relief that the cows were found even if the methods Mr. Wagner used weren't ones that garnered Mrs. Wagner's approval. She was just glad that the missing cows hadn't been part the madman's plot to hurt the family she had come to love.

Chapter 15

"*KOMMEN SIE SCHNELL!* MAMA'S BABY is coming. She asked for you, Mrs. Wagner."

Annaveta heard the words of the frantic boy at the door. It was so early in the morning that most of the family was still lying in their beds when they heard the loud banging on the door. Clara's parents had both rushed to answer it.

"Okay, I'll just gather what I need." Mrs. Wagner, who served as one of two midwives in the colony, reassured him. "Go tell your mama I'm coming."

Mrs. Wagner hurried into the girls' room, putting her hair up as she walked. "Annaveta, do you want to come with me?" With Annaveta's quick nod, she instructed her to go to the attic to get some herbs.

Annaveta rushed to grab bunches from each kind that were hung in the cramped attic space. She tried to remember the herbs Mrs. Wagner said she needed. With her hands full, she climbed back down and helped Mrs. Wagner put the many herbs in their separate pouches. Clean rags and cloths, scissors, and a sharp knife were also placed in the large medical bag. Mr. Wagner had the horse and wagon hitched by time they were ready.

Mrs. Burbach, who was in labor with her tenth child, was the mailman's wife. Her husband was called Poste Burbach so people in the colony could tell him apart from his two other relatives who had the same name. They lived on the other side of Pleve Colony. Mr. Wagner hurried the horse at a fast clip, the *click-clack* of horses' hooves sounding loud in the stillness of the morning.

"So how many children will this be for Frau Burbach?" Mr. Wagner questioned, lightly tapping the reins to the horse's back.

"This is number ten. They are all blessings, but God help her!" Mrs. Wagner whispered, fear edging her voice. "I remember the last one I delivered. She barely made it through that labor. I told her there couldn't be any more babies or she would surely die. Of course, she said it would be as God wills. *Ach*, we will be in for a time of it today!"

Annaveta put her hand on Mrs. Wagner's restless hands. "I'll help you with whatever you need. I helped my mama when she delivered my youngest brother."

"I know you will, my girl. I'm so glad that you are here to help." Mrs. Wagner patted her hand. "It helps that we have herbs ready should we need them. The yarrow will help with easy blood flow, and the raspberry leaves in tea will help with cramping." She started listing the herbs they had in the basket. "The black cohosh will give regular contractions, and shepherd's purse should stop large amounts of bleeding if there are problems with the delivery."

"We also have the motherwort. To keep her calm," Annaveta added.

"Yes, we'll need that." Mrs. Wagner nodded, handing the basket to Annaveta as Mr. Wagner helped them off the wagon. They hastened their steps to the bright-blue-painted house. Annaveta took in the red trim by the windows and door, appreciating the bright colors. Poste Burbach opened the door before they had a chance to knock.

"Please, this way. She's been in labor since yesterday morning. It's too much for her." The husband's furrowed brow was a picture of worry as he led the way. Annaveta gave a comforting smile to the children that were huddled together at the kitchen table. She patted the heads of the younger children as she passed by. She saw that the oldest girl was holding her younger sister in a blanket, shivering as if she was sick. Annaveta made a mental note to check on her later. She hurried after Mrs. Wagner, following the sound of the painful moans and screams of the woman in the back bedroom.

"Hurry here, Annaveta." Mrs. Wagner pulled Annaveta by her arm into the bedroom. Annaveta saw a distraught woman lying on the bed and clutching her bulging belly, writhing in pain. She heard the faint footsteps of Mr. Burbach as he returned to comfort his children. Mrs. Wagner walked to Mrs. Burbach's side and wiped her brow gently with a wet cloth, her soft words soothing her fears.

"Lena, looks like this new little one is having a hard time finding the way out. Not to worry. You'll be holding this sweet new baby in your arms soon." She smiled at the frightened woman squeezing her hand. Washing her hands in warm water, she continued. "I need to check to see how the baby is progressing, *ja?*"

"The babe . . . won't come," Mrs. Burbach gasped between contractions.

"We just have to help it along," Mama Wagner reassured her.

Annaveta watched as Mrs. Wagner moved her hands gently down Mrs. Burbach's swollen belly. Upon lifting her nightgown up to her waist, Mrs. Wagner frowned as she slipped her hand inside the opening to feel where the baby was.

"Seems like the baby is in breech position." Mrs. Wagner looked at Annaveta and then at Mrs. Burbach. "We need to see if we can turn your baby."

"Ahhh!" Mrs. Burbach screamed as the two midwives helped her to switch her weight to her hands and knees. Her face pinched red as boiled beets as waves of pain washed over her. Finally, on her hands and knees, her loud cries stopped. Annaveta reached her hands around the laboring mama to straighten her nightgown.

"That helps, doesn't it?" Mrs. Wagner encouraged. "The baby no longer is crushing your backbone." She gently rubbed the tired mama's back as her cries lessened to moans.

Annaveta wiped the woman's face with a cool, wet cloth and gently brushed the sweat-soaked strands of hair away from her face.

"Ahhh, the baby." Distress etched the lines of Mrs. Burbach's face. Mrs. Wagner used her hands to feel what was happening with the baby.

"The baby has turned slightly." Mama Wagner tried to move the baby with her hands. "My hands are too large. I think if the baby turns a little more, then Mama can push. Annaveta, your hands are much smaller. I'd like you to try."

"Okay, as long as you tell me how." Annaveta nodded, her face tight with tension. She followed Mrs. Wagner's instructions and placed a gentle hand inside the laboring woman to encourage the baby to turn so that the face was down. She found the baby's shoulder and helped loosen it. "I think it worked. I can feel the baby's face in my hands."

"The baby has switched position, Lena. When you feel the next contraction, try pushing again," Mrs. Wagner said as she saw fuzzy red hair emerge from the opening. "You are doing good. Your baby is ready to come out."

With Mrs. Wagner's encouragement, the weary mama pushed with each contraction. All it took was three big pushes, and the baby finally slipped out into Mrs. Wagner's waiting hands. Annaveta was amazed at the little red-haired boy who entered the world.

"Annaveta, find me a wet cloth."

Annaveta handed Mrs. Wagner the cloth and wiped the mucus from the baby's nose and mouth as she held him with one hand and rubbed his back with her other hand. After a few moments a lusty cry was heard. Annaveta looked at Mrs. Burbach's big smile of thankfulness when she heard the sound.

"Some string and linens. *Mach schnell.*" Mrs. Wagner's

crisp tone stirred Annaveta out of her trance. She reached for two equal lengths of string from off the small wooden chair in the corner. Mrs. Wagner held the wriggling baby close as Annaveta tied off and cut the baby's cord.

"I'll look after Lena now." Mrs. Wagner handed the baby to Annaveta and gave instructions. "Wash him in warm water, wrap him in fresh linens, then bring this new little man back to his mama."

Annaveta held the whimpering baby close to her as she walked to the small worn worktable on the other side of the room. She dipped the towel in the bowl of warm water and washed the tiny cone-shaped head. Her mama's words came back to her. *"Your head was peaked when you were born. A sign of strength. I knew then that I had been given a baby girl that would be able to walk through whatever came her way in this life."*

"You are a survivor." Annaveta repeated those same words in Russian to this new little boy. "You will grow up to be a gift to your mama, and you, too, will grow to be strong."

Washing and wrapping the baby in a warm blanket, she laid him in his mama's outstretched arms. Mrs. Wagner rubbed the worn-out woman's abdomen in circular motions to massage her womb. All the while she spoke in soft, soothing tones to her patient. It didn't take long to draw out the afterbirth.

"Thank you," she whispered, catching the tears at the corners of her eyes. She lay there exhausted as her weak, shaky fingers stroked her new son's downy softness. Both women smiled at each other in thankfulness.

Annaveta and Mrs. Wagner put fresh bedding on the bed and cleaned up the blood-soaked linens.

"I'll go call in your family. I know they have been anxiously waiting for the good news," Mrs. Wagner told Mrs. Burbach, whose tired eyes stared up at her. "Annaveta will make some tea for you."

Mrs. Wagner carried the news to the anxious papa and

children. The children rushed forward even though their papa tried to restrain them, excited to see their mama and their new brother. Annaveta followed behind them, not wanting to miss this moment. She stood in the doorway, absorbing their happiness.

"He looks kind of red and wrinkly," a little voice blurted out.

"Does he have a name?" a older softer voice asked.

"*Ja*. What do you think, Dietrich?" an exhausted mama asked her husband. "Should we call him young Heinrich?"

"We already have that name." This voice sounded like twelve-year-old Katherine.

"That's okay. There aren't that many names that are fitting for us German Lutherans to choose from, so we'll just call this new boy young Dietrich." Poste Burbach's proud voice echoed down the small hallway.

Letting the tea leaves steep in the teapot, Annaveta went to help Clara's mama wash the dirty linens. When they finished, they hung them up outside on the laundry line that was slung between two trees. They then came into the house to get the supper meal ready for the family. It was already late afternoon. Annaveta cut the vegetables for the stew while Mrs. Wagner made a quick dough of biscuits for the family. Soon a large pot was simmering on the big stove, enough for two meals.

They brought the tea to the bedroom, where they found the oldest girl holding the sleeping baby. She placed soft kisses on his head, acting like a little mama to her baby brother. Annaveta hurried, as she had left the sick little girl rolled up in a blanket huddled by the stove in the kitchen. Annaveta went over to touch her forehead.

"Your daughter has a fever," Annaveta told Mrs. Burbach. "I'll give her tea to help with the fever and cool her down so she can sleep."

"Little Elsa hasn't been well for two days now, and I'm worried about her. I would appreciate the kindness," Lena

Burbach said as she lay on the bed, lifting her tired head with a feeble smile. Poste Burbach sat on a chair beside his wife's bed, his large hands moving in soothing circles across her hands. Annaveta smiled at his care for his wife. Quietly she walked to the kitchen to pour tea for little girl and had her drink what she could. She dipped a clean cloth into cool water and sponged off the sweaty forehead and shivering body. She held her close and tucked the blanket in around her. When she heard Mrs. Wagner giving instructions as she walked out of the bedroom, she knew it was almost time to go.

"Thank you for coming today, Maria. Thanks to your new helper too." Unchecked tears escaped from the corners of her eyes. "I believe you both saved my life today."

"Thank the *gut* Lord, my friend." Mrs. Wagner smiled. "I am glad we could come. Lena, you need to have complete rest for at least a week. Your body is going to need lots of time to recover. Deitrich, I trust you'll see to it that she doesn't overdo?" She looked at Poste Burbach as he nodded.

"*Gut*, we'll be back in three days to see you. Have someone come get me if you feel feverish. Drink the tea, then have a long sleep. That will help you heal. I'll go see how it's going with your little Elsa." Mrs. Wagner went into the kitchen with Mr. Burbach close behind.

"I'll get the wagon ready while you gather your supplies." Poste Burbach got up, leaving the house in a hurry. Mrs. Wagner gave instructions to Katherine, the oldest girl, about supper and looking after her sick sister.

The sponge bath Annaveta gave little Elsa had cooled her body, and the child was now sleeping peacefully. Annaveta tiptoed out of the kitchen to the bedroom that one of the children showed her. Little Elsa slept peacefully now. When she got back to the kitchen, Mrs. Wagner was starting to collect their supplies. Annaveta went to help. It had been a long day, and they were ready to go home.

Once seated in the wagon, Mrs. Wagner told Poste

Burbach important things to watch for to help his wife get better. Since Mr. Wagner had dropped them off at the Burbachs' home and had taken the horse and wagon back home, Annaveta was thankful for the ride back to their home. Poste Burbach listened and nodded to Mrs. Wagner's instructions without saying a word until they reached home.

"*Ja*, well, I understand why he is the mailman here. His words match his height. Both are in very short supply. *Ach!*" Mrs. Wagner said, shaking her head in frustration as they watched Herr Burbach drive away. Annaveta put her hand over her mouth to quiet the giggles that escaped. Soon Mrs. Wagner's own laughter bubbled over. When their laughter faded, Mrs. Wagner reached into her pocket.

"I want to pay you for your help as my assistant at the different births we attend." Mrs. Wagner dropped five rubles into her hand. Annaveta eyes widened, and she looked up at Clara's mama in wonder. She had never been paid this much in her life. Throwing her arms around Mrs. Wagner, her eyes wet with tears of thankfulness. Clutching the money tightly in her hand, she nodded at her as together they walked to the house.

"Thank you. I will do my best to be a big help to you." Annaveta's emotion-rich voice stumbled over her words in gratitude.

"I know you will, my dear. I am so blessed to have you." Mrs. Wagner's words sounded like an echo of her mama's words. Her heart brimmed over with thankfulness.

Clara met them just outside the door.

"Sounds like it went well today." At her mama's nod, Clara smiled. "Well, we just finished eating, but supper's warming on the stove. I made it this time, Mama. I think it tastes pretty good."

"*Danke, Tochter*. It's so good to come home to a warm meal and welcome." Clara's mama kissed her on the cheek and hugged Erika and Katarina, who ran to meet her. Jacob, who wanted in on the fun, grabbed her hand to show her what he had built that day.

"Jacob. *Nein.* Oma's tired now," Inga scolded, the tight bun on her head not moving an inch as she shook her head at her son.

"*Ach,* it's okay, Inga. It won't take long to see what Jacob has made, and then I'll rest." Mrs. Wagner patted her daughter-in-law on the shoulder and grabbed Jacob's hand as they walked away.

Inga glared at Annaveta before she turned and walked off to the sitting room, where the men's voices were heard laughing and talking. Annaveta looked to Clara, a question lingering in her eyes.

"I don't know what's wrong." Clara shrugged. "Don't worry about it. Come taste my soup and see what you think."

Annaveta took a clean spoon and dipped it into the pot. "Umm, that's good. You make great soup." Moving her feet slowly, she went and sat at the wooden table, then rested her head in her arms. "I'm so tired. Almost too tired to eat. And I don't feel so good; my head and my stomach hurt."

"We'll have to put you to bed early tonight, but not before I tell you the good news," Clara whispered, her voice excited. "Tomorrow the Hoffs come for butchering. That means the handsome brothers will be here. Then right after that will be the Kerb harvest festival. Youths from the other villages come and join us. We'll be seeing all kinds of new faces."

"That's fun for you, Clara. It's great that the Hoffs will be here for butchering, but I don't think I want to go to the festival." Annaveta pushed away her bowl and frowned.

"Why not? It's the biggest festival around. It's where most couples meet their future husband or wife. Of course you need to be there." Clara crossed her arms as if daring her to argue.

"That's exactly why. I am an outsider here. I'm reminded of that all the time, especially by Catherine and Greta." Tears fell from Annaveta's tired eyes. Her hand went to her stomach to try to stop the unsettledness she had there. She tried to explain her thoughts to Clara. "Now with the new gossip that has spread, I'm sure, to every person on this colony, I will just be publicly humiliated again. I just don't think I can handle that again, especially now that I'm also living in fear for my life from that madman. Don't you see? It's just too much."

Clara dropped the spoon and hurried over to hug her friend. "I'm sorry. Of course you feel the danger, and I understand that you are fearful to risk coming, for all those reasons. You know my brothers and Papa will be there too, right? They will protect you, especially one brother, whom we both know will hardly leave your side," Clara teased, squeezing Annaveta's shoulders again. "We will all keep watch over you, Annaveta. I need you there with me. You are like a sister and best friend all rolled into one. It just wouldn't be any fun without you. So, please come?"

She listened to her friend's heartfelt words and smiled. "Okay. I'll come along."

Annaveta nearly toppled over from the force of Clara's embrace. Their loud peals of laughter brought Mrs. Wagner into the kitchen. She shook her head, put her hands on her hips, and sighed, but the smile that hovered on the corners of her lips betrayed her pleasure in the moment.

Chapter 16

SHIVERING AND MOANING, ANNAVETA TOSSED in her bed. Her body turned hot and then cold as if it couldn't make up its mind. In her dreams she relived the terror of Monsieur Arnaud's attack, smelled the fire that killed her parents, ran away from Misha's lewd clutches, and was paralyzed in fear of someone wanting to kill her. Her head, beady with perspiration, swung back and forth on the pillow. She cried out in fear.

"Shhhh, you are safe. You're going to be okay." She heard a low male voice comforting her. "I won't let anything happen to you."

Fingers combed through her hair and she tensed. In her mind she was back with the overseer in the shed, and he was touching her hair and her body and taking away her innocence. In her dream she put her knees up to her chest to protect herself, but it seemed like whatever she did, the man was still there touching her hair, her clothes, and her hands.

"Nooo!" Her loud scream seemed to stop him. Her cries turned into soft whimpers, and she heard his voice speaking to her again.

"Don't be scared. You know I would never hurt you. Open your eyes and you'll see it's me."

She heard his soft voice calling out to her from somewhere. Where had she heard that voice before? She remembered this man's gentle low tones as a place of safety. It was different than the harsh, demeaning voices she heard in her nightmares. It was as if she could hear him from someplace far away, but couldn't get close enough to see him or touch him. But oh, she wanted to — just to see if he was as real as he seemed.

"Even when you are sick, you're beautiful. You look like Sleeping Beauty lying there, with your long waves covering the pillow."

She stilled even more as she heard the male voice whisper. "Annaveta, my own sleeping beauty, please get better. I need to hear your laughter, feel the sting of your feisty words, and taste your sweet lips on mine again. Come back to me, my love."

A large calloused hand squeeze hers, and another hand continued massaging her head. Her tense body relaxed at the sound of his soothing words.

ALEX LET HIS FINGERS TRACE the soft russet-colored hair that fell in waves beneath her shoulders to her waist. He allowed his eyes to soak in every detail of the fragile beauty lying on the handcrafted wooden bed. He took in the creamy complexion of her oval face. Her dark-brown eyebrows framed the gentle slope of her freckled nose and high cheekbones. He knew her closed eyes hid those green eyes that made him feel like he was drowning. Her full pink lips, no longer crying out in fear, lay still in sleep. His knuckles gently touched the side of her cheeks as he watched her sleep. The blankets lay in disarray, revealing her threadbare white nightgown.

His thoughts strayed. He remembered their kisses. Holding her body close to his own had stirred him in a way nothing else did. When he was with her, he saw himself as strong, as if he could do anything. He could feel her love. She had yet to speak her heart to him, but he knew it just the same.

He pulled the quilt up to her shoulders. His thoughts about her lovely form and face were harder to control. Closing his eyes, he pictured Annaveta as his wife, with them waking up together, loving each other. She was more than he could ask for. He prayed that soon she would feel the same way about him. That thought alone made him impatient.

He put a stop to his straying thoughts. Some were best left for after the vows were spoken. He picked up her small hand and caressed the soft skin, willing her to get well.

"Is she finally asleep?"

Alex startled at his mama's quiet voice behind him. He looked at her and nodded.

"*Gut*. It's been two days now with this fever. Maybe tonight it will break. We will pray that it is so." His mama's caring for this non-German girl, a stranger, increased his respect and love for her.

"*Danke*, Mama." Alex's other hand reached over to squeeze hers.

"*Ach*, Son. You know we are doing our best. The rest is in God's hands." She squeezed his hand back. "Pray not just for her body, Son, but also for the rest of her to be whole. It's only then that she'll really be free to love deeply."

Alex nodded as he looked down at Annaveta lying there so still. He wasn't surprised that his mama had guessed at his love for this girl.

"It is late. You go to sleep now, and I'll keep watch the rest of the night." Mama spoke with determination. "She will get better; you'll see."

"I'll go. I've been building a new table in the shed for the Hoffs, and they want it done soon, so I need to get back to it. Make sure you wake me if things get worse." He looked at his mama until she nodded at his request. He rose from the chair, and with a last lingering look at the still form on the bed, he closed the door.

"Water, please?" Annaveta's raspy voice whispered into the stillness as she turned her aching head to see Mrs. Wagner nodding, her chin creeping toward her shoulder. Her head bobbed in time with the movement of the rocking chair.

Annaveta spoke again a little louder. Mrs. Wagner's body shook with sudden movement, and she opened her eyes.

"You are awake?" Mrs. Wagner raised her eyebrows in surprise as she ran her hand over her face in an effort to wake herself.

"Yes. Feeling thirsty." Annaveta's unused voice sounded hoarse. She smiled at Mrs. Wagner.

"Of course you are, my dear. I have water right here." She poured some in a cup and helped Annaveta sit up to drink.

"I feel as weak as a baby kitten and a little dizzy," Annaveta said, frowning as she used her hand to balance herself. She drank slowly, the moisture wetting her dry mouth.

"Thanks be to *Gott* that your fever is gone." Mama Wagner sighed in relief, as she touched Annaveta's cool forehead. "*Gott* has answered our prayers." Clara walked into the bedroom and smiled big when she saw her friend was awake. Before she could speak, her mama raised her hand. "Clara, go get your brother. Alex wanted to know as soon as Annaveta was awake."

Clara spoke quickly. "I'm so glad you're awake. We've all been worried about you."

"I do feel better." Annaveta closed her eyes and shuddered as fear flooded her thoughts. "I had a scary dream."

"Wait until I get back, and then you can tell us all about it," Clara urged her and rushed out of the room. Mrs. Wagner plumped two pillows behind Annaveta's head and straightened her blankets. She was drinking water when Alex and Clara came back. Her cheeks grew hot as Alex stared at her, a big smile on his face. She pulled up her bedcovers a little higher and squirmed beneath them, uncomfortable now that he was in the room. Her mind went to the vivid dreams she'd had, remembering a voice that sounded so much like Alex's and strong hands touching her hair, soothing her. Now that he was here, she wasn't sure what had been a dream and what had been real.

Clara sat beside her on the bed and grabbed her hand. "Tell us. Now that we're here, we want to hear about your scary dream."

"I was in this awful place where I could literally feel fear and hopelessness consume me. Thousands of people were standing still with their eyes glued to the never-ending blackness that surrounded them." Annaveta closed her eyes as if reliving the nightmare. "These people couldn't move, and neither could I. I had a sick feeling that it was all over for us. That it was too late. We were forever condemned to this place. Suddenly a man, bathed in light, came through the darkness. He walked toward me. I couldn't take my eyes off his face. He had such love in his eyes. He reached out his hand, and I put my mine in his. I knew I had been saved from something awful. I don't really understand what happened, but I feel more peace and love inside."

"What you are feeling is the peace and love of God," Mama Wagner said in a quiet tone.

"Peace and love. I need that."

"I'm so glad you are feeling better." Clara gave her another hug. "I do wonder, though, if you got sick just so you could get out of butchering."

"I forgot about that. How is that going?" Annaveta laughed, secretly glad to have missed the messy chore.

"Today is the last day. Supper will be in a few hours, and by that time the Hoffs will be headed home. You missed seeing the handsome brothers." Clara winked, laughing at her friend.

Annaveta just rolled her eyes.

"*Ach*, Clara. The things you say." Mrs. Wagner's half smile gave lie to her words. She went to the door and turned. "Daughter, you should let Annaveta rest now. She needs all the sleep she can get so she can heal faster." Looking at Annaveta, she smiled. "I'll bring you some broth when you wake."

"You do look tired. Let me help you lie down." Clara helped her settle under the blankets and quietly left Annaveta to her own thoughts.

Annaveta lay in bed thinking. She remembered sitting at the kitchen table, crying as she talked with Clara about feeling unwanted, and her next memory was a male voice telling her she was protected and loved. She was sure it must have been Alex's voice she heard. Warmth filled her as she thought of his soothing words and gentle hands. She savored the feeling, even though her head told her not to trust him or any man. But even though she was confused by her feelings, her uncertain heart was drawn to this man.

ANNAVETA WOKE UP FEELING BETTER than she had in days. Yesterday was the first day she had been up, taking meals with the family. Hearing the front door bang and the sound of milk sloshing in pails, she knew Clara and Mrs. Wagner had just finished the milking. The babbling hum of voices and dishes meant that breakfast would be ready soon. She quickly got out of bed and changed into her old work clothes. While brushing out her long hair, she suddenly remembered today was Thursday.

It was the start of the harvest festival — the Kerb Festival. This first week in October was a time for the villagers to celebrate. Clara had told her it was like a big party after all the months of working the fields. When the harvesting was finally done, it was a good excuse for a three-day celebration. Villagers from other colonies came to join them, especially young people. Clara said there was music, dancing, and lots of food and drink.

Annaveta frowned as she put her hair up. She hoped that there wouldn't be too many drunkards at the festival. Fear filled her as she thought about the sinister man who had been writing those awful notes. What if he hid in the crowd? He had come into the Wagners' yard, so what would stop him from coming to the festival? She knew Clara said she would have a lot of protectors, but they couldn't be with her every moment, could they? She would need to stay close to the Wagner family.

Breakfast was rushed because of all that needed to be done that day. Mr. Wagner told them they would wait until after lunch to leave because of the chores they needed to do. He took Helmut, little Jacob, Ernest, and Alex with him to clean the barn and toolshed to get them ready for winter. Clara's mama and oma cooked the sausage, while Annaveta and Clara made dough for a fresh batch of bread. Inga made dumplings and put them on the stove top to cook. By lunchtime everything was ready to go. Big baskets of sauerkraut, pickled watermelon, beets, cucumbers, and even extra portions of tea were placed by the door.

Annaveta went to change her clothes. She was glad that Mrs. Wagner had remade one of her dresses into a dark-blue outfit for her. The long dark skirt was a complement to the matching long-sleeved high-buttoned shirt. She looked at the cracked mirror that hung on the wall and brushed the thick reddish-brown waves that hung to her waist.

"Annaveta," Clara called as she walked into their room. "Here you are. Are you doing your hair again? It was fine. Here, let me help you. We have to hurry; it's time to go."

Clara hurried to make two braids. She then pulled Annaveta's hair up into a crown, adding extra combs to help her hair stay in place. Some loose tendrils escaped and hung in short wisps down her neck.

"There, all done. You look gorgeous no matter how you

do your hair. I'm sure my brother Alex won't be able to keep his eyes off of you," Clara teased.

"Oh, hush," said Annaveta, self-conscious at her words. In truth, she was both scared and excited for this day. She was excited to have a day of fun with Alex and with Clara. However, that fear of being snubbed, and anxiety over possibly meeting up with the unknown man who was after her, filled her thoughts.

"Papa and Mama took Oma, Helmut, Inga, Jacob, the girls, and all the supplies in the wagon to the schoolhouse already," Clara said as they put on their light jackets and boots. "So we are walking."

Alex and Ernest were waiting for them as they stepped outside the house. She noticed how Alex maneuvered his way to walk beside her. His shoulder brushed against hers with each step. As Clara talked about the many different people they would see, Annaveta steeled herself against the rude comments and gossip that she knew she would hear.

When they were still a ways away, she could hear the accordion and fiddles playing. The large brick schoolhouse beside the Lutheran church was filled with older and younger couples, and singles talking and laughing together. Clara and Alex waved at people they knew, and Annaveta smiled at a few girls her age. Ernest ran up the stairs. She knew he went to find Rachel.

Annaveta stayed close to Clara as they entered the schoolhouse. It was packed full of people. The older parents and some grandparents sat on the wooden benches along the wall, most of them holding sleeping babies. Young mamas were busy chasing toddlers, while they passed some papas talking about this year's crops.

"Can we go play outside with the other children, Mama?" Katarina asked, with Erika dancing excitedly at her side.

"Of course you can." Mrs. Wagner patted each daughter on the shoulder, then gave them a warning. "Stay close to the schoolhouse; no wandering around the streets."

"We'll stay close, Mama." The girls danced out the door with a few other girls their age. Annaveta hoped her evening would be as fun as the little girls' promised to be.

Annaveta followed Clara to the table of food and drinks. While pouring herself some tea, she said hi to some of the girls who were talking with Clara. Rachel smiled and welcomed Annaveta, but the other girls who were with Catherine and Greta wouldn't speak to her. She wore a pasted-on-smile despite the hurt over the way these girls shunned her.

"Aren't those young people over there from Kolb?" Clara asked Catherine and Greta, looking in the direction of a large group of men and women in their late teens and early twenties who were standing in the corner talking among themselves. "We should go over there and talk to them. Welcome them to our colony's festival."

"Some of those girls aren't worth the effort," Greta said. "They don't even know how to dress properly. I'll go say hi to those who seem like they're worth knowing." Catherine looked at Annaveta's clothes and smirked, her expression agreeing with Greta's harsh words. Catherine linked arms with Greta and left to meet some of the youth that came from Kolb, leaving Annaveta and Clara standing by themselves.

"Well, we should go over and say hi to the other girls, seeing as how Greta and Catherine probably won't include them," Clara said as she started walking toward the girls who were dressed in tattered black skirts and well-worn blouses. Others in the group were dressed in new hand-sewn colored long skirts and new embroidered blouses.

"*Wilkommen.* We are happy to have you here," Clara said as she shook their hands. Clara remembered most of their names from last year's harvest festival and introduced Annaveta as her friend.

They stood there talking about sewing and needlework for a long time. The young men were talking and laughing, standing by themselves, but it didn't take long until the men joined the ladies. Standing on the other side of the main room of the schoolhouse, Annaveta noticed that some of the well-dressed girls ignored her and Clara and the girls they were talking to. Annaveta tried to ignore their looks of distaste and scorn, but in her heart she knew she still cared too much what they thought. She moved to stand closer to Clara.

Suddenly she heard Katarina and Erika's loud voices as they ran into the schoolhouse. They were crying for their Mama. Annaveta went to them, and seeing the tears running down their cheeks she hugged them close and walked them to Mrs. Wagner.

"What's wrong, my *liebchens*?" Their mama pulled the two distressed girls close to her side. "You must tell me, so I can help."

"A bad man grabbed Katarina," Erika spouted before Katarina could speak.

"What? Tell us exactly what happened, Katarina," her mama said.

"We were outside playing hide-and-seek in the tall grasses and the bushes, when a strong hand grab my waist from behind. I tried screaming, but he covered my mouth with his large hand. Then he started speaking to me." Katarina was shaking with fear. "His words were in fast Russian, so I don't know if I remembered everything." She wiped away more tears from her red cheeks. He said 'tell Annaveta that I'm getting tired of waiting. Next time something worse will happen to one of your new friends.' He uncovered my mouth and looked at me and asked if I understood. I nodded my head, and then he ran away."

Katarina squeezed her mama tight around her waist, holding on to her place of safety. Annaveta gasped in horror at what had happened to Katarina. Now the man who was threatening her was now hurting the people who were closest to her.

"Can you describe what the man looked like?" Annaveta bent over so she was looking Katarina in the eyes.

"*Ja.* He had brown eyes, but the rest of his head was covered with a scarf and a hat." She closed her eyes, frowning.

Anger and fear grew inside Annaveta, both vying for equal attention. Fear won this time. Whoever the man was who was trying to hurt her had now targeted the young children in this family. The thought of someone harming a young child, made her so angry.

And then she felt sad, realizing she would have to leave the colony, and very soon. There was no other way. She didn't want to leave this wonderful family she had come to love, but she had to so they would be safe. Where would she go? There was no other person or place that she could run to and no way to support herself. She had promised to finish the lace for Rachel's wedding dress, so she could leave right after that. *I hope Mrs. Wagner will have a few more calls for a midwife, so I can help and earn more money. I'll need more in my little bag of savings if I'm going to leave here. It's my fault that Katarina was hurt. I'm to blame for all the bad things that happened in my family and now with the Wagner family. I've got to get out of here and soon.*

Annaveta saw that the girls were being comforted by their mama, so she turned to leave. Mrs. Wagner spoke up. "Don't tell Clara and Alex yet. No sense in ruining their evening. I'll tell them later."

She nodded and made her way back to Clara feeling the weight of guilt and blame. She listened to Clara's friends talk about their boyfriends, and she forced herself to listen and be cheerful. Guilt and anger gnawed at her as she thought about leaving Clara and this family she had come to love.

Someone tapped her on the shoulder.

"Do I get the first dance?" Alex put his hand out to accept her own. Deep sadness filled her as she thought of leaving Alex. He was the first man she every really cared about, and now she had to leave him. She didn't want to hurt him, but she knew she had no choice but to go away. And she worried that he might try to follow her. Well, she would tell no one where she was going. Then there would be less chance of Alex following her. She didn't want him getting hurt by the man who was after her.

Putting her hand in his, she walked to the center of the room where quite a few couples were dancing already. The music was a slow folksy tune that an old German man played skillfully on his accordion.

A tuft of Alex's blond hair fell over his forehead, hiding his eye. She pushed it away, her finger tracing the outline of his eyebrow. She wished she could tell him about his sisters, but Alex didn't seem like himself tonight, so maybe it was good she had promised his mama not to speak about it.

"You make me crazy." Alex pulled her closer and looked from her eyes to her lips. "I'm going kiss you right now."

"Not here." Annaveta frowned and moved her head to the side. He grazed her cheek. The stench of vodka on his breath made her mad. "Maybe you have had enough to drink, you don't want to overdo it."

He twirled her around and clutched her waist. "Hey, it's my turn to party. This is my reward for all my hard work this year. I'll drink as much as I please." He laughed off her concern as the last notes of the song drifted into the still air. Clara came up to them and tapped on Annaveta's arm.

"I want to introduce you to someone." Clara looked at her brother, shaking her head, the crease on her forehead increasing. Annaveta walked away from him, feeling anger at Alex for his eagerness to drink. At this moment it seemed like she was reliving her childhood with her drunk father. Even though Alex was wonderful in most ways, this was one flaw in him that she wouldn't be able to excuse. She had to get away from him.

A tall and dark handsome man stood waiting as she walked up to him with Clara. "Annaveta, this is Franz. He lives in the sister colony of Kolb." Clara wore a big smile on her face as she introduced them. Annaveta noticed she kept looking over her shoulder at Alex. Annaveta turned and saw

Alex glaring back at her. Clara continued talking to Franz, as Annaveta was only half listening. "This is my good friend Annaveta."

"It's not often I am able to dance with such a beautiful lady. May I?" He bowed slightly and held out his hand, his Russian heavily accented.

"Yes." Annaveta put her hand in his, hesitant to dance with this unknown man, but she wanted to get away from Alex. She had seen Clara frown at Alex, so she was sure Clara was helping her put some distance between her and her brother.

Franz led her to the middle of the dance floor, among many other young couples. He put one hand on her waist and with the other he held her hand. They moved together to the simple cadence of the waltz. She looked over Franz's shoulder to see Alex pouring himself another glass of alcohol at the drink table. Feeling perturbed, she looked back up to her dance partner.

"How come I've never seen you before here in Pleve Colony?" His dark-brown eyes questioned her.

"I haven't been here long. So you live in Kolb?" Annaveta asked, hoping to switch the subject to something other than herself.

"I first want to know your name and where you came from originally. You have a Russian accent when you speak German," he said firmly, then smiled widely. "You are most definitely the prettiest Russian girl I've ever seen."

Annaveta's face flushed, and she looked over Franz's shoulder and spotted Alex. He was glaring at the back of Franz's head. She ignored his angry look, as his eyes darted back and forth between her and her dance partner. Feeling disgust at seeing Alex guzzling so many glasses of strong drink, she turned away and looked up at Franz.

It wasn't long before other young men were cutting in and dancing with Annaveta. After what seemed like hours, she looked over again and saw Alex standing at the drink table with his friends, pouring glass after glass of vodka for them and for himself. As she danced with another young man, Alex got up and walked past the table toward her, swaying as he went. She smelled the vodka on his breath as he neared.

"It's my turn now," Alex said, trying to pull Annaveta away from the tall, broad-shouldered man she was dancing with. "Find someone else." He swayed on his feet as he tried to take her with him.

Annaveta pulled his hand from her arm. "No. I'm not dancing with a drunk. Go away." She tried to move away from him, but he squeezed her arm even tighter.

"What do you mean, no?" Alex's words slurred slightly and got louder as his face turned red with anger. "I should be the only man you are dancing with. Let's go."

"Stop it, Alex!" Annaveta's words came out louder than she intended. She whispered forcefully. "You are making a scene. Now, let go of me."

Alex let go of her arm, his lips tight in what looked like a mad pout. Before Annaveta could stop him, he stalked back to the man Annaveta had been dancing with and punched him in the face, his own face getting redder with each blow. Soon a fistfight was in full force.

Annaveta couldn't believe what she was seeing. Alex seemed out of control. Angry and more than a little scared, she looked around at the small group of people that encircled them. Younger men were prodding the two men to keep fighting, while some older men urged them to stop.

Soon the crowd grew in size, with both colonies gathered around the two men. There were many faces that looked at her, their eyes glinting with undisguised blame. The hate in the air, directed her way, was palpable. She crossed her arms in a protective gesture, shriveling inside with each accusing glare. She blamed herself. It was her fault Katarina had been grabbed, and because she refused to dance with Alex, it was her fault Alex was in this fight.

"Stay away from her," Alex warned in a loud enough voice for everyone in the schoolhouse to hear. With swaying steps he walked away.

Annaveta couldn't believe how drunk Alex was. And that he had gotten into a fight because he was mad she was dancing with someone else. Annaveta felt the cold coils of fear clog her throat as she watched the evening turn into a nightmare. For a moment it seemed as if she were reliving the past all over again. She could hardly breathe. Each condemning stare was like a hand pulling a rope tighter around her neck. She needed to get out of there.

Turning and pushing her way through the crowd, she rushed toward the door. Once outside, she ran all the way home, tears of anger, shame, and fear rolling down her cheeks.

Chapter 17

ANNAVETA SAT UP IN BED, her hand covering her mouth, stifling the scream that wanted to emerge. The nightmare had been so real. Her hands shook as she remembered. A man had chased after her, desperate to catch her. She ran from him, but there was no escape. She was out in the woods, and it seemed like someone was with her but she couldn't get a clear picture of who it was. The attacker came closer. She stood with her back pressed against a tree as she watched him move toward her, his right hand raised, a glint of metal in his hand. His face wasn't clear so she couldn't tell who this evil man was. She had been sentenced to die, and she couldn't even see her accuser's face.

She covered her face with her hands, her shoulders shaking with gut-wrenching sobs. The nightmare had seemed so real, as if it had actually happened.

"What's wrong, Annaveta?" Clara sat up in bed beside her, giving her a long hug until her cries had quieted to soft sniffles. "A bad dream?"

"Yes." Annaveta hiccupped, wiping tears on her nightgown. They sat there in the dark, hugging each other as Annaveta told her about her dream. "The bad part was, I didn't even see who was chasing after me." She pulled her knees up to her chest and wrapped her shaking arms around them in a protective move.

"Well, it's a good thing it was just a dream and not real." Clara rubbed Annaveta's arms, trying to calm her.

"That's just it. Ever since the dream I had of my family dying in a fire, all my dreams have come true." Annaveta put her hands in front of her face to stop the tears. "So I'm sure this dream is a warning. This will actually happen someday in my future. It's not like I can stop it either."

"You're right." Clara stared at her a thoughtful expression on her face. "Which means maybe we could make a plan that would either prevent it, or at the very least you could be prepared. Right?"

"I hadn't thought of that. It'd be good to have a plan." Annaveta shook her head, dispelling the fear.

Clara fingered her long braid for a long time before she spoke. "Here's a good plan for when this dream comes to pass in real life. When you are chased, don't make it easy for him to get to you. Don't run to a dead end." Clara moved to look her in the eyes. "Remember your angel? Ask him to guard you."

Yawning, Clara hugged her one last time and lay back down. "I'm going to get a couple more hours of sleep. You should too."

Annaveta lay in bed wide awake for a long time, wishing she could escape the nightmare of her dreams and dread that followed. Why did this always happen to her? First it was her papa, then the overseer, and now someone was chasing her. Her nightmare revealed her deepest fears and reminded her of Alex's drunken binge. The reality of what had happened last night showed her that Alex could become like her papa. She already lived through that once and was determined not to do it again.

As she wiped her tears away, she heard Clara's soft snores beside her. Annaveta was glad she had one friend who stuck with her. Two, if she counted Pavla. Clara had walked with Annaveta on Sunday last, to the meadow, to see if Pavla was there. She wasn't, but there was a note left in the log. Pavla had written to her telling her that Misha had been by their house twice asking about her. He had asked where she was living and where she was working. Pavla said she didn't tell him anything, but was worried because Misha seemed determined to find her.

Annaveta shivered as she remembered Misha. He had seemed so determined to make her his wife. Well, there was no way she was going to become the wife-slave of a drunkard. He would have to look elsewhere for his victim. But she also remembered Pavla telling her that Monsieur Arnaud had told the head gardener that because she had embarrassed him in front of his workers, she needed to be punished. If the goal was for her to be scared, then it was working. She didn't feel safe anymore. The notes had scared her, and being shot at in the Wagner's backyard had shaken her, but little Katarina getting hurt because of her really terrified her. She had hope, though, for she remembered the other vivid dream in which the angel protected her and led her on her journey.

She exhaled the big breath she had been holding. It was time she trusted the angel's words. It was time to believe God was speaking to her like Clara's papa said. Somehow He would show her the way through this.

THE EARLY MORNING SUNRISE LIT up the sky, giving the promise of a new day. A new day was exactly what she needed. This past week, ever since the harvest festival, she had avoided Alex as much as possible. She was still angry with him for letting himself get drunk and starting that fight at the Kerb Festival. Could he not control himself? Did his emotions and actions change with whichever way the wind was blowing? It was obvious she didn't know him as well as she'd first thought. She was a little more wary of him now.

As she stepped into the house, she gave the pail to Mama Wagner, who after finishing straining Clara's pail of milk took hers. Once the milk was poured into jars, Annaveta and

Clara took the jars and put them in a large bowl, then added cold water up to edge of the jars to keep the milk cool. Then they went back to the barn to let out the cows and calves. The bells attached to the cows jingled as they walked down their road with the herder. After letting the sheep out through the gate that enclosed the Wagners' yard, they followed the sheepherder. She was glad the herders came at the same time every day. It made it easier for the farmers to set their schedule by it.

She wiped the sweat from her brow with her sleeve and tucked a few loose strands of curls behind her ears as the last little lamb scurried after its mama down the lane. Her hurried steps took her back to the barn to help finish cleaning the stalls, but when she got there, Clara was hanging up the shovel and hurrying out the barn. She looked inside the barn and saw that the stalls were all clean with fresh straw laid down. Unbelievable. Clara had already finished.

Smiling, Annaveta turned around to follow her friend, when she bumped into a firm set of broad shoulders. She stopped her in her tracks. The smile left her face as she looked up at the same man who had been dominating her thoughts.

"I'm sorry." Annaveta blinked and moved to go around Alex. His arm blocked the barn's entrance. She tried to duck, but he moved to block her path and put both hands lightly on her shoulders.

"Annaveta, look at me." Alex's coaxing tone drew her eyes to his even as she tried to wriggle free of his grasp. She didn't like it that his touch still affected her. Anger toward him rose up within her.

"I've been wanting to talk to you for almost a week." His eyes looked pained as he searched hers.

"I know." Annaveta crossed her arms in a protective gesture. "I guess I don't see the point of talking. You showed your true colors at the dance, and I don't think I can take another reckless and angry outburst from you."

She backed up against the wall to remove herself from

his reach. He moved toward her, his eyes filled with such longing and sadness that her heart almost melted. Almost. She put her hands up to stop his progress.

"I'm so sorry for my actions. For fighting. For the embarrassment I was. For breaking your trust." Alex put his fingers under her chin and lifted her face so she had to look at him. "I'm so sorry. My jealousy got the better of me. I care about you, Annaveta, and more than anything in the world, I'm asking you to forgive me. To give me another chance to earn your trust."

Annaveta saw the yearning mixed with pain as he bit his lip and his forehead creased. He seemed afraid to hope. Her eyes welled up with tears. "I'm just scared of being hurt again." She wiped the tears and shook her head. "I don't think I can do this anymore. I need distance. Time to heal. I don't know."

Alex wrapped his arms around her as her shoulders shook with sobs. She knew he was regretful, but she was so scared. Her past had a way of catching up with her, winding its far-reaching tentacles around her neck as if coming in for the kill. But Alex's arms comforted her, and she gradually relaxed.

"Please forgive me, Annaveta." His warm breath tickled her ear as he held her close. "I never meant to hurt you. You mean the world to me. I would do anything for you."

He brought her even closer into his embrace as his lips kissed first her ear then moved to her forehead. Annaveta softened a little at his honeyed words and sweet caresses. His hand moved behind her head as he kissed one eyelid and then the other, trailing delicate kisses down her cheeks to her chin before he captured her lips with his. His warm mouth searched hers as he hungrily took more of her, devouring the sweetness of her lips with all the ardor of a lover who had been denied too long.

Suddenly a voice calling her name brought Annaveta to her senses. What was she doing? How could she let Alex kiss her like this? She was planning on leaving him, so she couldn't keep encouraging him. She pushed at his shoulders as his arms tightened. She pushed harder.

"No, we can't do this, Alex." Annaveta put her fingers over his lips to stop him from another kiss.

"I'm scared too, Annaveta." Alex pressed his forehead to hers, his breath heavy and quick as he still held her. He put her hand on his chest, and she felt the rapid beats of his heart. "See what you do to me? I can hardly catch my breath when I'm around you."

Annaveta smiled and tried to move back. His hands slid down her arms and grabbed her hands.

"I don't want to lose you." Alex's blue eyes were dark with desire and unfulfilled need. "Please say you forgive me. Do you?" One hand moved to caress her cheek.

"Yes, I do forgive you," Annaveta said as she pulled his hands back from her face and held them in her own. "But we do need to get going. Your mama will have breakfast on the table."

Annaveta looked at Alex, who put his hands down to his side and bowed to her, keeping his distance.

"My lady, your wish is my command." Alex swept his arm out in a courtly display of chivalry, encouraging her to go through the barn door first.

Annaveta walked toward the house, feeling like she had done the right thing. She had a hard time trusting her own emotions lately, but knew she needed some time and distance to sort through her feelings. Especially since she knew that it wouldn't be long now, and she would be out of his life for good.

CLIMBING INTO THE WAGON WITH Clara, Annaveta adjusted her dark-gray skirt and buttoned up her black wool jacket so the howling October wind wouldn't chill her skin. Mrs. Wagner had told them to bundle up with their warm jackets and boots today as they went to Pleve Market to buy extras like lamp oil and spices. Alex came out of the house holding a gun tucked close to his side. He shoved it under the bench quickly and hopped into the driver's seat. Mrs. Wagner frowned at him upon seeing the weapon.

"*Ach*, Alex. You know us colonists don't hold to much gun-toting." His mama shook her head and reached down to shove the gun further under the seat.

"Mama, it's for protection." Alex looked back at Annaveta as if to emphasize his point. "Just in case we need it."

"*Ja*, well, just keep it hidden." Mrs. Wagner shook her head and brought little Jacob closer to her.

Annaveta was glad when they stopped talking about the need for protection. She really didn't want to think about that right now. She was so tired of having to look over her shoulder to see if someone was following her. Fear seemed to be her constant companion these days. But she was thankful that Alex thought ahead to protect his family and her. He was a good man, always caring for those he loved. Her stomach fluttered as she thought of his kiss. He'd told her he didn't want to lose her. How could he still want her close by his side, when she had caused all these problems for his family? The faithfulness, courage, responsibility and the way he served those he loved were all traits that drew her to him. But she had to let him go. She shook her head, biting her lips.

"Stop it. You'll make your lips bleed." Clara poked her shoulder, then turned to look down the street. "So many wagons here today. I can't wait to see what new things people are selling. We'll have fun, so stop worrying."

"You're right. It will be a good day." Annaveta stopped biting her lip, bumping her shoulder with Clara's.

Annaveta couldn't wait to see the new clothes in the stores on Main Street. Katrina and Erika snuggled in on either side of her, and Clara to try to catch some warmth. Annaveta looked at Jacob's quivering body as he sidled up to his mama's warmth. They wouldn't get to the stores too soon.

"Bye-bye," Erika and Katrina said in unison as they jumped off the wagon and ran to catch up to their friends entering through the schoolhouse doors. Alex clucked to the horses and turned the wagon down Main Street, then stopped in front of the general store. They passed the big building they used for some community meetings. Today a wooden sign with the word *Bazaar* hung crookedly off to the side of the door.

"We should go see what the Russians brought to town to sell this year, Mama." Clara looked at her mama and pointed to the sign.

"We don't need anything else. Especially not from lazy Russians." Inga looked at Annaveta meaningfully, then frowned at the people coming in and out of the building.

"Inga, surely you don't mean that. We are to love our neighbors." Mama Wagner patted her hand and looked at Clara. "Well, it wouldn't hurt to look to see what they are selling today. Who knows what we'll find."

Alex moved behind another horse and wagon on the side of the street, parking where there was less traffic.

"Son, we should only be about an hour looking and getting our supplies before you come back for us," Mama Wagner said as Alex helped her down from the wagon. "Will you talk to Shoemaker Schmidt about sending his apprentice, Heinrich, to our home to fit us all with shoes for the winter?"

"*Ja,* Mama," Alex replied as he helped his mama, Inga, Clara, and then Annaveta from the wagon. Did she imagine it or did his hand linger overlong on her waist? She looked at him with her most firm expression on her face. He bent his head down, his humble apology filling his eyes. Her heart pained her as she looked into his kind eyes, knowing that she was in danger of liking him a little too much, but would soon have to let him go.

"I'll be back soon," Alex said as he finally let her go. Waving to the rest of his family, he got on the wagon and clucked at the horses to go.

"Come along, ladies. I've got a surprise to show you all." Mrs. Wagner led the way into the large general store, where there were many different things they didn't see at home.

"We need to look for a wedding present for Ernest and Rachel. Seems they want to get married with the rest of the couples at the start of November." Mama looked at them all with a twinkle in her eye. "Now don't look so surprised. You remember we went just a few days ago to Rachel's parents' place to discuss things. Looks like everything's in order."

"Oh, that's so exciting. Rachel didn't say a word." Clara giggled and clucked under her breath. "Well, let's see what we find."

Annaveta looked through the aisle, and high up on the shelf she saw a beautiful German-made striking bracket mantle clock. Walnut-colored wood cut with ornate designs surrounded the gold and silver numbers that were hidden behind the glass panel. She looked at the back and saw that it was made only a few years before in 1902.

She grabbed Clara's arm and pointed. "This clock is ever so nice."

Clara waved her mama over. "Mama, take a look what Annaveta found. This would be perfect."

"*Ja*, it is beautiful all right. I saw some mirrors and a new loom, but this would be even better." Mama Wagner ran her hand down the exquisite craftsmanship. "Besides, I think Papa was going to make them a wooden loom."

Annaveta smiled as she turned to look around the store. More people had entered the building. As they went through the store, many of them picked up extra oil and carried some of the fancy tea and coffee in their hands. Annaveta watched as they wandered the aisles.

Suddenly, behind one of the shoppers, a tall black-haired man turned his head to the side as he admired something.

From the back, he had looked vaguely like someone she knew, but she couldn't get a clear look at his face in the middle of all the other shoppers. Something about him set her heart pounding.

"Annaveta," Clara called. "We are going now. Hurry." Clara waved her hand, and Annaveta hurried her footsteps, her thoughts brooding over the unknown man.

Leaving the store, they were pelted by heavy rain. They hurried to the wagon and put their purchases under the tarp Alex had placed there. Alex helped her up onto the wagon, her teeth chattering with fear and cold. Loud booms of thunder and lightning seemed like a reflection of the sounds Annaveta heard in her heart.

Annaveta looked around the crowded street, hearing an eerie sound of laughter that sent a tremor up her spine. The howling wind mixed with the sudden deluge of rain made it difficult to see people as they ran for cover along the wooden sidewalk and into the stores. She had a tingling sensation of being watched.

Alex took the reins and clucked to the horses. The girls huddled together in the backseat using their coats as a barrier against the driving rain. The two bay mares hurried their steps with an eagerness to go home. She pressed closer to Clara for body warmth hoping that would calm the sense of foreboding that pulsed through her veins.

Chapter 18

"You seem nervous, Ernest." Alex laughed as he put on his winter coat and boots. The shoemaker had fitted him with new *filzstiefel* for his feet just this week.

"You would be too if you were about to have your brothers go to your girlfriend's house to ask for her papa's blessing on their marriage." Ernest glared at his brother. "But your time is coming, little brother."

At his brother's words, Alex looked over at Annaveta, who sat by the kitchen table stitching the intricate lace design she was making for Rachel's wedding dress. He heard Rachel talk excitedly over the lacing Annaveta had done for Clara's blouse, and so he wasn't surprised to see her making her fancy French lace for Rachel's wedding dress. Alex noticed her frown and shake her head as she did so often lately. Something had been troubling her since the last market day, and he needed to find out what it was. He would take her worries from her if he could, or at least be there for her to talk to.

He studied her beautiful face that was framed by wisps of hair that hung down in waves beside soft cheeks. She bit her lips in worry, and he heard her sigh. She raised her head and green eyes peered up at him with a question in her eyes. He just smiled and winked at her. Her innocent blush pleased him. He wished she was making lace for her own wedding dress. He knew he loved her and wanted to pour out his heart to her and ask her to marry him. It couldn't come soon enough for him.

He waited as Helmut put on his boots. They were going to the Hoffs' home tonight to deliver a speech. They were to bring Ernest's heartfelt devotion for Rachel to her parents and ask for her hand in marriage on their brother's behalf. He grinned at Ernest. He was so nervous this night, but he didn't really need to be anxious. Mr. and Mrs. Hoff already knew his brothers were coming, and even though they would pretend to be surprised, it was already established that the parents and bride-to-be would give their consent. The only ritual after this would be for them to meet with Pastor Sommelt to grill them in the basics of their faith. After that, they would go ahead with the wedding.

Mama had a smile that lit up her rosy cheeks as she put fresh bread on a plate for a snack. Alex wiggled his toes in the warm boots that were made from this year's sheepshearing. The outer material made from ox hide kept the feet warm even in very cold weather. The shoemaker had come to their house every day until all the boots for the family were finished. Now everyone was ready for winter.

"Do you not trust us, your only brothers, to speak well of you to Rachel's papa?" Alex lightly punched his brother's shoulder as he teased.

"You better do your best to convince her parents." Ernest swatted his hands away as he looked from one brother to the other.

"We all know that this is just a formality. Your marriage is already as good as done." Helmut, ever the practical son, grunted with impatience. "Let's go. With this much snow, I don't want to be gone too long and somehow find ourselves stuck."

Helmut and Alex left the house, out into the rush of cold air and snow. It was nearing the end of October, and already the snow was piling up good. Alex couldn't wait for this night to be over. He was discouraged that his efforts to win Annaveta over seemed to be wasted. She was holding him at arm's length, and he didn't understand it.

FROWNING, ANNAVETA TRIED TO FOCUS her tired eyes on the intricate French d'Alecon lace design her mama had taught her. She pulled out a few of the stitches and worked on it again. This time the flower with its tiny hanging leaf design looked evenly spaced. She tried to get rid of thoughts of fear and worry that had plagued her since Market Day. Mrs. Wagner had been teaching her that worry did no one any good. Why not use that energy to pray, instead? So she was trying.

She sighed and looked up, surprised to see Alex staring at her so intently. He winked at her. She pushed down the awareness that flooded her senses at the attention he paid her. She couldn't encourage him. Instead, she needed to make plans. Just this morning Mr. Wagner had read from the St.Petersburg newspaper nurses were needed at the hospitals there. She had casually asked Clara how far some of the cities were from their colony and if there was a train station near Pleve Colony. Clara had told her it was a five-day trip by train to St.Petersburg, and the nearest train station was twelve miles away. A friend of Clara's had gone to St.Petersburg and spoke of the differences in cost of food and rent and the hard time some people had living in that crowded city.

With these details that Clara had shared, Annaveta figured she had almost enough money saved for the train fare, but would need more before she could go. She glanced down at her ring. She would have to sell it — then she would have enough money. Her heart was heavy to lose the only reminder she had of her mama, but she had no choice. Of course she needed to plan what she would say in the note that she left for the family and in the notes for Clara and Alex.

She wouldn't tell them where she was going, but somehow she wanted to explain so they would know she appreciated and loved them.

Clara giggled at something her sisters said. Annaveta looked over to see them making faces at each other. She put down her lace and decided it was time to enjoy the fun of the moment. She didn't want worry and fear to crowd her thoughts so that she couldn't enjoy what was happening right now.

Alex and Helmut finally left to go to the Hoffs' home, leaving a blast of cold air in their wake. Mrs. Wagner hurried to the kitchen stove and added a little more fuel to the fire, setting the water to boil for tea.

"Well, that's that." Ernest's sigh was a mixture of worry and relief as he pushed the door closed behind his brothers. "I guess we'll know by the end of tonight if I will be getting married."

"Now then, Son. All will be well, *ja*?" Mrs. Wagner walked over, patting Ernest's shoulder. "Come, sit. We'll have some tea and talk while we wait for the good news." She pulled out a chair for him and went to pour tea into cups.

Mr. Wagner winked at his son and took the cup of licorice-scented tea from his wife's outstretched hand. "It'll be good to have another set of hands to add to our growing family."

Inga frowned and shifted on her chair as she looked across the table at Annaveta. "I don't know where we'll fit another person. It's already crowded in here."

"Now, Inga." Mama Wagner clucked at her daughter-in-law. "We will do as the good Lord asks us and be ready with a bed or meal when needed. We don't know when we might be entertaining angels without even knowing it. We are glad to have you here, Annaveta, and adding Rachel to the family is something we will look forward to."

Inga's face got red, and she put down her stitching and excused herself. Her quick movements, stomping footsteps, and door slamming said more than words ever could.

"I think Inga finds it hard to accept change," Clara whispered. "The fact that she lost two unborn babies after Jacob's birth hasn't made it any easier. Her heart is bitter and not quick to accept others."

Annaveta caught her breath at the news of Inga's loss. She was reminded of her own mama and how she often cried for the many babes that had died in the womb and those that had been stillborn. The heartache that Inga faced helped Annaveta understand her better.

"*Ja*, I know, Daughter." Clara's mama heaved a heavy sigh. "We will just keep loving her and pray that God will open her heart."

Mr. Wagner read from the newspaper while the women stitched and Ernest whittled. "This looks interesting. This article from the St. Petersburg paper says that Interior Minister Maklakov has urged the Tsar to overthrow the Duma. There's been so much arguing, especially now that the Bolsheviks have had a definite split with other Mensheviks in the Duma." Clara's papa shook his head silently as he took another sip of the strong tea. "This reporter seems to think that with the many riots in the streets and the splitting of these political groups, it won't be long before there will be an all-out war between the two. Doesn't seem to me like Tsar Nicholas has much control anymore—not with his wife agreeing with every word Rasputin says and the Duma making more of this country's decisions. It has even affected factory workers and laborers in the city. It says here that there have been more strikes of factory workers. They are demanding better conditions for work, but as a result quite a few of them are getting hurt, so the hospitals are overflowing with sick with not enough doctors and nurses to help them." He shook his head as he read a few more sections in silence.

"There is change in the wind." Mrs. Wagner frowned as she darned her husband's socks. "I wonder where it will take us?"

Annaveta picked up her tea thinking of all the changes that were taking place in this country. *All I need is one more midwifing job helping Mrs. Wagner, and I think I'll have enough money saved. It's got to be soon though, so no one else gets hurt.*

She picked up her lace and hook, weaving the delicate threads together, stitching in silence and wishing the broken pieces of her heart could be mended as easily.

It wasn't much later that Alex and Helmut burst through the door bringing the chilling wind with them. "*Gut*, you are home. And early too." Their mama kissed their cold cheeks. "*Ach*, come stand by the stove and warm up. You are both frozen." She shooed them over to the stove while she hung up the mitts and hats on the rope to dry.

"So, don't keep us in suspense." Clara's smile "What did they say?"

Alex laughed at Ernest, who sat on the edge of his seat looking up at him. "Not impatient for your bride, are you, Brother?" Alex teased. Ernest's neck and face turned bright red. "Okay, I'll tell you. Rachel's papa was quite agreeable to the wedding. We even negotiated the bride dowry that you and Mama agreed on." Alex nodded to his papa. "You'll all be happy to know he agreed to the terms."

"Looks like we'll need to build that middle wall in the large bedroom, to make more room for our growing family." Mr. Wagner winked at Ernest, whose face was still red. "We'll start tomorrow."

Annaveta sighed and put away her stitching. She bid everyone good night, her lips unsmiling, ignoring Alex's frown. It seemed like most of the family was looking forward to new beginnings, while she was simply biding her time until she had enough money to leave them. Her heart was breaking, and there was nothing anyone could do about it.

Chapter 19

ANNAVETA YAWNED AS SHE CARRIED the two heavy pails of milk in each hand and trudged across the fresh snow to the house. It would be a perfect day for sledding this afternoon. She hurried as she thought of Alex's promise to walk with her to the meadow this morning.

Last night she had stayed up late and finished the lace for Rachel's wedding dress. Now all that remained was for Clara to sew it onto the wedding dress. There were only a few days left before the wedding. It would be good to get away this morning. The four-mile walk would be worth it if she could put a note in the log for Pavla. Hopefully her friend from Noltava would hurry to the meadow to find it. Annaveta had written to ask Pavla if anyone had come to her house or if she had seen anyone at the Shremetev Estate or in Noltava who was asking about her. Maybe she had heard something about Monsieur Arnaud. If she could find out more about who was asking about her, maybe she could plan her next steps better. Fear of Misha and Monsieur Arnaud had her so anxious that she could hardly sleep at night.

It didn't take long for everyone to finish their breakfast. Annaveta helped wash the dishes while Alex talked to his mama about where they were going.

"Hurry home then, Son. You don't want to miss out on trying your new sled with the others this afternoon." Mrs. Wagner squeezed his shoulder and shook her head as she watched Alex grab the gun from behind the door. Annaveta knew it was for protection, but its presence filled her with a sense of foreboding.

Annaveta hurried to get her coat and boots on, tucking the note for Pavla in her pocket. They hurried out the gate taking a different way than usual. Annaveta looked up at Alex and frowned.

"This is a shortcut that will take us to the trail that leads to the meadow." Alex looked down at her.

"Truly?" Annaveta's eyebrows raised.

"You wound me, little doubter." He hit his chest with his fist, making a choking sound, from which he recovered quickly. "Since you're unsure, I guess you'll just have to trust me." She laughed as he nudged her shoulder, teasing her. "Ah, there's that beautiful smile that I've waited for all morning."

"I just haven't felt like smiling this morning. I have a bad feeling today. I'm sure it's nothing to worry about." Annaveta grimaced and followed him to the well-worn trail that took them to the meadow. As they hurried along, Annaveta noticed Alex kept turning his head to the side to listen to sounds. Twice they stopped walking and listened. Alex had signaled for her to be quiet, but the rustling noise they heard turned out to be a rabbit. They finally reached the meadow, and even though it was covered in with snow, it still seemed like a peaceful place to her.

She found the big hollow log by the tree and dusted away the snow with her gloved hand. Inside was a note from Pavla, and she quickly opened it. It had been over two months since she'd been to the meadow to give Pavla a note. She noticed that this letter was dated the end of August, just when they had finished the harvest. Pavla wrote about her mama's new baby and said that Sergei had asked her to marry him. She didn't say anything about anyone asking about Annaveta.

Annaveta placed the letter she had written to Pavla in the hollow log and stood up.

"Pavla wrote that there was no cause for worry, but her letter was written at the end of August, and a lot has changed since then." Annaveta shook her head. "I hope she comes soon to get this letter. "I told her to be careful of people asking about me. I don't want her or her family getting hurt either." She blinked back the tears that threatened to come.

Alex set the gun against a tree and pulled her close to him. Some of the tension drained away as he rubbed her back.

"You need to let go of your worry." Alex kissed her forehead and the tip of her cold nose. "Just like you need to let go of your guilt at what's happened to you or my family. If you hang on to it, it'll eat you alive." He pulled her close for a kiss. "You are beautiful, smart, talented, and very lovable. I know because I like everything about you. Just the way you are."

Annaveta was tired of trying to keep Alex at a distance. She couldn't help herself — she wanted to feel his lips on hers again. To hold him close. He was her one safe place.

Ignoring the nagging voice inside that reminded her this would hurt him in the end, she kissed him, without reserve. He moaned, putting his hand behind her neck and pulling her hair loose. His kisses grew more ardent, when without warning she heard a twig snap in the distance. She pushed herself free from his embrace and looked around. Alex grabbed his gun and pulled her behind the large tree. Together they stood there for a few minutes until no further sound was heard.

"It must have been another animal," Alex whispered. "We should get home." She looked around, not seeing anyone. All seemed quiet. They left the meadow, walking the trail that was covered with fresh snow. Annaveta noticed Alex kept both hands on his gun as they hurried down the trail.

Suddenly the sound of boots crunching in the snow reached Annaveta's ears. She tugged on Alex's arm and pulled him behind a large tree just off the trail. Behind her about thirty feet away, she saw a dark-haired man stick his head out from behind his hiding place, the glint of metal shining brightly in his hand.

The ear-piercing blast of gunshot burst through the air, startling Annaveta. She jumped back and ducked behind the tree again. She looked up at Alex just as he aimed his gun. The loud blast from his gun had her covering her ears with shaking hands. In an instant, he ducked back behind the tree but then slowly slid to the ground. Annaveta's gaze moved from his pale face to the small red stain that made a circle on the sleeve of his jacket. She gasped. With hurried movements she searched under his coat and saw the stain had begun to spread. His face grew whiter by the second.

"You're hurt." She lifted up the bottom of her petticoat and tore off strips of cloth, wrapping them around his arm to stop the bleeding. She looked around to see if she could spot their attacker and, to her horror, she spotted him dashing between trees, coming closer to them.

"I'll be okay. He just nicked my arm." Alex sat there taking deep breaths.

"He's coming closer," Annaveta whispered in his ear as she finished tying the last strip of cloth.

Alex stood up on shaky legs, loading his rifle. He took aim and fired again. This time Annaveta heard a groan. She saw the attacker run in the opposite direction holding his side with one hand.

"I'm going after him." Alex's nostrils flared, his breath coming rapidly as he spoke through tight lips.

"No. By the sounds of it, he's already wounded. I don't want something worse to happen to you." Annaveta looked up at him, hoping against hope that he would stay.

"I need to do this, Annaveta. Stay here." He loaded his rifle again, his hands shaking. With the gun held in his white-knuckled grip, Alex dodged their assailant.

She trembled as she watched him zigzag between the trees until he was just a speck in the distance. The thought of him chasing the man with his injured arm was more than she could stand, so she hurried to follow him. In that moment she realized that she couldn't bear to lose him. She wanted him to live and not die by some madman's hand.

She ran faster. When she arrived back at the meadow, she saw Alex walking toward her with his hand at his shoulder. Blood dripped from his wound. She ran up to him and hugged him, sighing with relief.

"Hey, what was that for?" He looked down at her, warmth in his words.

"I'm just glad you are okay." She ripped another strip of cloth from her petticoat and tied it around his arm.

"Whatever the reason, I'll take a hug from you anytime." He winked at her, his pale face belying his lightheartedness. He frowned and looked back. "I lost him. He ran too fast, and I just couldn't keep up with this injury." Alex winced as he touched his arm.

"Well, maybe you scared him off. You must have wounded him because I heard him moan. Maybe we won't see him again." She tried to cheer him up. "Come on. He's long gone. Let's get you home and fix up your arm." Annaveta put his good arm around her shoulders to help steady him. It seemed like hours passed as they followed the path, and the sun was high overhead by the time they made it home. The house was quiet as they entered the kitchen. Annaveta helped Alex onto a chair and took off his coat and then removed his shirt. The bleeding had slowed down, but the deep gash in his shoulder seemed more than just a nick to her.

She boiled water and found Mrs. Wagner's basket of clean cloths and herbs. She spied a small sharp knife at the bottom and cleaned it in the boiled water. Remembering where Mrs. Wagner kept the medicines, she grabbed the small bottle of whiskey from the pantry and hurried to kneel beside Alex. She poured some whiskey into a small glass and handed it to him. She looked at his strong arms and bare chest, and a wave of warmth stirred in her belly. She looked away and scolded herself. She was supposed to be helping him, not ogling his body. She changed the direction of her thoughts.

"Drink that. This is going to hurt," Annaveta warned him as she pressed her fingers around the wound. "I'm going to get the bullet out now." He gulped down the liquid in the glass, groaning as she gently put the small blade into the wound. It wasn't long before she found the bullet and worked it out.

"Almost done." Annaveta poured alcohol over the wound, cleaning it.

"That burns like fire." His whispered moan made her hesitate. She felt bad that she was hurting him, but it needed to be done so he had a better chance of getting well. Mrs. Wagner's teaching came back to her. After finding the needle and thread, she stitched up the small wound. Her quick fingers, used to delicate stitching, quickly finished sewing him up.

"It's all done." Annaveta loosely tied some clean strips of cloth around his wound to help keep it clean. "How do you feel?"

"Like I got kicked in the arm by an angry horse." Alex's smile seemed forced. "Thanks for stitching me up. I have a good nurse."

"Your mama left some extra buns with cold meat on the table. Do you want one?" Annaveta eyed the food knowing she should eat, but still felt the shock over the shooting this morning.

"Maybe I should eat a little, then I wouldn't feel so lightheaded." They both ate their sandwiches quickly, each deep in thought.

"You should rest now." Annaveta stood up to help him to his feet.

"No. I actually feel a lot better. Besides, I promised Papa I would check on the cows and maybe give them a little more feed before we went sledding." He smiled at her, his hand going to his shoulder. "I'll find a clean shirt and then we'll go."

"You can't be serious." Annaveta put her hands on her

hips and followed him. "You just got shot. You need to rest." She followed him into the boys' bedroom. He grabbed a shirt and pulled it over his head.

"Listen, I don't want my parents to worry about me right now; they have enough on their minds. We need to go and pretend like everything is normal. Besides, you cleaned me up, so everything will be fine." She followed him back to the kitchen frowning the whole way. "Let's go, so we're not too late."

"Okay, but if I see you showing any signs of getting dizzy or you start bleeding again, I'm going to bring you back home." She looked him in the eye as she put her coat back on.

"All right, my love. I'll do whatever you say." He took that moment to kiss her lips before he grabbed her hand to lead her to the barn.

The closer they got to the barn, the louder the bawls of the cows became.

"I wonder if something is wrong." Alex grabbed her hand with his good hand, and they ran to the back of the barn. They stopped and stared in horror at the scene before them. Their best milker, the cow that Annaveta usually milked, had been killed. Her neck had been slit from top to bottom, and her new baby calf lay dead beside her.

Annaveta's hand flew to her chest while her other hand tried to stifle the gasp of alarm that rushed out of her.

Alex knelt beside the remains, taking his gloves off to touch their necks.

"They are really cold. Someone must have done this in the morning after the milking." Alex got up and put both hands on his head as he paced back and forth. "Who would do this? What kind of madman kills animals just for sport?" He touched his arm and stared at Annaveta. "It's probably the same guy that took a shot at me. It makes me so angry, I wish I had shot him dead today when I had the chance!" Alex went into the barn and came out with a shovel.

221

They dragged the cow to the far end of the pasture, and Alex shoveled a hole to bury it. Annaveta dragged the small little calf to where he was digging. It didn't take long until Alex had dug a hole big enough to bury the animals.

"I'll need to tell Papa about this, but I'll do that after we come back from sledding." Alex stood there shaking his head. "This guy has to be found and brought to justice."

Annaveta watched as Alex finished shoveling the last of the dirt over the two animals who now lay deep in the ground. Alex's papa unexpectedly walked through the gate. His eyes grew wide as he saw what Alex was doing.

"What happened here?" Mr. Wagner stopped mid-stride, his posture stiffening as he looked around the yard.

"Someone killed Annaveta's milk cow and her calf. Their throats were slit wide open." Alex watched his papa run his hand through his hair as he stood stiffly absorbing the news. "We just found them a little while ago and bodies were cool already, so it must have happened this morning right after we finished milking."

"Did you look for footprints?"

"*Ja*, I followed them to the fence line, and then I lost his trail in the middle of all the other boot prints." Alex shook his head, letting out a frustrated sigh. "What do we do?"

"Since his trail is cold, we don't need to search right now. So go ahead and enjoy yourselves sledding. I will go talk to the colony elders about this and see what they have to say about what sort of action we should take." Mr. Wagner's set his jaw, nodding to them both before he walked away in a fast-paced stride.

Panic filled her as she thought of all that had happened. She realized that it wasn't just any cow whose throat had been cut, it was the cow she milked every day. Someone knew too much about her and was following her.

Terror made her go weak at the knees. The attacker would keep coming after the Wagner family as long as she lived with them — this she now knew. And no one really knew how to stop him.

Chapter 20

TRUDGING THROUGH THE BIG SNOWDRIFTS in her new boots, Annaveta walked in silence at Alex's side as they made their way to the small hill. With Alex's left hand he pulled the new sled he made. His grim, unsmiling face matched her own mood. It seemed like all the attacks happening one right after another was too much to take in for both of them. Besides losing her family in the fire and being molested by Monsieur Arnaud, this had been the worst day of her life. She looked up, hearing the sounds of laughter and teasing as the Wagner family and others in the colony brought their sleds to the top of the hill. This was supposed to be a happy, fun day. She decided she would wear a smile, even though on the inside she was anxious from the events of the day.

"We'll try to have a good rest of the day." She squeezed Alex's hand, trying to be gentle with his wounded arm. He squeezed her hand and gave her a lopsided smile.

"Yeah, we will. I'm glad we can be together today. I'd rather spend the day with you than anyone else." Alex lifted her gloved hand up to his lips, the strength of desire unmistakable in his voice. She admired this man. Even with his faults, he still had more integrity, character, and love for God and family than any man she had ever known. Her heart, it seemed, now overruled her mind. She realized that she could trust him. That he wasn't at all like the abusive and dishonorable men she had known in her past.

"I'd rather be with you too." She couldn't stop the

whispered words of longing that came out of her mouth. Her eyes fastened on Alex's blue ones, and her gloved hand softly flicked off the crystals that stood on his nose. He pulled her closer. The rustling noise of footsteps startled them both out of the spell that encircled them.

"Annaveta, Alex. There you are," Clara called to them as she ran down to meet them. "What took you so long? Never mind. I'm just glad you two are finally here to join the fun."

Clara walked between Alex and Annaveta as they climbed the hill. Annaveta saw other people from Pleve Colony and tried to stay close to Clara. She waved at Rachel and Ernest, who were holding hands and laughing together. Helmut was pulling Jacob in a big wooden sled. She didn't see Inga. Maybe she had gone home with Oma. Clara's parents were busy talking to their friends, and the little girls were just coming up the hill, pulling their sled. Alex grabbed Erika and Katarina's sled when they got to the top of the hill.

"Let's ride together." He sat behind the two girls, his long legs on either side of them forming a safe barrier between them and the snow.

"What fun." Erika yelled out. Katarina and Erika both helped their brother push against the snow-covered ground and got the sled to move. Annaveta watched as they laughed and screamed their way down the hill with their big brother.

"Hurry, Annaveta," Clara called to her. "We'll go down on this sled."

Annaveta quickened her pace to catch up to her friend, who was already getting on the sled. She reached the top of the hill and looked down. The long slope seemed to go down for at least a mile toward the river. There were several trees that they would have to go around and a few large bumps they needed to avoid. Little Erika and Katarina were climbing up the hill just as she sat down behind Clara.

"It's fun, Annaveta." Erika's said with a bright smile. She came up behind them and gave them a push down the hill. "Next turn I want to ride with you, okay?"

Annaveta waved her response as they flew down the hill. Laughing and screaming, they made it to the edge of the clearing without either of them falling off the sled.

"I'm so glad we didn't hit any trees. Thanks to a great driver." Annaveta pulled the sled, grabbing Clara's hand. She wiped snow from her eyes to look up the hill.

"It's a long way up." Clara sighed, stopping with her. She pointed to the top of the hill. "Hey, that looks like John. Let's go."

"All of a sudden you have your energy back, I see. Seeing your beloved's face can work miracles," Annaveta teased.

"He's not my beloved. At least not yet." Clara winked at her. They hiked to the top at a fast pace and stood for a few minutes to catch their breath.

"Hi, Clara. Good day for sledding." John's reddish-blond hair had curls that poked out of his winter cap and hung down over his forehead. His blue eyes shifted between the two women and landed back on Clara.

"You could come on my sled, Clara. If you want to." He fidgeted, putting his gloved hands in and out of his pockets. Clara nodded and put her hand on his arm.

"Go and have fun. I promised Erika I would have a turn with her." Annaveta moved to get out of the way of the two lovebirds, pulling the sled behind her.

Erika ran up to her as she walked along the ridge of the hill.

"Kat and I just had a turn with Alex. It was so much fun. He goes so fast. You need to go with him too." Erika pulled the sled string out of Annaveta's hand. "First Kat and I get a turn with you, then Alex will take you."

"Oh, I will, will I?" Her big brother walked up to her and tugged on his little sister's scarf.

"Won't you, Alex?" Erika looked up at him with her big brown eyes. "I promised Annaveta you would take her down the hill. She needs to have a fun, fast ride like you gave me when we went over those bumps and between the trees.

Please?"

"Since you asked so nice, how could I say no?" Alex pulled his sister's hat down over her eyes and winked at Annaveta.

"Oh goody. First, Annaveta is riding with me, so you have to wait your turn," Erika directed her brother, pointing her finger at him. "So you have to wait here for us."

Alex planted his winter boots firmly in the snow. Erika giggled at his antics.

"We can go now, Annaveta. Alex said he would wait for us," Erika said, tugging on her hand. "I see Kat over by Rachel. Kitty Kat!" Erika called out her nickname for her sister as she took hurried steps toward her. "It's our turn to sled with Annaveta now. Come."

Annaveta giggled as she watched the feisty little red-haired girl take charge. She felt like she was seeing a younger version of herself, before she had lost her self-confidence. Before her papa had started getting drunk all the time and hitting her mama. That was before the years of living every day in fear. She had been so young when she freely shared her opinions and thoughts, but that had all changed a long time ago. She had learned to remain silent except with trusted friends. She was glad that Erika didn't have to mask who she was on the inside. She hoped she would always have that kind of freedom.

Annaveta giggled with the two little sisters when they pulled her onto the waiting sled.

Erika sat with Katarina in front and Annaveta behind her on the long wooden sled. They pushed off, speeding down the hill with the younger sisters screaming until they finally came to a stop.

"That was fun. Can we go again?" Katarina said, her blond hair made even whiter by the snow.

"Sure we can," Annaveta gave her a big hug. She loved Clara's little sisters with their opposite personalities. Shy and quiet Katarina, who was so sensitive to others, followed her more talkative and feisty little sister, Erika, around. They got along so well together. Annaveta thought Clara was like the sister she had always wanted but never had. Of course, Pavla was still a good friend too, but she lived her life too much by the old ways. For some reason, Clara seemed more loving and free from the emotions and beliefs that limited others. She wanted to be more like that.

Annaveta hurried to catch up to the girls as they climbed up the hill, both of them pulling the sled together. When they reached the top, Alex was waiting.

"See, my brother is waiting for you," Erika said, eyeing the new sled Alex stood beside. "Can we try your new sled too, Alex?"

"After Annaveta has had a turn," Alex tweaked her nose and pulled Annaveta onto the waiting sled. She climbed into a sleek-looking sled that was flat with skis attached to the bottom. Hooks for four sets of feet were on each side of the sled, and there were curved metal handles in front for the driver that turned the front skis.

"Wow, I can't believe you made this sled. It is pretty fancy," Gingerly she sat down close to the front, unsure how this sled worked.

"Thanks. I love working with wood. Put your feet in the feet hooks," He showed her where to sit. "I saw a picture of this in the paper. They said that sleds like this were first made in Switzerland, and now it's a popular sport. It's called a bobsled. We'll be the first ones to try it."

"Well, it looks like an unusual sled. You could easily sell these." She rubbed her gloved hand over the smooth curve at the front end of the sled. "You're very good."

"I've thought about it. Maybe I will." He smiled at her and climbed on the sled behind her. His long legs stretched out on either side of her, his feet slipping into his foot stirrups. Annaveta's skin tingled with warmth as his arms brushed hers. He pulled himself closer to her so that his chest was snug against her back, and reached both arms around her, grabbing the handles. Her pulse raced at his touch.

"Ah, this is much better." Alex's warm breath tickled her ears. "Make sure you hold tight to the sides of the sled because I have a feeling we're about to go really fast."

"What do you mean by 'really fast'?" Annaveta crinkled her forehead in concern. She turned her head to the side, waiting for his answer.

"Don't worry, beautiful. I've got you." Alex nuzzled his cold nose against her cheek and laughed as he gave the sled a big push. Annaveta had no time to think before they took off.

She gripped the sides of the sled with all her might as they went speeding down the hill. They passed all the other sleds. Alex steered the sled around a small bush, then they went over a bump, gaining speed the closer they got to the bottom. They slid between the tall trees, and kept going past the place where most sleds stopped. They had slowed a little, but were still going at a fast pace, when they neared the river's edge.

Without warning, the sled hit a large bump. Annaveta flew off and landed on her backside on something hard. She thought she heard a crack as she landed. Sitting up, she tried to catch her breath. Looking around, she spotted Alex lifting his head up behind a snow-covered bank of the river. Hearing a loud crunch behind her, she froze.

She looked down and saw she was sitting on the ice. On the river. She panicked as she caught sight of the deep crack in the ice beside her. She moved to crawl away from the snapping sounds erupting around her. Russian folklore filled her mind. Mama had told her tales of the ghost of a young maiden, a *rusalka*, who walked the fields luring young men into her underwater palace, where they drowned. She shook her head dispelling the vivid image from her mind. She was no *rusalka*.

"Alex, help me. I'm on the ice." Her voice quivered in fear as she looked up, seeing his movements from behind the bushes. "Do you hear the cracking?" She saw Alex nod as he looked at the ice around her. He moved faster, getting closer to her with each step.

"I'm terrified. Please hurry. I don't know how to swim." Annaveta's whole body shook with fear. How would she get off the ice in time before it opened up and swallowed her? She was terror-stricken at the thought of going into icy water. It was a death trap.

Larger cracks formed on the surface like a spiderweb, trapping her. She inched forward.

"Annaveta, you have to start crawling forward. Move off the ice. Hurry." Alex ran, racing down to the river's edge.

"I'm trying," Annaveta half sobbed, half yelled at him. Crawling on her hands and knees, she slid carefully forward. Looking up she saw that solid ground was still ten feet away. Right now it seemed impossible to get there. Her heart jumped to her throat. Its pounding rang in her ears.

Another loud crack split the air, paralyzing her. The break in the ice beside her ruptured and grew wider. She forced herself to move faster. The background noises of the laughter of children on the hill seemed to taunt her. Would she make it off this ice alive? She felt powerless against the elements around her. Urging her stiff knees and hands forward, she inched her way closer to solid ground.

All of a sudden, the ice around her cracked wider. One knee fell through to the freezing water beneath. She tried to pull her body up with her hands, but before she could, her other leg fell through. Screaming, she went down, the frigid water swallowing her. Her hands reached up, fumbling for the edge of the ice. She pulled her head up out of the water and yelled.

"Alex! Help!" Water filled her ears, nose, and mouth as she went under the frozen river water again.

"Hang on!" Alex's shout of fear echoed across the ice as she came up for air again. She grabbed the ice with her hands, hanging on with all her might. She felt so tired, and her body was beginning to numb from the cold. With feeble movements she kicked her legs to help propel her body up onto the ice, but her sudden movement only made it worse. The weight of her heavy coat threatened to pull her further under.

The ice cracked even more under the heavy weight of her wet clothes, and she sank into the frigid water. The painfully cold water saturated her hair and numbed her face as she thrashed her arms, trying to free herself of the coat that strangled her. Kicking her feet, she managed to surface again, grasping wildly for something to hold onto. But her hands only slid off the ice.

She gasped for air before going under again.

Her legs seemed like unwilling players in her fight for survival. They hardly moved; her kicks got slower. She couldn't feel her arms even though she was reaching up. Somehow she couldn't find her way to the edge of the ice. Closing her eyes, she resigned herself to her fate.

So this is how it feels to die. The numbness just takes over until you can't feel anything anymore. There are so many things I wish I had told Clara and Alex, so many things I wish I had done, that now I'll never know . . .

Suddenly she felt a hand grab hers. It pulled her up until her head surfaced. She gasped for air, and her mouth burned from the cold.

"Annaveta, hang on to me. I've got you. I won't let you go. I promise." Alex tugged on her hands with all his might. Her upper body slid along the hard surface of the ice until finally her whole body lay sprawled on top of the ice. She could hardly move, unable to feel her limbs. Closing her eyes, shivers racked her body, and her teeth chattered so hard she thought her jaw would break. She just wanted to sleep.

"Wake up, my love." Alex patted her cheek with her hand. "You can't sleep. We need to get back to the river bank now. Then I'll warm you up. I promise."

"Can't move. So tired." She moaned, her eyelids feeling so heavy.

"If you can't move, then I'll pull you. We are getting off this unstable ice right now."

He tugged on her hands. She felt herself being pulled along the hard, cold surface. It seemed like it took forever, but in only a few minutes they made it to the river's edge.

He pulled her drenched coat off, but she couldn't move; she was so cold and numb. He wrapped her in his dry jacket and put her on his lap and sat down. His arms shook as he held her in a tight embrace, the warmth of his body binding her to him.

"You're cold. We can share," she said, opening up the coat he had wrapped around her.

"No. You keep that on. We need to get you warm." Alex turned her so she was facing him and started kissing her forehead, eyelids, and cheeks. He paused, his arms still trembling.

"That's not why I'm shaking," he murmured as his warm lips scattered kisses down her neck, pulling back her wet hair as he went.

"Why then?" Annaveta hated to ask, afraid he would stop the kisses that were warming her already.

"I'm shaking because I nearly lost you today." Alex looked into her eyes with a look so intense that the heat of it scorched her deep inside. "I realized today that I love you with all that's in me. I can't lose you, Annaveta; I just can't. You're in my blood. In my heart. In my soul."

Her body seemed to come to life at his words of love. She had almost drowned, and he had saved her life today—twice. He had done so much for her. She knew she loved him.

"I love you too. With all my heart, I do." She finally spoke the words that had been locked inside. The ice that had encased her heart melted from the heat of his love. His kisses pierced her skin like arrows finding their way straight to her heart.

"Ah, those are the words I've longed to hear from your pretty lips." He rained kisses on her hair, forehead, cheeks, and nose, leaving featherlight kisses all across her face until he found her lips. He kissed her until she could hardly catch her breath.

"You know my heart, my love." He stopped his kisses to looked deeply into her eyes, his voice calling to her heart like an impassioned plea. "Now I'm asking you to make a life with me. Will you marry me?"

She looked at him, wanting desperately to say yes. The impulsive voice inside her told her to run to the nearest church to get married. If she were to marry, she couldn't do better than Alex Wagner. She told herself maybe she didn't have to leave this family she had come to love. Maybe by now her attacker was dead or too scared to come back. The other voice told her that it was because she loved him that she could never consider marriage to him even as he asked. Alex Wagner was a man with dreams and ambitions. She was a Russian peasant girl with nothing to offer him, but a curse that followed her everywhere she went. There was nothing she could give him. She would only take away. And she couldn't do that to him. She loved him too much to offer him a life with someone who was being haunted by her past both from the inside and the outside. Most of all she needed him and his family to be safe. If she was out of his life, then he would be safe.

"I desperately want to say yes, but I can't. I just can't marry you. There's too many lives at stake." She kissed him slowly, pouring all the love she had in her heart into the kiss. Tears flooded her eyes and she stood up on shaking legs, looking at him one last time.

"What do you mean you can't marry—" Alex stopped when he heard someone calling for them.

"Alex, Annaveta, where are you?" The voice got louder as it came closer.

"This isn't over, Annaveta. We will talk this through, later. Now I've got to get you warm." His mouth had thinned into a straight line of irritation as he stared at her. The broken expression on his face as he picked her up in his arms broke her heart. With hurried steps he carried her toward the top of the hill toward the fire that someone had started for all the sledders. She felt weighted with sorrow but only nodded at him, too tired to argue, pretending to agree with his words. But she knew in her heart that she was letting him go for the last time.

Chapter 21

"ANNAVETA." MRS. WAGNER'S SOFT WHISPER echoed in the quiet room.

Annaveta looked up and saw the light from her lantern casting a soft glow in the dark. "Wake up."

"I'm awake. What's wrong?" Annaveta sat up in bed, wondering what had happened. She still felt the effects of yesterday's near drowning, but she was thankful she didn't seem to have a fever or cold. She had just woken up upon hearing Mrs. Wagner's footsteps. Her plan had been to leave this night after everyone was asleep, for she didn't want to have to face Alex only to hurt him again. But from the sound of Mrs. Wagner's voice, she needed her today.

"We have to go help a young woman who is about to deliver her first baby." Mrs. Wagner touched her arm. "Get dressed quickly. The new papa-to-be is waiting in the kitchen, and he's anxious to get back to his wife. I'll leave the lantern for you to find your way to the kitchen."

"I'm on my way." Annaveta found her worn but clean work blouse and skirt and slipped them on, then put on her warmest stockings as a barrier to the cold. With hurried movements she braided her hair into a crown, picked up the lantern, and walked to the kitchen. Mrs. Wagner was busy putting herbs and clean cloths into her basket. Annaveta was putting her boots on, when a man stood up from his chair and spoke.

"Why is she coming? I don't want this Russian helping

my wife." Blacksmith Kauffman's tone was filled with scorn. Annaveta stopped and waited for Mrs. Wagner to decide. She didn't want to go where she wasn't wanted.

"I see you've been listening to the rumors that have been spread around the colony about this girl." Mrs. Wagner looked him in the eye.

"Well, I just assumed—" Blacksmith Kauffman began.

"Well, don't believe everything you hear. Now, do you want us to come and help your wife or not?" Mrs. Wagner included her in her question, and it made Annaveta feel wanted and valued. Not many people had stood up for her before.

"*Ja,* she needs you." He looked at Mrs. Wagner and nodded his acceptance of her terms. Annaveta quickly put her coat and gloves on and followed Mrs. Wagner out the door.

Stepping out into the dark cold morning, they could barely see by the light of the moon, as the sun had yet to come over the horizon. They followed Blacksmith Kaufmann to the waiting wagon. Herr Kaufmann clucked for the horses to go as they made their way in the falling snow through the streets to his home.

Annaveta was thankful not only for another delivery to earn more money but that she could learn from Mrs. Wagner. She was so knowledgeable about bringing babies into the world and healing in general that already Annaveta had doubled what she knew since she first arrived.

"Annaveta," Mama Wagner nudged her arm. "We're here; time to get going."

"Oh, sorry. I was thinking." Annaveta grabbed the basket and jumped off the wagon. Herr Kaufmann helped Mrs. Wagner down and led them to the small house. Just as Herr Kaufmann opened the door, a scream split the air. The worried man ran to help his wife.

"Annaveta, you start the water to boil, then come to the bedroom," Mrs. Wagner said as she hurried to get her jacket and boots off.

Mrs. Wagner ran to the back bedroom, and Annaveta hurried to the kitchen. There she found an old stove with a large pot on the burner. She spied a big barrel of water and filled up the pot with water. Then she found wood to add to the stove to rekindle the dying fire. Leaving the water to heat, Annaveta rushed to help Mrs. Wagner. Sounds of screaming and moaning were getting louder as she approached the bedroom. Lying on the bed was a small woman, whose smooth skin and blond hair revealed her young age. She was turning her sweat-soaked head from side to side as she moaned, her body writhing in pain.

"You are doing good, Joanna," Mrs. Wagner said to the laboring woman. Her words had a calming effect on her. Her husband sat in a chair by her side, his eyes never leaving his wife's face. "Why don't you go check to see if that water is boiling, Mr. Kaufmann? We need to let nature take its course. From what I can tell, it shouldn't be too much longer until you'll have a new little one to hold."

With Blacksmith Kaufmann no longer in the room, Annaveta breathed a sigh of relief. Now she could concentrate without feeling like she was being judged. She dipped a clean cloth in the pail of tepid water and sponged off beads of moisture on Mrs. Kaufman's forehead. The weary woman now lay on the bed quiet.

All of a sudden shouts were heard, followed by loud knocking at the front door. Blacksmith Kauffman's gruff voice was heard arguing with whoever was at the door. They could hear the words from the bedroom.

'This is an emergency. My mama is dying." The boyish voice on the other side pleaded. "Papa said not to come home without the midwife."

"I will see what she says," The sound of Blacksmith Kauffman's heavy footsteps rang through the bedroom until they stopped at the bedroom door.

"Frau Wagner, may I talk to you a moment?" He looked

nervous as his eyes went from his weary wife to the midwife.

"*Ja.*" Mrs. Wagner turned to Annaveta. "I will be right back. Just keep talking to Mrs. Kauffmann."

Annaveta nodded, and after a few moments wished she could hear the whispered tones as they walked to the kitchen. It wasn't long before Mrs. Wagner came back to the birthing room.

"There is an emergency with Frau Zimmerman's eleventh child. They need me right away." Mrs. Wagner took hold of Johanna's hand. "You will be fine. It seems like everything is coming along smoothly here. Annaveta will see to you, and I'll be back as fast as I can."

"I need you too," The fear in Mrs. Kauffman's eyes was tangible.

"You will be fine, and I will be back as soon as I can. I promise. You're in good hands with Annaveta. She has helped deliver quite a few babies already and has done a fine job of it." Mrs. Wagner's words seemed to calm the woman's fears.

Mrs. Wagner nodded to Annaveta and followed Blacksmith Kauffmann to the boy who waited impatiently for her. When the door closed behind them, Mrs. Kauffmann started screaming in pain again. Worry tried to strangle Annaveta's throat. She swallowed and did her best to speak calmly.

"Let me see what is happening, okay?" Annaveta waited until the thrashing woman calmed, then placed her hand inside Johanna's birth canal. The size of this babe seemed much too large for this small woman. Annaveta blew out a breath. *I don't know if I can do this. It's worse than Mrs. Wagner thought. I'll just have to do my very best and try to remember what I've been taught. God, you've helped me before. I'm asking for Your help again.*

Let's move you into a better position." Annaveta helped the woman sit so her head was and back was a little higher. and placed more pillows behind her back. "This will help." When she saw Mrs. Kauffmann nod, she massaged her bulging belly to encourage movement. Patiently her hands worked until there was another contraction.

"Something has changed." The woman's worn-out face was chalk white from the strain of the labor. "I feel so tired."

"You can rest once this little one has made its way into the world. You need to try pushing now," Annaveta encouraged. She pushed back panic again. Her patient's body was becoming listless, and she just lay there moaning, her pale face beaded with moisture.

"You have to get this baby out now. When you feel the next contraction, you need to push—hard. If you don't, either the baby or you will die." Annaveta's earnest words ignited a final burst of energy in the exhausted mama.

"I need to push," she said through gritted teeth, bearing down with all the strength left in her. Blue veins on her face protruded as she gave a fierce thrust. Annaveta moved to see what was happening.

"I see the baby's head. One more push and your baby will be here."

The weary mama gasped for air between each push.

The last thrust was one that shook the bed. Mrs. Kauffmann's whole body trembled as a red wrinkled baby came out of her small, tired body. Annaveta caught the slippery blond-haired baby boy in her hands. Looking down, she noticed that the baby wasn't the only thing that spilled out of the Mrs. Kauffmann's body. Annaveta was horrified as she saw blood pouring onto the sheets in an ever-widening circle.

"My baby?" The woman's eyes closed as her whispered words carried to Annaveta.

"You have a handsome baby boy." Annaveta forced herself to smile and act like nothing was wrong. She cut the cord and cleaned out the baby's mouth. He still wasn't crying, so she hurried to dip him into the cool water, then into the warm water, again and again until finally a whimpered cry was heard.

She wrapped him in a warm blanket and brought him to his mama. Mrs. Kauffman's arm moved slightly to embrace her baby, but it seemed to Annaveta that this woman's life was draining away. She moved to see if the flow of blood had ceased, but to her shock, the darkening circle was twice as large as it had been. She removed the soiled sheets and added some new ones, which were soon stained blood red. Massaging her patient's abdomen, she hoped the afterbirth would expel quickly. More blood gushed out. A sudden coldness hit Annaveta at her core as she realized this woman would most likely die. Today.

"Call my husband." Mrs. Kauffmann's whispered words rang like funeral bells in Annaveta's ears. She hurried to the kitchen and found Blacksmith Kauffmann pacing the floor.

"Come quick. Your wife is asking for you," Annaveta croaked out, panic lacing her words. "You have a new baby boy."

He hurried to the birthing room with Annaveta at his heels. She saw him stop at the sight of all the blood.

"What happened?" He pointed to the bloody sheet and without waiting for an answer looked up at his wife's pale face. He walked to his wife's side and cradled her face, kissing her cheeks. "My Johanna, I love you. Don't leave me." Tears poured down his cheeks as he sat beside his dying wife's side.

"Take care . . . our son, John. I love . . . you." Elsa Kauffman whispered her last words, and closed her eyes.

Annaveta looked at the girl-woman lying so still on the bed. Her sweat-soaked blond curls lying over the pillow made her skin look even whiter, the way Annaveta imagined an angel would look.

She could hardly stand to listen to Blacksmith Kauffmann's heartrending sobs as he laid his head on his wife's bosom. The little baby's cries reached her ears, and she reached over and gently lifted him away from the lifeless body of his mama. Walking to the kitchen, she held him close and whispered in his ear. Still the little one cried. She spied a jar of milk sitting in the cold box and found a clean cloth and dipped it in the milk. Using her finger, she put the milk-covered cloth to his mouth. Sure enough, he sucked every drop out of it and cried when it was gone. She gave him more until at last he fell asleep in her arms.

The house had gone quiet. There was no more sobbing. With slow steps, she tiptoed back to the bedroom to see what happened. Blacksmith Kauffman looked like he was in shock to see her there. Within moments his face changed from sadness to an ugly, angry red. She took a few steps back.

"You! It's your fault. You made my wife die," He got up, his walk and tone threatening. He saw her holding his son and grabbed him. "Give me my son." Annaveta backed further away, her limbs shaking with fear.

"I'm sorry, Mr. Kauffman. I tried my best." Annaveta's tears covered her cheeks. Her lips trembled, and she tasted blood as she bit her lip.

"Well, sorry doesn't bring her back, does it?" His finger shook as he pointed to the still form of his wife. "I should never have let Mrs. Wagner bring a Russian along to tend to my wife. All of you Ruskies are lazy and worthless. You should not have come here or to this colony."

"I tried to—"Annaveta began, but her words were cut off by the enraged man.

"There is no excuse." His whole body shook, causing the babe to cry in alarm, his cries filling the room. "Get your things and get out of this house. Now!"

Annaveta moved past him, her feet stumbling in her haste. She gathered the scissors and other dirty cloths that were on the chair in the corner put them in her basket, and moved as fast as she could out of the room. He followed her to the front door, his face still red with anger. She grabbed her coat and boots, barely putting them on before he opened the door.

"I'll see to it that you never help birth another baby in this colony ever again." His words pierced her heart as she stumbled outside. "You are not a midwife. You are a murderer."

Tears streamed down her cheeks like a dense waterfall; she could barely see her way on the road ahead. She ran through the icy streets, slipping and falling to her knees as she reached the Wagner home. How would she explain what happened today? It was bad enough that most of the girls her age in Pleve Colony spoke against her, but now everyone who lived here would brand her as something much worse than a loose woman—they would call her a murderer.

Chapter 22

ANNAVETA HUGGED HER SMALL BUNDLE of clothes closely to her chest as she forced her numb legs forward on the snow-covered streets. Her legs were still sore from nearly drowning, but she had been determined to go ahead with her plans to leave. With a heavy heart she trudged the first few miles from Pleve Colony toward the nearest train station in Sursk. Each step took her farther away from Alex. She had left him a note explaining that she needed to leave so he and his family would be safe. She poured her heart out in her note, telling him she loved him and that she hoped he would find someone else he could love to fulfill all his hopes and dreams. But she didn't tell him where she was going, because she knew he would try to search for her.

No matter how hard she tried, she couldn't stop the tears that flowed freely down her cold cheeks. She had lost the one true love of her life. But she had no choice; she had to let him go. It was the hardest thing she had ever had to do.

Last night she had told Mrs. Wagner of Mrs. Kauffman's death and had explained everything she had done. Mrs. Wagner had held her as she cried and told her there was nothing she would have done differently herself. She didn't want Annaveta to worry. But having a woman die under her care was the last straw for Annaveta. Now the Wagners's good name would be questioned because they had harbored her in their home. In this colony she would be branded a murderer. Her fate was sealed.

Looking up, her eyes widened at the ribbons of yellow and cinnamon light scattered across the early dawn sky. A portal of light beckoned her from above and reached down to the earth below. It was a sign. Even if she couldn't see it now, there was a sliver of hope of something new. Hearing the clacking sound of hooves and the squeak of wagon wheels, she turned. The old farmer driving the wagon offered her a ride to the village. It was noon by the time the man dropped her off near the train station.

She reached inside her coat pocket and fingered the money she had there. She hoped she had enough rubles to take her as far as Moscow, but secretly she wanted to go to St. Petersburg. She thought of what Mr. Wagner had read in the newspaper, that they needed nurses. Maybe she could find work there. She hurried past the few people she saw, keeping her head lowered so she would not be recognized by anyone from Pleve Colony.

Her steps were as heavy as her heart as she walked along the wooden boardwalk toward the station's small cabin-like building. She pulled open the creaky wood-slatted door.

Warmth greeted her as she entered the dimly lit room. She walked to the stove, pulling her hands out of Mrs. Wagner's homemade mittens and rubbing them together so she could feel her fingers again. Looking around the room, she relaxed a little, as it was empty of people except for the dark-haired clerk standing behind the counter.

"Can I help you, miss?" He placed his eyeglass by his right eye as if to get a better look at her.

"Uh, yes." Annaveta made her way to the counter, feeling a little nervous. She didn't know if the money she'd counted in her pocket would cover the cost of the train ride.

"I am looking for a one-way ticket to St. Petersburg. Could you tell me the cost?" Her nervous fingers plucked invisible lint off her coat as she awaited his reply.

"Let me check my list of train fares." The clerk's brown eye bulged with the weight of the eyeglass as it wavered on its delicate perch. "When were you wanting to leave?"

"Today, if possible." Annaveta jerked a little as the door squeaked open. She lowered and turned her head to see who stood behind her. It was an old man, someone she didn't recognize. Letting out the breath she held, she turned to look at the clerk and hoped he couldn't read the fear in her eyes. There was no one she could talk to and rely on. No one was by her side to protect her. Missing Alex more than she believed was possible, she swallowed the fear that tried to paralyze her. She forced herself to control her breathing and calm down. She lifted her head and squared her shoulders, then looked the clerk in the eye.

"The train is scheduled to arrive in one hour. It will take a few days before it arrives in St. Petersburg. There will be scheduled stops on the way." The clerk eyed her with doubt as he named the price. This trip would take almost all the money she had, but she needed to do it. There wasn't any way she could stay here.

She had left a note for the Wagner family too, explaining that she couldn't stay and risk bringing anymore harm to their family. She told them she didn't want to let them know where she was going in case trouble followed, but she would write them later. Annaveta thanked them for all they had done for her, but now she needed to make her own way. She hoped Clara's Papa and Mama would understand that it was time for her to leave.

Warm tears trailed down her cheeks as she handed over the rubles to the clerk in exchange for a passenger ticket. Drying her eyes, she walked over to the wooden bench near the warmth of the woodstove, and sat down.

Not too much later the sound of the rumbling train accompanied by its shrill whistle pierced the air. Annaveta jumped to her feet, glad that the train had finally arrived. She stood in the short lineup as the conductor checked the tickets of the three people ahead of her. Then, he punched a hole in her ticket, and she found her seat number. The elderly couple across the aisle frowned at her as she sat down and let out a heavy sigh of relief. She gave them a faint look of apology before she laid her head against the seat. Still clutching the small bundle of clothes in her hands, she let her weary body rest.

THE JOSTLE OF PEOPLE BUMPING into her seat startled Annaveta awake. She opened her eyes to a long line of people headed to their seats and moved over as a young couple with two small children sat down across from her. She moved closer to the window. Looking outside, she saw the sun beginning to rise. A steady flow of horse-drawn carriages moved in front of the many rows of buildings. Annaveta guessed by the large buildings she saw surrounding a big square in the distance that they had arrived in Moscow.

She turned back and gave a little smile to the couple and their children. The mama was busy pulling out sandwiches from her handmade bag. The smell of the sandwiches made Annaveta's stomach growl. It had been a whole day since she had eaten anything. She had a little bit of bread and cheese that she had stuffed into her bag from Mrs. Wagner's pantry, but she would save that for later. Instead, she pulled out her small jar of water and took a deep drink. That would have to keep her for a little while longer.

"I am so exhausted. Get me out of this crush of people. I need my private berth immediately." The shrill demand of a cultured lady's voice rose above the others.

Annaveta watched as a very pregnant lady in a expensive green silk dress walked past her seat. She was followed by two porters and a maid carrying the heavy bags and extras that most ladies of quality would bring.

"Countess Tashkova, let me help you to your seat." The conductor offered his arm to the lady as she wobbled toward the first-class berths. Annaveta shook her head as she watched the countess surrounded by people vying for her attention.

Annaveta was glad that no one besides the conductor knew who she was. She wanted to keep it that way. She thought of the madman who had scared her these past few months with the note, the attack, and the mutilated cow. She hoped that by going as far away as possible she would no longer need to worry about someone coming after her. Dark thoughts of the two most likely people who could be after her — Misha and Monsieur Arnaud, filled her. Maybe it was someone else after her. But who? She ran a shaky hand lightly along her hair, putting stray wisps back into her bun. How she missed Alex and wished he was there to protect her.

Annaveta's eyes filled with tears at the thought. She'd also had to leave Clara, her one true friend in the world. Yet, she knew that she would understand. Annaveta had explained to Clara about Blacksmith Kauffman's cruel words and how she felt she had to leave before their family name was ruined.

Annaveta's mind raced with all the feelings of hurt, pain, and fear that mingled with the devastating loss of family — something she had now suffered not just once but twice. Tears flowed down her cheeks as her heart ached from the weight of it all. Turning her head toward the window, she gently dabbed at her cheeks with her fingers at the tears that she couldn't seem to stop. The dull-gray sky from which dark clouds dangled over miles of farmland mirrored her dark mood. Spatters of rain dropped on the window, keeping time with her own tears. Looking out at the vast land, she hoped there would be something in St. Petersburg for her. Maybe she might even find a friend. But most of all she hoped she wouldn't cause anyone else pain and that she wouldn't be bothered by anyone. She hoped Monsieur Arnaud and Misha wouldn't be able to find her. Maybe she would be able to get lost in a city the size of St. Petersburg.

Since being branded a murderer in Pleve Colony by the

grieving Herr Kauffman, she was scared to be a midwife again. To her, it seemed that everywhere she went all she caused was pain, and most of it was to ones she loved. It would have been better for everyone if she had died in the fire alongside her family.

"Here you go." The little girl from the seat across from her could barely be heard over the loud sounds of the rumbling train. With her dark-brown curls bobbing from the swaying train, her hand reached out to Annaveta, a handkerchief hanging from her small fingers. Her papa pulled her back to sit on his knee, holding her tight.

"Thank you."

The mama handed Annaveta a slice of bread. "I could hear your stomach rumbling. We don't have much, but what we have we can share." The woman's kind eyes were similar to her daughter's.

"I couldn't." Annaveta shook her head as she looked at the children.

"Please, take it." Her eyes pleaded. "We have enough for our little family."

Annaveta took the bread, savoring every bite until her stomach felt comfortable again.

"Thank you." Annaveta nodded at the couple, who smiled back at her. She drew some animal pictures for the children until they got tired. The constant movement of the train lulled the children to sleep, and it wasn't long until Annaveta's eyes closed.

"Is there a doctor on the train?" The conductor walked along the rows of seats, holding a speakerphone in front of his mouth. He looked at the people on both sides of the aisle to see if anyone would come out. Annaveta could hear his booming voice as he called out throughout the length of the train. She wondered what was wrong, until she heard whispers among the passengers.

"She is having labor pains right now. I overheard her maid talking to the conductor," a gray-haired matron said to a friend across the aisle.

"Who? The countess?" A plump red-haired lady put her gloved hands to her mouth in shock as her voice resonated in a stage whisper.

"Yes. That's why the conductor is desperately trying to find a doctor. If no one steps forward, they'll start asking for midwives next. Just you wait and see." The matron adjusted her hat as she continued to talk about Countess Tashkova's husband, their grand estate, and their connections to the imperial family. Annaveta thought of the countess having a baby on the train and quivered in fear. Memories of the last birthing filled her mind with terror of going through that again. She squeezed her eyes shut and forced herself to think of something else.

"Does anyone here have experience as a midwife?" the conductor now asked in an anxious voice as he walked back through the middle of the train where Annaveta was seated. Annaveta didn't look up. There was no way she was going to be responsible for another woman's death. She didn't want more blood on her hands. So she sat there looking down and then out the window at the scenery. Anything to keep the conductor from noticing her as he continued to the front of the chugging train.

It was quiet again in her section, so she relaxed and put her head back to rest. Without warning the bang of the door between the train cars jerked her whole body and made her sit up.

"Listen, everyone, we are desperate here. I have a woman in labor who will die if she doesn't get some help right now." The conductor's eyes anxiously searched the occupants' faces hoping for some sign. "Please, if you can do anything at all, come help."

Annaveta's stomach clenched as she battled within herself. Her palms grew sweaty as she remembered what had happened last time. Fear warred against using the gift she knew she'd been given.

"You need to help this woman. Do not fear. I will be with you. I will show you the way."

Surprised, she looked around to see who had spoken to her. The family across from her were busy talking to each other. The older couple across the aisle were sleeping, and the people on the seat in front were eating. None of them had spoken to her. She wondered, who had spoken?

"I am here with you. Go now and use the gift I have given you."

She closed her eyes as she realized God was speaking to her. He wanted her to help this woman. She wouldn't be alone.

"I will help the woman." Annaveta looked up, her voice shaking. Fear and insecurity wrapped themselves around her throat as she spoke. "I have had a little training as a midwife."

"Oh, thank God." The conductor held out his hand to help her up. "Please, let's hurry."

She followed the conductor through the next train car to the front, where the first-class passengers were located. She could hear the sounds of a woman screaming in pain before she entered. He threw the door open as they hurried to follow the sound.

Annaveta stepped through the door of the berth to the cries of the woman on the bed. Watching the countess writhing in pain, her face twisted in agony, was more than Annaveta's soft heart could handle. She went to the woman and held her hand. She sponged her face as she talked to her.

"I am here to help you," Annaveta said confidently. "We will deliver this baby safely and with all speed, but I need your help."

The countess gripped her hand tightly with her own and nodded, letting out another moan.

"Now then, let me see what is going on." Annaveta's gentle hands moved along the pregnant woman's belly to find out the position of the baby. Everything seemed in order from what she could tell by touching the countess's belly. But somehow she felt compelled to check inside the birth canal. There, she could tell the baby's shoulder was somehow stuck behind the mama's pelvic bone. She remembered Mrs. Wagner had mentioned different birthing positions that had helped with another woman's labor and delivery.

Annaveta spoke to the maid who was sponging the countess's face and arms. "If you could go ask for boiled water, scissors, and some clean cloths, and bring them here, that would be helpful." The young dark-haired maid left to see what she could find.

"The babe needs a little more room." Annaveta stopped and waited. The next contraction caused Countess Tashkova's eyes to widen as waves of pain overwhelmed her body.

"I need you to lift your knees up to the abdomen. That should help," Annaveta instructed as soon as the pains had gone. Wearily the countess gave a small nod. The maid entered the room with the necessary supplies, and Annaveta asked for her help to move the countess. With both of them working together, they managed to get her into position.

"How does that feel?" Annaveta rubbed her hand in soothing circular motions on the Countess's protruding stomach.

"Feels much better. Here comes — " Countess Tashkova didn't finish her words as another big contraction came. She pushed this time, and when Annaveta looked at the opening to the birth canal, she saw little tufts of dark hair sticking out.

"I can see the baby's head." Annaveta encouraged the panting woman. "A few more pushes, and you will hold your precious babe in your arms."

Countess Tashkova pushed as hard as she could two more times before the baby slipped into Annaveta's waiting hands.

"You have a big beautiful baby boy, Countess." Annaveta removed the phlegm from the baby's mouth and nose, then tied off and snipped the cord. The baby boy started crying, his face changing from a shade of blue to a nice healthy pink. After giving instructions to the maid to clean the little one and wrap him in clean blankets, she turned her attention to the countess. She rubbed her womb in circular motions until the afterbirth came out. The maid helped her clean up the soiled linens.

"I'll help you get comfortable." Annaveta shifted her so that a few pillows cushioned her head. "How do you feel?"

"So much better." Countess Tashkova looked weary as the maid handed the little baby boy to her. "He's just beautiful. The count will be pleased."

Annaveta smiled in wonder — not only in gratitude for the beautiful baby boy but for the mama's good health. Annaveta's heart whispered a prayer upward. *Thank you for helping me and showing me how.*

"Thank you for helping me today. I wouldn't have survived without your help." The countess's blue eyes filled with tears as she kissed her baby's head. "You saved my life and the life of my little boy." Countess Tashkova's shaky hand reached out took Annaveta's hand in hers. Then she closed her eyes, letting out a long sigh.

Annaveta's face flushed at the praise, relieved that the birthing was over and had gone so smoothly. "I am glad I was here to help."

"Do you have family expecting you when you get off the train?" Countess Tashkova looked up from staring at her baby's face to see her response.

She wasn't sure why the countess would ask her if she had family in the city, but she decided she would answer.

"No. I will be looking for work," It felt a little odd answering these questions to a stranger, but she was careful not to give too much information. And the countess seemed grateful that she had helped with her son's birth. She poured water into a cup and handed it to the countess.

The countess took a small sip and studied Annaveta for a moment. "I would like to offer you a position as nanny at our estate in St. Petersburg. You see, our old nanny is retiring in a couple of weeks to go help her daughter. I can tell you must be great with children with your gentle ways. You would be in charge of our three-year-old daughter, Ekaterina, and now our new baby boy, Nicholas, as well."

Countess Tashkova's compliment and kinds words sent a wave of relief through Annaveta's heart. Now she would have a job and a safe place to live.

"I would like that." Annaveta's eyes filled with tears as she nodded. She was so grateful for this new opportunity. All her anxious thoughts about where she would live and what work she might find had worried her as she started this journey, and now the solution was right in front of her. Someone was watching out for her.

She smiled as she watched Countess Tashkova and her new little one drift off to sleep.

Chapter 23

ALEX WOKE UP WITH A pounding headache, his body weak and muscles sore. The burning feeling he had in his right arm yesterday was like a dull throb now. He remembered being shot and pulling Annaveta out from the icy river water, then he closed his eyes, smiling as he relived holding her close and kissing her sweet lips. She had finally told him that she loved him. It seemed like he had been waiting forever to hear those words. His heart hurt from her refusal to marry him, but he wasn't planning on giving up on her—on them. He would talk to her today and convince her that she needed to marry him.

He hoped she was okay after her near drowning accident. He had hurried her to the fire they had going at the top of the hill, and the women had helped her get dry. She seemed tired, but there was no signs of fever when they had brought her home. He couldn't wait to see her today.

"*Ach*, Alex, you're awake." His mama came into his room carrying a cup of tea. "We've all been so worried about you. You've been lying here sick with fever for three days and just last night the fever broke. *Gott* be thanked. But by the look of the bandage on your arm you have some explaining to do."

"Wait, I've been lying here for three days?" He moved to sit up on the lumpy mattress, his head dizzy with the movement. He lifted his eyes to look at his mama. "I can't believe I've been sick for so long. I've got to get up. There are a few things I need to take care of." He really hoped his mama wouldn't want to talk for too long. Impatiently he ran his fingers through his hair.

"First, I would like to hear about what happened to your arm." Mama's calm voice reminded him again of why she was the colony's most trusted midwife and healer.

"Annaveta and I were shot at by a man on our way back from the meadow. It was clear he had been following us, waiting for his opportunity to strike." He told her what happened. "So, don't let Annaveta go anywhere by herself. It's too dangerous."

"What? Oh, Son, how could this happen to you?" His mama jerked her head back with a loud gasp. Her eyes were wide with what looked like fear. "Someone nearly killed you. Do you know who it was?"

"No, his face was hidden behind a large scarf." Alex reached over and rubbed the top of his mama's hand. "We'll find whoever it is, Mama. I'll talk to Papa today so he can talk to the the colony elders about the threat to the colony."

"Just promise me you'll be careful, with whatever you do." She scrunched her forehead, giving her that worried look he knew so well. He nodded and rubbed his throbbing arm, thinking about his attacker. He then smiled at his mama, hoping to shake off some of her worry.

She shook her head and sat down on the chair near his bed. Hastily she changed the subject. "About Annaveta, Son. There's something you should know." Mama spoke softly, the way she usually did when she had something serious to talk about.

"What is it?" He looked into his mama's eyes and saw worry written there. He'd seen that look before when their first dog, Wolf, had died when he was a little boy. He had been attached to that brown dog who had been so loyal to him. How she was acting made him wonder if someone had died. Then he thought of Annaveta. "Did she get sick from her fall in the water?"

"No, Son, it isn't that."

He let out the breath he'd been holding and relaxed. "Well, what is it then? Everyone else in the family is good?"

"*Ja*, Son. Now stop asking questions so I can tell you." Mama plucked off imaginary crumbs on her apron, not speaking for a few moments. She looked up, a determined look in her eyes. "Well, you'll find out soon enough, so I'll tell you now." She took a big breath and continued. "Annaveta has left us. It was the night after Mrs. Kauffman died in childbirth. We woke up the next morning and she was gone. She left us a note thanking us for taking her into our home, but she said she needed to leave us, so our family would be safe. Now that you told me about the man who attacked you on the trail to the meadow, it is starting to make sense why she would want to leave. As hard as it is to admit it, she really is not safe here."

"What!" He stood up, running his hand through his hair. He then searched frantically for his clothes and said, "I've got to go find her."

"Look at me. I need you to listen." His mama put her hands on his shoulders. He stopped and looked into her worried eyes. "Son, you have to get completely better before you start searching for her. You are still too weak. If you go now, you won't last a day, and then what good will you be to Annaveta? Drink this tea; it'll help you feel better. And don't do anything drastic. We'll talk more when Papa comes in for lunch."

She walked over to the door, stopping suddenly to pull an envelope from her pocket. "Before I forget, here's the note she left for you."

He took the folded, water-stained letter from his mama's hand with his own shaking one. His name scripted so neatly on the top of the fold beckoned him. A part of him worried about being rejected, while another part of him ached to know what she said. He heard the faint click of the door closing in his mama's wake as he pulled open the single sheet written with precise penmanship. He read:

Dear Alex,

I know you will be shocked by this letter, and I'm sorry. By now you will know I have left your wonderful family—and you. I couldn't stay and see you or your family hurt anymore by whoever has been chasing me, hurting your family, and shooting you. I needed to do what I could to help ensure your safety. My heart is breaking, Alex, surely you must know this, but how can I stay? I love you with all that's in me, but it seems once again that life has stepped in and forced me to lose the ones I love. I'm asking you to forget about me and find someone you can love, who will love you more than you ever thought possible. Someone who will help you fulfill all your hopes and dreams. Someone with whom you'll find happiness. I'm so sorry for all the pain I've caused you and your family and would give anything if I could undo the heartache. But know this—I wouldn't have traded getting to know you and your family for the world. For your own safety, I won't tell you where I am going, but know that I will always love you.

Annaveta

Wiping his eyes with the back of his hand, he told himself the tears were the after effects of the fever. He reeled with the shock that she was actually gone. Many emotions warred inside him. He threw the note against the wall, angry that she'd left without telling him. He feared for her safety because she was out there all alone somewhere. Squeezing his eyes shut he relived the precious moments he had with her, and his heart broke as he was reminded that she had asked him to forget about her. How did she think that he would be able to forget her? Annaveta was the only woman who had made his world come alive. Her courage as she faced her family's death, her loyalty to her friends both old and new, and her sacrifice for those she loved topped his list as his reasons why he loved her. It would be impossible to forget her. He needed to find her, and he wouldn't stop until he did. Today he would begin his search.

He dressed in a hurry, making sure the cloth that covered his wound remained in place. His thoughts were on where he needed to begin his search. First, he would ask people in town if they had spotted her leaving the colony. Then he would go to Noltava and talk to Pavla. After brushing his hair, he put Annaveta's letter in his pocket. He would keep her close by.

Inga and Clara were helping Mama with lunch preparations when he walked into the kitchen.

"You are up! How are you feeling?" Inga looked at him in amazement. Clara ran up to him and put her arms around his waist, giving him a big hug.

"I'm so glad you are better." Clara pulled back, and he wiped the tears that came from the corners of her eyes.

"Aw, Clara. You know us Wagners. We're made of hearty stock. Not much can keep us down for long." He put his arm around her shoulders and led her to the table. They sat down, and Alex looked at his sister, wanting answers to his questions.

"Did you know Annaveta was planning to leave, or where she planned to go?"

"*Nein*. She didn't say anything about leaving the colony other than saying that someday she wanted to travel to different places." His sister wiped away the tears that spilled from her eyes. "I'd hoped she would stay here with us."

"Me too, Sister. Me too." He reached over and squeezed her hand. He understood her sadness. "I'll find her, don't worry."

Soon the men were called in for lunch. His mama smiled as she watched him eat heartily. It didn't take long until the children finished and went outside to play.

"Glad you are feeling better, Son." His papa winked at him. "So why don't you tell us the story. Mama says it's a good one."

Alex began with the story of being chased in the meadow

and shot at by an unknown attacker. He had wounded their assailant and chased him, but lost him. Then he reminded his papa of the time he had found Annaveta and him in the pasture shoveling the graves for the cow and calf that had their throats cut.

"This is an violent act done by a very desperate man." Papa's vein became engorged on the side of his face, and his voice deepened in anger. "I did talk with the colony leaders about this. They were shocked that something like this would happen in our peaceful colony, and some blamed us for having a Russian girl stay with us in the first place. But, in the end, they thought it would be better if you went and searched for whoever this person is. They said you would have more information about who would want to come after Annaveta and our family. A couple of men even offered to come with you if you want."

"I think I'll go by myself. I know some of the first places I'm going to look. I'll start with Annaveta's old village of Noltava." Alex shifted in his chair, hesitating before he went on. "Also, I must try to find Annaveta." He saw his parents eye each other. "I love her, and before she left I asked her to be my wife."

"Does she love you? If she loved you, wouldn't she have stayed?" Helmut smirked as he popped one eyebrow up looking at his brother.

"Listen, you idiot. She does love me; she told me so. She also told me the reason she felt she had to leave was so our family would be safe. So there would be no more bloody cows, or shootings at people in our household. She sacrificed herself, for the good of our family." Angry words spewed from his mouth at Helmut. He took a few breaths to calm himself down.

"She's not German, Alex. That might not make for an easy marriage." His mama's soft words were what he already knew.

"I love her, Mama." Alex saw them shaking their heads.

"Besides it's not like it hasn't been done before, a German marrying a Russian."

"That is true. And she is a good, hardworking girl who believes in *Gott*. Those are all things in her favor." Mama Wagner spoke out loud, as if thinking it all through.

"You know we had planned for you to take over the family farm, Alex." Papa's words felt like a dash of cold water on all his dreams. He loved and wanted to honor his parents, but he had dreams in him that wouldn't be denied.

"I know, Papa." Alex considered his next words carefully. "I've learned I really like building furniture more than I like farming. Give the farm to Helmut, Papa." Alex felt like he was pleading his case and winning. "And maybe this is too soon to speak of this. You know I love and want to honor your wishes. I guess I'm asking for your blessing to bring her home. Because right now all I know is that I need to find Annaveta so I can marry her."

His parents looked at each other for a long while before they nodded at each other.

"Then you have our blessing, Son. Find her and bring her safely back home. We will pray *Gott* will help you and for his will to be done." His papa stood, walked over to him, and shook his hand. "You've grown up son. I'm proud of you."

"I love you, Papa." Alex pulled him into a hug, happy that they had resolved some things. "Well, I need to go. Do you mind if I take Blackie?" The large black gelding was Alex's favorite horse and could run fast for longer distances than the others. He didn't feel bad about asking, because all the fieldwork was finished now for the year.

"*Ja*, go ahead. You'll get where you're going quicker with him." His brothers stood up and slapped in on the back, Inga patted him on the shoulder, and Clara squeezed him in a big hug. He brought his bag of clothes from his bedroom, not knowing how long he would be gone.

"Wait. Here's some food to take with you." Mama had packed a bag bulging with food. "Keep warm, and make sure you get your sleep. You are still healing." Her firm tone didn't match the tears he saw in her eyes as she reached for a hug.

"I love you. I'll be back soon." He gave his mama a tight hug and kissed her cheek. After putting on his winter clothes and boots, he looked at his family one last time before he went out into the cold winter air. In his bag, he also carried some cash from his earnings in his furniture-making business. He wanted to be prepared the best he could be for when he found Annaveta.

He hurried to the barn and saddled Blackie, packing a big bag of feed for the large horse. Giving Blackie free rein, they set off at a brisk trot toward the main street of Pleve Colony. Alex asked around at the general store, at the shoemaker's, the bazaar, and every place he could think of if anyone had seen Annaveta. None had, but told him they would keep watch and let him know if they did see her.

Disappointed, Alex turned the horse westward toward Noltava. The air suddenly turned colder, and the falling snow combined with the driving wind, made it hard for him to see his way. He had his hood up and his mama's knitted scarf wrapped tightly around his head, but still his cheeks were numb by the time he made it to the small village. In the dark, he searched out the house that Annaveta had said was Pavla's home.

Tying the horse to a pole outside the house, he knocked, uncertain of his welcome. The raging wind threatened to blow him away from his sure-footed stance by the knotted wooden door in front of him. He knocked again, louder this time.

A woman opened the door a crack, peeking her head around the corner. "What you want? It's late."

"I've come to ask you about a girl named Annaveta. She told me she had stayed in your home a few months ago." Alex was relieved when she waved him to come inside.

Walking into their small home, Alex looked around at the many pairs of eyes staring back at him. He remembered

Annaveta telling him that Pavla had a lot of brothers and sisters, but he didn't expect this many. He saw a large man sitting at the table, holding two children on his knee.

"So, my wife says you have come to ask about Annaveta? Where are you from and how do you know her?" The man clanged his cup on the table a few times, and his wife came running with strong drink, bringing another cup with her. She poured half a glass for each of them. Alex, was about to say no, when he remembered Annaveta telling him that relationships or business wasn't done in Russian culture without some form of strong drink.

"I am Alex Wagner from the German colony east of here — Pleve Colony. Annaveta stayed in our home for the past few months, but a few days ago she left. I'm asking around to see if anyone has seen her."

The large man wagged his bushy eyebrows and laughed. "So you've gotten to know her independent ways too, have you? She did the same to us, a few months back — only, that time it was because she didn't want to be married."

"We think she might be in real danger, sir." Alex told him about the threats and attacks that she'd had in the past few months. "So now you know why I really need to find her. I know your daughter Pavla was friends with Annaveta. Would she have ideas as to where I could look for her?" Alex looked around the room and saw a young girl about Annaveta's age stand up holding a baby in one arm with a little boy's arms tight around her legs.

"Daughter, come and tell this man what you know." The man's commanding tone had his daughter hurry to the table to obey.

"I haven't talked to her for a long time. I received two notes from her, but none of them said she was leaving Pleve Colony." Pavla looked at him as if getting his measure. "But if there was a real reason, like the possibility of your family being hurt, sir, then she would have left. Come to think of it, Misha stopped by here last month asking about Annaveta, remember, Papa? He said he really wanted her back and that he couldn't wait to marry her. Of course, I know she didn't want to marry him last time, so I can't imagine that she would have changed her mind."

Alex thought about this new bit of information. "Do you happen to know where Misha Ivanov lives? Maybe he has seen her." Alex wanted to meet this man who seemed to be obsessed with Annaveta.

"He lives in a village to the west. The name is Molkov," Mr. Baranova said, a smile still lingering over his lips. "You won't be going tonight though, with the weather like it is. You are welcome to stay with us for the night. Though you'll have to find a place on the floor."

"That would be so good. Thank you." Alex nodded and got up. "I would like to give my horse some water and feed and settle him down for the night."

"We have an old barn out back. It's small, but it would fit your horse. You can find Mr. Ivanov's place in the morning." Mr. Baranova waved his hand toward the door in a gesture of good will.

Alex quickly put his winter coat and boats on again and went out to see to Blackie. The wind had picked up again, as they walked to the barn. Once inside, Alex took his saddle off and found a stall in which to keep the horse for the night. He poured feed for the horse into a bucket, and after running to the house, he found the water barrel. Pouring a pailful, he brought it back to Blackie, who eagerly drank until the bucket was half gone. Brushing his horse down, he thought about all that Pavla and her papa had said. He knew he would need to find Misha. There was a reason Annaveta was afraid of him, and in his mind it had to be more than just his demanding ways.

THE HEAT OF THE SUN warmed Alex's face as he approached the Ivanovs' prosperous home. He was thankful that the wind had stopped blowing. Shielding his eyes from the reflection of sunbeams off the freshly fallen snow, he stared at the property belonging to the Ivanov family whom Mr. Baranova had described as too wealthy for their own good.

Their *izba* gave the appearance of being a showcase to each passersby of the wealth some peasants could secure for themselves. Neatly fitted wood shutters covered the many windows that surrounded their brick home. He counted four windows on one side of the house and six down another.

He tied Blackie to a new wood fence that surrounded their large yard, then walked up to the sturdy front door and knocked. The only sounds he heard were from a few chickens clucking and some cows mooing. He tried again, knocking louder this time. Looking at the footprints and wagon trail that made a new path in the fresh fallen snow, he wondered if anyone was home. The neighbors' much smaller wood huts in the village were quiet as well. So, when no one answered, he walked behind the house to the backyard.

He was surprised to see a large barn, another small hut, and a toolshed there. He knocked at the small house and didn't get a response there either. As he headed to the toolshed, he noticed the door slightly ajar. The door squeaked on its hinges as he pulled on the door. When he opened it wide, he could see by the light of the sun, and was amazed at the sight that greeted his eyes.

Lined up against both sides of the walls were many kinds of guns. He saw a few pistols he recognized, like Browning, and Smith & Wesson models. Many were large rifles, most of which were much newer than his Berdan single shot rifle. He gave a low whistle as he walked inside and looked at the many rifles, including the Winchester Model 1895 and the smaller Nagant M1895 seven-shot revolver. The back of the shed was stacked with many varieties of ammunition.

Why would Misha need all these guns? What or who

was he involved with, and what were they planning to do? Whatever it was, it looked like it wasn't a game. He meant business. Alex looked around the shed for a long time before he spotted a note tucked behind an ammunitions box. Most of it he couldn't make out because of water stains; however, some phrases seemed highlighted on the page. Words like *Serbian unity* and *I insist you contact other members of the Black Hand*, and *find Baron Yakov* really got his attention. The symbol of a skull with crossbones with the words *Black Hand* encircling it was stamped on the bottom right side of the page.

A chill ran up his spine. Taking the page with him, he hurried to his horse. He needed to find Annaveta.

Chapter 24

ANNAVETA PLACED ONE HAND IN the footman's outstretched hand as she stepped down from the luxurious carriage. She cradled baby Nicholas in one hand, lifting her long dress with the other as she followed Count and Countess Tashkova up the wide steps of their stately mansion. Count Tashkova had met them at the train station with two carriages, one for the master and mistress of the house and the other for the servants, as was the custom. Annaveta was perplexed that the well-dressed count didn't even ask to hold his new son. She looked down at the sweet face of this new baby, who was sleeping contentedly in her arms.

Wide-eyed, her gaze moved upward toward the massive white two-story brick mansion that extended in a semicircle to fill one acre of the large estate. The palace-like entrance was surrounded by eight Greek-styled columns with a large balcony overlooking the courtyard. Annaveta stood on the landing taking it all in.

"Come now, Nanny. It's time for you to meet Ekaterina." Countess Tashkova walked ahead with Annaveta following, her mouth hanging open in awe. Stepping through the open ten-foot-tall double doors, she could hardly take it all in. Sixteen-foot-tall ceilings were surrounded with ornamental scenes from Greek mythology, and plastered white pillars were braced against oversized curved windows. The curved staircase that led to the second floor was made of rich cherrywood that dipped down to a polished gray marble floor.

A stout grave-looking man in a gentleman's black coat and trousers helped the master and mistress with their coats. Annaveta surmised he must be the butler. Another older gloomy-faced matron with a high-necked dark-gray gown stood beside him.

"Welcome back, my lord and my lady." The older lady curtsied and bowed her head, not once cracking a smile. "Shall I have Cook prepare the dining room for a late supper?"

"No, Mrs. Ilchenko. Just send one of the maids upstairs with a light supper." Countess Tashkova turned from the housekeeper to motion Annaveta forward. "This is our new nanny, Annaveta Travotsky. I will introduce her to Ekaterina and Nanny Klokov, and then you can see to it that she gets settled." The countess stopped and spoke to the older lady one more time. "Also, Baron Yakov's housekeeper has recommended a wet nurse. See to it that she arrives tonight."

"I'll see to it." Mrs. Ilchenko curtsied once more to her mistress and gave Annaveta a calculating look. Annaveta curtsied and then trailed behind the countess holding the little babe close to her chest. She hoped she hadn't done anything to displease the housekeeper. She would try to be extra nice to her the next time she saw her.

Annaveta followed her employer up the grand staircase to the left wing of the house, where the children's bedrooms and nursery was located. She looked down from the top of the grand staircase, and her mouth fell open in awe at the display of large paintings and gold-trimmed windows that adorned the walls. She never imagined a house could look like this or that she would ever be in one.

Seeing the countess far ahead of her, she hurried her pace to follow down the hallway. Sounds of a little girl singing a nursery rhyme greeted their entry to one of the large rooms.

"Ekaterina, Mama's back." Countess Tashkova stood there waiting for her daughter. Annaveta watched as the little three-year-old curtsied to her mama and gave her a dutiful kiss on the cheek. Annaveta looked up to see a plump gray-haired woman with her hair pulled back into a bun smile at the excitement of her young charge.

"Now, Ekaterina, I would like you to meet your new nanny. You can call her Nanny Travotsky. Remember, your Nanny Klokov is going to live with her daughter. So Nanny Travotsky will take care of you now." Annaveta watched the interchange between the countess and her daughter and was sad when Ekaterina's eyes filled with tears. She guessed the older nanny must be pretty wonderful to inspire such love in her young charge. Countess Tashkova tried to distract her daughter. "There is a nice surprise for you. Do you want to see your new baby brother?"

"Oh yes." Ekaterina put down the dolly she held in her hand. Annaveta sat down on the nearest chair so the little girl could look at her sleeping brother. She ran her chubby fingers over his soft curls and skin and grew excited as the baby stretched and yawned, his tiny hands touching hers.

"Oh, I love him. Can I play with him?" She clapped her hands and jumped up and down.

"He's too small, love. You'll have to wait until he's a little bigger before you can play with him." Nanny Klokov put a little doll in her hands. "You can practice with your dolly first, and then when your brother is a little bigger, you can hold him and play with him."

"All right." Ekaterina walked toward her little chair holding her baby doll in her hands, imitating her new nanny.

"I should introduce you two. Nanny Klokov, this is Annaveta Travotsky, who will be taking your place as you move to your daughter's home soon." Annaveta smiled and nodded at the older lady, feeling the warmth of her smile. "Good. That's all settled then. I need to rest. Oh, there is a new wet nurse who will arrive later tonight. Nanny Klokov, if you would give Nanny Travotsky and the new wet nurse instructions on how things are done here, I would appreciate it. Also, Nanny Travotsky, you may have Wednesdays as your day off." Her new mistress nodded and swept out of the room.

Annaveta sat at the table holding little Nicholas while Nanny Klokov spoke of the rules Countess Tashkova asked them to follow.

"You'll need to keep an eye out, if you're to stay here." Nanny Klokov's tone held a note of warning.

"Keep an eye out for what?" Annaveta frowned, not understanding.

"For the groomsman and some of the other single men, or married noblemen, who often come to the estate." Nanny Klokov looked at Annaveta with a gleam in her eye. "They will definitely be looking at you, with your big green eyes and fine features."

"I will be taking care of the children, so they will hardly know I'm here," Annaveta reassured her. "Now, why don't you show me what I need to learn." Annaveta hoped she could veer Nanny Klokov off the subject of men and onto other things.

Nanny Klokov just shrugged her shoulders and started talking about the expectations of the upstairs staff. They were to eat most of their meals upstairs in the nursery, or they could breakfast in the small dining room beside the kitchen. The children were to be kept out of sight unless the master or mistress called for them. They were to get fresh air daily unless the weather was bad.

Soon little Nicholas started whimpering, and it wasn't long before his tiny cries echoed in the room. Annaveta sang a Russian lullaby and dried the baby's tears as she rocked him in her arms.

"You have many talents, I see." Nanny Klokov stood at the door listening to her song. "It seems to have worked. The little prince is sleeping again." Annaveta looked down, glad the little babe finally slept.

Footsteps echoed in the hallway, coming closer until a light tap on the door interrupted their conversation. A maid entered carrying a large tray of food. She was followed by a disheveled girl. Her tattered brown dress and red scratches and welts on her arms and neck called out to Annaveta's compassionate heart. The girl was holding a little baby in her arms.

The maid put the food on the table and picked up the tray looking at them. "This is the new wet nurse." The maid frowned as she stared at the rumpled new arrival. "I have already shown her the connecting room where the wet nurse sleeps. And the countess said she doesn't want to be disturbed." She hurried out of the room as if she couldn't leave fast enough.

"Glad you could come on such short notice." Nanny Klokov nodded to the girl.

"I ain't got no other place ta be." The newcomer tightened her grip on her own swaddled babe. "Besides, I need the money to help feed me other wee ones and my mama."

"Well, the countess will be glad you came to help with little Nicholas. What is your name?"

"I am Elenya." The look she gave them both was a cautious one. Her bent head with all its scars looked like she carried the weight of the world on her shoulders.

"I am glad you came. I'm Annaveta." Annaveta walked over to Elenya and removed the blankets from baby Nicholas. "See, here is little Nicholas. He's the one who needs you most."

"This wee one is so innocent and unscarred." Elenya's broken whisper pierced Annaveta's heart. The wet nurse touched his cheek and little hand. "Me family thanks ye for this."

"You will get a chance to thank the countess tomorrow." Annaveta smiled, hoping that Elenya would let down her guard enough to let her be a friend. Elenya wiped the tears from her cheeks and gave a small smile to both nannies.

"Come and sit at the table; you must be hungry." Nanny Klokov ladled the chicken soup into three bowls, placing a fresh bun beside each. All three of them sat at the table. The nervous wet nurse sat down and took a spoonful of soup. It seemed like she hadn't eaten in days as she finished her portion at a hurried pace. When she had finished two bowls of soup and two buns, she sat back in her chair with a smile.

"It 'as been a long time since I had somet'ing that good." Elenya's smile showed nice white straight teeth that somehow shone brighter against the tapestry of her sullied looks. "Me two other wee ones would gobble up this soup, they would. With the rubles I'll make from nursing this wee one, it will help put decent food on the table."

Little Nicholas started whimpering, putting his fist to his mouth as though searching for food. "Where should I lay my sleeping girl, then? I see the little man is hungry, with 'im eatin''is fists and all." Nanny Klokov took Elenya to the connecting room, and it wasn't too much later that she came back and took the hungry babe from her arms.

With both children being looked after, Annaveta decided she would bring the dishes downstairs and go to bed. Going into the hallway, she spotted the housekeeper coming her direction.

"I'll take that downstairs. But first let me show you to your room." She followed the stern matron to the room that was next to the nursery. It was small and plain with a bed that Annaveta wanted to sink into. She thanked the housekeeper as she left and thought about Elenya as she changed into her nightgown. She couldn't help but wonder what or who had caused the scars on her body. Did she have anyone to protect her, or had the one who was supposed to protect her become her abuser? Annaveta felt tears slip down her cheeks at the thought. Crawling under the covers, she determined that somehow she would learn Elenya's story.

ANNAVETA WOKE UP REMEMBERING THE vivid dream.

She had walked into an old large brick building that had been turned into a hospital. When she walked through the hospital, many sick and pregnant women reached out their hands to her. They were asking for her help. *God, show me where this building is, if you are wanting me to go to this place.* She quickly got dressed and went to the nursery.

She greeted Elenya, who was up feeding little Nicholas. "How was he last night?" She sat at the table and helped Ekaterina finish her porridge. Elenya seemed less nervous than she was last night and was able to look her in the eye.

"He only woke up twice." Elenya smiled looking down at her charge. "Me own little one woke up three times, so between the two of em, I's tired." The two babies were sleeping soundly in the nursery, so she had a little time for breakfast. Ekaterina took another bite.

"How are your other two children doing?" Annaveta really wanted to get to know her better. She hoped they could be friends.

"Me sister has 'em. She will be glad for the money I can send her, she will." Elenya's eyes misted. "We've 'ardly 'ad enough food. Factory work doesn't pay much."

"You are lucky you have family close by." Annaveta swallowed back tears that threatened to come as she thought of the loss of her family and of having to leave Alex.

"Well, I 'ave two sisters. The other one is on strike from the factory now. She and I worked there together for a few years. At least until a man got me in the family way again." Elenya frowned, her fingers moving softly over the scars on her face. "If I never meet another man again, I will live a 'appy life."

"Does the children's papa help?" Annaveta wondered what bad things she had gone through with men that made her so angry with them.

"'Eaven help us, not at all. Not that 'e doesn't 'ave more rubles than he knows what to do with." Elenya smirked. "'E struts around fooling all the ladies into thinking 'e's a gentleman in those 'lordly' clothes of his. When all the while 'e's ruining innocent girls and making more money in shady places."

Annaveta wondered what man she was talking about. It sounded as if she'd been ruined by an aristocrat who got rid of her. She felt sorry for her and all the abuse she had suffered.

'That's not all." Elenya went on as if needing to get it off her chest. "I know so many young girls that were used by 'im and 'is fancy friends, who are in the family way. The girls' families have rejected them, and they are so poor they don't have any rubles to pay the doctor when their time comes." Elenya's eyes had a hopeless look in them as they met her own.

"Do you know which hospital they usually go to for help?" Annaveta was curious now. She was reminded of her dream.

"Sure, it's not far from here—right off of Nevsky Prospekt Street." Elenya looked at her with a curious expression. "Why—do you want to go there?"

"I was thinking I might see if they need volunteer help." Annaveta described the building she had seen in her dream. She nearly laughed when Elenya's mouth dropped open in surprise.

"Sure, and it must be a sign from up above." The wet nurse crossed herself. "One of me friends last week had to go to another 'ospital because they didn't 'ave enough nurses and doctors to 'elp 'er. That's the Alexander II 'omeopathic 'ospital. I will tell you 'ow to get there." Elenya gave Annaveta simple directions to the hospital. It was only a few streets over from the Tashkova estate. "I'm 'appy that you've come to 'elp."

Elenya clasped her hands to her chest, a wide smile lighting up her features. Annaveta sighed in contentment, her thoughts fixed on the positive ways she could help ladies like Elenya's friends in this city.

"Countess Tashkova asked me to bring you this uniform, Nanny Travotsky. She wants to introduce her children at the dinner party she's having tonight." The housekeeper handed her a long dark-green skirt with a new cream-colored linen blouse that had a high-buttoned neck. It was plain but crisp and clean. "You are to wait outside the doors at seven sharp."

Annaveta took the clothes, adjusting them nervously in her hands at Mrs. Ilchenko's stern voice. The housekeeper's unsmiling gaze looked her over with narrowed eyes.

"Thank you." Annaveta's smile didn't seem to soften Mrs. Ilchenko. The housekeeper turned and quickly walked away. She knew she didn't have a lot of time to get the children ready.

With Elenya's help, the children were washed and put in clean clothes in short order. Ekaterina was wearing a long white dress, with lace around the neck that went down to the sash at her waist. She looked every inch the little princess. Baby Nicholas was put in a off-white gown that was hemmed with lace. Annaveta changed into her new uniform, looking in the small mirror to adjust her hair. Pulling up stray wisps of hair that had loosened from her bun, she took one last look at herself. Her eyes seemed greener today, and she like the cream color next to her ivory skin tones. She was glad the freckles on her nose and cheeks were fading. Alex had told her he loved the freckles — that they went perfectly with her beautiful copper-toned hair. A great longing filled her as she thought of her lost love. The ache began in her chest and moved upward to her head. She swallowed back the tears that threatened to come as she turned away from the mirror and went to get the children.

She carried baby Nicholas in one arm and held on to Ekaterina's hand in the other as they went down the staircase to the dining room. The butler went inside the noisy room, only to return a minute later.

"The countess has asked if you would bring the children, Nanny Travotsky," the staid butler announced after he opened the massive doors to the dining room. Laughter and the delicious aroma of roasted chicken wafted through the air. Annaveta pasted on a smile and entered with Ekaterina hanging tightly to her hand. She followed the butler, and noticed that most of the elegantly dressed people who sat at the massive cherrywood table watched her with curiosity. Pulling the baby closer, like a shield, she walked past women whose hands, hair, and clothes sparkled with pearls and diamonds. The gentlemen had their hair slicked back, and their black suits were highlighted with gold and diamond cufflinks on their expensive French-cuffed shirts. She walked directly up to Countess Tashkova, then paled when she saw the woman who sat beside her.

Countess Shremetev was here. Annaveta looked at the floor and took deep breaths trying to quell her panic. Maybe the countess wouldn't recognize her from when she worked at their estate. She didn't want to have to explain why Monsieur Arnaud had gotten rid of her and her family.

"Ah, here are our children, my friends." Countess Tashkova waved Annaveta over to where she was seated at Count Tashkova's right side at the head of the table.

"This is Ekaterina—the oldest, and a most beautiful girl." The countess smiled serenely when her daughter gave a nice curtsy to all the lords and ladies in attendance. "The wee babe in his nanny's arms is the future Count Nicholas Tashkova."

"To the future count." A handsome but bold man with brown eyes and long dark hair tied at the back of his neck lifted his wine glass as a toast. "My lady, do introduce the maid in charge of your children."

"Ah, yes. This is our new nanny, Annaveta Travotsky," Countess Tashkova announced as she pointed her wine glass in Annaveta's direction. Looking at the couple next to her, she tinkled a little laugh. "Lady Shremetev, our new nanny comes from your village. Noltava, I believe?" Annaveta shrank back in fear.

"Did you work at the estate?" The countess raised her eyebrows as she eyed Annaveta with interest.

"Yes, my lady." Annaveta somehow remembered to curtsy despite the waves of panic that rushed over her.

"Well then, I will have to ask our overseer, Monsieur Arnaud, why he ever let a good girl like you get away." The countess smiled at Annaveta, then turned to talk with the lady on her other side.

Annaveta felt the color drain from her face at hearing the name of her attacker. She wished she could run away right now. Now Monsieur Arnaud would know where she was. *I shouldn't have used my real name or mentioned where I used to live to the countess. I should have been more careful. Now what am I going to do?* Her hands trembled as she held baby Nicholas a little tighter. The babe whimpered, and soon his soft cries got louder.

"I'll meet you in the hall, Nanny," Lady Tashkova said as her son's cries disturbed their dinner.

"Yes, my lady." Annaveta held little Nicholas with one hand as she tugged on Ekaterina's hand with the other. "Come. I think your baby brother is getting hungry." Annaveta's words helped the little girl walk a little faster.

"He's hung'y, just like me, Nanny." Ekaterina glanced back one more time at the people and food in the dining room.

"I'll ask the maid to bring you some food." Annaveta let out a big sigh of relief when the butler closed the doors behind them. A maid walked by about to go upstairs. Annaveta asked her if she would go get Elenya to come take the children.

Countess Tashkova came out of the dining room and looked at her children. "They did so well. I was pleased to introduce them, and you, Nanny." She smiled and kissed both children on the forehead. "Now, it's bedtime for you both."

"My lady, may I speak freely for a moment?" Annaveta asked her mistress just as Elenya came and took the children with her upstairs to the nursery. Annaveta smiled nervously at the countess as she nodded. "I just wanted to explain how important it is that Monsieur Arnaud not discover where I am.

"Oh? Why is that?" She had the countess's full attention now.

"While I worked at the Shremetev estate, their overseer, Monsieur Arnaud, tried to rape me and threatened to come after me, but it was a long time ago. So I just would rather not see or talk to him." The words came out of Annaveta's mouth in a rush, and she stared at the floor, not knowing what the countess would say.

"Oh, I didn't know. I'm sorry I brought it up at the table." Countess Tashkova thought for a minute, and then her eyes brightened. "I will go get Countess Shremetev, and you can tell her what you told me. I'm sure she'll want to know what their hired man has been doing behind their backs." She looked with concern into Annaveta's eyes. "Don't worry — I'm sure she'll keep your secret." Her mistress walked back into the dining room while Annaveta nervously paced up and down the hallway. The side door opened, and she stopped when the same distinguished, handsome man who had asked to know her name walked out. She turned to go the other way, when he called her name.

"Miss Travotsky." She turned around and waited for him to come closer. He towered over her and looked down at her with dark-brown eyes that were framed by thick brown eyebrows. His long brown hair tied back in the French style gave him a playful look. "I wanted to introduce myself." She waited, a slight smile hovering on her lips, unsure why he would want to make himself known to her.

"I am Baron Vassily Yakov." His leaned in closer.

"My lord." She dipped into a curtsey as expected, eyeing him warily.

"Don't look so frightened. I just had to see for myself if you were as beautiful up close as you looked in the dining room." Baron Yakov lowered his voice and stared into her eyes as he brought her hand up to his lips. "Annaveta. Your name is like beauty and grace all rolled into one."

A hot flush stole up her neck to her face as she heard his compliments. His admiring gaze penetrated her skin. She felt as if she had stepped into the realm of the rich, and she was very unsure of herself. She looked into his brown eyes and relaxed, and her limbs were like melting chocolate. The thump of a door opening sounded in the background, and Annaveta stiffened

"I must see you again. Don't worry — I'll find a way," Baron Yakov whispered and put down her hand. Winking at her, he stood back.

"Nanny Travotsky, there you are." Countess Shremetev glided over to where she stood with Baron Yakov. "My lord, shouldn't you be having port with the other gentlemen?"

Baron Yakov bowed graciously to both ladies and walked away.

"Now, my dear. Countess Tashkova asked me to come talk to you, that you had something to tell me?" Lady Shremetev, looking regal in her red evening gown and pearls, intimidated Annaveta. She took a big breath and told the countess all that had happened when she had worked in the gardens on their estate and that Monsieur Arnaud had forced her family out of their home. Annaveta told her that, from what she had heard and seen from other girls who worked there, she wasn't the first girl the overseer had treated badly.

"So I'm asking you if you would please not tell Monsieur Arnaud where I am." She implored Countess Shremetev as she wrung her hands together waiting for her answer.

"What! We employed him in good faith from the recommendation of good friends. They will hear about this, and so will the overseer. He will be punished. Of course I won't tell Monsieur Arnaud that you told me this or where you are — you can be sure of that." Lady Shremetev told her, her hand still held tightly against her stomach as if digesting the news was too much to bear. "Thank you for your honesty, my dear. I'm sure it wasn't easy for you to tell me. But I will somehow get to the bottom of this. We won't have such wicked things going on any longer on our estate."

Annaveta curtsied and watched as Lady Shremetev went back to the dining room. She hoped with all her heart that she had done the right thing and didn't make the situation with Monsieur Arnaud worse. She held her breath and prayed that the countess didn't tell anyone else where she was now working.

Chapter 25

MISHA'S LARGE FOOTPRINTS MADE DEEP imprints in the snow as he paced in front of the shed in the backyard of his family's home. He hoped Larue Arnaud would come soon. They had a lot to discuss regarding their business with the Black Hand. He kicked at a rock as his thoughts turned to Annaveta. He had been to Pleve Colony last week, staying in hiding for a few days and hadn't seen Annaveta at all. He wondered if she had really left that family's home that she'd been staying in. He would have to check again. He wanted her to come running to him, but if she didn't, he would think of another way to bring her to him. It wasn't over.

He clenched his fists. He couldn't believe he had missed killing the blond man when he and Annaveta had been walking along the trail to the meadow. Well, he may have suffered a little, but not as much as he was going to in the end. He rubbed his own wound, eyes narrowing as he heard his cousin's heavy footsteps coming closer.

"Bonjour, Cousin. Sorry I'm late, but I needed to finish hauling my things from the Shremetev estate." Monsieur Arnaud grabbed both his arms in a gesture of camaraderie. Misha couldn't believe this roly-poly little man was his cousin. He didn't want to claim that he even knew him, but he had served his purpose a few times already. Their mamas were sisters, originally from Serbia. His papa had cleared the way for Monsieur Arnaud to work as overseer on the Shremetev estate. So, really, his plump little cousin owed him a lot.

"Wait. Why were you packing your things?" Misha lifted an eyebrow, wondering what new scheme he was planning.

"Count Shremetev fired me, just this morning." His arms made sweeping gestures, his nostrils flaring in anger as he told his story. "He told me he had heard evidence from three different witnesses that I have mishandled the finances, among other things."

"Well, is it true?" Misha stared at his cousin, expecting him to try to blubber his way around the truth. He could read him like a book.

"Ah, well some of it true." He raised an eyebrow questioning his statement. "Oh, all right. It's all true, but I didn't think Count Shremetev would believe other people over me. I think I know who told on me too. It was either that cocky Alex Wagner from Pleve Colony or the beautiful yet sly quiet girl Annaveta, who I fired from the estate, that did this to me. I want to kill them both." He punched his fist into the side wall of the toolshed.

"Hey, that's not going to help. But I know a way that we can both get what we want." Misha waited until his cousin calmed down enough to listen. "Listen, I want to get rid of Alex just as much as you do. But my plan is slightly different when it comes to Annaveta. I want to marry her, but that'll mean she'll still be out of your hair, right?"

"Yeah, I suppose so. What's my part in all of this?" He could tell his cousin was warming up to the subject.

"Well, you remember we go in another week to our meeting at Baron Yakov's estate in St. Petersburg with the Black Hand members?" Seeing his cousin nod, he continued. "I say we scout out Pleve Colony this next week before we go and see what Alex and Annaveta are up to. Maybe we'll find our opportunity to get it done then."

"*Oui.* I don't have anything else to do right now, anyway." Larue Arnaud's pudgy face turned into a dissatisfied pout. Misha heaved a sigh of frustration at his moody cousin and waved him into the toolshed to show him the newest shipment of guns and ammunition.

MISHA HAD SPENT SIX DAYS watching the Wagner home in Pleve Colony with nothing new happening and he and Arnaud were both getting tired. Misha crouched down to a sitting position, his back against a tree in the Wagner's pasture waiting for some sign of action from Alex or Annaveta. Soon it was high noon, and still nothing.

"Maybe we should pack up for today. We need to leave on the train tomorrow anyway." He looked at down at his cousin, who shrugged his shoulders.

"Wait, I see Alex and his brother coming out of the house. Looks like they are getting the horses hitched to the wagon to go somewhere. We'll stay close to Alex. He'll lead us to Annaveta." Misha thought maybe now they would see what he was up to.

They walked trying to keep up with the wagon as it headed eastward out of town. Misha waved at a wagon that was about a mile behind the Wagner brothers, and they caught a ride with the farmer. They went as far as the next town, and they jumped off the wagon when they saw Alex hop off at the train station.

"He's headed somewhere. I'll go listen and see where he's headed." Misha pulled his coat up around his neck and lowered his hat on his forehead and entered the ticket office. He sat on a chair, trying to make himself as invisible as possible. He overheard Alex asking the clerk for a one-way ticket to St. Petersburg. Misha heard the time that the train would be leaving and left the office. He found his cousin busy eating by the side of the building.

"You need to sit somewhere else where Alex won't recognize you. He knows you, remember?" Misha grimaced, disgusted at his gluttonous cousin. "Looks like we are going to St. Petersburg a day early. Let's think about some disguises so Alex doesn't recognize us."

ALEX STEPPED OFF THE TRAIN, hurrying to the nearest trolley with his small bag of clothes and a few other necessities. He picked up a newspaper and read the headlines. There was lots of disturbing news. Minister Maklakov was urging the Tzar to overthrow the Duma, and they were refurbishing all the equipment used by the Navy, preparing for possible war. In the arts section he read that author Belyi's apocalyptic novel *Petersburg* was now available. It was the story of the son of a diplomat who had been chosen to assassinate a high-ranking official—his papa. He read the reviews, and most of them raved about the puns that the author used. Folding the newspaper, he decided he would need to read the book.

Tucking the paper under one arm, he hurried to the electric tram car that was already overflowing with people. Hopping on, he paid a ruble for a ride to Nevsky Prospekt Street. He knew there would be businesses along that street where he would be able to find work, at least until he found Annaveta. So far he'd only been given clues. When he had returned from searching Misha's toolshed, Clara had just been sent a letter from Annaveta. Her words laid bare the fact that she was in St. Petersburg because she mentioned going to bakery shops on Nevsky Prospekt Street. He knew she was a nanny, but she didn't say at which house she was employed. He was disappointed he didn't know more details. One of the colonists had admitted to giving her a ride to the train station, but that's all the information he had.

His parents had talked to him again about marriage to Annaveta, and voiced their objections. In the end they told him they trusted him and gave their blessing. They had a hard time letting him go to St. Petersburg but knew it was what he needed to do. He smiled at the memory of his mama telling him to "bring that girl home."

Seeing the many businesses bustling with patrons, Alex jumped off the tram car and headed to a bakery. He hoped he would spot Annaveta somewhere, maybe even today. Dodging his way between peasants, middle-class business people, and wealthy aristocrats, he made his way down the street. The heavenly smell of rising bread drew him in before he saw the sign on the store front. Walking in, he looked around and didn't see her. He then went to all the bakeries and shops on the street, and still there was no sign of her.

While chewing on the small loaf of bread, he thought of his next steps. He needed to save his money, and as he walked the streets looking in different markets, bazaars, and boarding houses, he knew he would need a job if he stayed here and looked for Annaveta. He wanted to be somewhere down this street, so he applied at the general store and a few other businesses, but they all told him they weren't hiring. Late in the day, he came to Poda's Tavern. He inquired about a job, and thankfully, Savva Poda, the owner, hired him right away. Mr. Poda said Alex might as well starting work today, because his other worker had just quit the day before.

"Oskar will show you where we keep our supplies and what needs to be done around here." Mr. Poda spoke as he filled up the beer mugs for the men who sat at stools around the bar.

Alex worked with Oskar, learning where they got their supplies of wine and how Mr. Poda made his beer. Oskar a big man with red hair and freckles, and looked more like a fighter than a bartender. They talked about the news, and they each mentioned a little about their families. Oskar's papa had died a couple of years ago, so he looked after his seven brothers and sisters and mama. Alex admired a man who took on such a big responsibility at his age.

He worked side by side with Oskar until late at night, then he asked him, "Would you know of a boardinghouse or place where I could stay for a few nights until I can get on my feet?" Alex finished washing the last of the beer mugs and put them on their trays while they talked.

"If you don't mind a bunch of little children waking you in the morning, you could come stay with my family in our apartment. Mama won't mind another mouth to feed. If you plan to stay awhile, all I ask is that you help pay for food and rent." Oskar put the last of the empty bottles in the crate near the back door, ready for pickup by their supplier.

"Thanks, and I don't mind little ones. I'm used to my own little sisters and nephew." They finished up and said good night to Mr. Poda, then walked through the darkened streets to Oskar's apartment. Alex was thankful he had found a new friend in this city.

EAGER TO GO LOOKING FOR Annaveta this morning, he washed his face in the small bowl that Oskar's mama, Mrs. Rodchenko, had put on their small table. It was still early, the sun hadn't risen, and yet all seven children were sitting around the table waiting for their breakfast. Mrs. Rodchenko brought the steaming pot of *kasha* to the table and put a scoop into each of her children's bowls. She waved her hand to an empty chair beside Oskar.

"Come. Eat. Food is warm." Oskar's mama patted her hand on the worn-out handmade wooden chair. He sat down, frowning when it wobbled on unsteady legs. He decided he would need to get wood and make a new set of chairs for their family. The steaming bowl of *kasha* was placed in front of him along with a cup of tea — typical Russian peasant fare. Mrs. Rodchenko nodded at him and looked at Oskar as if waiting for something. He bowed his head, and they all were silent for a moment and crossed themselves. As soon as Oskar said "amen," the chatter began again. The children with their unwashed faces and scruffy hair looked tired and worn-out even before the day had begun.

"So what are you children doing today?" Alex teased, thinking that would each have little chores to do for their mama.

The oldest boy spoke up. "We older three work at the factory. We have to be there early and stay there for ten hours a day, six days a week. Vanya and Andrei are more tired than I am when we've finished for the day." He straightened his shoulders as if proud of how big he was.

"It's no good them working in that awful place." Their mama shook her head, her double chin wobbling with the slightest movement. "There have been way too many accidents in that awful spinning mill. Children getting their hands caught in the gears, or even worse. And all for the small wage of fifteen kopeks a month."

"I know, Mama." Oskar looked at his mama. "Maybe Mr. Poda will give me a raise soon. Then you and the children can come home to work and start your sewing business like you've always wanted. At least we have it better than many other factory workers who live in the filthy and crowded factory barracks or tenement housing. We don't have to live in Khitrovka's *trushchoby*—the large townhouse where anyone who pays five kopeks a night can sleep on double- and triple-decked platforms that are shoved close together. They are packed in like sardines. The city's beggars, thieves, whores, and unemployed workers gather there to guzzle raw vodka and cheap wine. We have lots to be thankful for."

Shaking her head, Mrs. Rodchenko stood up, her gray face and slumped shoulders revealing her thoughts of hopelessness. She organized all the children so they were ready to go. Holding the little two-year-old in her arms, she left the apartment.

Thoughts about drunks and cruel men reminded him of Annaveta's papa, who had showed he was both. Only eight months had passed since the house fire that had taken

Annaveta's family, and once again he remembered what Annaveta had said about the mysterious footsteps she had heard outside their small *izba* the night before the fire. He knew Annaveta still thought the fire had been deliberately set, but how would they ever find out who did it? After all this time, the guilty person would be long gone. There seemed to be injustice everywhere he turned. He clenched his fists as he thought of the cruelty shown to Oskar's brothers and sisters and other children who worked in the factories.

"What happens to the littlest ones?" Alex asked Oskar.

"Sometimes Mama has to take them with her, which makes it hard because they have to play away from the machines. Most of the time there's an old gramma who lives down the hall from us in this apartment building who takes care of them for a small wage." Oskar stood and gathered the dirty dishes, then washed them quickly. "I'm hoping for a raise, then Mama can come home with the other children."

Alex thought of all that he had learned about this family and wanted to help. There must be something he could do to help change their situation. He was still deep in thought when he left the apartment to search for Annaveta.

HE CONTINUED TO LOOK FOR Annaveta for many months. He had asked at the many different hospitals in the city, and he'd kept his eyes open as he went into different shops down the main streets of St. Petersburg, but couldn't find her anywhere. A few weeks ago he wrote to his family telling them that he was doing good, but didn't have enough money to afford the train fare home. He let them know he still hadn't found Annaveta, but he was still looking. He told them he had bought tools and had been building sturdy wood chairs for Mrs. Rodchenko and her family. The oldest boy, Dmitry, had been helping him when he had time and had a real knack for working with wood.

He thought of the letter from his parents. They told him to get enough sleep and to eat right, and that they missed him. His thoughts turned wistful as he thought of their concern and their description of the meals and fun they had with neighbors. The biggest surprise was that Ernest and Rachel had applied to immigrate to Canada. They were still waiting for the paperwork. Mama said she hadn't heard any more news from Annaveta, so she hoped he found her soon.

He was discouraged from not being able to find Annaveta as he walked to work one day in the middle of June.

Poda's tavern was crowded when he got there. Loud singing and bawdy laughter came from the men and women gathered at the piano. An older red-haired woman dressed in a low-cut red satin dress swayed her hips and sang to the off-color songs. The men responded by raising their beer jugs to cheer her on. A few drunks were passed out, and others had their lecherous hands around some of the tavern girls who worked upstairs. Alex went behind the bar to talk to the tall bald man with the beer belly. Savva Poda was pouring more drinks for newcomers, who sat on the bar stools drinking their troubles away.

"Sir, what's to be done with the drunks who have passed out on the floor?" Alex asked as he hung up his coat and hat and tied the small white apron around his waist.

"You and Oskar can drag them out the back door and leave them there. I'm not their mama."

Mr. Poda was abrupt with all his workers. Alex hadn't seen him smile since he started working for him. He nodded at his boss and went to find Oskar.

His friend was busy washing cups in the back room. "Oskar, Mr. Poda wants us to haul the drunks outside." Oskar dried his hands as he finished his task and shrugged.

"Does he really want them to go outside in the cold snow?" Alex frowned and walked with Oskar to the front room. "It just doesn't seem friendly."

"Savva Poda hasn't been friendly ever since his wife died in childbirth three years ago." Oskar spoke in quiet tones. "Heck, I don't think I've ever seen him smile. Not even when his only son stops by during his days off from the Navy." He lifted his hands with his palms up as if to say "who cares?" "I wouldn't worry about it. We just do what we're told."

They found four drunks passed out on the floor between chairs and under tables. They dragged them out through the back door one by one, until the human carcasses all lay on the cold snow outside.

Alex had just brought the many racks of clean cups to the front bar, when the tavern door flew open. He looked up in time to see four men coming through. One was a small dark-haired man who was talking with a well-dressed gentleman. One of the two men who followed on their heels was paunchy with a sallow complexion. Alex took a closer look. It was Monsieur Arnaud.

What was he doing here in the city? And who were the men he was with? Alex backed up and tried to think of a way he could disguise himself so he wouldn't be so easily recognized. He then remembered Mr. Poda's wide-brimmed fedora hat and his black horn-rimmed glasses that he used for reading. He saw the men walk to the table at the far corner of the room.

"Alex, go see what Baron Yakov and his friends want to drink," Mr. Poda barked in his ear. "They are the newcomers at the corner table." His boss pointed to the table where Monsieur Arnaud sat. Well, it looked like he would have to take his chances.

Mr. Poda was busy with customers at the far end of the bar, so Alex quickly put on the wide-brimmed hat and pulled it down so it covered his eyebrows. He placed the glasses on his nose and squinted from the strong prescription. Focusing on the men's hazy features through the lens, he walked up to the table.

"Can I get something for you?" He pulled out his pad

and pen and waited, looking down at the paper. When no one spoke he repeated the question, glancing up at them and looking down again. His chest tightened with anxiety, and his legs tingled as he waited.

The well-dressed gentlemen spoke to him. "I like your hat."

"Thanks." Alex nodded, his face unsmiling as he glanced up. This man was the baron that his boss spoke of. He did his best to remain well-mannered being so close to Monsieur Arnaud. He noticed that the overseer watched him closely. "We will each have a glass of Mr. Poda's special brew of beer. That will be all, for now."

Alex gave a slight bow as he'd been taught and went back to the bar to get their drinks.

"Hey, what are you doing wearing my hat and glasses?" Mr. Poda asked as he walked passed him, his arms full of dirty mugs.

"Just trying them on. You don't mind, do you?" Alex called after his boss, and seeing him shrug, he finished filling the last of the glasses and walked to the table. With his head down and his hat pulled low, he handed each of them their beers. Seeing them nod, he walked to the back room to grab a clean cloth and water bucket. He was determined to listen in on what these men were talking about. If Monsieur Arnaud was a part of their group, they must be up to no good.

He started wiping the first empty table that the drunkards had abandoned. He saw a couple of men look in his direction, but they dismissed him when he started stacking the dirty dishes and wiping the table.

"This radical action against Austria will cause war. Mark my words." This voice sounded like a superior tone. Most likely the words of Baron Yakov.

The firm tone of a much younger voice joined in. "Good. I'm ready for it. We need to remember Colonel Dimitrievic's words three years ago when he formed the Black Hand."

Alex listened to the young man's passionate voice with

his back turned so they were less likely to recognize him. He had caught a glimpse of who was speaking. It was the small dark-haired man. "We have sworn to fight all enemies outside Serbia with every weapon at our disposal. We pledged our lives to be faithful unto death for the cause of Serbian freedom and unity. We all have Serbian blood running through our veins, and that is enough of a reason to fight. And I, for one, am ready. I have seen our people being ruined more and more. That is why I must take revenge. There can be no regrets."

"Hear, hear, Gavrilo." After the unknown voice spoke, the clinking of glasses followed.

"Misha, have you found a place to store the weapons so they'll be ready when we need them?" This from the young passionate voice.

Alex stopped wiping upon hearing the name Misha. Was this the same man whose shed was filled with guns and ammunition? The same man who had wanted to marry Annaveta? He wiped slowly again, but managed to turn his head for a quick glance at who was speaking. The cocky tone of his voice matched his fashionable clothes.

"I'm still waiting for some special pistols." Misha shrugged. "They'll come soon, I'm sure. If my papa wasn't so strict about where I spend my time and his money, I would have gone to get the guns myself. It's a good thing Count Shremetev is such good friends with my papa. That's the reason I can come to St. Petersburg three times a year to buy new horse flesh and look at new investments. Of course, when I tell him that Baron Yakov has invited me to his home to talk about investments, he is more than willing to have me come here."

"Well, I'm glad you're here to help us, Misha." The superior tone of Baron Yakov filled the air. "Your loyalty to the Black Hand does you credit."

"Your drawing of the Black Hand symbol is quite good." Monsieur Arnaud's French accent was easily heard. Alex turned slightly, as he had already started cleaning the last table, which was closest to the four men. He pulled his hat lower and turned to see what they were looking at. Misha was drawing on a notebook in front of him. It was a picture of a human skull with two long crossbones under it. He remembered where he had seen this picture before. This same symbol had been stamped on the bottom of the letter in Misha's shed. The same place he had also found all the guns and ammunition. This picture was the seal of death.

"Let's toast to our success," the man with the young passionate voice said. Alex shuddered as he wondered what they were planning with all the guns and ammunition. He hurried to bring the dirty dishes to the sink, to let them soak a minute as he stood there thinking. So they all wanted Serbian freedom and unity. And by the look of the symbol Misha drew tonight, they were willing to fight for it. At any cost.

Chapter 26

ANNAVETA STARED OUT THE LUXURIOUS carriage window, mouth gaping wide at the tall brick castle-like building that was Baron Yakov's home. She could hardly believe that it had been only two weeks since the last dinner party and already she'd gotten an invitation from the baron. He had invited not only Count and Countess Tashkova but also their children and maids and the nanny. Normally the children stayed home when their parents went out to one of their dinner parties, but Mrs. Ilchenko assured Annaveta that this time Baron Yakov had entertainment coming especially for the children.

The carriage stopped. Annaveta helped Ekaterina down and walked with the other nannies in through the back entrance of the baron's large home. She missed Elenya. The wet nurse had stayed at home because of a nasty headache, so she kept little Nicholas with her along with her own little one. Annaveta followed the other nannies into a big room where there were lots of toys and tables filled with snacks. Ekaterina soon let go of her hand to go play with another girl that was close to her age.

Baron Yakov had hired actors and actresses to perform a play for the children and it had just started, so Ekaterina was enjoying herself. The baron was introducing the new play *Peter Pan*, by J. M. Barrie, and was in the middle of telling the story to the children when she left the room to find the washroom. She quietly went down the long hallway, passing the library and an office until she finally came to a washroom.

When she was done, she tried to remember her way back, but went down a different hallway, this one with portraits of Baron Yakov's ancestors. She had just started looking at them, when she heard footsteps behind her.

"Admiring my many ancestors?" He looked up at the long wall where many portraits were lined up. They walked down the hall together. "I'm glad you came tonight."

"Well, I was needed. I am in charge of Countess Tashkova's children." She eyed him uncertainly when he stopped and turned her to face him.

"I hoped you would come. I needed to see your exquisite face again." Baron Yakov put a hand up to play with her loose tendrils of hair and lowered his head so she could see his deep-gray eyes. "You've betwitched me." One hand settled around her waist while the other hand cupped the back of her head and pulled up close against him, and before she knew it, he kissed her. At first he was gentle, then his lips moved hard against her own with increasing ardor. Annaveta pushed against his chest, freeing herself from his uninvited touch. She backed up, her gaze darting behind him, trying to calm her anger.

"No more." Feelings of betrayal and guilt sifted through her mind. She was shocked that the baron would take advantage of her and that she hadn't stopped him before he kissed her. She loved Alex. She needed to get away from this man; he was starting to scare her. "We shouldn't be doing this. I hardly know you." Annaveta took another step back to distance herself from him.

"So you're a shy one, are you? That's okay; I like a challenge." Baron Yakov nudged her playfully and put her hand through his arm as they walked back to the nursery.

"Until next time." He bowed to her. She curtsied back, schooling her emotions to remain expressionless. She looked back as she opened the nursery door to see him looking fixedly on her form and face. She was relieved when, not too much later, the butler announced to her that Count and

Countess Tashkova were ready to leave.

Annaveta was glad to finally be going home. Her thoughts were muddled as she got Ekaterina ready to go. She had been uncomfortable most of the evening, but since those few revealing moments with the baron, she had been angry. Now she knew she couldn't trust him. His bold kisses and easy familiarity with her — someone he didn't really know — confused and frightened her. Guilt came over her as she thought of Alex and his tender kisses and loving ways with her. She missed him so much.

ANNAVETA WOKE UP HAPPY. TODAY was her day off. She planned to go to the hospital that Elenya gave her directions for, but first she wanted to see how Elenya was feeling. She hurried through her morning dressing and washing and made it to the nursery just as the maid walked in with a tray of toast and eggs for breakfast. With Nanny Klokov gone these past three weeks, it was only Elenya, Ekaterina, and herself eating together. Soon Ekaterina finished her food, and she excused herself to go play with her dolls.

"How is your head feeling today?" She watched Elenya gently pat her baby daughter's back with one hand and eat with the other.

"It's doing a lot better, it is." Elenya's smile turned to a frown in a hurry. "Ow was it at the baron's house, then?"

"It was okay, I guess." Annaveta twirled her food around on her plate. "Have you heard much about Baron Yakov? There's something about him that doesn't seem trustworthy."

"Oh, miss, you mustn't 'ave anything more to do with 'im. 'E's a bad man, 'e is." Her face had turned pale, and the hand that patted her daughter's back was shaking.

"What is it, Elenya? You must tell me, and don't hold anything back." Annaveta put her hand softly on her friend's

295

wrist. "Is he the reason you stayed home last night?" She looked into her eyes and grimaced at the slow nod that followed.

"Baron Yakov is the devil's spawn. Don't ya know—'e's the one who got me with child." Her voice wobbled with the memory.

Dropping her mouth open with her hand to her chest, Annaveta stood up and paced, not knowing what to say. Then she stopped. Looking back at Elenya again, she hugged her when she saw the tears silently streaming down her cheeks. Questions plagued her mind. A new thought sent chills running up her spine.

"Was it the baron who gave you those scars, Elenya?" Annaveta whispered her question, hoping against hope that it wasn't true. She decided she was prepared to accept the truth, no matter what it was.

"When I was a maid in 'is 'ouse, that's when it happened." Elenya wiped away fresh tears and nodded as she remembered. "It was after me man 'ad left me, and I needed to work. My friend tol' me to go to the baron's estate and to ask the 'ousekeeper if there was work. I 'ad two little ones at 'ome and was desperate for a job. So I went."

Annaveta sat down, her stomach clenched, listening to her story.

"Anyway, the baron took a liking to me. I was jus' the maid, so 'ow could I say no, right? So 'e 'ad 'is way with me many times. One day 'e had come back drunk from 'is meeting with what 'e called 'is comrades with the Black Hand, and 'e shows me his new dagger. 'E tol' me, 'e swore, that 'e would be faithful till death to this cause. I got scared and tol' 'im I needed to go home 'cause I was feeling poorly. 'E asked if I was breeding, an' I told 'im that it was 'is child. I should've known better. 'E flew into a rage and grabbed me and made small cuts along my face an' neck with 'is dagger as 'e threatened me. 'E tol' me if anyone ever found out about the child, or that it was 'is child, 'e'd find me and kill me. I 'aven't seen 'im since."

Elenya wiped her tears away, her features becoming stiff and resolved. "I'm pleading with you, I am. Don't 'ave anything more to do with 'im."

"I promise, my plan is not to get closer to him. Thanks for telling me what happened to you." Annaveta took her hand in hers and held it. She couldn't keep down the anger that rose from deep within. "Why do some people think they need to control and hurt others? It makes me angry. Baron Yakov needs to be brought to justice for what's he's done to you and others. I don't know if he'll pay for any of his bad deeds, but I plan to do what I can to uncover the evil he's done. I'm just not sure right now how to do that."

"I promise I will be extra careful when I see him next. But I have to find out more." Annaveta thought for a moment and stood up. "Well, since it's my day off, I'm going to to see if they need help at the hospital. I'll let you know how it went when I get back. Wish me luck."

Annaveta hugged Ekaterina and squeezed Elenya's hand before she left the room. After grabbing her coat and slipping on her sturdy shoes, she hurried down the servant staircase and out the back door.

She picked up her long skirt and walked faster in her hurry to get to the Alexander II Homeopathic Hospital. It was quite a long walk, as it was located on Litseiskaia Street in the center of St. Petersburg. It was good to have Wednesdays off from her nanny duties at the Tashkova estate. It gave her a day away from the children, even though she loved baby Nicholas and little Ekaterina more and more each day. She wanted to do more things that she was good at and to somehow use those gifts to help others.

She walked by the maze of factory workers on strike with dirty faces and tattered clothes. They marched along the street calling out their protests with each step. Annaveta hurried to get closer to the building to avoid being struck by a sign held too loosely by a man who looked to be a little older than herself. She had learned that Nevsky Prospekt

Street had been full of striking workers since 1911, but now the number of people striking every day had tripled.

"Factories don't pay us enough rubles to feed our families! We need higher wages!" A gaunt-looking older man with patched clothes and no shoes waved his sign high in the air as he chanted.

A woman who was skin and bones held up a sign. "Need better housing. Our children are dying from disease and poverty." Another hollow-cheeked woman beside her had a crying baby strapped to the front of her baggy dress, and she was being jostled by the erratic crowd.

Annaveta hurried as she neared the end of the street. The noise around her was deafening. She turned her head to see just how many people were behind her and around her, when she spotted a tall dark-haired man whose swaggering stride looked familiar. He wore a light-brown trenchcoat, with a deerstalker cap on his head. The brim was pulled down low over his forehead, so she couldn't see his eyes. She then spotted a mole on the lefthand side of his mouth. Jerking her head forward, she hurried her steps.

Misha! What was he doing here in St. Petersburg? Her hand flew to her throat at the sour taste that came into her mouth. One more block to go and she'd be there. Thankfully, when she rounded the corner, the crowd thinned, and she couldn't spot him anywhere. She hoped she wouldn't see him again, but was worried. He was probably angry that she had left Noltava before they could marry. But she would have rather died than marry him, a man like her papa. She could only hope and pray she wouldn't see him again.

Breathing a sigh of relief that she'd made it to the hospital, she rushed up to the stately brick building in front of her. It was massive with well over a hundred windows on both floors. Several carriages moved past her and came to a stop on the packed ground in front of the large hospital. Her steps quickened as she saw a young woman, large with child, waddle toward the entryway. The pregnant woman was gasping for air and leaning on the arm of an older woman. They both wore tattered patched skirts and blouses that were loose on their bony frames.

"Let me hold the door for you," Annaveta offered as she met them at the front doors. She smiled at the two women as they moved into the front room.

"Thank you for your help." The older woman nodded, her gap-toothed smile showing her gratitude. The young woman panted for breath and held her large belly as if she would give birth right there.

Annaveta saw that there was a woman dressed in a white nursing uniform, so she stepped forward to help the laboring woman get the care she needed. "Please, this young woman is about to have a baby. Could you direct them to the women's section?"

The nurse, sizing up the situation, moved both women as fast as she could to the right-hand side and down the hall to the women's wing. Seeing that they were being cared for, Annaveta looked around and found a man who was approaching the women's wing pushing a wheeled bed cart.

Annaveta hurried to catch him. "Excuse me." He stopped in front of the closed doors to the wing. "I'm wondering if you could tell me who is in charge of volunteers? I would like to help."

"You probably want to talk to Dr. Rubkin or his head nurse, Mrs. Mihailov. Just follow me." Annaveta opened the door for the large orderly so he could bring the bed through. She stayed close behind him as they passed the many patient beds. Many of the women lying in this room looked and sounded as if they were suffering pains in their stomachs or backs. Annaveta was curious as to what they used in this homeopathic hospital to help the heal the sick. She hoped she would be able to help here.

Annaveta followed the orderly through two connecting doors to another smaller room, where many women were nursing newborn babies. The man found an empty spot in the corner and placed the bed there, then found sheets to cover the mattress. Annaveta stepped in to help, but he waved her away.

"Now, I'll show you where Dr. Rubkin most likely is." His whisper sounded loud in her ears, but she followed his steps through another couple of small rooms. Annaveta looked into the first room that had a desk and files and books stacked from one end to the other. Hearing loud groans coming through the connecting door, she entered.

"I'm not going in there," the orderly told her. "That's the new lady who just came in. I'm sure Dr. Rubkin is with her." He eyed her clothes. "Here. You'll need to put this long white apron over the top of your skirt and wear this nurse's cap. Dr. Rubkin says it's to keep things clean."

Annaveta hurried to tie the apron on and adjusted her hair pins to hold the cap securely in place. She nodded her thanks to the orderly as she opened the door. The first thing she saw was a bright light shining over the bed on which the pregnant lady lay. The lady's face was red with pain as she pushed and screamed at the same time. Annaveta's head went up as she heard the doctor's voice.

"Come on now, Mrs. Miirsky." The doctor used soothing tones to try to calm his patient. "All mamas go through this. You will be fine. Now try pushing again."

"Baby won't . . . come," rasped the laboring woman as she tried pushing again. This time she lay back on the bed, frail and exhausted with no energy left. Annaveta felt the fear rise within her. As fearful as she was of helping with childbirth, this doctor and woman clearly needed help. She respected the fact that the doctor was more knowledgeable than she in many areas of the healing arts, but perhaps she could help a little.

She walked to a nearby water spout and washed her hands with soap.

"Could I help?" Annaveta spoke calmly, looking at Dr. Rubkin and rubbing the patient's arm at the same time. The doctor looked at her skeptically, as if trying to figure out who she was.

"I've trained as a midwife, and a few weeks ago I helped in the safe delivery of Countess Tashkova's baby." Annaveta smiled when she saw the doctor's eyebrows move up at her words.

"I've tried all that I know to do, Nurse. I'm not the official delivery doctor at this hospital; it's not my specialty. I'm just covering until a new doctor comes in. So if you know of a better way to deliver this baby, we need to do it quickly." The doctor gave her a look that indicated the life of this patient was on the line.

"Mrs. Miirsky, the good doctor would like us to try something a bit different. But I'm going to need your help." Annaveta talked in soothing tones to the patient, whose eyes were closing. Her face was pale and layered with tiny beads of perspiration. The laboring woman nodded slightly.

"I want to move you to the birthing chair." Annaveta nodded at another nurse to help move her. "First, I want to feel the position of the baby." She discovered that with only a little turn, the baby's head would be facedown. "This will hurt a little while we are moving you, but you will feel so much better after your baby moves off your back."

The doctor frowned with a skeptical look in his eyes, but he followed her lead. Annaveta went on the opposite side of the doctor, and with arms under the woman's shoulders and legs, they managed to move her so she sat in the birthing chair. The worn-out woman was shaking, so the doctor tried to steady her.

"Does that feel a little better?" The moaning woman nodded. "Good. So now we want to see if the baby has turned, so he's ready for his grand entrance into this world."

She looked at the doctor and saw that he was just watching her. Annaveta lifted up the bedclothes to see what was happening.

"You will feel my hands now. They are cool." Annaveta

put her hand inside the opening and slowly reached in through the cervix until she found the baby. "I feel the head, and it's in position. That's good news." She pulled her hand out, pleased with how the baby was coming along.

"Does that feel better? The baby just needed a little nudge to move to the right place." Annaveta smiled even though inside she knew it wasn't over. She still remembered the mama who had died from loss of blood — at her hands. She shook her head. Somehow she needed get past her own fears and get this baby out. One thing was sure — if the baby didn't come out now, both mama and baby would die.

"Feels better." The soft words came out as a whimper from the weary mama-to-be.

"When you feel the next contraction, push." Annaveta hoped her trembling voice didn't betray her anxiety.

"Ahh . . ." The woman's loud cries echoed off the ceiling as she pushed the baby forward.

"I can see the baby's red hair. One more push and we'll have the head out," Annaveta coaxed the weary mama. With the next contraction, the baby's head appeared.

She took the clean cloth and wiped off the mucus from the baby's nose and mouth. With the next contraction, Annaveta helped to maneuver the tiny shoulders through the small opening. Soon the slippery little babe spilled into her waiting hands.

"Mrs. Miirsky, you have a fine baby boy," Annaveta announced as the doctor took the sterilized scissors and cut the cord. Then he helped the bone-weary mama lie down on the bed. As she moved, Annaveta noticed excessive bleeding coming from the mama. She remembered Mrs. Wagner's instructions and the steps to take when this happened.

Handing the baby to the nurse's aide that had come into the room a few minutes before, Annaveta massaged the woman's uterus using circular motions. The afterbirth hadn't come yet, so after a few minutes of massaging, she reached inside and pulled the cord attached to the placenta to try to stimulate it. It didn't take long before it came out, but the bleeding still continued, so she placed one hand inside her vagina, and with the other hand on her belly she compressed Mrs. Miirsky's uterus between her two hands. It seemed to help the uterus contract because the bleeding lessened until it finally stopped.

Annaveta breathed a sigh of relief, and she and the doctor cleaned up.

"Your wee one has a good set of lungs. Maybe he'll be a singer." Annaveta spoke as she covered the shaking mama with warm blankets.

"Here he is. A fine son you have, Mrs. Miirsky." Annaveta handed the little babe to his mama, then she fluffed the pillows behind her back so she could rest more comfortably. It didn't take long for the tired woman and little boy to close their eyes, snuggled together under the warmth.

Annaveta cleaned up the blood from the floor, then took the dirty instruments to the sink to be washed. She assumed a nurse's aide would come later to wash the instruments.

Her hands started shaking as she realized what she had just done. Things could have turned out much worse for mama and baby. *Thank you for your help*, she prayed to God.

"You seem too young to know so much about childbirth." The doctor's comment startled her out of her thoughts. "You were quite good at calming this laboring mama. And it was nothing short of a miracle how you turned that baby around from the inside. I didn't know if they would make it. How did you do it?"

He looked at her as if he had never seen anyone like her before.

"I learned about herbs and healing from my mama when I was young. For the last year I worked alongside a midwife and learned many things from her." With hurried movements, Annaveta washed her hands and dried them as she explained. "I learned that healing is something that I seem to have a gift for. For some reason — well, most of the time anyway — women in the throes of labor respond to my small hands." Annaveta lowered her eyes as he intensely gazed at her. "It's just something I can do." She shrugged, feeling uncomfortable with his many questions.

"Well, you're a natural." The tall young doctor moved forward to shake her hand. "I'm Dr. Joseph Rubkin." His hand lingered on hers for a moment longer than necessary as he stared into her eyes.

"I am Annaveta Travotsky." Her face reddened with embarrassment as she suddenly realized what she'd done — came into his hospital and took over the patient he was working with. "I'm sorry for barging in here. I had originally come to find you, Dr. Rubkin, to ask you if you needed more volunteers. I have one day off a week from my nanny position and thought to help if you needed it. Forgive me if I overstepped."

"Don't be sorry. You saved this mama and baby today. So I thank you." Dr. Rubkin let go of her hand as a nurse entered the room.

"Mrs. Mihailov, there you are." Dr. Rubkin put his hand on the small of Annaveta's back to move her closer to the tall, angular woman. Her gray hair was pulled back in a tight bun that held her nurse's cap tightly in place. "I would like to introduce you to Annaveta Travotsky, our new part-time assistant nurse. She just saved the life of a woman and baby. We need more nurses like that here. Annaveta, this my head nurse, Mrs. Mihailov, who keeps things running smoothly at this hospital."

The nurse's eyes lit up at the good word from the doctor, but she responded stoically. "Well, I'll take your word for it, Doctor. And we do need more help around here," she said primly, then frowned as she spied Annaveta's bloodied apron. She walked over to a cabinet and found a clean apron, which she handed to Annaveta. "Let's put a clean apron on you."

Annaveta was relieved when Dr. Rubkin went to check on the new mama. Mrs. Mihailov then put the clean apron on Annaveta, who was glad the doctor had made room for her here.

"All right, now you look presentable, Nurse Travotsky." Annaveta's stomach fluttered with pleasure at her new title. "Next, it looks like we need to move the mama and babe to their new bed in ward three. Come with me, and I'll show you where we keep the wheelchairs."

The nurse's brisk walk had Annaveta almost running to keep up. She led Annaveta down the hall to another storage area, where there were canes and wheelchairs. Annaveta pushed a wheelchair to the surgery room, hurrying after the nurse.

Annaveta was kept busy for the rest of the day. She moved the new mama and baby to the maternity ward and helped with another woman in labor. Just like the woman she'd helped earlier, this one seemed to come from the poor side of town. Because Annaveta knew what it was like to be poor, she wanted to help as much as she could.

She gave an asthmatic little girl her homeopathic herbs and met an elderly widow, Mrs. Rabinovich, who was in the hospital with a bad case of the flu. She listened to her tell her story, and Annaveta gave her tea.

Without warning, a loud commotion filled the hallway. She gave her last patient for the day a book to read, then hurried out of the ward toward the loud voices.

"I be well. No need for doctor. No money."

A older man with gray streaks in his brown hair keep repeating these words, his voice becoming louder and more insistent. The right side of his cheek and neck was bloody and bruised, and his right arm had a long, deep cut. He was trying to pull his left arm away from a tall, broad-shouldered blond man who hung on to him.

"I will treat you for free." Dr. Rubkin had just arrived and spoke to the injured man. "Don't worry." Dr. Rubkin's kind tones to the older man seemed to calm him. Then the doctor spoke to the tall blond man, who wore a hat low on his head and who Annaveta assumed had escorted the old man to the hospital. "Looks like you have a few cuts and bruises as well, but not as bad. My nurse will take care of your wounds."

They all followed Dr. Rubkin to a examination area, where he cleaned the wound. Annaveta handed the doctor clean cloths, then turned around to see to the blond man take off his hat.

Her eyes flew open as she got a good look at his face.

Alex. Here.

His hands touched her shoulders and pulled her forward in a big hug as soon as he recognized her. She pushed him back, struggling to think clearly but smiling up at him, glad that he was here. She said the first thing that came to mind.

"What are you doing here?" Annaveta managed to sputter the words out as she looked into his intense blue gaze. "I mean—I'm sorry you are hurt. What happened?"

She blinked, tightening her grip on the clean cloths. Was this really Alex? It was, but she could hardly believe it.

"I can't believe I've found you at last. I've searched and searched the city for the past couple of months and couldn't find you anywhere." She cleaned a big gash on his arm and looked up at him, her eyes full of questions. "I must have gotten too close to the mob of angry striking workers on the streets today." He shrugged off his wounds as if they were nothing.

He pulled a cloth out of her hand with one hand and with the other reached for hers. Their fingers touched. She tingled with awareness as his strong calloused hand enclosed hers with a soft caress. She stood there looking into his eyes that darkened with longing as he reached up and skimmed her cheek with the back of his fingers.

"You're actually here." Alex sighed as he pulled her in a tight embrace, as if he couldn't get enough of her.

"How—?"

"Your letter to Clara said that you were working as a nanny close to Nevsky Prospekt Street. So I knew you were in

St. Petersburg," Alex explained. "I was so worried I wouldn't be able to find you in this big city, but it seems God led me straight to you."

Annaveta shook her head. She couldn't believe that the man who had nearly lost his life saving her and had declared his love to her only a few months ago was standing in front of her. Didn't he know that being near her was dangerous? If Alex had found her, then the man who was chasing her would find her too. She shuddered at the thought.

"I can't do this again, Alex." Annaveta's hoarse whisper could barely be heard. "You and your family are the reason I left your colony in the first place. We can't be what we once were. It's not safe."

"Annaveta, listen to me. I don't care. I want to protect you. I need you desperately." He touched her hand, rubbing his thumb across the smooth surface. "Don't you see? I love you."

Dr. Rubkin came over to them and lifted up Alex's sleeve, placing himself between her and Alex. The doctor took a look at the gash on his arm and began cleaning it.

"I can't do this to you, Alex. I just can't. I'm so sorry." She squeezed her eyes shut with regret. The knots in her stomach spread, and it felt like she could hardly catch her breath. She looked at him one last time and turned away.

Her quick steps took her as far away from him as she could get. She didn't stop walking. Her eyes burned with tears that fell down her cheeks. Her mind told her there were too many reasons they couldn't be together. That she couldn't love him. Why they couldn't be together. But her heart wouldn't listen.

Chapter 27

ALEX STARED AFTER HER, REELING in shock that he had actually found her. Annaveta's words echoed in his mind as he stood in frustration as the woman he loved bolted away from him like a startled horse. Suddenly reality hit him. Annaveta was disappearing again when he'd only just now found her. He looked at the doctor, who was putting some cream and gauze on his cuts. He waited anxiously for him to finish so he could find Annaveta.

As soon as the doctor finished, he ran out, determined to catch her. Somehow he needed to woo her back into his arms. He knew she was running scared. Scared to fully trust. Scared of rejection. Scared of being abandoned, again. He needed to show her that she didn't need to run anymore.

His hurried steps took him down the hall toward the front doors. He couldn't see her anywhere, so he rushed outside looking both ways down the street. There, on the right side, he could see the wisps of her auburn hair coming loose from her nurse's cap. In her hurry, she had forgotten to take it off, and that made her easy to spot. There was only one woman around with long, thick waves that shone like burnished copper. She turned and disappeared around the corner of the brick building onto Nevsky Prospekt Street.

He sprinted forward, desperate to catch her before she got lost in the crowd. When he rounded the corner, she was halfway down the street. She turned her head and saw him running toward her, so she lifted her skirts and quickened her steps. But he caught up with her just as she turned down the street where many wealthy estates lay hidden behind rows of trees.

"Annaveta, stop. I just want to talk to you," Alex said, touching her shoulder with a gentle hand. With his other hand he reached for her hand. She stopped. She tried to put her nurse's cap back in place, but as she did her thick hair fell loose from the bun. She looked beautiful. With her chest heaving from her run and her hair hanging loose framing her innocent face, Alex wanted to kiss her right there.

Annaveta turned and peered up at him, her eyes filled with confusion and entreaty. She stood under a cusp of trees looking for all the world like she had just lost her best friend. Fresh tears poured down her rosy cheeks. Alex took his fill of her. He watched in fascination as the red-gold colors of the evening sun weaved their way through her long hair and like slender fingers wrapped her in a warm embrace. He was jealous of the sun and its freedom to do so. He reached for her other hand as he stood there trying to see into her heart.

Catching his breath, Alex's heart pounded at a fast pace as he tried to think of words to say. The right words, to open her heart to him once again.

"I've missed you." Alex came a little closer as his thumbs caressed her soft skin. She moved back until her shoulders touched the trees. "Annaveta, you don't know how hard I've tried to look for you. I left the family farm months ago to come find you. I told my parents I needed to find you because I love you and want to marry you." He bent his head, his forehead touching hers. "I was afraid for you, that whoever was chasing you would find you and harm you. Most of all, I missed you. Your laughter, your quick wit, your compassion, your friendship, and even your clever tongue. I adore you, Annaveta. Don't keep running away from me."

"Oh, Alex." She closed her eyes and sighed. "I don't want to be separated from you either. I don't know what to do. I'm so scared." She opened her eyes and looked around, her face pale. Alex ran his hands up and down her shoulders hoping that would help calm her fears. "How do you know you weren't followed when you came to the city? What if they find us again? Remember what they did last time? They hurt your sister, they killed the cows, and they shot you, Alex. I just don't think we should be seen together anymore. Whoever is after us will hurt you or worse, and I couldn't live with that."

"I know you're scared and I admit I've had many moments of fear too." He pulled her close and kissed the top of her head. "But the worst thing to do right now is to abandon each other. We need to stand together, be committed to each other and to fighting whoever is trying to ruin our lives." He looked into her eyes with determination. "I just spent months trying to find you, and I'm not about to give up on us now. I won't give up on our love and our life together. You can't give up either."

Alex kissed her eyelids and cheeks until he found her lips. He pulled her closer to his chest, his fingers stroking the silky length of her hair. He deepened the kiss, tasting the sweetness of her as if he would never let her go. He could feel her responding to his touch and opening up to him. His passion ignited as she slowly lifted her hands, caressing the back of his head. Her slender fingers moved through his hair, while her other hand moved in featherlight motions across his cheek and neck, then came to rest on his shoulder. He tasted her tongue while his hands moved with a mind of their own, wandering from her waist to her back and upward, moving in circles over her soft curves.

Without warning, she pulled herself away from him.

"Alex, don't." Annaveta pulled her arms from around his neck and put her hands on his. She tugged his hands away from her waist and held them. "We can't do this." She was breathing hard, just like he was. He tried to tug her back into his arms, but she stepped back. "Alex, I missed you too, but we need to stop."

"All right." Alex smiled at her stern expression. "I just

needed to hold you again, my love." He felt vulnerable exposing his heart to her, but wanted only truth in their relationship. He didn't need any more half-truths or hidden thoughts to stop them from what they could have.

"Let me tell you of the life I dream of for us." He grabbed her hand and kissed it. "I dream of us getting married, and maybe not too far in the future leaving this country. To go live in a peaceful country like Canada, where hardworking people can prosper and live in peace. We would live on our own land and have beautiful children that looked like their mama. I would make fine furniture, but the most important thing is that we would be together."

Her big green eyes shimmered with what looked like hope for the first time in a very long while. Alex was encouraged by what he saw.

"That would be good to go to a new country, but hard to be away from your family and all those you love." She hesitated. "But you're right — it would be wonderful to be together without living in fear for our lives. Right now, I just want this nightmare to end. I'm so tired of always looking around every corner and watching my back."

"Well, we need to just take one day at a time—with everything." Alex kissed the back of her other hand. "We'll trust that somehow God will work everything out for good in the end."

"I have my doubts, Alex." She looked past him, letting out a big sigh. "I've seen too many hard things so far in life. But we'll see. Meanwhile, I am committed to work as a nanny and now as a part-time nurse. So I need to stay here."

Alex admired the resolve in her face. "You tell me you are staying, so I'll stay too. We'll see this sinister plot through— till all the trouble is finally over. We'll stick together and believe together."

She nodded, her eyes still clouded over with a look of uneasiness.

He looked around at the snow-covered cobblestone

streets that led to many large houses. "So are you going to tell me what we're doing in this wealthy area of St. Petersburg? Or do you just like to walk here?" He looked at the tree-lined estates, where towering castle-like turrets and high brick walls peered over the tops of the trees. He saw at least ten estates down this street, and each had well-groomed yards. On many he could see stables and servants' quarters and other buildings he couldn't name. Yes, definitely a place for aristocrats.

She looked past him. Alex watched her. She seemed deep in thought as if weighing her words before she spoke.

"I have a position as a nanny at one of the estates here." He raised his eyebrows in surprise as she continued. "Coming on the train here, I helped deliver a son to Countess Tashkova. She needed a new nanny and offered me the service position. It was just what I needed to get started in a new city. Today is my one day off a week, and it was the first day I volunteered at the hospital. So that is why you found me there. Now I really need to get back to the estate, as the sun is going down. I don't think they would take too kindly to my returning after dark." Her half smile seemed to hold a mixture of tenderness and regret as she moved to go past him.

"Wait," he implored as he put his hands on her shoulders and looked into her eyes. The rhythmic *clip-clop* of horses' hooves and the creak of a slow-moving carriage bumping along the cobblestone street beside them were ignored as they stared at each other. "When can I see you again?" His eyes probed hers as she looked down and then up at him.

"I want to see you too, Alex," she whispered. "But you can't come see me at the estate; it's just not proper. The next time I'm at the hospital is a week from today. We could talk again when I'm done at work. Also I take the children for a walk every afternoon around three o'clock. We could meet then."

Alex pulled her close one last time. "Good. I'll come find you tomorrow. I miss you already." Wrapping his arms around her waist, he leaned down and kissed her lips. He savored their sweetness until he knew it was time to let her go. He lifted her hands to his lips and slowly let her hands go as he gazed intently into her eyes, revealing his heart. "Be careful." He smiled at the flush of red that grew from her neck to her cheeks. She started to leave, then turned and blew him a kiss. He stood there staring at her until she disappeared behind the trees on the estate.

ANNAVETA WATCHED EKATERINA SKIP ACROSS the pathway to the park that was nearest to the Tashkova estate. Stopping the pram that held the sleeping baby Nicholas, she pushed back her wide-brimmed straw hat that she had bought with her wages. Her simple long gray skirt and ivory-colored long-sleeve blouse were too warm for this hot June day. Watching Ekaterina pick some wildflowers and hearing her giggle brightened her day. She pushed the pram to the nearby bench and had just sat down when she saw Alex come into view as he walked between other people who were leaving Catherine Garden park. He saw her wave and hurried to meet her.

"Sorry, I'm a little late." He sat down beside her. "I was dodging my way through the striking factory workers again today. Seems like each week there're more strikes breaking out. Now that I've been staying with Oskar's family, I understand the real need for better working conditions and wages among workers." He stopped, raising her hand to his lips. "Forgive me. I don't mean to go on and on about all that. I'm so glad to see you."

"I'm happy you're here too." Annaveta moved so she was more in the shade of the tree. "So, have you heard anything from your family lately?"

"*Ja*, I just got a letter from Mama." Alex looked up a wistful look crossing his features. "She mentioned that since

Ernest and Rachel had been married last fall, they've been talking about moving to Canada. So they will stop by anyday now to say good-bye and then they'll take the train to Latvia to board a ship there to take them to Canada."

"That's exciting. There will be lots of changes for your parents with Clara and John marrying in the fall." Annaveta smiled at the thought.

"Changes like that are good, but since working at the tavern, I've overheard some conversations that might suggest bad changes." Alex frowned.

"What do you mean? What have your heard?" Curious now, she urged him on, wanting to know more.

"Well, a few weeks ago, I saw four men come into Poda's Tavern." Alex's worried look caused Annaveta to sit up on the edge of the bench.

"Who were they?" she asked, torn between needing to know more and fearful of what she would discover.

"Monsieur Arnaud, Misha, a man they called Baron Yakov, and a guy named Gavrilo."

Annaveta gasped, her arms going rigid by her side as he went on.

"I overheard what they were talking about. It had something to do with a strategy to smuggle guns and ammunition from Russia to Serbia. I saw the guns for myself when I went to Misha's home a few months ago. I also heard them mention a group called the Black Hand. This group wants unity for Serbia at all costs, according to what I overheard them say. The symbol Misha drew of a skull and crossbones was a picture of death."

Annaveta wrapped her arms tightly around her stomach and moaned. "Misha and Monsieur Arnaud are both in the city? And they're involved with smuggling guns? I wonder what hateful thing they are a part of now. I'm scared, Alex." She squeezed her eyes shut as the pain in her chest increased. He reached for her hands and massaged them gently. She continued.

"You don't know the worst of it. There've been two times that I've suspected I was being followed when I went to the hospital. Both times it was the same man, who I'm afraid looked very much like Misha." She felt the blood drain from her face, and she shook uncontrollably. "I'm terrified of what he might have planned. Or what new scheme Monsieur Arnaud might be plotting."

Alex put his arms around her, murmuring unintelligible words of comfort into her ear, but she couldn't hold back the dread that filled the pit of her stomach at what was to come.

Chapter 28

MISHA DRESSED FOR HIS DINNER at Baron Yakov's estate. His thoughts were more on Annaveta than the plans they were setting in motion with the Black Hand. She had looked as beautiful as ever, even while wearing her dark-gray nurse's uniform the other day. The long white apron with the black cross on the front and the long white head covering that hid her glorious hair couldn't take away from the delightful innocence of her big green eyes and the smooth skin of her oval face. Once this plot with the Black Hand was done, he would take Annaveta home with him as his wife. He was sure he could woo her so she would come around to his way of thinking.

But since he had arrived in St. Petersburg two weeks ago, he had seen a man, and he was sure it must be Alex — the same man who had been a snag in his plans since the beginning. After their last meeting tonight, he would figure out a way to get rid of Alex once and for all.

HOLDING EKATERINA'S HAND, ANNAVETA HELPED her descend the carriage. They had been invited once again to Baron Yakov's elegant home for a dinner party. Her mind wasn't on the party but was dwelling on the dream she had last night. She had been locked in a room by Misha and told that she wouldn't be let out until she agreed to marry him. He was waving the Star of David in front of her face that he'd found in the burned pile of ashes of her family's *izba*. Suddenly Alex was there trying to free her, and Misha pulled out a gun. She had woken up crying, her body shaking from the horrible nightmare, when she heard that familiar Voice speak. *Don't be afraid. I am with you in trouble and will show you a way out.* Remembering the calm voice soothed her fears.

Ekaterina ran to play with her friend as they entered the big playroom. Elenya walked ahead of her carrying little Nicholas, while Annaveta carried Elenya's baby girl. Elenya glanced nervously at Annaveta. Countess Tashkova insisted that Elenya come so that she could introduce her new son to her friends that would be here tonight. Annaveta knew she had been scared to come to Baron Yakov's home. For her, this home was the place of terror. Annaveta touched her shoulder hoping it would help calm her.

Elenya leaned over to whisper in her ear. "'ere's a room in the back. I could feed the wee ones an' settle 'em down."

"Sure. I think it's a large storage room, but I'll bring the rocking chair so you have a place to sit." Annaveta gave Elenya the baby and dragged the heavy chair into the storage room. She brought a lantern and set it on top of a shelf so there'd be a little bit of light.

"'ank ye. It's feeling better about it all, I am. You'll get me if I'm needed?" Elenya eased into the rocking chair, and it wasn't long before baby Nicholas was sucking greedily.

"I will. Now relax." Annaveta smiled and closed the door, glad she could help Elenya in some small way.

Three clowns emerged onto the stage in the large room. It looked like Baron Yakov had brought more fun for the children to enjoy. The clowns carried balls, and she heard the coins jiggling in the pockets of their oversized polka-dotted baggy clown suits. Many of the children jumped up and down in excitement, eager to see the show. She sat down close to Ekaterina and enjoyed the show. Maids came in with large trays of food that they set up on the tables along with drinks for the children. Annaveta helped Ekaterina get a plateful of cold meats, buns, and fruit, and then brought a plate to Elenya.

She sat down and listened to the other nannies as they talked about their employers and the children they took care of. Most of the talk was gossip about all the bad things that happened in the houses where they worked. Annaveta didn't really want to hear any of it, so she turned and talked with Ekaterina's new little friends instead. She started thinking about Baron Yakov and what Elenya had said about him. He acted the role of a gentleman when he was with her. Inwardly she seethed, knowing that was all an act. The thought of Elenya's scars and her little baby reminded her of that fact. They were proof of his bad behavior.

Annaveta could hardly keep her food down. Her stomach was in knots. She needed to find the washroom quickly. *What is wrong with me? Why am I so tense tonight?*

Annaveta got up and followed a maid to the bathroom, which was located down two separate hallways. She had just made it in time as she got rid of everything she ate. She washed her face until she felt better, then left the room. Seeing no one in the dimly lit hallway, she tried to remember the way back to the children's playroom. Then she heard men's voices, so she followed the sound down the long hallway. Maybe one of them would be able to help her find her way back.

A door was open a crack to a large room as she came closer, but she was only able to hear two voices. *I must have made a wrong turn. I need to go back.* She was about to leave, when the voices got louder. She stepped forward so she could hear what they were saying.

"Everything's in place for Sunday. In two days we will ride the train through the Austrian border to Sarajevo." A passionate voice that sounded so familiar carried through the crack in the door.

"Ah, *oui*. I have the weapons packed that we received from other friends of the Black Hand. We already arranged for the four Browning semiautomatic pistols and six hand grenades to be sent to Sarajevo with Gavrilo. They were undetected by the Austrian border police."

Annaveta's heart raced a little faster at this man's familiar French accent. Monsieur Arnaud was here in the baron's house! And worse, what were they doing with all the weapons?

"We couldn't have planned this day better. Four days from now, this Sunday, is the Festival of St. Vitus. It is the 525th anniversary of a Serb killing a Turkish sultan after they were defeated at Kossovo. It seems like a strange coincidence that Archduke Franz Ferdinand will also be assassinated by a Serb on the same day. It was meant to be." The fire in his voice sent chills up Annaveta's spine. "Nedeljko Cabrinovic and Trifko Grabez, who are Bosnian patriots, will each have their own guns and grenades. It will be a sweet victory for Serbs everywhere."

"Just make sure things go as planned. I hope your friends know we can't afford mistakes, Misha." Baron Yakov's aristocratic command came through loud and clear.

Her legs grew weak, and she could hear the sound of her hearbeat thrashing in her ears. Misha was here at Baron Yakov's home? The low din of his voice brought back painful memories of her family and of Misha's arrogant and forceful ways. Then she remembered what Alex had said about the meeting at the tavern and Misha's involvement with the baron and the Black Hand.

She set her jaw and pushed her shoulders back. She had to find out what they were doing. The voices in the next room grew quieter, and Annaveta moved her head closer so she could hear better. But as she moved forward, she lost her balance. Her foot instinctively stepped ahead, and she bumped into a hall table. A loud sound like glass breaking followed in the shadowed hallway. The door to the room

319

where the men were opened, and she trembled as one by one the men came to see what had broken. Baron Yakov looked at her and frowned when he saw a treasure of his shattered on the floor. He looked up and down the hallway as if expecting to see more people with her.

Annaveta was about to tell him she was alone, but her lips pressed together in a tight grimace as a mixture and fear and anger washed over her at the sight of Misha and Monsieur Arnaud together.

"Annaveta. You shouldn't be in this part of the house. Were you not enjoying the entertainment I provided for the children?" Baron Yakov glared at her, a black look on his face.

"I'm sorry, my lord. I think I got lost. If you would show me to the children's playroom, I will get out of your way." Annaveta looked at the vase."Sorry about breaking the vase. I'll ask one of the maids to come and clean it up." She nervously looked up at him.

He shook his head. "Sorry, I just can't be sure that you didn't hear all the details of our plans. You'll need to stay with me until I think of a plan." The baron looked behind him and saw his friends. "Ah, I should introduce you to Monsieur Arnaud and Misha Ivanov. My business partners."

Annaveta just stared at them wide-eyed. No words came to her.

"Ah, *alors*. So we meet again. Trouble seems to follow you, doesn't it?" Monsieur Arnaud raised bushy eyebrows that shadowed his beady eyes and looked down at the pieces of the vase lying on the floor. His puffy cheeks turn a shade darker as he taunted her. "Here is someone else you know." Monsieur Arnaud looked behind him at Misha.

Annaveta stood there in silence and put her shaky hand against the wall to hold herself up. She felt faint. How could both of these men be here in St. Petersburg, at Baron Yakov's home? She was living her worst nightmare. She was too unnerved to move a muscle. The picture in her mind was all too clear of the trauma she had lived through at Monsieur

Arnaud's hands. Misha's controlling, arrogant, drunken tendencies and threats also rushed back to her mind in vivid clarity.

Fear rose, choking her breath. She gulped for air and willed herself to breathe deep and slowly.

"You're breathless, my dear." Misha walked closer to her, his hips swaying to the rhythm of his own self-importance. "It makes me happy that you missed me so much. It's been a year, hasn't it?" When she didn't say anything, he went on. "What, my fiancée has nothing to say? I'm shocked."

Annaveta mustered the courage to speak. "I did not accept your offer. My papa did and he's dead. The contract wasn't final." She stepped back when he tried to touch her cheek with his fingers. She felt like a trapped animal — just like last time.

"I thought a good girl like you would honor her papa's last request. Too bad you had to listen to our discussion, my lovely." Misha ran his fingers down her arm to provoke her. She tried to move away, but he kept at it. "I think she might be trouble, Vassily. She might tell what she knows." Misha turned around and looked at Baron Yakov, who was frowning as if considering this new turn of events.

"Well, we can't have that, now can we?" Baron Yakov looked at her, deciding her fate. "I'm not sure you heard everything, but even if you heard a little bit of our discussion, we can't have you slipping and saying something by accident. So that means you won't be attending to the children for the rest of the party either."

"Well then, take me home." Annaveta nodded as if to reinforce her idea.

"Sorry, that won't do." Baron Yakov stood thinking. "We need to hide you somewhere for a few days, until the deed is done."

"What? Where are you going to put me?" Annaveta tried to keep the panic out of her voice, but it didn't work. "Count and Countess Tashkova will miss me. I take care of their children. The people at the children's party will wonder where I've gone. What will you tell them?"

"I'll just tell them the truth, my darling. That you suddenly didn't feel well and needed to lie down." Baron Yakov nodded at Misha and he grabbed her arm. Annaveta tried to pull away from his grip, but he was too strong and pulled her forward.

"Looks like you need to learn a lesson. I believe there is a room in the basement you'll find to your liking." The baron's cold eyes looked from her to Misha as he handed him keys. "You shouldn't have deceived me, my dear. Take her away."

Misha's strong arm went around her waist and crushed her tightly to his side as he forced her to move with him. He found the stairs and dragged her down the dark and musty brick staircase to a cold, desolate basement. Her heart beat wildly, and she felt nausea rise in her throat, threatening to choke her. She was descending into hell.

"I know just the place for you, Annaveta." Misha walked her to the farthest corner room and unlocked the door. It opened to a small brick windowless room.

"Maybe a night's stay here will help you change your mind about marrying me. If you agree to my terms, I'll find a way to free you. If not — well, look around you. There's no way out. Think about it, my dear." His lips curled in a wicked sneer. "Oh, there's something else you need to see." He pulled an object out of his pocket.

Annaveta gasped as she realized her dream of the man locking her in a room and sentencing her to die was about to come true. "How did you get Mama's star?" Her eyes filled with tears mixed with anger. "Give it to me — it's mine."

"You only get it back once we're married, my dear." His voice mocked her. "I know more about you than you do. For instance, do you know your papa was working at the docks along Odessa's port during the time of the 1905 pogrom? You knew he hated your Mama's Jewish family, didn't you? Well, enough said. I'm sure you'll come to your senses soon."

He lowered his head to hers.

"I won't — "

Misha kissed her hard, bruising her lips with his anger. Then he shoved her into the room so that she fell on the cold, hard floor. "Don't say anything you'll regret. You can tell me the happy news next time I see you."

"Never." She crossed her arms across her chest, her eyes piercing daggers into his. He gave her a look of arrogant displeasure before he closed the door. The scraping of the key as it turned in the lock clanged loudly in her ears. She sat there in desperation, tears rolling down her cheeks. She knew of Mama's Jewish heritage, but would her papa have been part of the killings of so many Jews in Odessa? She felt the nausea rise again in her throat. Her grandmama and grandpapa killed by her papa's own hand?

The bile spilled over, and she spewed out the little bit of food that remained from her supper. She was sick until there was nothing left.

Maybe someone would find her. But Alex wouldn't know she was missing until tomorrow afternoon when she failed to show up at the park. Elenya would know something had happened to her. No doubt Countess Tashkova would believe Baron Yakov was telling the truth, that she was very ill. They might come to the baron's house to inquire, but they would probably believe whatever he told them because he was a wealthy baron of the realm. They wouldn't want to offend him. There was no way out.

"What have I done to deserve this? Where are you, God?" With shoulders shaking and hands running through her hair, she cried tears of abandonment, rejection, and fear until there were no more tears left.

Chapter 29

ALEX RAN SHAKY HANDS THROUGH his hair as he paced in front of his and Annaveta's meeting bench at the park. She was very late. On Tuesday, when he had last seen her, she seemed preoccupied with something. She had reassured him it was nothing. Yesterday was her day to work at the hospital, and she said Countess Tashkova expected her home promptly afterwards to help with the children. So he had looked forward to seeing her today. He grew restless realizing she wasn't coming and decided he would go to the Tashkova manor to see what was the matter.

He walked up to the servant's entrance of the big house. His quick knocks on the large door mimicked the rapid increase of his heartbeat.

"Yes, may I help you?" A tidy-looking maid wearing a black dress with a white apron answered the door.

"I was wondering if I could please speak with Nanny Travotsky? I'm a friend — Alex Wagner." His foot tapped in impatience.

"I'll go see if she's available to speak with you." The maid told him to wait, and he heard her footsteps moving quickly up the servant staircase. He stood there for what seemed to his anxious mind a very long time before he heard the footsteps return.

The maid stood before him frowning. "I'm sorry to say, Annaveta is not here."

"What?" He heard the stress of his emotion-choked

voice and took a deep breath. He ran a shaky hand along his new gray shirt, picking off imaginary lint, trying to calm his emotions. In a calmer tone, he spoke again. "Can you tell me where she has gone?"

"I spoke to Elenya, the wet nurse and Annaveta's friend. She said that she was worried for Annaveta, especially when she didn't return from the dinner party at Baron Yakov's place last night. Countess Tashkova said the baron told her, she hadn't been feeling well at all."

Alex stared at the maid, his eyes wide and fists clenched. "They were at Baron Yakov's last night and she stayed there all night? I've got to go to her." Pulling the door handle to rush out, he stopped when he heard the maid call out to him. He turned his head, his movements jerky and his lips tight with anger.

"You might not want to go over there. Elenya said the countess had a footman sent over to Baron Yakov's estate to see how Annaveta was feeling. The maid there said the doctor told everyone in the house that Annaveta was very ill and was to receive no visitors." The maid barely finished her speech, when Alex nodded and took off running.

Annaveta was in danger. He knew he needed to get to her fast. He didn't believe a word of what the doctor said. She had been feeling fine when he saw her two days ago, so something was very wrong with this whole situation. Alarm filled him and he ran faster. He remembered delivering wine to Baron Yakov's mansion, so he knew it was about three miles to his estate.

Finally he reached the baron's estate and ran up to the castle-like building. Breathing heavy from his run, he knocked on the door by the servants' entrance. A older woman came to the door, her apron splattered with flour.

"I'm here to see Annaveta Travotsky." He got the words out one at a time as he panted for breath, hoping she could understand him.

"I'm sorry. Baron Yakov told us the doctor said she was to

receive no visitors. You'll have to wait until she's better." Her curt nod punctuated her words. She started to close the door, when Alex put his hand there.

"Wait. I really need to speak—" His words were cut short as she shook her head, slamming the door in his face.

He stepped back, his muscles clenching along his jawline. He walked around the manor to see if there might be another way in. The few doors he found and tried to open were all locked.

With a fast-paced stride, he made his way toward the tavern, his thoughts churning with a mixture of anger and determination. Somehow he would get Annaveta out of there, if it was the last thing he did.

Crossing the street just before Poda's Tavern he spotted a policeman. Hope squeezed its way into his troubled thoughts as he hurried toward him.

"Sir! I have a friend who needs help." Alex looked the policeman in the eye as he explained the situation.

"Ah, I'm acquainted with Baron Yakov. She'll be safe in his home. No need to worry." The policeman walked forward and blew his whistle at some men who had started a drunken brawl just outside one of the taverns.

"But—" Alex hurried up to him, wanting desperately to explain the urgency of the matter.

"Can't you see I'm busy? Now be gone with you." The police officer's curt dismal as he waved him off set Alex's teeth on edge. He kicked some stones on the sidewalk to vent his anger. He remembered Annaveta telling him about the great lack of respect and trust for constables. One woman had protested to the governor when a hundred rubles went missing after a police captain and members of the rural guards searched her home. Despite an investigation of her charges, which was done by the precinct commandant, the case was dismissed because of lack of evidence and the plaintiff's bad reputation.

Alex shook his head as he remembered other stories

about the lack of police protection from theft, robbery, and arson, and that more often than not they only showed up in villages for tax collection. Well, there wouldn't be any help from that quarter. He knew he would have to take matters into his own hands.

After reaching the tavern a little late for his shift, he worked at filling up the stock and serving customers. During the few moments he had working in the back with Oskar, he told him what had been going on with Annaveta. Alex told him after his shift was done he was going to wear a disguise to try to get into the baron's manor house. His worry over Annaveta increased as the day went on, so that by the time his shift was over, he scrambled to get to Baron Yakov's estate.

Dressed in a low-lying black hat, sporting a fake mustache, and wearing the clothes of an old man, he walked as quietly as he could. He hoped the disguise would work. He had borrowed most of the attire from Oskar and had made the mustache himself. When he arrived at Baron Yakov's estate, he tried all the doors and windows again, hoping to find a way inside. Everything was locked tight.

When a man with a gun came out the door holding a lantern high in the air to see who was out there, Alex hid behind some trees. But the guard remained at his post all night long, so Alex never got a chance to sneak inside.

Alex fell asleep sometime in the wee hours of the morning, tired from waiting for the guard to fall asleep. When Alex woke up, the sun was high in the sky.

He rubbed tired eyes that were sore from lack of sleep. He saw that a different guard had taken over and paced in front of the manor with his gun slung over his shoulder.

Alex slipped away between the trees and headed back to the tavern. He was desperate. There had to be some way to get into the baron's house today to see Annaveta.

While he was talking with Oskar, his friend had had come up with the idea to deliver a small box of vodka to

Baron Yakov's house so he could get inside. This really needed to work. Alex didn't know how much longer he could go without seeing Annaveta. He was frantic to know that she was well. Anxious thoughts mixed with anger at his own inability to find and rescue her plagued his days and nights.

"I borrowed this from my friend Yuri, who runs a bakery just three streets over." Oskar was breathing heavily as he steered the sturdy wooden pushcart to where the vodka was stacked in rows.

He stopped and wiped the sweat from his forehead. "I sure could use a drink right about now." Oskar eyed the box of vodka and rubbed his large belly.

"If this works, I'll buy you a drink later, my friend." Alex picked up the heavy case of vodka and loaded it onto the cart. It had cost him a week's wages for these drinks, so this had to work. "Thanks for covering my shift for me and for finding the cart."

"We are comrades. We help each other." Oskar swatted him on the back. Alex took the handles of the pushcart with a determined grip and walked away.

About an hour later, he reached the baron's large estate. It was early evening, and the shadow of the large castle loomed over him like a predator about to catch its prey. With his shoulders back he hurried toward what he thought was the servants' entrance. He wouldn't let thoughts of doom scare him away. He needed to find her and bring her back to him. It was time to do whatever it took.

His quick knocks on the wooden door at the back of the house brought the sound of hasty footsteps to the door.

"What do you want?" A timid maid poked her head through a crack in the door and frowned when she saw him standing there. She looked down at his pushcart. "We have strict instructions not to buy anything while the baron's away."

"I'm not selling anything. This case of vodka is being delivered compliments of Poda's Tavern." He hoped she would let him in. "If you could lead me in the direction of the wine cellar?"

"Uh, I guess that would be all right, since it's compliments of Mr. Poda." The tense lines on the maid's face relaxed a little as she opened the door so he could come through. Alex followed her through the kitchen and into a hallway that led to the basement.

"The wine cellar is down the stairs and to the left." The maid opened the basement door for him. "I'm not going any further. There have been too many strange sounds lately, and I don't want to go down there."

"That's all right. I'll find it." Alex tightened his grip on the box as he walked down the stairs into the dark basement. There were a few small windows to his right where the light of the evening moon lit up the brick floor. His heavy steps took him toward the cellar door. He opened the door and stopped as he heard the faint sound of someone crying.

Moving swiftly, he put down the heavy case of vodka in a corner of the large cellar. He turned around and left the room, closing the door with a loud thud. He listened again for the sound of weeping. Now all around him it was silent. Where had the crying come from? The maid had heard strange sounds down here too.

He walked toward the west hall, which got darker the farther he walked. Toward the end of the long narrow hall he heard whimpering. It sounded like Annaveta's voice. He rushed to the door and tried to open it. It was locked.

"Annaveta. Annaveta, is that you in there?" Alex heard a faint rustling of clothes and a thud, followed by a small cry. "It's me — Alex."

"Alex, please get me out of here." He heard her feeble cry for help and he groaned inside. He was wondering how he could break down the door, when he felt cold steel against the back of his head with the sound of a click. The sound was unmistakable.

"So you are Alex. The one she keeps talking about." He

329

recognized the arrogant voice behind him as one of the three men who was at Poda's Tavern that night with Baron Yakov. "Move away from the door. Looks like I'll need to find a way to silence you. Although, if you remember, you've seen me with this pistol aimed at you before. I admit, I was a poor shot that time. Next time I won't miss." His laugh sounded like a madman's cackle. "Come with me. I know just the place to put you."

So it had been Misha who had shot him on their way back from the meadow. Alex's hands balled into a fist, his muscles quivering. "I think my aim was a little better than yours." Alex's comeback must have hit a nerve with his captor, because the force of the blow from the butt of Misha's gun momentarily stunned him.

"Next time it'll be worse. Now move!"

Alex turned away from the room where Annaveta was being held prisoner. He heard her calling his name, and dread filled him at the anguish he heard in her voice. The cold steel pressed hard against the back of his head reminded him that he needed to try to stay alive so he could rescue her. He prayed. He tried to think of a plan.

"Why are you doing this?" Alex needed to know the answer.

"Walk faster. I don't have all night." Alex was waiting for the man behind him to make some sort of blunder so he could beat him to a pulp. The steel gun threatened to pierce the skin on his head as his captor pushed the gun to speed up his pace. They walked toward an unused part of the basement, where there were stairs leading up to a large outside door.

"Did you know Annaveta's papa consented to my request to marry her before he died? In case you think she's available, she's not. She's mine."

"And if she doesn't want to marry you? She's not a dog that will come just because you call. She can make up her own mind." Alex's anger spilled over at the arrogance he heard in the man's voice.

Misha pressed the hard pistol roughly against Alex's head. "Listen, I can shoot you right here, if you don't shut up." Misha's tone had turned to quiet rage. "She will come to me willingly, or she'll be sorry in the end."

Alex stopped taunting him, not wanting things to go worse for Annaveta. He could feel the cold chill of evil coming from this madman.

Misha pushed the door open to a moonlit night sky. They walked to a grove of thick trees, where a small shed sat hidden. The guard from last night appeared out of nowhere. He grabbed Alex's arms and yanked them behind his back.

"I've wanted to do this since the first time I saw you embracing my fiancée." Misha starting punching his stomach, ribs, and face, hitting him with all the rage he had in him. Alex tried to move from side to side, out of the way, but the guard held him tightly. By the time Misha was done with him, Alex could hardly see or stand on his own. Blood spilled out of his nose, and his ribs felt like they were bruised or broken.

"Perhaps now you'll stop trying to take what's mine or question my right to my own fiancée." Misha gave him a hard look, then motioned to the guard. "Throw him in."

The guard opened the door and threw him down, blood from his nose dripping all over the wooden floor.

"Here you will stay until I get back from my little trip. My wish for you is that you die a slow agonizing death. But that will have to wait until I get back." Misha taunted him with a cruel laugh. "Just know this — Annaveta is mine to do with as I please. She might not accept that quite yet, but in time she will realize I'm the best man for her. I guess now that you're here, I really don't have to worry about you getting in my way, do I?" He threw Alex a one last smile that seemed to mock his powerlessness and inability to help the woman he loved, then slammed the door as he left. He heard the faint click of the key in the lock.

"Antov, guard him well. See to it that he doesn't escape. I

will return in three days." Misha's commanding voice echoed through the shed walls.

"Yes sir."

Alex bemoaned his fate at having a watchdog standing like a sentry over his last chance at escape. He sat there in the dark, wiping his nose on his sleeve. Hopefully the bleeding would stop soon. He tried to stand, and on his third try he was able to wobble to the door. He pushed on it, but it didn't budge. He threw his weight against it to break it down, but that didn't work either. Finally he sat down against the cold, wet wall. *I must think. There must be a way out of here. God help me.* He moaned and held his head in his hands as dizziness overcame him.

Anger consumed him like a raging fire as he thought of Misha. This man had a sick, twisted mind — claiming that Annaveta was his fiancée, yet treating her like a stray dog that needed to be locked up and taught a lesson. It seemed Misha couldn't handle having someone challenge his way of thinking either, if the throbbing in Alex's head was any indication. He would have to get out of here and find him. Get him to stay out of Annaveta's life somehow, along with Monsieur Arnaud and Baron Yakov. Something had to be done; they each in their own way had destroyed her life. They had caused her to think less of who she was, and hurt her physically and emotionally so every day she lived in fear.

Well, it would stop now. Or at least it would as soon as he got out of here. He would do everything he could to protect her.

He felt his way around the shed, feeling closed in and without control. Fear rose up inside him, and with it came an overwhelming desire to lash out at God. These past few months, with all that had happened to Annaveta — with Monsieur Arnaud's attack, her family dying, and all the scary threats against her — he wondered where God was in it all. Now both of them were locked up waiting to face death by the hands of a madman.

He didn't know how long he sat there blaming God for everything that had gone wrong, but when he got it all said, he was exhausted.

Then, in the silence that followed, he heard God speak. *Trust me. I will bring you through to safety and peace.*

His tense shoulders relaxed against the wall. He surrendered his need to be in control of every circumstance to God. *I'm sorry for always taking situations into my own hands and going my own way. I give in to you. Show me your way.* Peace enveloped him like a giant hug, something he'd never felt before. A weight was lifted off his shoulders, and he felt more freedom than he's ever known before. Somehow Alex knew it would be all right. He was ready to move on.

He dozed as darkness filled the shed. He had restless dreams of Annaveta getting free from her prison. He dreamed of being back at the tavern and overhearing all four men talking together, conspiring to bring weapons onto the train.

He rubbed his eyes and tried to peer through the cracks that let in slivers of light, but the light blinded him. He looked through a small hole and couldn't tell if the guard was asleep. There had to be a way out. He needed to find a way. He felt around and picked up a shovel that he found on the floor, when he heard the whisper of soft footsteps on the grass. Who could that be? He needed to take a chance. It was now or never.

"Help me out of here." The booming sound of his voice in the quietness of the morning seemed to startle his own ears.

Misha smiled to himself at his victory. He had won Annaveta. From the few times he had seen Annaveta before he left, he could tell the princess wasn't liking the lonely, cold basement floor that he had personally chosen for her. Good.

Her emotions were wearing down, and soon she would surrender to him. Of course her boyfriend Alex had to go. He would send her lover to Siberia on the first train out. But all of his plans needed to wait until he got back from Sarajevo. He was glad that Antov was loyal and could be trusted to keep to his post. Others had learned the hard way. Misha had no mercy when mistakes were made. Those who committed them didn't live to make any more mistakes. He was glad he was feared by all who knew him. He felt power over those people and liked it.

He had an important role to play in Sunday's assassination. He couldn't let Gavrilo and his friends, or even Baron Yakov, take all the credit. He deserved to be recognized and respected for his part in freeing the Serb people from Austrian rule, and he would make sure he got it.

He looked out his window and imagined himself being awarded a medal for his bravery in helping to kill the heir to the throne of Austria. He kissed the medal and waved to his smiling admirers.

His lips touched the cold window, mirroring his daydream, and he pulled back with satisfaction. He could taste and smell victory. It couldn't come soon enough.

Chapter 30

CURLED UP IN A TIGHT ball, Annaveta tried to embrace whatever warmth was left in her shivering body. She didn't know how long she had been here in this cold, dark room. The days and nights blended together in this prison cell of constant darkness. Held captive in the cold dungeon-like room with no food for days had weakened her already thin body. She vaguely remembered Misha coming to the door. Was that yesterday?

Misha had come to the door and demanded she agree to marry him. She remembered her eyes hurting from the dim light of the lantern he held in his hands. Anger at his arrogance overshadowed her fears. She was tired of how he treated her. That he demanded his own way instead of asking what she thought. She finally saw his handsome looks for what they really were—a glossy mask for his cruel, evil ways. She had told him she would never marry him and sat there staring at him with cold determination. He stood there for the longest time, his face twitching with anger. He then told her she needed more time to think about it, to make the right decision. She would get no food until she had given him the right answer. Then he slammed the door and locked it.

Annaveta rubbed her eyes as she shook off the memory of Misha's cruelty. She leaned against the wall. With a shaky hand she wiped away a few stray tears while pulling her soiled blue dress tighter against her trembling legs. The memories caused a flood of tears to pour down her cheeks again. She

335

was surprised she had any tears left after crying herself to sleep the first day he put her in this cell. She remembered Alex's gentle voice outside her door, but she didn't know how he could have found her here. His voice had calmed her and soothed her fears, but then Misha's voice had ordered him away. She had been filled with anxiety ever since Misha took him away. Where had he taken Alex? What had happened to him? Her stomach was in knots thinking of all the possibilities.

So, here she sat in this dank basement. Abandoned. Annaveta shook her head trying to drive away the deep hurts that stayed in her memory. *No, no this can't be happening. Not again. What is wrong with me, that everyone close to me hurts me? They either hurt me physically or they walk away forever. Just like so many people in my life. Was it true about my papa? Would he have done something so horrible as to murder my mama's family? Had he hated them all that much?*

She pulled her knees close to her, and her shoulders shook with fresh sobs as the pain of her past washed over her once again. She could feel a cold, dark presence hovering over her, as if trying to touch her skin and crowd into her mind. She heard the memories come back to life, taunting her. Voices in her head whispered words that she had been told most of her life. "*You are nothing but a poor peasant girl. You will never amount to much. You are a girl men use and throw away. You're not the keeping kind. You might as well accept it . . .*"

"No! Please help me." She cried out into the darkness, her heart calling out for the man who had saved her in her dream. Suddenly, she startled as the cold tentacles lifted off her skin. The icy sensation was soon replaced by a soothing warmth that started in her stomach and spread to her toes and then to her heart. She stopped shivering, wondering what had changed. A calmness settled over her mind, and she opened her eyes. Before her stood the shimmering form of a giant man who was dressed in common clothes but had large wings bulging out from his back, by his shoulders. He stood there, smiling at her.

The aura of light around him didn't frighten her as he reached out and touched her. His embrace felt like a big hug. She closed her eyes basking in its warmth. She rubbed her eyes. *Am I dreaming? I am seeing an angel. I know I should be scared, but all I feel is peace. How can this be real?*

She closed her eyes, sure she must be dreaming. He was still there smiling at her when she opened her eyes, but this time he held out his hand. This giant's arm was so long that it almost reached to where she was curled up against the wall. She just stared at him for the longest time, not knowing what to do or say. Something drew her to stretch out her hand to his. Instantly she was on her feet and walking toward the door. The angel's massive hand rested on the door when he spoke.

"You are not cursed, but blessed. You are loved." His eyes glowed like embers. Their warmth filled Annaveta with the truth of his words. In that moment, every breath she took was like breathing in love. It covered her completely and washed away all the insecurity, rejection, loneliness, hurt, and pain she had endured. She was made whole. She was finally free.

She looked up at the angel, amazed. A tingling feeling flowed through her body, and she felt new strength and joy returning to her in that moment. He placed a gentle hand on her head. "Now, go free Alex."

"Where is he?" As soon as she asked the question, she saw a picture of him, with cuts and bruises over his body. He was sitting in a dark shed behind Baron Yakov's mansion with his head in his hands. A guard sat against the shed with his eyes closed and body relaxed in what looked like a sound sleep. She looked up at the angel, and her eyes widened with a clear understanding of what she needed to do next.

The angel nodded at her, and with a twist of his hand the door was unlocked. He opened the door and urged her forward with a gentle nudge. Annaveta stared ahead. Scarcely believing she was free from that tomb-like cell, her slow steps took her forward into the hallway in a daze. When she turned around to thank him, he was gone. All she could see was the cold, empty cell where she had been imprisoned. She stood there for a moment, in shock at what had just happened. Then she turned with her heart full of song, she walked toward the stairs. She was finally free.

Annaveta reached the top of the stairs and listened. Not hearing any sounds, she found the back entrance in the small hallway close to the kitchen. With no more noise than a whisper, she slipped out of the house into the early dawn. She wanted to stand there and soak up the light after living in darkness for so long, but she knew she needed to hurry. As she crept along between the bushes beside the mansion, she spied a small building almost hidden by a circle of thick bushes. *This is the building the angel showed me. Alex is in there.*

She crouched behind the trees so she could see where the guard was. Pressing flat against the building, she inched her way forward until she reached the corner. She could hear loud snores. Peeking around the corner she saw the guard with his head slanted and mouth gaping open as he slept against the front of the shed. She tiptoed over to where he lay and saw the shiny glint of keys dangling from his pocket. With a light touch, she reached over and pulled them out, gripping them in her fist. Since he wasn't moving and his snores were still as loud as ever, Annaveta went to the door and softly slipped the key into the lock. Her eyes adjusted to the darkness as she opened the door.

She stood still and watched as Alex peered up at her, his hand shielding his eyes from the sliver of light reflected in the morning sun. He sat there in the dark, hunched over in the corner. His eyes and smile grew large as he saw her standing there. She smiled at him and put her finger to her mouth to signal him to be quiet.

Alex got up and grabbed her in a big hug. Together they left the shed and ran as fast as their legs would carry them until they got to the road.

"I'm so amazed and relieved you're here. How did you get out, and how did you know where I was?" Alex's words came out stilted between breaths.

"You might find this hard to believe, but an angel came into my cold basement room, just when I thought there was no hope." She kept describing what happened even as she saw his chin drop in disbelief. "I know, it sounds unbelievable, but it's true. He was tall, his head reached the ceiling, and he had the most amazing eyes that looked like circles of fire. I was scared at first, but then he touched me, and all I felt was peace and love. It was when he touched me that I had a picture of where I would find you. I'm so thankful we made it out alive."

Annaveta slowed to a walk behind Alex. "Wait. I'm a little weak from lack of nourishment." She stumbled a little, and Alex caught her as her legs buckled beneath her.

"It's been too much for you. I'll carry you the rest of the way. It's not safe here. We must get farther away."

Alex picked her up, her soiled dress hanging limply on her body. She shivered and bounced as he walked fast, away from their prison. He looked down at her and kissed her lips. She touched his bruised cheek, so thankful that he was here with her.

Alex looked at her in wonder at her words and shook his head. He remained silent for a long time, thinking as he carried her. They were now one street over from Nevsky Prospekt Street. Stores were still closed. The sun was just starting to rise in the sky. He walked until they came to a park that was close to the hospital where she worked.

He stopped by a hedge of bushes that flanked the corner of the property. Annaveta took a few deep breaths and hung on to a tree branch to steady herself. Alex put his hands on her shoulders. He frowned as he took in her beautiful dress that had been soiled and ripped in places. His hand moved down the length of her windblown hair, trailing the thick bunch of hair to her waist. He pulled her close.

"I'm so glad you're here." Annaveta felt a delicious warmth stir in her belly as she saw his eyes fill with what looked like intense relief. Alex moved his hands up and down her back in soothing circles. "I don't know what I would have done if something happened to you. I nearly went crazy trying to find you. I couldn't sleep. I couldn't even eat for worrying about you. I finally made it inside the baron's house and would've gotten you out of that cold dungeon but for that madman. I'm so thankful that you're safe."

"I don't know what to say. I'm grateful that you were so worried that you risked your life to find me." Annaveta looked up at him with a new sense of wonder at his love for her. "I'm so thankful to God for helping me make it through the last few days and for sending the angel to get me out of there." Tears poured down her face as she relived the horror of being locked in that spine-chilling room.

"What is it? Tell me your thoughts, my love." He cupped his hand under her chin so she would look up at him. "Why all the tears?"

"I was just remembering the overpowering sense of despair and hopelessness I experienced in that dungeon. I thought about the many hard things I've gone through, but the worst of it is I've built walls of distrust around my heart because of it. There have been so many times when you've been kind to me, Alex, and I repaid you wrongly when I misjudged you, feared you, or treated you unfairly. I'm sorry."

"Ah, my love. Of course I forgive you." He wiped her tears as he pressed his lips to hers with a sweetness that she wished would last forever. "But I need to ask your forgiveness also. I've been critical of you and have tried to stifle your freedom in many ways. I'll admit, sometimes it was because of jealousy, but the other times it was my way of trying to have control. So, I'm sorry." His look of sorrow combined with his boyish appeal made her want to kiss him again.

"How could I not forgive the man who has put his life at risk so many times for me?" She then frowned as she thought of the man who had made her life so miserable. "Misha told me some terrible things about my papa." She explained to Alex what that vile man had said to her. "Not that I trust anything Misha says. But if what he says is true, how do I forgive that, Alex? I know it's eating me up on the inside, but I don't know how to get rid of the hate and unforgiveness I hold toward him." She covered her face with her hands, sobs shaking her shoulders.

"Oh, my love. What a horrible thing to learn about your own papa. And you're right, Misha's vicious enough to tell you something like that just to spite you." He kissed her hair. "The only thing I know to do is to ask God to help take all the hate from you. That's what my mama would tell you."

"I will try, but I can't promise anything." Annaveta wiped her eyes on his shirt. "There, now you've helped to dry my tears." She giggled a little as she looked at him.

"I don't mind. You must know by now I would do anything for you. You are so special to me." Alex pulled her close and held her for a long time.

Feeling weak from lack of food and the pain of her ordeal, Annaveta suggested they sit down. They found a bench sheltered by a few large bushes. She was enjoying Alex's attention, when unexpectedly she saw a man she recognized. He was walking across the grass, away from the hospital and past Alex and herself. She had seen this same dark-haired man with the neatly trimmed mustache come to Baron Yakov's house the few times she had been there. She had accidentally overheard the baron and this man speaking of helping the Black Hand.

Fear gripped her. Would he see her and recognize her? Would they never be free?

Alex looked into her eyes, concern written on his face. "What is it? You look like you've seen a ghost."

"Look. See that man over there?" Annaveta pointed to the man who was now a lot closer to them. Alex nodded and she continued. "He's also with that bad group of men that Misha, Baron Yakov, and Monsieur Arnaud are a part of. I overheard them talking about how they were planning something for Archduke Ferdinand. That he would be in Sarajevo on Sunday. That man was saying he had heard from Apis, their leader, that six men would be positioned along the motorcade route. I don't know what they're planning, but it didn't sound good."

"That man knows Baron Yakov and the others?" Alex sat up straight on the bench and ran his hand through his hair, a crease forming on his forehead. When she nodded, he went on. "Do you remember when I told you I overheard those men talking in Poda's Tavern a few weeks ago? If the Archduke will be in Sarajevo this Sunday, then it all makes sense. That's what their plan is." He stood up and walked back and forth as if agitated.

"Alex, what is it? I don't understand," Annaveta whispered even though the man she'd seen had long since walked past them.

"Don't you see?" Alex took her hands in his own and helped her to her feet. "Those men aren't just planning some new military plan, my dear. No, it's much worse than that. They are planning to assassinate the heir to the throne of Austria, Archduke Franz Ferdinand. And they plan to do it tomorrow."

Annaveta eyes grew large as the import of his words hit her. "I didn't realize those men were involved in something so sinister, but I should have known. Can anything be done to stop it, or is it too late?"

"No, it's not too late." Alex set his jaw in determination. "I need to get on the train to Sarajevo as soon as possible. I need to let the police in Sarajevo know what is happening." Alex looked at her as if gauging her response. "I have to try, Annaveta. They are going to murder the heir to the throne of Austria."

"I can't believe they are planning something so hateful. I just wish you didn't have to go." She looked at him, thinking of a plan. "I could come with you and help."

"No, absolutely not." He grabbed her hands and kissed them. "You must stay here where you will be safe. Out of the reach of cruel men."

"You aren't trying to control me again, are you?" Annaveta teased as one eyebrow lifted. She crossed her arms in front of her.

"No. This is different. I want to keep you safe to give your body a chance to heal." Alex spoke in his most convincing tone. "Look how weak you are. You must rest."

"I suppose you're right." Annaveta grimaced. "If you really want me safe, then I probably shouldn't be at the Tashkova estate for now. Everyone knows that's where I live. I will need to contact the countess soon."

"Why do you think I brought you here?" Alex turned her around so she could see the hospital behind her. "I thought you might know someone here who could take you in for a while."

"So you already had this all worked out, convinced I would just go along with whatever you planned?" Annaveta frowned but didn't leave the cocoon of his arms.

"Now, my love. I just thought to bring you here as we were leaving Baron Yakov's estate. Are you willing to trust me that I'm trying to do what is best for you?" Alex nuzzled her neck from behind her, and she giggled.

"Yes, I trust you, Alex. Oh, all right. I will ask my friend Malina if I can stay with her for a while. Then I'll send a note to Countess Tashkova and ask if I can come explain what happened." Annaveta turned around to face him. She pulled his head down and kissed him on his lips.

"All I ask is that you be careful. Baron Yakov or Misha's guards might be looking for you, so I don't want you going anywhere by yourself. Promise me?" He glanced behind her and to the side, rubbing his neck as though tense.

"If it will make you feel better, I promise." Leaning forward, she gently put her hand on his. Alex caught her hand and pulled her to a secluded little corner among the trees. She wondered what he was up to, when he stuck his hand in his pants pocket.

"Remember when you first came to stay with my family, and Mama and Papa talked about the handmade bracelets they made as a promise of their love?" Alex looked at her with a nervous and vulnerable look in his eyes.

"Of course. I loved the story of their romance." Annaveta smiled at the memory.

"Well, I made something for you." Alex's intense blue eyes took in all of her. She wanted to run her fingers through the curl in his wind-tossed hair, to help calm his nerves. Instead, she moved closer and held his hands. "You are the light in my dark days and the song in my heart." He put his hand in his pocket and brought out a handmade bracelet with her name on it. He placed it in her hand. "I knew I loved you from the moment I found you broken and crying in that garden shed. It was that evening, after you came to stay with us, that I made this bracelet. The circumstances right now don't allow me to ask you to be mine, yet. However, this is my token for you that comes with a promise. I promise to love you. Even though we need to part for a little while, my love for you will not fade but only grow stronger with time."

"Oh, Alex, what a wonderful gift. I love it almost as much as I love you. I will treasure it always because it was made not only with your hands but with your heart." She stared at the handmade bracelet, braided together in dark green, blue, and purple. Her favorite colors. She looked up at him with tears in her eyes, emotion clogging her throat. The look in his eyes intensified, and he reached his strong arms around her, pulling her close to him in a close embrace.

"I will miss you. But I'll be back." He seemed to see deep into her soul.

Annaveta felt a new bond forming between them. She put her hands on his cheeks and pulled his lips down to hers, drawing from the strength of his love. His gentle hands pulled her close to his heart, and he kissed her fully, deeply, as if he would never let her go. His hands went under her thick hair to hold her head as his passion increased. His tongue swirled with hers in a new dance that she didn't want to end. She could feel his heart racing, and it matched the rhythm of her own. His featherlight touch on her shoulders pushed her back as he gave her one last kiss and pressed his forehead to hers.

"You make me crazy with longing for you. Thoughts of running away together flood my mind when I'm with you." Alex whispered, his breathing fast. "But I must go, before the guard or someone comes after us again. You go stay with Malina. Be safe. I must go and inform the authorities in Sarajevo. We need to find these madmen and try to stop their plans of murder."

"I'm scared for you." Annaveta's eyes were filled with fear at what the future held.

"Listen to me. Remember your dream? You will be kept safe. We both will make it through this because there is a bigger plan than what we see right now. You are loved in every way possible. I will come back as soon as I can. Will you wait for me?"

"Yes." Annaveta closed her eyes as his gentle lips touched hers one last time with a sweetness that took her breath away. He ran his hands down her arms until he held her hands. He kissed each hand and then backed away looking into her eyes.

"Until we meet again, my love." Alex blew one last kiss. She caught it with her hand and brought it to her lips with a smile.

"Until then . . ." Tears filled her eyes as he walked away from her. She stood there and watched until he was a speck in distance. She wondered when she would see him again. Her heart hoped it would be soon.

Chapter 31

"Next stop, Sarajevo." The conductor walked down the aisle, his uniform black cap with the attached Russian Railway insignia pressed tight against his head. He glanced at the passengers, staring longer than usual at Alex, as he announced the next stop to each train car.

Alex fumbled for his dark leather billfold in his back pocket, making sure he still had it. After he paid for his ticket, there would only be enough rubles left over for food, so long as he didn't stay here too long. Good it was still there. He opened the folded newspaper so he could see when the heir to the Austrian throne would arrive in this city. Archduke Ferdinand and his wife, Sophie, the Duchess of Hohenberg, were expected to be in Sarajevo on Sunday, June 28. They were expected to arrive at ten o'clock in the morning, and they were to leave for the town hall by way of Appel Quay Street. That was today. He wrapped up the last remaining cheese and bread that Oskar's mama had given him, after he had grabbed his money from their apartment. He had eaten most of it last night. His stomach was too tense to eat anything this morning.

He stretched his neck to see the old clock on the wall of the rail car. It was nine forty-five. He mentally urged the train to hurry so he could follow their progress. To be one step ahead of them, to get to the police in time was his goal. He was desperate for the police to catch the men involved.

The train slowed, then rumbled to a stop. The conductor

had barely announced their stop, when Alex's quick steps took him through the side door and out onto the wooden platform. He ran as fast as he could to the street. He hurried to catch up to ask an older gentleman for directions.

"Could you tell me the way to the city hall?" Alex listened and watched as the man pointed the way.

He barely got the words out before he was running again. He knew he didn't have much time and remembered from the newspaper that the Archduke was scheduled to be at the town hall midmorning. The hot sun's rays felt like a branding iron as it peppered his sweat-soaked skin. He heard the noise of the motorcade before he saw them.

Two cars were parked in front of the town hall. Their engines were just being turned off as he hurried to get as close to the front of the crowd as possible. He saw the archduke and his wife standing beside Mayor Curcic as he began his speech.

He moved forward to listen to the closing remarks of the nervous mayor, who gushed about how proud he was of their fine city of Sarajevo and how they were all so honored to have the archduke and his wife visiting their city. Archduke Ferdinand stood up to the podium after the mayor finished his speech.

"I assure you of my regard and favor."

Alex supposed the archduke's last comment was meant to place the people's mind at ease. The mayor and the rest of the diplomats saluted Archduke Ferdinand and his wife as they went down the stairs to the waiting cars.

Even though he was still tired from running in the heat, Alex knew he needed to try to keep a step ahead of the motorcade. The mayor's driver in the first car took off, followed by the archduke's chauffeur-driven car. The cars were moving slow enough that it was easy for him to keep up. It looked like they were going to the Imperial Bridge.

Alex ran ahead to see if any of the men he knew were lurking on the street to complete their murderous scheme.

He crossed the bridge and stood waiting on Appel Quay Street, where the procession would most likely come. He looked around him and spotted a policeman a couple of blocks up the street.

The loud sounds of the cars filled the street. He saw many people moving forward, all hoping for a glimpse of Archduke Ferdinand and his wife. The laughter and thunderous cheers of the crowd for their leader seemed an ironic backdrop to the fate that might be in store for the Archduke.

With hurried steps he tried to get to the policeman before anything bad could happen. He looked around to see if he could spot any of the other men he had seen at the tavern and then spotted Gavrilo Princep only a street away. Remembering Gavrilo's passionate speech about Serbian unity and getting rid of whoever stood in their way caused an anxious frown to settle on Alex's face. Alex had almost reached the gray-haired officer, when the policeman put his hand out as if to stop him in his tracks.

"Officer, there's a man over there who is planning to assassinate Archduke Ferdinand today." The puzzled officer looked to where Alex was pointing and turned back to stare at him with undisguised suspicion.

Alex started walking, gesturing for the policeman to follow, but the officer grabbed onto his arm.

"Hold on, who are you and how do you know that information?"

Alex told him his name and where he was from, but the officer stood there squeezing his arm tighter, his eyes narrowing in disbelief.

Alex tried to convince the officer of the truth of his words. "I overheard four men talking about guns and ammunition they were smuggling into Sarajevo a couple of months ago. They spoke of getting rid of Archduke Franz Ferdinand on this day. They planned it. If you would follow me to the man, I'm sure he will have a gun on his person somewhere. That will be all the proof you need." Alex waited impatiently for the man to move, but he did nothing. "Officer, there's no time to waste."

The policeman put his hands on his hips, widening his stance. "Neither of us is moving until all my questions are answered." His fingers grazed the handle of his revolver as if daring him to make a wrong move. "In fact, I would like you to empty your pockets. Show me that you have nothing on you that is intended to harm someone."

Alex felt heat rising up to his cheeks. He couldn't believe his ears. His Imperial Highness was about to die, and this policeman wanted to stand there talking and checking his pockets? He bit back the angry words that formed on his tongue as he handed him his train ticket, his money, and the newspaper clippings that he kept there. As the policeman looked through his papers, more people walked past them following the route of the motorcade. Alex saw one man taking pictures of the river and landscape. He had turned to face the crowd and began setting up his Brownie camera and his powder flash as if waiting for the right moment for his picture. Alex looked back at the officer and saw his mouth moving, but couldn't hear what he was saying because of the noise of the crowd.

The loud procession of cars passed them like a whirlwind. Alex saw the first car carrying the mayor turn down Joseph Street. The second car that carried the archduke and his wife, followed, but came to a sudden stop. It seemed as if the driver had made a wrong turn, so he began immediately backing up. Then the car stopped again. Maybe it had stalled. Alex tried to move forward, but the policeman held his arm.

Without warning two shots pierced the air. One shot came right after the first. Yelling and screaming erupted from the ever-growing crowd mixed with shouts of policemen.

A young boy ran down the street yelling to anyone who would listen. "Archduke Ferdinand and his wife have been shot. I saw the blood myself."

Alex stopped to look for the shooter. The car carrying the

archduke was about a block away, and he could see a small dark-haired man try to put a gun to his head. A policeman pulled the gun away just in time.

He saw more policemen arrive. They started beating the assassin. The driver of the car that held the archduke and his wife sped away, returning across Lateiner Bridge, which was only ten feet from where Alex was standing. He saw General Potoirek sitting in the front seat of the archduke's car, pointing the way and shouting orders to the driver while trying to help the two wounded who were with him.

Many onlookers walked around confused and in shock, some with their hands on their heads or covering their mouths, too shaken to think straight. Alex shook his head, trying to make sense of what just happened. He turned to the policeman who hadn't done anything to help, stiffening in anger.

"Why didn't you help me? I told you this was going to happen, and you didn't do anything. Now someone will most likely die because you didn't listen!" Both of Alex's hands formed into fists, and he narrowed his eyes at the officer.

The policeman tightened his grip on Alex's arm. "It was my job to wait until the deed was done."

The officer's self-satisfied smirk and his sinister laugh left a heavy feeling in the pit of Alex's stomach. "What are you talking about?"

"Those shots. The killing of the archduke and his beloved wife. It's the sound of victory. I had to stop you from bringing an end to the biggest moment in Serbia's history. My friends who worked so hard for this moment would've been very angry." The policeman's mocking voice took on a threatening tone. "It is rather convenient that you came just before His Imperial Highness was shot, don't you think? Now you will be charged with conspiracy to commit murder."

Alex tried to back away as he realized this officer was trying to frame him. He couldn't believe this was happening. His pulse raced, and fear sent chills up his spine as the impact of this man's words finally hit him. His friends would've been angry? The assassination was the biggest moment in Serbian history? It was at that moment that he realized that this man was a member of the Black Hand. And Alex had played right into his hands.

He looked around trying to find a way of escape. Most of the crowd had thinned, having moved down the street to where the policemen were arresting the shooter. Alex then noticed the man with the camera facing them. He was busy mixing the powders he would use to ignite the flash. Alex remembered reading in the newspaper a few years ago about the use of flash powder in photography. The article had said if people looked directly into the light, they were momentarily blinded. He knew if he didn't act now, the officer would arrest him for something he didn't do. Unexpectedly his chance came.

The officer gripped his arm harder and fumbled in his back pocket searching for something. He pulled out handcuffs from his back pocket and dangled them in front of Alex's face. "You're going to jail," he told Alex.

Suddenly the powder flash went off. Alex twisted and turned his body to get out of his grip and finally got free. He ran in the opposite direction of the crowd as fast as he could. He heard some yelling behind him, but as he rounded the corner to run across the bridge, he saw that he had outdistanced the officer by a couple of blocks.

What would happen now? The officer had his billfold and his train ticket back to St. Petersburg. He would need to hide somewhere until the police and Black Hand members stopped searching for him. Somehow he needed to find a way to get back to Annaveta.

Annaveta poured a cup of tea for Mrs. Rabinovich. The

older lady had come to the hospital with pneumonia this time and needed a long rest. Annaveta had been working at the hospital for the past couple of days because Dr. Rubkin insisted they needed the extra help. Annaveta missed taking care of little Ekaterina, but when Annaveta had sent a short letter to Countess Tashkova explaining what had happened, she had insisted that Annaveta take some time away from her duties to rest.

Her friend Malina had invited her to live at her house with her five younger brothers and sisters. It was crowded with all of them in the small house, but Annaveta liked being with Malina's family. However, after three days of doing nothing, she told Malina she couldn't stand it anymore, being cooped up in the house. So Malina's brother, seventeen-year-old Andrei, had been walking her the five blocks to and from their house to the hospital.

It had been five days since Alex had left for Sarajevo, and he still hadn't returned. She was concerned about him. Something was wrong — she knew it. Knots in her stomach formed from the fear over what may have happened to him. She could hardly sleep at night or eat for worrying. At least when she worked she had a little relief from her despairing thoughts.

"Dear, could you see if the newspaper has arrived today? I would like to read while I drink my tea, if you please."

Annaveta plumped the widow's pillows behind her back and handed her the freshly brewed tea made with lilac leaves. She remembered Mrs. Wagner's herbal remedies well. This would help treat her cough.

"Of course." Annaveta walked to the front of the hospital, where patients were admitted. There on the desk was the *St. Petersburg Times*. She picked it up and looked at the front page. The headline stated that Archduke Franz Ferdinand and his wife had been assassinated on Sunday.

Annaveta tried to swallow the fear that rose in her throat. She stood there reading further how the assassination happened and all the police that were involved. The paper mentioned the arrests of some members of the Black Hand, including Baron Yakov, Misha Ivanov, and Monsieur Arnaud. Annaveta read on, amazed that those cruel men had been captured. She hoped they would spend a long time in jail for their parts in the assassination plot. She wanted justice done for what they had done to her and to the people she had come to love.

Breathing a deep sigh of relief, she closed her eyes and savored the moment. She hoped she wouldn't have to live in fear of them ever again.

She read on, hoping to find news that might give her some idea of where to look for Alex. When she turned the page, she gripped the side of the desk. There before her was a picture of a policeman dangling handcuffs in the air in front of Alex's face. Alex's arm was in the officer's tight clutches. She put her hand to her mouth in shock. He was in trouble. They must have arrested him.

I must go to Alex. He's all alone and probably sitting in a jail cell in Sarajevo by now. I've got to try to help him.

Chapter 32

THE CUP OF TEA SHOOK in Annaveta's hands as she stared out the window, so she set it down before any more of it spilled on her white apron. Forced to take a week off work by Nurse Denisov, she sat in Malina's kitchen drinking tea, hoping that would calm her nerves. In the last week, ever since she saw that picture of Alex with the policeman in the newspaper, she had spilled hot tea on patients, cut herself with a scalpel, and accidently mixed up medicine between patients. Nurse Denisov told her she wasn't herself, that she needed a break to try to get her feelings sorted.

She couldn't stop thinking about Alex. So many thoughts had coursed through her mind in the two weeks that Alex had been gone. Biting her lip, she recalled the photograph. Surely he was suffering in a jail cell in Sarajevo somewhere. Some of the attendants and nurses at the hospital had spread rumors stating that many others had been killed in Sarajevo the day of the archduke's assassination. She had also overheard stories about the cruel treatment inmates received there, that imprisonment in Serbia was a death sentence.

Staring at the bracelet Alex made for her, tears slid slowly down her cheeks. At last she had found the one man who understood her, knew her faults and still loved her for who she was, and now he was gone. She was convinced he was either dead or imprisoned. Either way it looked as if Alex was lost to her. Forever.

She picked up a clean cloth and started cleaning the

small home Malina shared with her five younger brothers and sisters. As she wiped the cloth over the small mirror, she looked at herself. A pained stare gaped back at her. The dark circles under her eyes had only become larger and her face thinner because worry and fear had all but stolen her appetite.

Papa's words came back to haunt her. *You're stupid, worthless, and ugly. You'll be lucky if a man wants to marry someone with the reputation of a whore.* The hateful words of rejection and abandonment had been seared like a hot iron brand on her heart, bringing what had been spoken to life. It only confirmed what she believed about herself. She was cursed. Papa was right when he said she would never find happiness. Insecurity covered her in its deceptive mantle, causing the doubts to mushroom.

Then Alex's words of love came back to her. She brushed them off as kind words spoken to a poor peasant girl. Maybe she'd lost him. It would be her own fault if she had. Right now, it seemed like all she had dreamed of was dead. Hopeless. With a bent head, she sat on the old chair by the window and sobbed until she had no tears left. Rocking her body back and forth, she hugged herself, but found no comfort to quell the voices in her head.

Unexpectedly another voice pierced through her senses. She could see the glowing eyes of her angel and hear his soothing voice as she remembered. *You are not cursed, but blessed. You are loved.* Shivering, she remembered breathing in love and the peace that had encircled her with his words. Alex's last words came to her unbidden. She rubbed her fingers repeatedly along the frayed bracelet as she remembered.

A knock interrupted her brooding. She wiped her tears using the bottom of her apron, then stood, wondering who could be at the door at this time of day. It was still an hour before Malina or her siblings would be home.

As she opened the creaky wooden door, her breath caught in her throat. It was him.

Alex.

A flush of adrenaline tingled through her body as his blue eyes devoured hers. She stepped back to let him in, not taking her eyes off his face and pushed aside the insecurities that lingered in her mind. He stood in the door, his rugged form silhouetted against the light.

The wind blew in, ruffling the hem of her skirt before he stepped inside. Abruptly the door closed behind him, and throwing his cloth cap to the floor, he stepped toward her. A rush of relief coursed through her as she saw a small flame of tenderness and love that stirred the embers to life in the depths of his blue eyes.

"I'm so glad you're back." Tears brimmed over and wet her cheeks, and abruptly the breath she'd been holding came out as a loud sigh.

"I was delayed." Alex gripped her tightly around her waist, looking into her eyes in understanding. He pulled her close to his heart. They held each other as though to let go would mean to be torn apart forever.

"Annaveta, I love you," he whispered fiercely in her ear. "Nothing could have kept me away for long." He spoke between kisses.

"Oh, Alex, I've been so worried, so fearful and so blind. I thought you had been arrested, because of the picture I saw in the paper. And then I heard rumors that you had been killed. When it took you so long to return, I thought the worst had happened and I lost you. I'm so sorry — " Annaveta tried to go on, but Alex put his finger on her mouth to silence her.

"Little doubter." His teasing grin dispelled the last of her worries. "We're together now, and that's all that matters. Some other time I'll explain the adventures I had with many different farmers and city workers in order to get here."

"I want you to know that I love you." She reached up, lacing her fingers behind his head, and kissed him with all the tenderness she had in her heart for him. He pulled her close, and the strength of his embrace gave her confidence.

Their kiss was in defiance of anything that would come between them again.

"Alex, do you love me no matter what?"

"Yes, Annaveta, no matter what."

"Always?"

"Always."

The wind rattled the windows in the old house, Alex pulled her close, resting her head against his chest. They held each other for a long time, content to let the moments slip by without a word.

"Alex, what do we do now? About the future, I mean." Annaveta pulled back, thinking of all they had been through recently, unsure about their next steps.

"We do need to talk about that, because there's been a slight change of plans." He kissed her and led her to a chair by the kitchen table. "Let's sit down. I need to explain a little of what happened in Sarajevo." Alex sat across from her, holding her hands in his.

"What is it? What happened?" Her muscles tightened at his serious tone, and she sat on the edge of her chair as he explained.

"When I got to Sarajevo, I followed the motorcar of the archduke and his wife and finally managed to speak to a policeman. The police officer — you know, the one you saw with me in the newspaper?" She nodded, remembering the dangling handcuffs. "*Ja*, well, it turns out that as I was telling him that he needed to stop an assassination, he was trying to divert my attention and stall for time. Because, as you know, Gavrilo Princep ended up shooting and killing the archduke and his wife."

"Yes, I read about that." Her furrowed brow revealed her questions.

"The murder isn't the worst of it. The officer told me that he couldn't let me stop his friends because this assassination was their greatest moment of victory. Then he said that it was convenient that I was there, because he was going to arrest me for conspiracy to commit murder."

"Are you saying the policeman was a member of the Black Hand?" She touched her temple and closed her eyes for a moment as she thought of the officer's treachery.

"Yes, one of many." Alex shook his head, his jaw clenched in anger.

"But I saw in the paper that they arrested Misha, Monsieur Arnaud, Baron Yakov, and Gavrilo Princep. So we shouldn't have to worry anymore right?" Annaveta gently bit her lip as she waited for him to speak. When she saw him shake his head, a low moan erupted from her throat. Her stomach clenched as nausea loomed ever nearer.

"Listen, Annaveta. I'll do everything I can to keep you safe." He tilted her chin up so her eyes met his once more. She saw hope and belief there, and needing both desperately, she held her tongue. "Even though they have arrested the people we knew were part of the Black Hand, I know there are more people involved, like this police officer. He might have followed me here; I don't know." Alex's eyes held hers. "That means we need to leave this city for a while and go someplace where they won't think to look for us. Right now, we aren't safe here."

"Where would we go?" Insecurity threatened to untie the thread of hope that had weaved around her heart and mind.

"I've thought of that, and I think I know a place where no one would think to look for us. A place where we would be safe."

His confidence gave her hope. "Where?"

"To your aunt's home in the port city of Odessa." Leaning back in his chair, he smiled broadly, like the cat who had just drank a bowlful of cream. "Don't you see? It's perfect. You can connect again with your mama's sister, I'll find work, and no one will know where we are. We'll be safe, and we'll be together. It's our chance for a new future."

She stared at him for the longest time and thought about all the changes that would mean. But there really was no choice, not if there were others of the Black Hand determined to hunt them down.

"You're right; we're not safe here anymore. But what about your family? They will wonder why we haven't come back home." As she combed her fingers through hair that had escaped the loose bun, she thought of his parents and Clara. She didn't want to be the cause of their worry.

"We'll let them know what happened. I know my parents. They will be sad that they'll have to wait a little longer to see us, but above all else, they'll want us to be safe."

Alex's sense of calm and ease about the whole situation quieted her worries.

Annaveta stood and grabbed his hand, pulling him toward her. She had made her decision. "I will go wherever you go. I love you and trust you."

He held her tightly to himself, and his kiss promised more happiness than her heart could hold. Even with the uncertainty of the future staring down at them, she knew she had Alex, and he was not afraid of the future. They would go hand in hand into the unknown, knowing that whatever waited, they would have one another, and that God had both of them.

"I don't deserve you. You are so much more than I could ever ask for, or imagine." Alex picked up her left hand and kissed her palm, planting a trail of kisses to her ring finger. "You are without a doubt worth waiting for. I love you so much."

"Oh, Alex . . ." she whispered.

Author's Note

When the idea for this series of books came to my mind a few years ago, my first thought was to write a story based on the true life stories of my dad's parents who were Volga Germans in Russia. Much to my surprise and delight the story grew to include the Russian peasants, neighbours to many German colonists in Russia in the early 1900's.

Perusing through history books like *In War's Dark Shadow* by W. Bruce Lincoln, I learned about the terrorist group known as the *Black Hand,* who were responsible for the assassination of Archduke Ferdinand and his wife Sophie. As I researched details of the Volga Germans, I discovered an excellent book by Fred C. Koch called *The Volga Germans* which helped tremendously. These books and many others gave the real details of midwifery, childbirth, Herb Lore and the differences between German and Russian cultures in the early twentieth century.

I took creative liberty with some details of the book. I added more trees and hills than they actually had in the area near Pleve colony(based loosely on the real village of Frank, Russia). Also, I couldn't find evidence that Russia actually smuggled weapons into Serbia, although they did support Serbia when war finally came.

I wanted to say thanks to a lot of people who helped make this book possible. Thanks to Leona Eby for lending me her many photographs and for taking the time to tell me stories of her family's history in Russia. I would also like to thank my mom-in-law, Erna(Kopp)Siemens and my dad, Edward Amendt for all the stories they shared in letters and conversations about life in Russia as they remembered them. My dad has since passed away, but I'll treasure the stories forever.

I'm very grateful to my editor, Susanne Lakin for all the many hours she put into this debut author, teaching me story and character development. The cover of this book was done by New Dimension Design; Designer: Valerie Gagnon. Thanks for a job well done.

To my husband, Murray, and my sons Qualan and Saejal and daughters Atlee and Coral, thanks for being my first and last readers and for riding the writing roller coaster with me. You give me daily inspiration.

I'm deeply grateful to all the people God has placed in my path.

My story is about history, which I love, but more importantly my story is "His story." It began many years ago when God planted a dream to write books in the heart of a farm girl. When she'd grown up and almost given up, He began fulfilling that dream. His timing is perfect. And I'm so very thankful.

Thank You Readers

Thank you, Readers, for taking the time to join me on Annaveta and Alex's perilous journey. Watch for their new adventures coming soon in Book #2.

Please consider leaving a review on Amazon. I would really appreciate it!

I would love to hear from you. Here are several ways you can connect with me:

Website: www.lornafaith.com
Email: lornafaith@gmail.com
Facebook: http://www.facebook.com/lornafaithauthor
Twitter: https://twitter.com/

Glossary

French Words

Monsieur – *Mister*

oui – *yes*

Mon Dieu – *My God*

Russian Words

lapti – *bark shoes*

khorvody – *round dance*

posidelki – *work bee*

shchi – *cabbage soup*

izba – *peasant hut*

kasha – *porridge made from buckwheat groats*

German Words

Ja – *yes*

Mach Schnell – *do quickly*

Gut – *good*

Kommen sie – *come*

Bitte – *please*

Ich fuhle mich nicht gut – *I don't feel good*

Hinnerhof – *back yard*

Mein sohn – my son

Wachen sie auf – wake up you

Meine kostbarer sohn – my precious son

Wenden – turn

Mistholz – manure wood made for winter's fuel supply

Meine liebe – my love

Wir stoppen hier – we will stop here

Danke – thank you

Tochter –daughter

Nein – no

Gott – God

Wilkommen – welcome

Filzstiefel – winter boots

Reff – a frame for carrying loads on a person's back. Usually attached to the reff was a cradle scythe.

Kirghiz–Turko-Tatar – tribesmen who captured or killed over one thousand Volga Germans in 1700's